MW00776300

Sword of Shadows

by

C.N. Lesley

www.kristell-ink.com

ISBN 978-1-909845-62-6 (Paperback)
ISBN 978-1-909845-63-3 (EPUB)
ISBN 978-1-909845-64-0 (Kindle E-book)

Cover art by Evelinn Enoksen
Cover design by Ken Dawson
Typesetting by Book Polishers

Kristell Ink
An Imprint of Grimbold Books
4 Woodhall Drive
Banbury
Oxon
OX16 9TY
United Kingdom

www.kristell-ink.com

To my long-suffering family for giving
me time when the muse bites.

Chapter 1

FREEZING RAIN LASHED down at Arthur, sending chill runnels over his fighting men where they huddled in a gully. Forked lightning crackled around them, charging the air with a stink of destruction. He eased higher to see through this unnatural deluge and choked back a string of foul oaths at the sight of a Nestine skyship positioned over trapped victims in the distance.

Well-oiled leather clothing hung heavy from hours of pounding rain that ran off his hybrid skin. A faint tingle made him duck for cover seconds before another bolt zapped to ground, feet from his former position. Thunder hammered his eardrums, leaving him shaken by the violence of its detonation. Not one man broke for cover. Pride flushed through him at their discipline and courage. A storm like this one came as a shock to even the Terran Outcasts in his unit, conditioned as they were to foul weather. As for his Submariners, unused to electrical storms, he could imagine the calming mantras they used to hold position.

Water forced between his neck and the collar of his tunic making a cold pocket of wetness. His flesh moved in automatic response to pry open gill flaps under his ears. All Arthur's senses came on full alert. That shouldn't happen.

He tasted salt on his lips. Seawater scooped up to form an artificial storm directed as a weapon? What a brilliant strategy. Arthur envisioned precisely where he wanted to return the compliment.

Caught between both races as a fulcrum, he had elected to wear Brethren clothing as a counter to his Submariner skin.

Without the Brethren leathers, no pocket of water could have given forewarning. His hated mixed ancestry proved its worth this time. A double-edged sword; he stood between human Brethren and mutant Submariners as a living shield.

Responsibility for his unit weighed like a rock on his soul. They crouched in misery, waiting for the end of a timeless storm. Copper-haired Kai, his younger brother, with their mother's deep violet eyes, resembled her second mate. Arthur, by contrast, wore the features and the rich, dark hair of her first. He pictured the Submariner faces of half his men, just a little different from a Terrans, with their aquatic mutation and psi factor that he shared. The Brethren, those Terrans cast out from surface habitation by birth or circumstance, were shock-troopers of the unit, now he had to make a hard choice. When he looked down at his brother crouching in the rocks, Kai's expression told him all he wished to know.

Kai's mouth turned up into the slow smile of Brethren. Calm acceptance radiated from his brother's casual stance and the cold, flat stare that made others think Outcasts could see through rock. Arthur didn't need Kai to voice the grim odds against surviving through the night. He had the others to consider, all comrades gleaned from amongst the ranks of Brethren and Submariners. All dead men, soon.

A violent rumble shocked though his body. He ducked for cover as lightning struck. Thunder hit him like a stun blast again, leaving him shaken and partly deafened. He had to admire this battle tactic. Defense against weather control orchestrated from an off-world location represented an impossible scenario for Submariners. The Nestines held the winning hand . . . for the present.

The ringing in his ears eased into a hiss while he searched his memory for every detail that brief glance over the terrain afforded him. Outcasts belonging to Rowan's rival faction hid amongst boulders approximately a thousand paces from this location, pinned down by the skyship. Arthur reckoned about three of them still survived; caught without Submariner fire-power apparently. His face settled into grim lines.

Yesterday evening, Kai reported sensing an event horizon, another candidate about to be made into an Outcast. Arthur needed recruits just as much as Rowan did. He experienced a bitter sense of irony that his orders had led them into this death trap.

An animal scream of pain sounded from the direction of the trapped victims. He looked over the rim, blinking against shafts of moisture. A green ray shone earthward from the skyship. Flashes of white flickered within, followed by howls of someone dying in slow agony in that light. The terrorized scream from the moor ended in a howl of unspeakable animal anguish that brought a flood of bile into Arthur's mouth. This was the fifth poor bastard losing his nerve to run into death. Blind with terror, stumbling over rocks in panic, caught in a holding beam and carved up into gobbets of meat for the Nestines in the hovering skyship.

The burden of leadership hung like a leaden noose around Arthur's neck. Even Kai thought the Nestines just killed their victims. He could not, and would not now, tell these people the truth. Emrys, his long departed mentor judged aright in this case. The knowledge of such horror must remain his silent load. Of all here, only Kai possessed strength enough to fight with his eyes wide open. Arthur refused to share and thus destroy Kai's peace of mind.

Something wasn't right about the way they fell into this trap. Rowan's men were beyond help, and then the skyship would come for his storm-trapped group. No Outcast wore his original slave bracelet; all had Submariner supplied replicas, so the Nestines weren't using those to track them. Something else was the lure. Something gave the director of the storm a homing beacon to trap them.

3

"Hey, the odds . . ." Kai didn't finish the sentence. Arthur guessed the remainder, grateful for his brother's fey ability to see threat in possible alternative time lines.

". . . are altering in our favor," Arthur said. His mind slipped back to a training session with Emrys in the cave of his dreams. Sometimes sacrifices, however horrific their fate must be offered. Three hundred paces to their right lay a deep river. Each Terran in his party carried a standard issue stasis device. Counting himself, that meant three Submariners to ferry five Terrans to the depths and safety.

"Arthur?" Kai's hand gripped his upper arm.

"I know. The odds." He watched Kai's eyebrow quirk up in question as lightning flashed again. Thunder rattled their bones moments later.

"What are you planning?"

"Give me a moment." Arthur reached up to cover Kai's hand with his own. "I almost have it."

"Commander?" A voice came out of the gloom. One of the Brethren, his tone sounding troubled. "We'll be next."

"Patience, Stalker." Kai cautioned. His voice larded with relaxants learned from Arthur. "We will make a move soon."

Arthur heard the anxiety in Stalker's voice: some of them came to breaking point. His mind shifted with abrupt clarity into a higher mode. Special quartz earrings prevented Brethren succumbing to mind control of the Nestines, and the psi powers of his Submariners blocked thought raid attempts. So which now failed? Not psi power, as his ability was the strongest of all and he would have felt a challenge. The Nestines would target him if they knew he existed. That left the earrings. With mostly Terran physiology, even Kai needed his earring for protection. That clinched it.

"Listen well." Arthur looked to the shadows of rocks concealing his men. "We have a problem. I think Nestines track us by a connection to the earrings some of you wear. Bury them in mud as deeply as you can. I will shield your minds from any intrusion."

"What if you can't?" Stalker's voice sounded from the darkness. "What if there are too many to shield?"

"I guess you will be going to sleep if that happens," Kai suggested, sounding almost friendly.

"Kill us, you mean?" Stalker edged out from around a rock. "It is our right to die in combat."

"Enough!" Authority of conviction rang in Arthur's command. He let the lesson sink in for a few moments before he continued, "No man of mine remains here. We win through, or we die together."

"Commander? Your orders?" Haystack's voice held tones of trust as it carried over the deluge.

"No triads. We go as a group." Arthur sensed rather than heard the reluctant removal of jewelry. He reached out with his mind to encircle all of them in a link. Now he waited for another sacrifice to fate from the trapped group in the distance.

A flash of lightning streaked down from angry clouds. Thunder cut off the sound of a shriek of agony from one of Rowan's remaining men. Arthur used this moment to send an order directly into the minds of his troops. A close-knit group of shadows flitted to the safety of water.

*

Five hours later, Arthur and the exhausted Submariners finished dragging all the Terran warriors into a vast, air-filled cavern under Dozary Lake. Looking up, he just managed to grab the wrist of a weary man about to remove stasis devices.

"No. Leave them, Huber. They are getting the rest they need." Arthur's hand shook where it gripped the Submariner. He forced it to stillness. "They have just lost a battle advantage. They do not need time to brood over it."

"Will you leave them here, Arthur?" Huber sank to his knees, trembling with the same fatigue. The raw scent of ketones,

5

the by-product of protein breakdown, wafted through the air around him.

"All of us must rest." Arthur looked around at what he could see of their dank and noise-some bolthole. It offered little beyond safety. He faced a decision he did not want to make. "Then we visit Avalon."

When his Submariners crawled to sleeping places in the sand, Arthur used every last ounce of his willpower to stand and walk to his own bedroll. He knew it as a pointless gesture when he added to the scent of ketones on the air. He also guessed at the nature of the reception he could expect from the rulers of Avalon and his mother after an absence of two years. Tomorrow they would board the submersible vessel and return to the place of its theft, under the southern ocean. Sleep came as a soothing blanket of darkness.

*

Transport lights gave the empty ocean a blue hue, for at this depth few life forms could withstand the crushing pressure. Arthur's thoughts drifted as Kai piloted the craft. Their journey, with Terrans still in stasis, from the cavern to this transport had further drained his Submariners. They lay sleeping at the back of the cabin. Arthur felt his own need, yet resisted. Guilt colored his reasons because he wanted a genuine excuse to escape from his mother's expected chilling wrath.

Over the past two years, many messages from her regarding his abrupt departure reached him through a variety of messengers. However phrased, each one held the same command, 'Come back immediately.' He knew Kai shouldered a similar burden of demands from her. Neither of them replied and so risked giving a clue to their location. Now they must face her.

A brighter blue glow appeared ahead, signaling their proximity to Avalon. He glanced across at Kai. His brother's face remained expressionless. Information of their discovery must be shared despite any personal cost. The lethal storm had remained anchored over the earrings while the group made their escape. Without the earrings and their strange emissions, all the Outcasts were helpless to fend off a mind attack from the Nestines. If the earrings no longer worked, then the Outcasts might be used to kill their Submariner allies.

"Avalon wants an identification code." Kai passed the information relayed through his earpiece in an offhand tone as if it didn't matter. The sound of his voice roused Submariners into reluctant wakefulness.

"Break comm-silence." Arthur glanced back at his unit, seeing the strain and fatigue showing on each face. "Tell control who we are. At least some of us can hope for a shower and a hot meal."

"Commander?" Haystack, an Outcast with untidy blond hair edged closer to Arthur. "What will happen to us now?"

"You all get a respite for a time." Arthur looked towards Kai, who only shrugged. Respite was their personal code for nothing changed.

"No." Haystack looked tense, unusual for any of the Brethren. "I meant this unit including our leaders."

"Unknown." Arthur pushed aside his own misgivings to appear confident. "No Brethren, whether born into the state or created an Outcast, can function on the surface without risking his comrades until this is resolved."

Haystack looked back towards the others. Subtle adjustments of posture among Brethren and slight nods from Submariners seemed to give him input. "We won't go to Rowan. We will share whatever punishment is decreed for those we trust."

"The strength of the valorous," Kai quipped, catching Arthur's eye.

"Sir?" Haystack raised one eyebrow.

"Keys to the Kingdom." Arthur struggled to keep his voice steady as a fierce pride in his fighting men surged through him. "One mainstay of any kingdom, however small, is the strength of the valorous."

7

"The cries of the oppressed demand the wisdom of the wise," Stalker joined in, coming to stand beside Haystack.

"Who dares lock the doors of wisdom?" Merrick, a Submariner, continued this surface-world game of children's logic, gaining himself a startled glance from the Brethren.

"Those who wish to suppress truth," Kai continued on to the next phase, looking hard at Arthur.

"Shall the truth be hidden from those oppressed?" Stalker jumped a level, leading them closer to the final gambit.

"The people cry out for justice from those who must judge," Haystack responded, also looking at Arthur.

"The valorous must fight to ensure truth is given to the one who must hold the keys to the kingdom." Kai smiled the slow smile of Brethren.

"Who is the one?" Haystack matched Kai in expressions.

"He who would sacrifice his all for the sake of the oppressed." Merrick finished the game.

"We will not stand down. We will not be dispersed. We will continue our mission together."

Arthur looked from one trusting and resolute face to another, aware of the same commitment from all. For the first time, it hit him how much they knew of the burden he bore. Looking into those eyes, he saw acceptance. It made him want to kneel before them and beg their forgiveness. A lump formed in his throat.

Kai's console began blinking with an incoming message that diffused the moment. He reattached his earpiece.

"They say they are sending a security detail to 'assist' us in debriefing. Once we dock, we are to exit the submersible and wait for further instructions." Kai terminated the connection. "How much assistance are we prepared to let them give us?"

"We stay together," Merrick answered for all of them, and then a slow smile peculiar to Brethren lighted a Submariner face.

A slight thud warned them all of docking clamps securing their transport. The faint hiss of airway breathers activating brought a smell of dust and mold to Arthur. His nostrils flared in protest at this contamination of their clean if recycled air, with Avalon's best offering. It smelled of home to him and his Submariners, but he knew how much the Brethren Outcasts hated this stink of ages as he also did now. He suppressed a yearning for the fresh bite of a keen, crisp wind on his face, bringing with it a rich aroma of growth and life. How many years must he live without experiencing the full array of natural odors this time?

Automatic processes thudded, entrapping their craft and preparing to open it like a hapless clamshell. Faint stirrings behind Arthur told him the men formed up into position for disembarkation. Tiny betrayals of sound indicated that they moved into fighting triads. He isolated the creak of Brethren leather clothing from the almost soundless rustle of Submariner water-repellent garments. Not one footfall though, not from these stealth-trained warriors. By the deeps, he must be wound to snapping point to notice these niceties.

Kai closed down all engines and came to stand at his side, an unspoken question in those violet eyes that matched his own, down to the color and shape. He guessed Kai sensed his tension since he shared the concerns and consequences. Even as he took that first deep breath to start a calming mantra, Kai's muscles slid into the fluid stance of battle-ready Brethren. They turned to move as one as if sharing the same soul. Icy chills washed over Arthur as he recalled when this happened in fact. No one had ever survived a gestalt before.

The main doors opened onto a deserted docking bay. Metal walkways gleamed in the perpetual day of Avalon. Buildings cast harsh shadows in their thrust upward to the transparent bubble of plas-glass that kept out the crush of water, fathoms deep and fading into blackness. Arthur moved his hand in Brethren sign language to order halt and scan.

His flesh crept in the unnatural quiet of the area. No ground runners rumbled by carrying workers. No railpods hissed from overhead tracks. No people walked to their destinations as they should during a day split into multiple shifts. Faint sounds in the distance warned him of an area cleared for combat.

"I can't sense any change, yet there is something." Kai caught at his arm, looking as if he concentrated. "I'm beginning to feel very sleepy."

"Stop probing ahead." Arthur caught sight of a partial shadow in an alleyway. "We have a shy welcoming committee. Some of them are Seers."

"They set an ambush?" Kai hawked and spat. An action calculated to upset the social instincts of any Seer. He grinned at Arthur.

"If I find that a primitive example of coarse behavior, the Seers who witnessed will want to roast you over a slow fire." Arthur matched his smile. "We wait." Behind him, he heard similar expulsions, normally against his expressed orders. Brethren knew how and when to disgust others to their own advantage. Liquid sounds splashed against a hard surface and the smell of fresh urine made his nostrils flare.

With hypersensitive olfactory organs possessed by most of the Seers, the aroma must reach them soon if they hadn't already connected the sound with the action. No one in Avalon had ever before witnessed Brethren living up to their role of insentient animals ascribed to them by forts. The sound of a similar splashing to the right of the first sound caused him to check a laugh. This aroma held the pheromones of a Submariner. Was it going to take the formation of an outside urinal to make Seers break?

Pile all your weapons in a heap and move away from them, a multi-toned voice in Arthur's head whispered. An octet of Seers and he guessed Elite trooper backups. He eased his hand behind his back to sign for more offensive behavior. Two more of his unit obliged.

We can order you shot down where you stand. The tone of the multiple voices held a note of anger.

And forgo the benefit of information brought to you at personal risk? Arthur let traces of amused irony infuse his return thoughts.

10

A scream of pain spun him around. Haystack thrashed on the ground, frothing in his agony. Arthur linked with him to feel a white-hot rod of flame piercing into his head for the moment it took to trace the attack back to its perpetrators. Then he counter-struck.

Two howls sounded from around the corner of a building. A brief glimpse of a leg in spasm appeared, to be pulled back from view with some speed. Haystack groaned shaking his head and easing up to his former battle stance.

Care to try that again? Arthur taunted his unseen enemies.

We have a combined psi factor strong enough to destroy you, the multi-toned voice warned.

Chapter 2

S HADOW SCANNED THE warriors disembarking from their transport. Would she recognize both her sons now they wore the faces of adults? Why no message from either of them during their two years of absence? Was there a new threat from the Nestines, and had her sons become Nestine drones? She didn't want to face that thought.

A mother's eye picked out Kai. By the deeps, he looked like a younger version of his father. The same flame-colored hair and strong, even features, as yet unmarked by battle. How proud Copper would have been with this son at his side. Would Copper's spirit hold the same pride after this day was done?

Arthur now, where was he? Shadow scanned the Submariners in the party. Light shimmered off the silver tones in their skin. None looked like the young man seen so briefly before he vanished from her life a second time. Sick fear clenched at her stomach. Desperate now, she picked through the last of them exiting, and then she saw . . . Uther.

The dragon duke stood at Kai's side. Shadow fought against a rushing sound in her ears. She recalled each feature of her first mate, the way his dark hair waved like a raven's wing at rest; the hawk-like nose, his firm jawline and the sheer presence of the man. A strong arm encircled her waist as her legs started to buckle.

"Steady, love. I see him, too," Ector whispered in her ear. "He has become his father's son."

"Uther . . . ?"

"No. Look again," Ector urged. "Uther does not age at our slow pace. That is Arthur."

"But he looks Terran."

"He's a hybrid who has spent two years in a place with natural daylight." He made her face the group once more. "Look at your son. There are bound to be changes."

"You mean he has developed the power to alter his appearance?"

"No." Ector tightened his grip on her, preventing her moving out of cover. "He was never conscious of his looks. Wait and see what they intend."

"What if . . . ?"

"Leave it alone. Let's see how they respond."

Heartsick, Shadow recognized Brethren battle tactics overlaid by Elite training, and then anger surged through her at Kai's disgusting expulsion. Amazement followed when several warriors urinated with apparent unconcern.

"Evegena's going to eat them alive for that," Shadow said.

"Let it run the course. They are testing the limits," Ector murmured. "Arthur is aware of how much offense his men are causing. I don't think he would bother with this if he had become a drone."

"Oh Ector, I can't bear to lose my sons."

Both of them stiffened when the watching Seers broke under outrage. Arthur's answering thoughts of challenge and negation increased the tensions.

"Shadow, go to him. Get him to stand down his fighting men or we will have a bloodbath here."

"And if he won't?"

"He'll listen to you. Treat him as a man, or you'll put him on the defensive, and stay linked to my thoughts."

Shadow stepped into the light, sending her challenge. She advanced to the center of that empty plaza willing her sons to come to her. Only Arthur moved forward. Kai remained behind.

Each step Arthur took sent a spear of pain to her heart. Why did he have to look so much like his sire? His violet eyes, the only part of him resembling her, peered down from his father's height. His almost Terran skin now lacked the silver tone, but she could still see the fine interlocking scales of a Submariner. His gaze remained steady, if wary and defensive. She wanted to gather his tall frame into her arms to hug him. The doubt held her back.

"Not one word in two years and now you signal you have a problem?" Hurt dictated her words more than anger. Fear rode over all else.

"What could I say, except no?" Arthur gave her that slow Brethren smile colored with overtones of the dragon duke. "We received the same request over and over."

"And you didn't think how worried I was?" She caught a trace of guilt in his expression. Hope surged within her.

"We sort of thought we might be called in for an accounting if you pinpointed our location." Arthur glanced over his shoulder at Kai. "We were busy."

"And now?"

"The Nestines have developed an edge." Arthur glanced to the darkened alleys where a contingent of Seers lurked. "We wanted to share our data, but our welcome is . . . indifferent."

"How is Avalon to treat those who renege on duty, and then return after a total lack of contact? How do we reconcile this doubt?"

"You want to pick through my thoughts to test my commitment to our joint cause?" Arthur's eyes crinkled at the corners, bringing more memories of Uther.

"Will you let me?"

"I would like it to be that simple." Again Arthur looked at Kai, making eye contact before he turned back to her. "Who would best whom, if it came down to it? How far can I trust an indifferent welcome with the lives of my men at stake?"

"That is something your father would also consider." Shadow took a deep breath, willing calm. Someone had to back down, and he had always held back from mind contact with equals. Even now, he positioned himself to draw the fire while his fighting unit could escape into their transport if they were prepared to damage Avalon in the process. She thought they might be willing.

"Arthur, take your men in peace to Elite barracks. You will be made welcome."

"No Seer interference?"

"The streets are being cleared as we speak. Go get some rest while we work on a solution." Shadow stood back, aching to hug her son for the man he had become, but not diminish him in the eyes of his warriors. Personal feelings must wait. She turned to rejoin Ector.

*

"Well?" Kai's question spoke for all of them.

"We are 'invited' to rest and recuperate at Elite barracks while they sort out a fix."

"Can they?" Haystack caught Arthur with a hard, searching glance.

"Do you want to go back to the surface if they don't?" He noted the grave expressions. Without the electromagnetic lodestone in their earrings, every Nestine-created Outcast lost his ability for coherent speech inside Terran forts, and to some extent, in general. After twenty years of normal talking whilst wearing earrings, the practice of sign language had dwindled into disuse for Rowan's men if not his own, aside from around the vortai swamps near Haven. Earrings also gave them protection from mind scans, or at least they had, until now. Arthur wondered if the thoughts, as well as the location of wearers, were open to Nestine marauders.

"Arthur?" Kai glanced at Elite troops emerging from cover to stand guard from a distance. "They don't look like an honor guard. Something is wrong here."

"I guess we will find out soon enough." Arthur signed his men to move out in tight formation, relieved that he and Kai had decided to make silent language a part of training when they formed their renegade force.

Tension mounted as Arthur and his force started out to barracks through deserted thoroughfares. The fact that the ruling council felt a need to clear an entire section of Avalon warned him of the enormity of their concern. The blue-lit canopy of Avalon's roof seemed to crush down upon him. He found himself breathing deeply as though it were his last breath.

What of the others? Arthur tight-linked to receive multiple impressions of anxiety from men pushed to the limits. His fingers snapped out behind him in the sign for calm and wait.

They all stood down from breaking point, if only by half a heartbeat.

He welcomed the sight of the gray façade of barracks as a place of safety after what felt like the passage of an eternity. A fully armed Elite guard waited by the door. Whatever followed might not be pleasant, but it would clear the air.

Elite troopers directed Arthur and his force down into the bowels of barracks to cleansing units. Crisp orders barked out to instruct them to strip and shower. Arthur didn't buy the ploy. He faced-off against the troop leader.

"My men have a responsibility for the safety of their weapons. While none of us have any personal objection to losing a few parasites, we will retain our equipment."

"We need to process your weapons also." The man's face held no trace of expression.

"And the sun rises due west," Arthur suggested, establishing eye contact. "Every one of us can kill in unarmed combat. Did you want to pursue an exercise in futility?"

It seemed not. The troop leader withdrew his men, leaving Arthur and his party to shower in peace. They emerged clean to find neat piles of Elite uniforms had replaced every shred of their clothing. The weapons lay untouched.

"Why take our gear?" Stalker objected.

"Avalon is over sensitive about personal parasites." Kai shot a look filled with humor at Arthur. "Isn't that so, brother?"

"This is a closed environment." Arthur reached for what looked like a reasonable fit of clothing while he wondered how to phrase the next shock for his Terrans. This was a first visit for all of them. "Bugs tend to get out of hand."

"And they call this place clean?" Haystack pointed to a scuttling roach. "That bug is the size of any half-grown rat."

"Which is part of the problem," Arthur agreed. "There are no natural predators to balance the scales. Be prepared to drink whatever is offered. Medi-techs will want to flush out any internal bugs we might carry."

"I haven't got no bugs inside," Linden, the youngest Terran Outcast objected, his eyes big with outrage.

"We drank from streams on the surface, lad," Huber pointed out. "We have all probably picked up our share of worms. A thorough flush out will improve your energy level . . . later." His face took on a martyred expression as he began to dress.

Guards waited outside the cleansing rooms to escort them to a large dormitory where Arthur bit back his surprise. Until this moment, he had not realized how much privilege he scored during his brief time with the Elite before leaving Avalon.

Food and drinks rested ready on a long table in the center of a room that had bunks lined against the two longest walls.

The guard commander fixed Arthur with a measuring stare. "Did you tell the newcomers what to expect? We don't need anyone panicking."

"They will all take medication." Arthur looked back at the man on noticing one of the drinks to be of a different color than the rest. He raised one eyebrow in query.

"Shadow told me you could flush yourself," the officer said

"I don't want special treatment."

"Suit yourself. Your guts . . . your problem." The officer motioned to one of his men to replace the drink with a substitute from a food dispenser in the wall. His expression altered to one of respect as the replacement glass arrived from a lower level. "Make sure all of them are dosed. I wouldn't like to take the element of choice out of this." He looked around one final time and then motioned for his men to leave. The door shut behind them with the loud click of a locking mechanism.

"What did he mean?" Stalker pushed his long shanks to the front of the group.

Arthur looked around, spotting another door at the far end of the dormitory. He guessed it led to latrines. "That we are going to get guts ache, and then we will be sprinting for a place to relieve our very urgent need. It is through that door if I don't mistake my guess."

A very subdued unit sat down to enjoy their dubious meal. Arthur noted their reluctance to touch their drinks. He downed his first, and then picked up on the fragments of conversation as he tackled his meal of reconstituted plankton.

"Why didn't our commander need to dose?" That was Linden from the far end of their table.

"Because his psi factor is so high that he can control his body functions," Huber replied.

"Then why choose a painful path?" Haystack questioned.

"Because I know what is in your drink, and I don't know what they might have put in my first one," Arthur cut in. "You might as well down it. They have probably laced your food with the purgative too. Why else trust my honorable intentions?"

That comment created a set of grins and put them all on the same standing again. Something Arthur needed.

*

By the time his night of misery was over, Arthur strongly suspected Seers of ordering an extra dose of purge for all of them, a petty payback for public urination. His guts felt as though a blast of fire had passed through them. He vaguely remembered passing fellow victims in the night, and now wanted about three

18

days of sleep. Not that he was going to get it. The Seers would want to grill him in a weakened state if he guessed right.

Sure enough, a squad of Elite troops marched into the dormitory on the first waking hour to 'request' his presence. Faced with an array of charged blasters, he chose not to argue, signing for his group to stand down. He didn't want any casualties from either side.

Not one of the Elite glanced at him on the trek through deserted corridors. Arthur began to feel wary at this lack of personnel, who should be abroad and were not. Something warned him just before the troop reached a grav lift. He started to slow down, and then they swamped him; hands and arms grabbed at him. Thought probes hammered in his mind. A wet and strange smelling cloth covered his nose and mouth. His reactions slowed as light faded. Sounds of shouting muted into a hiss and then nothing.

*

Warmth, but continued darkness scared Arthur on his return to consciousness. His body was spread-eagle in water. His gill membranes expanded and contracted at a regular interval. He couldn't move and couldn't see. No sound except bubbling water broke through the eerie silence. Waves of panic rose within him. Desperate, he reached out with his mind towards Kai. A solid wall of blocking barred his probe.

He knew now where he was. A Hakara chamber meant total sensory deprivation and Sanctuary had one such. Here he must remain until he lost his mind, or gained a reprieve. What did they want? Time passed.

Arthur? A thought probe flavored with Ector's essence touched his mind. He grasped at it, desperate for contact.

Why? Panic surged through him. What was Ector doing?

We caught an infiltrator controlled by the Nestines. You have not contacted Avalon, or Haven since you left us.

I fought Nestines. Damn you.

19

Prove it. Ector's thought carried concern and implacable resolve. *Open your mind to me.*

Go freeze in the seventh hell.

Of course, with you out of action, we could question the others. The threat hung, pregnant, between them. *Shall I give you time to think about it?*

Wait. Arthur couldn't let them pick his men apart. Not to save himself from a mind raid. He let down all his barriers.

Just try to relax. I will be as quick as I can, Ector promised.

Arthur now fought an inner battle to keep his shields down while the layers of his thoughts lay bare for inspection. If it had been Evegena picking through . . . he felt Ector's wry amusement as they shared that notion. Somehow it helped him get through the rest until Ector withdrew, leaving him alone in this man-made hell.

Sensation and sound returned first with the draining of water from the chamber. He hung suspended from restraining straps while the panels of his cage retracted into floor sockets. He caught the stink of algae as light increased from an overhead fixture. Arthur crashed to his knees when restraining clamps released him. He breathed in a great lungful of air, shivering in the sudden cold against his bare flesh, his eyes tight shut.

The scent of another person came across the air when a door opened. He caught pheromones of a woman and enjoyed the warmth of a towel drying him. It was good to be touched.

Slender hands became more personal. His body reacted as if severed from his mind. Soft lips pressed against his, insistent and teasing. He pushed her away, opening his eyes to see Circe.

Her deep blue gaze looked hurt and inviting at the same time. She wore a transparent robe that set his pulse racing. The fabric stuck to her breasts where she had rubbed against his wet chest.

Fury welled up from deep within him. How could they send a Breeding Mistress to him at such a time? His question gave him an answer, because he was weakened and they thought he would give her the viable seed they coveted even before his escape from Avalon. They were right. Arthur's concentration levels were lacking for the internal adjustment he needed to make.

"Did you miss me?" She breathed the words in a low, intimate whisper, moving closer to him again.

"Circe, my sweet? Come any nearer and I will make you loathe every aspect of sexual union for the rest of your life."

"Arthur. You wouldn't? You can't?" Her voice squeaked her fright and the conviction that he had the power to do just what he had threatened.

"I can and I will." He let her see the slow Brethren smile that left his eyes cold.

"I make good children," she pleaded.

"But not from me."

"Why not? We are good together, and you want me now."

"Still the same reasons. I will not sire a child for Evegena's amusement. Sex is different. If I am given freedom of movement, I will scratch this itch that bothers both of us."

"I care for you. I want your child." Tears pearled her long blonde lashes. "I won't be used by you again." A sob choked her. She scrambled up to flee, crying.

Great, now he felt like the lowest life form he could envisage. In addition to this, his loins ached in frustration. This day, badly begun, had progressed downhill at an alarming rate. Trapped into giving out every detail of his covert operations, and now this? He wanted to pound into the person responsible, but knew he had no grounds to attack an individual trying to protect Avalon. He stalked through the door Circe left open to find a neatly folded gray Elite uniform on a side table in an otherwise bare anteroom. It didn't help his temper.

He had just finished dressing when the outer door opened to admit Shadow closely followed by Ector. They were alone.

"Satisfied?" Arthur glared a hole in both of them.

21

"Technicians are working on a solution based on your input, however acquired," Ector supplied. He moved to stand slightly in front of Shadow. "We had to know if you could be trusted."

"And Circe?" Arthur let the accusation fly at his mother.

Shadow looked at Ector. He shrugged. Both of them wore an expression of puzzlement.

"Who sent a Breeding Mistress to help with my 'recovery'?"

"Evegena," Shadow said, more to herself than anyone else. She squared her shoulders to meet his furious stare. "And was Circe successful?"

"Negative. It is entirely possible that I might have ruined her." He took no pride in his admission. "I am sorry for that. And no, I didn't touch her."

"Ector, I think I had better deal with her right now." Shadow ran her eyes over Arthur as if she didn't approve of what she saw. "Take him to the medi-techs. Have them check him over, and then make sure he has a nourishing meal." She spun around to leave them with her instructions.

Arthur met Ector's hard accusing stare, about to further explain his actions when a gripping gut pain doubled him over. Another spasm forced a groan from his lips. Beads of cold sweat broke out on his forehead as he tried to compensate for pain with the release of endorphins. Ector's arm snaked around his waist, holding him upright.

"Damn fool. What did you want to go and take a dose for when you don't need one?" Ector grumbled, almost dragging him forward. "You're lucky. There is a relief station just a few steps more. Think you can hold out that long?"

"Ah huh," Arthur mumbled, hoping he could. The fire in his guts made his legs feel like strands of wet seaweed. A door opened, and he caught sight of hope.

Half a lifetime later, Arthur emerged, trembling in every limb to see Ector leaning against a wall and grinning. He wanted to throw a punch at that face, but he hadn't the strength.

"Ah, the many joys of leadership," Ector quipped, throwing an arm around Arthur to help him walk.

"I spent the better part of last night ridding my body of purge. Why send Circe if I downed a double dose?" He didn't see the point of trying to trap him into sex when the act would be interrupted before completion.

"Do you mean you took two drafts of the stuff as a test of courage?" Ector's muscles tensed as he quickened their pace.

"Not by choice. I think mine was spiked."

"Then we get out of here as quick as you can manage." Now Ector almost dragged him down the long, bland corridor.

Arthur committed all his remaining energy to speed. Something was very wrong here. He allowed Ector's light mental contact and accepted it as he accepted physical help.

Together and linked they stood a better chance of reaching barracks.

A door opened at the end of that long corridor to admit Evegena.

Chapter 3

CTOR HESITATED FOR a moment before he half carried Arthur toward Evegena and the door to freedom. Linked in thought as they were, Arthur discounted his own physical weakness since he could draw on Ector's strength if it came to a test of wills with the matriarch.

"Where are you going?" Evegena said as she glided to meet them, her swaying skeletal gait even more apparent than usual under her long gray robe of office.

"Out." Ector didn't falter in his pace until she stepped in his path. "Stand aside."

"Oh no." She smiled, a mere stretching of skin over bone. "Arthur reneged on Elite enlistment, which means he reverts to me. There is a certain function I require him to perform if he wants to attain free choice again."

"And you might have achieved your goal already if you hadn't given him a double dose of purgatives."

Evegena's smile faded. She directed a mind probe at Arthur that he allowed far enough inside to see his memories of what had happened since he took the dose.

"Now do you understand?" Ector demanded, aware of the exchanged from his link.

The Seer matriarch not only stood aside, but she joined Ector to help the unfortunate victim walk. Both the men sensed a flash of fear that she tried to hide. She glanced at Arthur.

"This isn't over. I am helping you now to preserve your genome. Remember this."

Now balanced between them, Arthur didn't bother gracing her remarks with an answer. He did let her stay in the link, aware that he might need her psi power to win them freedom.

Thoughts flew between the three as they headed toward the door. The multiple minds agreed the Nestines must have compromised a Seer. Evegena's thoughts snapped with fury and determination to catch the new drone. She demanded and received agreement that she would be the focus of power if they were challenged.

Suddenly the final door swung open to admit an octet of Seers bearing the flavor of the outside world in their questing minds, along with a sense of glee. All of them wore the long, gray hooded robes of Sanctuary, bearing witness that they had not just arrived from the surface world. The minds joined to bear down on Arthur and his companions.

Evegena knew all of them and their psi ratings. Her thoughts began to register her fears as Arthur and Ector fed her strength and willpower.

"Would there be a problem, here?" Shadow stepped out of a side door between Arthur and the hostile Seers.

"Get her," one of the Seers cried.

A knife aimed at Shadow's heart arrested mid throw, caught in the power of her will. It turned around, flashing back to deliver the sender a death blow. She smiled at the survivors, a slow smile, without any warmth, while she joined her mind with Arthur's party.

"I think that evens the odds. Evegena? Your choice?" She raised one eyebrow reviewing various possible punishments.

The matriarch sucked will from all of them to send a devastating sensory overload at the opposition. A skull crushing pain hit as the seven fought back, but they faced greater power than their own. One by one they crumpled, dropping into fetal positions. Evegena broadcast a general call for a security squad, her face reflecting the inner turmoil of her mind.

"The power . . ." She relinquished her hold on Arthur to Shadow with an expression of relief.

"Is very near to gestalt when my son links into a mind meld." Shadow looked down at the still figures huddled on the floor. "You need to do some house cleaning."

Evegena's face set into hard lines. "And I doubted your son. While I am sorry for that, I still must have his genome. Do you see how important it is now?

"Talk to him, Evegena. He is a man who will make his own choices."

"Arthur?" Evegena moved to face him, forcing eye contact.

"Rot in hell," Arthur suggested in a pleasant tone of voice, offended to be discussed as an object for procreation. He would see them all damned before he gave them another hostage to fate to serve in his stead.

"We can't afford to lose any advantage." Evegena shifted her facial muscles into a semblance of reasonable patience, belied by the straight line of her mouth. "What just happened here proves my point. Suppose you become a casualty of this war?"

"Then I will discover which one of the seven hells most fits my requirement." Arthur met her glare with one of his own.

Arthur looked from Evegena to Shadow and back again. He raised one eyebrow in silent question and tightened his hold around the shoulders of his supporters, ready to move out of this place.

"She is Brethren." The matriarch spat the word out like a curse in answer to Arthur's unspoken suggestion. "Besides, we want your genome, not half of it."

"And you think that breeding me with one such as Circe will achieve this purpose?"

Shadow shifted her hold on Arthur to a more supporting grip when a belated security staff appeared on the scene.

"Seems you will be tied up for a while. When you have time, the ruling council will be delighted to read your report on how those eight managed to escape your detection," Shadow said, reminding the matriarch of her position on that body.

The walk between Sanctuary and barracks tested Arthur to his limits despite help from Shadow and Ector. They delivered him, white-faced and shaking with exhaustion, straight to his dormitory, where the rest of his men met him with concern written deep on their faces. He heard Shadow calling Kai for a private meeting while Ector set him on his bunk.

"No," Kai said in a quiet, but firm tone. "Arthur walked out of here this morning, fit and alert. He returned a wreck. I don't care who is responsible. I'm not leaving him."

"Kai, be reasonable." Ector looked up from tucking Arthur into bed. "We need to discuss strategy."

"What you really want from me is an in-depth picking over of whatever you managed to wring out of him." Kai sat down on the end of Arthur's bed. "I'm not playing this game. Leave us be."

Those were the last words Arthur heard. Sleep wrapped around him with a gentle embrace, drawing him into darkness.

*

Thirst clawed, rousing Arthur from warmth and peace. He moaned, restless, and then a firm arm slid under his shoulders to lift him up into a sitting position. A cup pressed against his parched lips. Welcome moisture seeped into his mouth and throat.

"Easy. Take it slowly," Kai said.

Arthur took more sips, savoring the wetness. "How long did I sleep?" he asked after a while.

"A good fourteen time units. Feel like talking?" Kai released him to fill his cup and passed it across.

Arthur drained the second vessel slowly, taking time to glance around the room. No one met his eyes, yet all of them had positioned themselves to where they could get a good look at his face.

"I didn't get a choice." He swilled the dregs of water in the depths of his cup. "I made a bad decision separating from all of you. Once they caught me, it left the rest vulnerable."

"So Avalon knows all our boltholes and stashes?" Kai's eyes held an angry glitter.

"Just Ector, and by implication, our mother."

"We could have held out." Kai's hand closed around Arthur's wrist in a hard grip. "You took that away from us."

"They used a Hakara chamber." The words fell into absolute silence. Now he met their eyes to see horror and pity reflected in every face. "I couldn't break through the mind blocks to warn you. Just as well, as it panned out."

Haystack stalked over with catlike grace to within arms-reach. His face bore the Brethren lack of expression many enemies ignored to their peril. In the harsh overhead lighting Avalon provided, he resembled a predator about to make a kill. Arthur met the flat-eyed stare.

"Sanctuary held some Seers reduced to Nestine drones. They tried for me," he told the Outcast.

"And?" Haystack threw the question as if it were a knife.

"It could have succeeded if the Seer Matriarch hadn't had her own plans for me, and Shadow hadn't arrived to spoil those plans." Arthur felt a twinge of guilt on remembering Circe's tear-filled eyes.

"Who dealt with the problem?" Kai cut to the crucial issue.

"We linked. I channeled. Shadow gave of her power, Ector his strength and Evegena dealt out retribution." He had an idea that the Hakara chamber might be fully operational for quite a while.

"Avalon has internal problems and our news is old." Haystack looked at Kai over Arthur's bed, matching one hard expression for another.

"No one knew about the earrings." Arthur sat up higher to swing his legs out of bed, wincing when a sharp pain passed through his skull and the room spun. Haystack gripped his forearm, heaving him upright. Bright sparkles of light danced across his line of vision. Arthur took a deep breath and it cleared.

With Haystack's help, Arthur managed to struggle to the showers. He felt sure Kai could handle damage control better with him gone. Fresh water washed off the salt clogging his skin, but not the memories associated with his recent experience. Those stayed with him like a bad taste in his mouth. He accepted that he should pass on his genome, and while he enjoyed Circe's company and experienced excitement in her presence, he could not justify siring a child by her. Not with the amount of Seer intrusion such a child would receive.

The Outcast flowed out of a hunkered position and tossed over a towel when Arthur emerged, dripping. Haystack also grabbed a bottle of oil and signed to lie on a bench. Startled, Arthur lay face down, not sure what to expect. For one moment, he was tempted to scan, but Haystack would feel his intrusion.

Some Brethren preferred liaisons with their own gender. If that were the motive behind this exercise, then his psi strength would be enough to dampen flames of desire. He gasped, feeling cool liquid spilled on his back. Firm, calloused hands began an expert massage. Not the cloying caress of a would-be lover, but the hard touch of a soldier relieving a comrade after battle.

Tension began to ease out of his neck and shoulders under the rough hands. As it did, Arthur reviewed all he knew of Haystack, one of Kai's acquisitions.

They located the man near High fort just before the hunters burst into a clearing where he lay, bleeding and exhausted. He still attempted to crawl into bushes when Arthur, Kai and two other Brethren left cover to face down the fort men. Three Submariners waited, hidden, to come if needed.

Twenty hunters brought up short by four seeming Brethren. Arthur remembered the thrill of power that coursed through him when the superior force sheathed their weapons and turned about to slink home to base. Not one word passed any lips of his troop during the journey back to a bolthole. None of them chose to question why this new member had the marks of fire torture burned on his flesh. That crossed into a forbidden zone. Whatever a man did to earn his new status remained his own business.

Arthur began speculating while Haystack dug into his calf muscles. This man had been a soldier before sentence. Certainly, he needed extra training to bring him up to Brethren standards, but the now exposed skills marked him as a former warrior rather than a guard.

The ministration stopped. Arthur flipped over, just in time to catch a pile of clothing. For a second, he caught the look of deep injury in Haystack's eyes.

"Why?" Arthur meant all of it, the aid, the care, and the stance of a would-be bodyguard.

"Because." Haystack shrugged off the question to begin clearing up.

"Not good enough."

"Torture leaves marks on a man even if his skin is still intact." The Outcast bundled up wet towels and used clothing to thrust them into a laundry hamper with more force than he needed.

The question still hung in the air between them. Arthur met those ice blue eyes, repeating his inquiry with a look.

"She was as beautiful as the first day of spring, and she returned my love." The man's face set in hard lines of pain. "Someone higher up wanted to play love games and didn't like seconds. He laid false charges, and then decided to have fun before sentence was carried out. The pain made sure I had total recall for what happened next. I didn't have the fortune of having my memory diminished by the procedure, unlike most Brethren. The fort people didn't see, couldn't see, what the Nestines did to her. She carried our child."

"I'm sorry." Arthur looked away from the raw pain, aware his words sounded trite in the face of such suffering.

"I knew you would come for me. Brethren claim their own. I wanted my chance to get revenge. That is why you won't leave my sight again."

Arthur recalled how close Stalker stood to Kai as Haystack helped him into the cleansing unit. These two were Nestine made Outcasts, not the children bred from Outcast unions, like Kai. He wondered how Kai felt about having a bodyguard.

"Arthur?" Haystack's mouth set in a hard line, as if he relived the past still. "I don't want the others knowing."

"They won't." He yanked on a soft Elite boot, glancing up in time to catch a rare genuine smile from the handsome blond Brethren. Now he knew why Haystack avoided women. Not because the man didn't care for them, but that he did.

A thrum of urgent warning vibrated in his skull. One of the Submariners called to him. "We have a problem," he said, not needing more words to alert an Outcast.

An extraordinary sight confronted the pair on return to their dormitory. Shadow stood just inside the threshold from the corridor. She was alone and unarmed but dressed in her Brethren gear of black leather pants and a studded hip-length tunic. The reminder of her background had not the effect she must have assumed it would. His men stood in loose fighting triads. Both Stalker and Huber restrained Kai, keeping him well away from her. Half the troop began a careful backward movement in his direction without taking their eyes off Shadow.

"Arthur. Call them off." Shadow's quiet voice held the ring of authority that sent his men into tighter formation.

"I am sorry, Mother. I don't think I can." He sensed the antagonism and tension emanating from all of them. They were not prepared to back down.

"Look, we only want you and Kai to come to a family meal." Her limpid violet eyes took on a look of hurt bewilderment. "What more pleasant way to be debriefed?"

31

Again the formations tightened. Arthur's legs began to tremble from the effort to stand. Haystack's arm snaked around him once more, helping him remain steady.

"I swear there will not be a repeat of what happened before." She looked at Kai now, her slight form radiating a trust that Arthur knew came from use of psi power.

"The problem is only Kai, and I will believe you." Arthur looked at his brother to get a slight nod of agreement. "And yes, I could twist the minds of my comrades to make them comply, but I won't. The basic element of trust has gone for them. I will not force them to my will."

"Maybe later, then?" Now her attention focused on Arthur.

The power of her thoughts pushed against his mind. He wanted to do what she suggested. He started to move toward her.

"Arthur!" Haystack held him back. "I will not fight a mind meld with you. Take what strength you need from me."

That brought him to a standstill. Brethren guarded privacy beyond life. He established contact to suck at Haystack's energy, feeling it as it flowed into him, giving him the edge he needed.

"Maybe we will discuss meeting you after you have found a solution to our earring problem." He straightened, now free of Haystack's support, to give her a curt half-bow identical to one of his father's. It afforded him no pleasure to see her face drain of color. She broke eye contact and left without another word.

"Arthur?" Haystack's voice trembled with fatigue. His skin held the gray tone of total exhaustion.

"Rest easy. You have my word." Now Arthur returned the support he had been given, helping the Outcast to a cot. "I took strength only, not any of your memories. Sleep now."

*

The slow drip of a pearl of moisture splashing into wetness disturbed Arthur from his pleasant dream of a fresh spring morning. Darkness replaced light, and a green smell of growth faded to one of wet earth. He knew this place. He fought to awaken, but it clawed at him, holding him trapped.

A shaft of brilliant light flashed into existence, hurting his eyes. Slowly, the image condensed, shifting into a sword. Arthur made another futile attempt to wake, recognizing the blade. In another lifetime, he knew how this weapon handled. A large, two-handed sword, it had a single red gem encrusted near the hilt. Runes ran up the blade, seeming to writhe as they might have done on the day this weapon was forged out of sky metal. He felt again the power flowing from that blade into his hand.

Behind this unearthly vision, eyes watched in the dark. *I know you're there, Emrys.* He sent the thought towards a sense of presence. *Stop playing games.*

The scene changed so fast it shook him. A fire now flickered in the place of that sword. It lit a cavern that disappeared into gloom in its immensity. Across from the blaze sat Emrys, his youthful face strange looking together with snow-white hair and an old man's beard. The press of ages hovered over this cave sitter, along with a mantle of power too great to contemplate.

"You've grown stronger," the old-young man said. "I didn't think you would feel my hand behind the dream I sent." He poked at his ethereal fire with a stick, making flames burn bright on a fuel not of this world; a human gesture from one who was not mortal.

'Why not try varying the location?' Arthur couched his words into a sneer, furious to be trapped in the schemes of this being again, but curious to see if it snooped into his mind still.

"And there I was thinking that physical weakness might have dulled your senses." Emrys looked up from his blaze to catch Arthur's expression. No reflection of flames lighted those coal-black orbs.

"So the point of this dream is?" Arthur found his dream-self could move. He walked across the cavern to hunker down across the fire from Emrys. A rich scent of burning wood gave this dream more than a touch of reality.

"The battle for survival of humanity wavers on the point of a needle. You are going to lose if you don't make progress soon." Emrys reached out his hand to will a cup into existence. The chalice glowed with a life of its own as the strange entity looked into its depths. "There are four talismans of power in this realm. The sword of shadows for a warrior. A chalice of mystery for a seer. The pentacle of might for a world builder and the wand of power to be wielded by a mage. The last two are hidden from my sight. The sword belongs to you."

"Fine." Arthur glared at Emrys, aware he wasn't going to get more than token aid. Still, he needed to play this out. "So why don't you just give it to me."

"Where lays the value of that which has not been won?"

"Can you, or can't you give it to me?"

"My link to the sword is through you." Emrys tossed the glowing cup into nothingness. "I cannot feel a trace of its location unless you are on the surface world."

"You could be a god if you wanted," Arthur argued. "Use that power."

"We had that discussion before." The old-young man looked deep into firelight as if seeing countless possibilities unfold. "I have other realms to aid, and my ties here are very weak."

"What if I order my men to worship you?" Now Arthur began to enjoy himself, aware of how much the entity hated groveling worship. Emrys stiffened, spearing Arthur with his dreadful gaze.

"What if I just left you to your fate?" He called Arthur's bluff. "I created you. You have enough strength to see it through. Get moving."

Darkness engulfed Arthur, drawing him down into velvet folds of silence.

Chapter 4

ARTHUR AWOKE CRACKLING with energy. A single glimpse of the sword filled his being with power. He flowed out of his bunk, heading towards the showers. A gray-faced Haystack shuffled out of sleep to trail after him. Arthur sent a flow of energy to the Outcast.

"You didn't have to do that," Haystack said. The color began to return to his face.

"Yes. I did. We share what we have." Watching the Brethren straighten his back made a small sacrifice of energy worthwhile. "You would have dragged my footsteps in your self-appointed role if you hadn't received payback for what you gave." Arthur hoped he wasn't going to get an argument. "Come on. Let's beat the others to the showers."

A second real smile transformed Haystack from Brethren to Terran. Then the race was on.

*

The day dragged on for those confined in barracks. Arthur and Haystack played dice with Huber, while Kai honed his unarmed combat skills against Stalker in a cleared area. A crowd gathered around the fighters to offer friendly advice or catcalls for a maneuver gone wrong.

Arthur lost his wager and parted with a gutting knife. He hadn't been able to concentrate on the rolls with the tension from all of them bearing down on him. The thought of his dream also intruded. Why was a sword important? He saw the use for such a weapon against fort Terrans controlled by the Nestines, but those skirmishes were not what his group battled by choice. He

35

preferred to use hi-tech weapons against skyships, or psi strength and fey power to draw new Outcasts from forts.

What could a blade contribute? The sword of shadows for the fighter, Emrys had named it. A talisman? Arthur considered accessing Avalon's database for a brief moment. He had no idea how much useful information remained after Emrys' release from entrapment in the Archive circuits. Then there was the problem of Nestine infiltrators. The risk outweighed any potential gain.

A sudden silence made him look up. Shadow, Ector, and Evegena stood within the threshold. They seemed ill at ease, although their faces looked calm. The way they held themselves betrayed inner tension. Evegena carried a box as though it contained liquid fire. Every eye in the room watched the intruders . . . waiting . . . ready.

"Arthur," Shadow said. "We think we have a fix for the earrings, but we need to test it . . . on you."

No one spoke. Warriors inched into position; battle ready. Arthur made to stand, but both Huber and Haystack grabbed his forearms, denying his move.

"Why him?" Kai spoke from his own protective circle. "Arthur isn't Brethren. He doesn't need an earring to counter mind control."

"He is the strongest." Evegena took half a pace forward. She stopped when hands went to weapons. "We must test our improvement to the limits, and this can be done from where we stand."

"Why is she here?" Arthur looked at his mother for an answer to Evegena's presence.

"Because she has a psi rating of fifteen." Shadow opened the box held by Evegena. She hooked out one earring that looked no different at a distance from those the Brethren had left in a muddy grave. "Besides, Evegena has proven her integrity. Now, do you want to return to your chosen roles on the surface, or not?"

Arthur struggled, but the other two still held him firm in their grip.

"Throw an earring over," Huber called.

Shadow tossed the trinket toward one of the Brethren triads. The youngest, Linden, caught it. He began to edge back without taking his eyes off the intruders.

Arthur felt control slipping from him. He didn't stand a chance. Neither his men nor Avalon's representatives, headed by his mother, considered his wishes. Not since his days in Sanctuary as an Acolyte had he experienced the sensation of being the object of an experiment. And he did not have opened piercings to accept the device, either.

Linden closed the gap to take Haystack's position holding Arthur. The older man turned to dig in his pack for an implement. He advanced with a bodkin and a piece of soft bark.

"Hold still," the Outcast said, bringing the two items into position. "This will give you access to a fort if it functions as they claim."

Arthur heard and felt the scrunching as it pierced the gristle in his ear, not once, but three times. He wondered about Haystack's comment. Had exposure to sunlight made him look Terran enough to pass as one? But then Brethren never bothered to lie when they expressed an opinion. Either a thing was or it was not.

The feel of metal attaching to his ear brought a different sensation into full focus. Warm tingling came from the device now fixed to him. Ector, his mother, and Evegena moved closer to each other as they established a link. Logic told him they had more psi power between them than he had the strength to fight.

"Are you ready, Arthur?" Shadow called, giving him fair warning to brace himself.

They struck with a combined force, the power behind those collective minds trying to shred his barriers. A sizzling sensation spread out from the trinket, almost like an electrical discharge, but at a cellular level. Pressure mounted, pushing in at him.

Arthur used his psi power, increasing it at a slow rate. A sudden shaft of pain stabbed inside his head. Psi power rose to meet the challenge, but something wasn't right. His vision clouded with blue and white bands of sparkling particles that throbbed with life. Arthur sensed his testers at their limits. Now their efforts slid off a blue-banded shield encasing him. His own psi power grew to a new strength. The contest ended as suddenly as it started.

Strange visual disturbances vanished, making him blink in the increased light. Now Arthur saw the hard lines on Evegena's face that she normally manipulated out of existence. Ector breathed in ragged gasps as if he had run the race of his life.

Shadow alone seemed unaffected, apart from subtle nuances of expression. Pain registered in the thin line of her mouth and the slight narrowing between her brows. Arthur expected that. The sight of him, a replica of his father, always hurt her. He had her memories of the dragon duke, especially the last meeting between them. Dragon and his damned pride couldn't accept her as a Black Band Outcast, still less, Brethren. Shadow wore a scar on her soul from Dragon's desire to slay her. The sight of Arthur opened that wound.

Something else caught his attention about her. She held her head high, her shoulders set square, and she looked him in the eye, almost as if she felt proud of him. Arthur wanted to believe that she did.

A slow shoulder clap began with Stalker pounding his left palm against his own right shoulder. Within moments, each Brethren joined the salute. They all wore an air of approval as if Arthur had passed some skill level. His Submariners, by comparison, looked awestruck. Always before, the Submariners had accepted his differences first, before any Brethren.

"I think . . . I think we all now know why the Nestines want Arthur dead." Evegena's voice trembled with fatigue.

Arthur spoke into the sudden silence, "I don't understand."

"You glowed blue, Boy," Ector told him.

Arthur raised one eyebrow. "Boy?"

"Sorry. Slip of the tongue." Ector walked over to him, unchallenged by any of the warriors, to slap him on the back. "We hoped you would gain a shield, but we hadn't anticipated a meld with the blue-john stone emissions. No one has ever done that."

"Kai?" Arthur looked toward his brother. Kai, raised as Brethren, knew more about the jewel in the earrings than he did.

"Every Brethren present, except mother, is fey to a greater or lesser degree. We all felt a shift in future possibilities. We got a sense of safety around you."

"Dragon is fey." Shadow's words dropped like stones into a quiet pool. "He found his own way to hide his talent from the Nestines. How else does he still rule his territory?"

"Arthur . . . ?" Evegena began.

"No!"

"All right. Not with a breeding mistress." Evegena let her tone remain flat, devoid of soothants. "Get a base established on the surface and take your pick of any Seer Acolyte. I will release her unconditionally to you." She took a deep breath. "If not an Acolyte, then choose a Brethren woman. One with a fey sire. We cannot risk losing this genome."

"And have you waiting to grab the child? As you did with me?" Arthur let all the hurt and anger of his own upbringing tone his voice.

"No." The denial came quiet but firm. "I have found Sanctuary not as safe as I imagined. Breed from love, if you believe such exists. I care not, as long as you ensure the product of your union reaches maturity."

"You will never know if I do."

"Arthur." Shadow's voice cut at him like a brand of fire. "I know how you feel about this, none better. Evegena has proven her worth to us. She has made enormous concessions. Put aside old grudges. At least consider what we stand to gain."

"When can my unit ship out?" Public discussion of his stud capabilities both embarrassed and angered him. He wasn't in the mood to listen to anymore.

"We still need another volunteer," Ector said. "Now we know that our modified earring worked on the strongest, we need to test it on the weakest." He tossed an earring to Kai.

Shadow's other son beckoned to Linden, the youngest. He came over to have his new earring fitted.

"We will only test him to the limits of Nestine interference," Evegena said, before Arthur could object.

Linden faced them, unafraid. His expression remained calm during the next while. Evegena began to wear her predatory look, just before she called for a halt.

"He is beyond Nestine control," the matriarch declared. "I would suggest all of this troop wear the earrings. Arthur must be protected from any Drones, and we have already witnessed Seer subversions."

Despite resentful expressions, every Submariner soon sported a bauble attached to his ear.

"Can we leave in the morning?" Arthur wanted to be gone from this place now that his men had protection.

"No. You leave now." Shadow answered. "There might be other Drones in Sanctuary, or in Barracks. Someone gave you a double dose of purgatives. That someone might assume a rest time for you all after our experiment. Go now. Catch them off guard. We will be watching for any signs of agitation."

Each man turned to his own sleeping area to pack. In a matter of minutes, they formed up ready to leave. Arthur looked around for one last check. Half-filled cups stood on the tables, food remnants littered plates. Beds showed signs of a haphazard tidying that indicated the user gave guest courtesy of keeping his place of rest in some order. They had done their part to establish the fiction of their continuing presence.

"Got a plan to get us to our submersible, or do we pretend we are training and jog there?" Arthur directed his question to Ector as the best tactician from the Avalon group.

"You disappear." Ector looked at Shadow, who nodded. "Evegena and Shadow will link to send a suggestion into the minds of every conscious inhabitant along the route that there is nothing unusual happening. I have a railpod with 'inexplicable' problems stuck near barracks. The pod will take all of us to the southern plaza where you disembarked."

"That cuts down the number of minds we need to invade," Evegena said.

"We serviced and stocked your vessel some time ago," Ector said. "Anyone watching will have become very bored by now."

"As we learned from your own abrupt departure from Avalon, when you stole that submersible." Shadow gave Arthur a pointed look.

"We borrowed it." Arthur swung his pack over his shoulder, trying not to look uncomfortable.

"Did either of you intend to return it?"

"We haven't finished borrowing it yet." Kai gave her a big grin, and she matched it with one of her own.

"I guess I am going to have to wait for a visit with my boys." She glanced at Ector and sighed. "Morgan so wanted to meet her big brothers. So be it. Let's get this over with."

*

The railpod clung like a sleek, tubular gray waterbug to its overhead track. At the front end, sensors resembling mandibles wavered, questing in still air. The dark plas-glass view ports gave the vehicle the appearance of multiple eyes. Arthur caught an expression of concern from Kai as his brother glanced back at the troop. Submariners looked around at the sights of home, maybe trying to see someone familiar. Brethren though . . . they edged toward the pod, eyes riveted to it.

How would they react when the transport started? The thought passed between them in one second of eye contact that spoke of mutual concern, but their minds did not touch, leaving him with a strange sense of isolation. He caught the distant outside thoughts from ordinary citizens. They came to him in a droning

41

buzz. Nothing from his men though. He hoped the loneliness would be justified by the gain.

"Look." Kai gestured toward the interior of the pod. "They are sorting themselves out."

Following Kai's glance, Arthur saw the Submariners arrange themselves around window ports to leave the interior roof hanging holds for their Brethren comrades. They also faced inward to obscure as much of the view as possible with their bodies. The brothers took up position at the front, just behind Ector, who settled into the operator's seat. Evegena and Shadow stood to either side of him, effectively blocking the forward view from other passengers.

Doors slid shut, and the sharp hiss of compressed air from the overhead rail sounded as the craft started forward. Several muttered curses came from the center section. Calm, firm voices began soothing. The forward velocity increased, causing the pod to tilt as it rounded corners. Then came a hiss of airbrakes, and the doors slid open to show an assembly platform on the edge of the southern plaza.

Citizens on leisure time strolled amid booths where craftsmen displayed their wares. People sat on the steps of a broken fountain to consume snacks. A mother watched her tiny child take a few unsteady steps before being caught in her arms. Everything appeared normal.

Ector stood, turning to face the men as Arthur and Kai stepped out on the platform. "Go in groups of twos and threes. Pretend you are enjoying a free-time period. Make your way indirectly to your submersible and embark at once."

Groups of men went down the stairs to the plaza at intervals. No one appeared to take notice of warriors off duty enjoying a stroll. The last of them disappeared through the submersible hatch, and then Arthur turned to Kai. His brother was making private farewells to Shadow and Ector.

A sharp intake of breath from Evegena caught his attention. Color drained from the matriarch's face, leaving her silvery-sheened flesh looking like a death mask. She turned haunted eyes toward him and quickly looked away.

"Evegena?" He caught at her arm, preventing her moving onto the platform. "You've just had a private transmission. One that concerns me, I guess."

"Those renegade Seers." She closed her eyes and took a deep breath, seeming to draw strength. She looked to have aged twenty years in twenty seconds. "They weren't entirely Nestine drones."

"What do you mean?" Arthur made himself release her sticklike arm, afraid of hurting her.

"The thought started with a Nestine drone. She infected others. Many others." A shudder shook the ancient Seer.

Arthur glanced into the cabin of the pod, where a normal family visited to share thoughts and wishes. He hadn't the heart to break them up. Evegena pushed past him onto the platform, where she looked out at the scene with blind eyes. Arthur joined her.

"I've held my rank for many more years than you can imagine." Her clawed hands gripped the guardrail with a pressure that turned her knuckles white. "I took over on the death of one who trained me for this position." One tear wove down her age-seamed face. "He drilled into me, over and over, never to permit any religion to flourish other than veneration for the Archive."

She looked small, frail and frightened. Shocked at her weakness and struggling against years of resentment, Arthur put his arm around her, wanting to give whatever comfort he could offer.

"We never thought . . ." Evegena's voice trailed off. She shivered.

"What do you want from me?" He took her hand with his free one. All the animosity between them no longer seemed important. "If it is within my power, I will help."

43

"Arthur . . . I took you from your mother as a baby because I decided it was in your best interests. I still stand by my choice." She brushed another tear away with an angry swipe. "I watched you grow. I oversaw your education. I ignored your misbehavior. You were the son I would have chosen had that been my role to play. Now I must send you away."

"I'll be back from time to time." Arthur didn't see why she made an issue of his leaving. He could feel her body trembling in the shelter of his arm.

"No." The word came out a flat negative. "I have to banish both you and Kai." She pulled away to face him. "Those Seers we took worship the spirit you released from Archives. They believe you committed a crime against the godhead by releasing it. They intend to offer the pair of you as sacrifices to entice it back."

"But that's . . ." Words failed him.

"That is why we tried to prevent any religious trends. Fanatics don't think. They follow blindly along the course set out for them."

"Shadow and Ector? What about Ambrose, too? Are they at risk?"

Evegena looked away, giving him an answer before she spoke. "Too important to the running of Avalon to be allowed to leave. There will have to be security measures."

"How long must we stay away?" Arthur tried to shake off a sinking feeling, his thoughts centering on Shadow's probable reaction.

"I can't answer. I don't know how far this madness has spread." Evegena looked once towards the pod and then back at him. "Stay away, both of you, for her sake. She will be at risk if you defy me to visit. Someday this will change."

"How do we know when it is safe once more?"

"Shadow or Ector will find you on the surface. Don't trust anyone else and don't recruit more men. The group you have is loyal to you. Others might be enemy plants."

Kai emerged, followed by Shadow, who came over to give him a hug. He saw a strange look pass between Ector and Evegena over his mother's head. Knowing this might be his last sight of her, he held her at arm's length to take in every detail of her face.

"Let's not keep the men waiting," he said to Kai, releasing his hold on Shadow to Ector. She would need all the comfort she could get in the months and years to come.

Together the brothers descended to the plaza. Neither looked back. The skin between Arthur's shoulder blades crawled as they ambled around stalls. He couldn't sense threat with the damned earring attached and dared not take the thing off in case Shadow saw him. He wanted to give her as many seconds of peace as he could before she learned the truth. Only when the submersible hatch closed, and Kai released docking clamps did he relax.

Kai reversed the craft and then laid in a course. He turned, smiling at Arthur. "Well, that ended better than I thought, despite getting booted out before we got to visit with our little sister." He leaned back in his pilot's chair, stretching out his long legs. "We will have to take her a trinket the next time we visit."

Arthur squared his shoulders, trying to steel himself. "There won't be a next time. We can't go back . . . ever," he said, facing a truth Evegena hadn't been able to bring herself to utter.

Chapter 5

SILENCE ECHOED AROUND the craft to bounce off plush seating, off control panels, off men. *By the deep, this feels like being sucked into a blanket bog in fall.* From the appearance of Kai's back, his brother seemed ready to snap from the tension.

Kai made a course shift that lacked finesse, and a shudder rocked through the craft. Not one of them had spoken since Arthur had shared Evegena's news. Submariners faced permanent exile, aware they were marked men. Brethren, outcasts from their own homes, stayed quiet out of fellow feeling.

What did Emrys think of his new worshipers? No comfort came from imagining the entity's biting irritation at any genuflection or other forms of religious groveling. *Is that why he sent the dreams of the sword?* Emrys called it the sword of truth, a talisman. Talisman translated into a special symbol or magical artifact.

Out of the front port a leaf-like fish glowed bright blue to fool lurking predators of the deeps. Reminded of the need to eat, Arthur got up from his seat to go to a rear compartment. Ector had stocked the craft well for their departure, but Arthur had no appetite. He didn't think the others would either and so selected energy bar field rations, giving them out to each man as he made his way forward. Kai accepted his share, looking at it in distaste before cramming it down in silence.

Arthur bit into the bar, not tasting it. His thoughts returned to the sword. Emrys came from another world. So what if he had brought talismans with him? A laser rifle looked magical to a fort dweller. Could not a sword have properties other than

46

the obvious? That made sense. He needed to contact Emrys. Maybe a place of power on the surface? Arthur couldn't think of any. What about the spectral gods of the Brethren? They had a meeting place, but he only recalled the location from a past life.

"Kai, what do you know of the Wild Hunt?" Arthur's voice lacerated the wall of silence.

"I don't imagine any renegade Seer would consider trading non-belief just to get close to us for a god who glorifies death by combat." Kai looked around, his mouth curved in a smile betraying bitter humor. "I haven't noticed any of them leaping into the forefront of a sortie."

"Forget the Seers for a moment. What else do you know?"

"We need to figure out what we are going to do with the rest of our lives." Kai set the controls to autopilot and swiveled his chair to face Arthur. "As I see it, we are cut off from all supplies but those we find for ourselves. We can't contact any Brethren in case they are Nestine drones. We are banished from Avalon, and we dare not recruit for the same reason. Shouldn't we be thinking about finding a quiet valley where we can settle down? If we hunt and farm, we can sustain ourselves. What about stealing some women so that we can set up a future generation to continue our fight? That is the only way I can see we are going to get a battle force now."

So this was what his brother had been planning in the silence of this journey. Given what they could and couldn't do, his suggestion presented a logical resolution for an impossible set of circumstances. Brethren had founded Haven for similar reasons.

"I agree in principle," Arthur said.

"But?" Kai truncated a whole conversation in that one word. A Brethren trait.

"I had a visitation while we were in Avalon." Arthur glanced back to see who might be listening. The men either dozed in their seats or stared out of ports. "Emrys told me to find a sword." Kai's expression warned him. "No, I don't mean he sent a nightmare like he did before. I don't think he has his own agenda and needs to draw us into a trap. I think he is trying to help this time. So yes, we need a home, but we also need hope."

"A sword?" Kai quirked up one eyebrow, doubt written on his face.

"That is what he said." Arthur shrugged. "We can't recruit. Nor can we fight the Nestines, without eventually running out of ammunition. Dying in battle is acceptable. Being sucked up to a skyship is not. We need a goal, why not this one?"

"Trust." Kai's flat statement of negation didn't bring any surprises.

"So he tried to kill us. If you had been trapped for millennia in circuitry, wouldn't that make you a trifle ruthless if you found a way out?"

Kai considered the idea for a few moments. "Fine, but what does he stand to gain if you find this weapon?"

"I got the impression he doesn't care all that much what happens. He sounded like he wanted to repay a favor. If we choose otherwise, then that is our funeral pyre."

"Where does the Wild Hunt come into this?"

"They materialize more often where the lines of earth force are most powerful." Arthur suppressed a shudder, trying to obliterate a memory of riding with that spectral band in the pursuit of lost souls. "I need a place where magnetic forces are strong if I am to contact Emrys again. I wondered if Brethren had a special place."

"The standing stones," a deep voice said from behind. Haystack moved forward to take a seat next to Arthur.

"How long have you been listening?" Kai asked. "You looked fast asleep."

"I was." Haystack shrugged. "I needed to relieve myself, and I listened to see if we were getting near land. I'm not fond of using a tiny hole in a lurching ship."

"You said standing stones?" Arthur said.

"That is where the Wild Hunt is said to meet on the nights of Samhain and Beltane. Those are the old names for the first days of year end and spring. Is that what you wanted?"

"We aren't anywhere near fall, and we have missed spring." Kai turned to check position, having made his point.

"Seasons are important, then?" Arthur mused. "Summer solstice is ten days away by my reckoning. Where are these stones?"

"South and east of High fort." Haystack settled into a more comfortable position in his chair. "I went there once when I was a fort soldier. Someone had a notion that the 'special' powers of lumps of rock would make his own spear stay rigid between the sheets. The lord's young wife didn't appreciate the benefit. Rumor had it she fell down a well after he caught her with a Silver Band."

Kai passed Haystack an electronic map palm pad. "Show me approximately where this place is." The Outcast pointed. "I can get us near." Kai tapped a black line on the pad. "If we travel by this river we have enough Submariners with us to get underwater if we have problems. It will leave us a one-day march overland."

"You're in agreement then?" Arthur wondered at Kai's change of opinion.

"Maybe Emrys will tell us of a place where we could make a good base. Who knows?"

*

Morning mist wafted upward to make a haze on the horizon. Brilliant dewdrops clinging to grass soaked everyone to knee level and Submariners squinted more with each extra lumen factor the rising sun created. Despite argument, Arthur insisted on a daylight march. While detection from fort patrols was a real threat, he needed landscape details for Haystack to navigate.

The troop moved forward at a soldier's pacing for long distance travel on foot. Twenty paces running, twenty walking for over an hour, and no end in sight. He knew that nothing could disguise the nature of his force if they were spotted. Submariners made poor horsemen when mounted. They preferred technology or river journeys to any overland trek. In addition to the Submariner's lack of equestrian skills, his band was the only mixed group on land not to have horses as they didn't have a land base. This must be rectified soon, or they risked betraying the nature of their differences from ordinary Brethren parties.

While they had the luxury of trading with the regular Brethren force, maintenance supplies for Submariner technology hadn't been a problem. Ector's careful restocking of the submersible would give them a breathing space. After that they were on their own. Who knew how many Submariners on the surface subscribed to the new religion? As much as he wanted to bury the thought, Arthur made an effort to face this as he traveled.

Kai cracked out a command for a silent halt. All of them crouched in instant response. Stalker, the nearest Brethren to Arthur, edged closer. The man's concentration appeared to be centered to the right of their position. Feeling blind by comparison, when all the Brethren searched ahead with their fey sense, Arthur waited, trusting their instincts to probe in time for danger. He caught the musky scent of a saurian upwind. Reason enough for a sudden halt. If compelled, they could take one down, but at the risk of injury or death in a senseless fight.

Repeated thuds of something heavy running shook the ground under their feet. A sudden shriek of pain and crash of contact shattered the silence. A wild pig screamed out its last agony. The sound of tearing flesh and breaking bones carried on the wind, along with a sharp metallic scent of fresh blood.

Kai signaled for them to move left, off the pack train route to keep them downwind of the predator. Every man ran without a care for sound. They had the time it took a saurian to eat a pig before it started hunting again. Arthur noticed the tension leach from all Brethren some time later. He didn't need to ask. He guessed the saurian to have found more prey.

*

Haystack's standing stones came into sight that afternoon. Arthur experienced a sudden stab of recognition, but one image overlaid another. He had memories of them in a complete state, not the tumbled ruins he saw now. Three sets of uprights still had their capstones in place. He knew the middle one of the trio would channel the first ray of sunshine to an altar stone on summer solstice. The dim shapes of long dead people out of time moved in a ghostly observation of the rites held here in distant ages and then Emrys materialized, standing by the keystone.

"Arthur? Why did you stop?" Kai stood in front of him, blocking the view and looking concerned.

Arthur caught a glimpse of a fragment of stone over Kai's shoulder. The second, ancient image was gone. "Just admiring the view. It must have taken a lot of effort to build them, and now they are almost gone." He didn't feel comfortable giving Kai the real reason; not wanting the others starting to give him strange looks again. More than that, Arthur didn't want any barrier ruining the family sense he shared with his brother.

Just for a moment Kai lost all facial expression. His eyes seemed to be deprived of light, the way his pupils expanded. A closed set to his mouth warned Arthur that Kai experienced a moment of future time, but Kai turned away to set about organizing a camp as if nothing had happened.

Expanding frames formed the core of two-men dwelling units. Once a rounded skeleton made the frame, a waterproof, lightweight fabric of grass and earth tones fitted into place over the top and sides. Seen from a distance, the camp resembled natural landscape. While Arthur would have preferred it to be set up inside the standing stones, something held him back from questioning his brother's decision. His big surprise came when the group paired off for sleep. Where he expected Haystack

51

to share with him; Kai's fiery thatch of hair appeared in the opening. Ever since Avalon, both Haystack and Stalker had become self-appointed guardians for the brothers.

Kai unrolled his bedding, a certain stiff formality in his movements. Arthur wasn't quick enough to evade Kai's hand clamping on his wrist, or the instant of minds joining; an impossible, unpredictable joining that left him stunned.

Kai's mind held images of the stones surrounded by a violent swirl of danger in the form of angry-colored spinning lights. The images ceased when Kai released him.

"Now you know, as do I. Why did you think I would hide from you if you told me of your vision?" Kai's face resembled a pale blur in the dying light, but Arthur read anger in the way his brother held himself.

"I've always had to conceal what I can do." Arthur looked away, remembering his childhood, Seers always at him, constantly trying to find his limits. Scared of him, yet full of authority designed to intimidate the child. "Why spoil what we have?"

"Honesty. Trust." Kai cut through whole conversations around a difficult subject Arthur wanted to avoid with a terse Brethren economy of words.

"Have you any idea what it feels like to be so different that you wonder if you're going mad?"

"Have you ever experienced looks from those who age at a normal Terran rate and suspect you will not?" Kai countered into the gloom. "I have the longevity gene and the accelerated healing from our mother. Then there is us. Different sires but the same dam. Two halves of the same whole, who can share thoughts at a touch, despite earrings designed to keep us separated."

"What do you mean?" Arthur guessed a deeper import to Kai's bitter statement and shivered.

"Why do you think Avalon wanted those earrings tested on you, the strongest?" Kai wriggled into his blankets to settle into a sleep position. "Testing the weakest link is more logical."

The breath whooshed out of Arthur. Every piece fitted into place. The picture came into focus. "You mean we were not exiled just for the danger of attracting zealots' attention? Evegena is playing a double game again. She is threatened by us?" He imagined that wrinkled neck in his hands as he squeezed tightly.

"I watched her face when you started glowing. I have never before seen fear so clearly etched in the expression of a living person. I've seen that look on a few dead people though."

"Kai, does our mother know? Did she have a part of this?"

"She wants us safe. I don't think she cares how different we are. I didn't get that impression when I said goodbye." Kai rolled so that he faced towards Arthur. "Why didn't you make your peace with her? She was waiting for you to come to her."

"How can I?" Arthur moved a rock out of the place he intended to lay. He didn't like where the conversation was going. "You know how much we each resemble our sires. She loved yours. Mine tried to kill her."

"He did. You didn't. So stop acting guilty around her. Assuming we ever get the chance to see her again."

Arthur settled down into his blankets. The feeling of being cut off seeped into him like slow poison. How long could they hold out? "What do you think we should do? Is this sword idea a waste of resources? Am I pulling rank for my own benefit?"

"A quest will keep us focused." Kai let out a sigh. "No, I don't think you are being selfish. I'm not happy with this idea because it came from Emrys. Maybe it will pan out and maybe it won't. It gives us a direction while we adjust to what has happened."

"So what did you really see in future time?" Arthur had an idea Kai concealed some of it in the exchange.

"That danger comes from being in this place. It is not immediate, so whatever you intend to do here will affect the intensity. I'll be happier when we leave."

Kai started to breathe in the deep regular way of a sleeper soon after, but Arthur lay awake. Images of Shadow's look of pain upon sighting him nagged at his conscience. He had avoided her because of the memories he stirred up. *By the deeps, why couldn't I have taken after the maternal side?* He had Shadow's memories of the dragon duke. *What is this man really like now?* Could physical attraction be the only tie between his parents? Why had Dragon wanted Shadow dead? Arthur turned over possible reasons, yet without knowing the man, he couldn't pin down any one as a true cause. Meeting Dragon to ask for a reason seemed as likely as making peace with the Nestines.

The hooting call of a nocturnal saurian sounded in the distance. Arthur held his breath, waiting. Brethren fey sense alerted any gifted Outcast to full battle readiness in seconds. Kai remained in a deep sleep that eluded Arthur. He lay listening to the sounds of the night until he could bear no more. Careful not to disturb Kai, he crept from shelter to keep vigil outside.

In the darkest hour before dawn, when every star faded, Arthur moved into position to satisfy a need to watch sunrise strike through the standing stones. The image of an ages old ceremony flooded through his mind; long dead fires and the stink of sweat overlaid with fear. Drums beat in time with his heart.

The star of impending morning brightened a misty land to outline the stones like grim sentinels. Soon – whatever came crept slowly on the wings of time out of memory.

Silver light in the east blushed pink, and then red. Caught in another world, Arthur moved forward. He entered the ring of stones, every one intact to his eyes. A single beam of light stabbed through a star stone to illuminate an altar. The flat rectangle glowed blue.

"Arthur—no!" Kai's shout came from a great distance. The blue-charged light drew him like a moth to flame. A two-handed sword hung suspended in that light, glowing with power.

*

For one instant, darkness shrouded all. The mournful sigh of wind over empty lands whispered in Arthur's soul. He floated

54

forward . . . a glow appeared in the distance. Firelight and a figure hunkered down beside it. Arthur glided to a halt in front of Emrys. The cave sitter's black upon black eyes bored into his own.

"Welcome, Arthur."

"Somehow, I expected a more original setting than this." He waved a hand around, aware the residue of anger had forced this snide remark out. Memories of being a sacrificial victim remained too fresh in Arthur for any polite veneer.

"Old is often better." Emrys threw another log on a fire that did not exist, except in Arthur's mind. Desolate moorland grass bowed before a strong breeze that brought faint tangs of ocean to mix with the smell of wood smoke. "This is our place out of time. Why create a new one? We need to talk, not admire the scenery."

"Point taken," Arthur conceded.

Emrys pushed back his cowl to reveal hair as white as his beard. It looked out of place on a youthful face. The eyes, those eyes, held no light, yet they thrummed with power. "I am impressed. I didn't think you would find a conjugation of ley lines so swiftly."

"Um, what lines?" Arthur looked around for threads or markers.

"Ley lines. Channels of power that run through land to connect into a network of force. The place you chose is the most powerful convergence."

"So I am here. Why?" Kai's warning sounded in Arthur's thoughts. *Can I trust Emrys?* "Is this another game of yours we play? What are the stakes this time? My life again?"

"Yes. The lives of all Humans, whether Terran or Submariner." Emrys held out his hand. A chalice appeared in his grasp from nowhere. He looked into the depths. "Your enemies are tired of conflict. Their numbers are now sufficient to destroy Avalon and enslave all land dwellers."

"How so? Is this a guess?" Arthur recalled Emrys saying he lacked the power to predict with certainty.

"That thought was accurate once." A smile brightened the face of this timeless entity. "Yes, I can read your mind, despite whatever trinket you choose to wear."

"What changed?"

"Spite has an uncanny knack of biting the sender." Shaking shoulders betrayed laughter. He seemed to make an effort to gain some control. "Was discomforting me worth what you unleashed on yourself?"

"No!" Arthur got a sinking feeling. Did Emrys merely want to gloat?

"When you reinstated worship, you also increased my power on this plane of existence."

"Then why don't you wipe out the Nestines?"

"Listen. I said increased. I didn't say restored. You are out of time, even if you survive the new disciples." Emrys looked into the chalice once more. "I see only one way to freedom for your people. Find the sword."

"Why?" Tired of playing word games, Arthur resorted to a Brethren speech pattern.

"I showed you what happened when the Nestine species came into being. Now I will show you their current plans. You will see through my eyes. Be prepared to jump from one individual's thoughts to another. They are far more telepathically advanced than Submariners. That means I have easy access, if almost no control. Brace yourself."

Chapter 6

A CHANGE IN THE air pressure alerted Kiri Ung to the silent doors of his workroom sliding aside to admit a life form. He continued his study of the planet's landmasses from his personal console screen until the stink of prey caused his claws to extend. Drawing the scent in through his mouth, he savored the telltale clues on his palate. A human drone in his presence? As the flavor circulated, he detected faint differences in the pheromones. Not a surface human – a mutated aquatic variety and one of the ones he wanted to question. Kiri Ung didn't care for the taste of fish all that much. His claws retracted, and he continued his study isolating the required zones with a sense of satisfaction, ignoring the interruption until he felt ready to deal with it.

Of all landmasses on the planet, only two harbored uncontaminated prey. Each of these island formations enjoyed similar climates, both being wet and temperate, if at distal ends of the globe. Those Terrans in the southern hemisphere represented true prey. The thrill of the hunt unleashed his claws again. Just looking at the northern set of islands made his head crest rise, as these prey beasts should be domesticated; had been domesticated. The mutant drone served to remind Kiri Ung why those circumstances no longer existed. The killing rage began to throb within him, but he needed this creature.

Shutting his eyes in an attempt to calm himself, Kiri Ung pictured his workroom. The smooth gray metal walls eased his eyes. His desk and chair of refined silicate amalgam emitted no disturbing aroma. Soundproof corking on the floor gave him the peace he needed to concentrate and he liked the solid matte-black color. Now more contented, he opened his eyes to pin the intruder with a stare.

The creature offended him. It needed artificial layers of covering to maintain body temperature. While hairless skin made eating more enjoyable, a glimpse of scales reminded him of the fish taste. Perhaps he had better deal with this creature, but not on a mind link level, like land drones.

"Report?" It must have something to say, or it would not have contaminated his peace.

"The new Submariner religion is making data acquisition difficult."

Kiri Ung digested a fact that displeased him in a minor way. Already established data indicated a serious lack of resources for the aquatic humanoid habitat. Fifty revolutions of the planet, a hundred at the most with careful planning, and that base would not sustain life. None of those mutant prey possessed surface survival skills. Thus, the problem solved itself.

"How does this affect land Terrans?" He didn't need another religion encouraging prey to think. They must worship Nestines with the aid of the priest-drone provided to every domesticated fort. Nothing must interfere with the priest-drone's effective elimination of all telepaths born to Terrans.

"It doesn't, except where rebel forces infringe on our territory."

The monotone flatness of the drone's voice pleased him. Kiri Ung hated the warble of unaltered prey voices. "How is this a problem?"

"It gives the rebels a sense of purpose beyond mere survival."

Now that interested him. A cause increased fight potential in the domesticated prey. "Outline origin?"

"Primary indication suggests a probable cause to be the release of a sentient life force from the database in Avalon," the creature reported, looking into the distance with disinterest. "The half-breed mutant named Arthur, who affected this release, deliberately started a religion based on the deification of this entity. As the life form hasn't answered any prayers, the worshipers are blaming the half-breed and intend to sacrifice him so they can get the entity to return."

Kiri Ung leaned forward in his chair. A half-breed capable of comprehensive thought processes? What had been the plan of this one? What made the scheme backfire? This mutant might be an interesting study. "The Seers let this happen?"

"The half-breed is more powerful than any Seer. He terrifies them just by existing."

"Why?" Kiri Ung decided this ranked as prime data. His crest erected. The Queen must be told this information at once.

"The Seers believe he formed a viable gestalt. Previous attempts have always resulted in death for both participants. We also have reason to believe they formulated technology to limit him before he was exiled from Avalon."

Kiri Ung suppressed a rush of pure adrenalin. He leaned back in his chair to stare at the creature, needing more data. "This half-breed? What else is he accused of doing?"

"His pain threshold is beyond thinkable parameters. He can multitask telepathically by projecting the essence of himself into many places simultaneously."

"Proven, or supposition?" Could this be the one? Kiri Ung wanted to squeeze every last shred of detail out of his drone. *The potential . . .*

"Documented."

"Where is he now?" Kiri Ung caught the scent of his own pheromones in the air.

"On land. The exiles did not record any projected designation."

"Conjecture?" At least these mutant drones could form opinions as well as hold a reasonable conversation; it made up in part for their bad flavor.

"Resources will run out. The exiles will need to replenish their weapons charges from Brethren bases."

Kiri Ung allowed himself the pleasure of imagining the drone's head being slowly pulled off. Of course, the technology required replenishment, but given a new religion, would this happen? In those circumstances, what actions would the half-breed choose? Extreme caution and conservation of firepower? He dismissed the drone with a curt flick of his hand before he succumbed to the urge of dismembering it.

As the odor of prey faded, Kiri Ung considered the half-breed's problem. What if the creature contacted Brethren bases? Then the chances of being killed by a worshiper increased. And the worshiper would be aquatic, which made a falling out with Brethren very likely should such an attempt succeed. Without that alliance Nestine command could pick off each group, so that is just what this half-breed would not attempt to compromise.

No visiting with either rebel faction for the exiled few then. But they must have supplies. Ah yes, they would attack the forts under control. How could a slave race have bred one so gifted? An urgent need to acquire this specimen flowed through his bones. With such a creature held in bondage, Kiri Ung possessed the ultimate opportunity to mate. Only those with the best Terran alleles to add to their own genetic material could have a chance with the Queen. He needed calm thoughts before he could enter her presence though. A few sharp commands to the intercom initiated the delivery of a light snack.

An immature Terran female entered under mind control. She saw and felt nothing. Kiri Ung rectified the problem. He started to feed slowly, with a care to preserve life for as long as possible. Shrieks of agony improved his digestion.

Much later, after cleansing from his meal, he made his way from his office into the heart of the moon base. Spotless steel passageways, unrelieved by any clutter, brought a sense of well-being to Kiri Ung. Absence of any aroma, apart from Nestine pheromones, also pleased him after the stink of terrified prey. Once past the feeding frenzy, he found the aftermath offensive.

He detected the Queen's wonderful scent. One final set of doors slid open to admit him to her presence. He thought he might burst from the mere sight of her. She glowed with health. Her elongated cream abdomen glistened with a slick sheen as it hovered over the hexagonal egg receptacles beneath her. Young larvae crawled around and over her, some sleeping in the fur on her torso. Large, compound eyes turned towards him, sending shivers of sexual pleasure thrilling through his body. Her pheromones created an instant erection. He knew she could sense this and that he had no human alleles contained in his phronx organ to complete an insemination.

"Kiri Ung?" The Queen's sibilant whisper increased his excitement. She had named him.

"I bring news." He bowed low before her.

*

Shi Nom observed the male making his obeisance with interest. Kiri Ung possessed a ruthless drive that made him stand apart from the rest. She wondered if he would relieve her boredom for a few moments. Trapped in her vast nursery chamber for over a millennium by her increased size, she lived for the brief glimpses of other places that her males brought with them embedded in their minds. She hated this chamber and kept the lumen level low so that she did not need to see the extreme corners of it.

He had a powerful physique with a well-muscled frame, although bipedal. Shi Nom hoped for more legs on each male larva before it metamorphosed, but that hadn't happened so far. Still, as males went, he had a more developed jaw. It held a faint resemblance to her mandibles with his tusks larger than usual.

"How does the war progress?" She sensed that he had become calm once more.

"We are gaining ground. Five more Terran forts wrested from Brethren control."

"And the bad news?" *What is he hiding in the secret areas in his mind?*

"There is a new leader amongst the rebels."

"Eat him." The command produced a sense of dismay in Kiri Ung. His thoughts revealed themselves to her.

"So you think he would improve our race. I agree. The most powerful Seer in existence will make a good source. When do you expect to acquire him?"

The male had run through awe, excitement, to become calm once more. "Soon. He is on land. He cannot evade us for long."

"See that he doesn't. We might approve the reward you have in mind if the task is conducted with alacrity."

*

Swirling shafts of brilliant crystalline light resolved into a softer flame radiance of a campfire. Arthur shivered, chilled to his soul. He wanted to scrub down his body in a cleansing unit in Avalon. Perhaps that might come a little way to removing the filth he now wore like a second skin. The feeding frenzy of Kiri Ung turned his insides to mush. Arthur's stomach responded accordingly – he heaved out his last meal.

"I did warn you." Emrys was there, holding him until the spasm passed, easing him back into a sitting position and pulling a glass of spring water out of the air to hand to Arthur.

The water tasted good, cold and pure, with a faint suggestion of sweetness. He took careful sips, concentrating on the water and not what had made the drink necessary. Control returned in spurts and with it came anger; a white-hot anger that blazed through him, burning disgust in its wake. How long could he elude the Nestines? Would his comrades obey an order to incinerate him if he were about to be captured? Is that what it would take to stop these creatures?

"Think about the broader picture, not your own issues," Emrys advised, moving back to his former position opposite Arthur.

The Nestine creature was convinced Avalon would fail. Why? Resources? Trade with the surface took care of mineral needs now.

"What Avalon gets from the Brethren barely touches the surface of what is needed." Emrys threw a log on his fire, seemingly unaware that he picked thoughts from Arthur's mind. The sparks swirled upwards into the night sky, making shadows on his face. "There is a metal, found only on the moon that is needed to build a replacement moisture seal over the city."

"But the dome has no weak spots." Arthur searched his memories for any recollection of cracks or leaks in the transparent dome shielding Avalon from the crushing pressure of deep-sea water.

"There are not one or two spots. All of it is weakened. That is why I had to reach out to the surface for fresh chromosomes to make a host body for my essence. I thought that was the only way to get out of encrypted circuitry."

"Couldn't the shell be reinforced?" He didn't want to remember how close Emrys had come to eliminating his mind.

"With what, Arthur? And by whom?"

If we captured a Nestine skyship . . . if we overran their moon base for the metals . . . and then what? Emrys was right. Who could fix the dome? Maintenance engineers couldn't make complex amalgams. Medi-techs dealt with flesh and robotics. A list of all other skills flashed through his mind. Then he thought of the makers of the Nestines and what had happened to them, to all the innovators who had suddenly become a waste of space when space became an expensive luxury. They got left behind on a surface that Nestine creator Greenley sterilized of life. Avalon didn't get any scientists. A cold chill ran down his back. They had only got people to maintain a structure and environment already established. The skills no longer existed.

"Accept your losses. You can't change what is going to happen to the city. Your actions can affect whether the inhabitants survive or not, and you are almost out of time."

"So you keep telling me." Arthur thrust his hands towards the blaze, wanting something to take the chill off his body. "I can't trade for weapons. I don't have enough men to attack a

63

fort, even if they had anything useful, except women. And I can't return to Avalon. So I go hunting for a sword? Why? What difference is it going to make?"

"The weapon represents pure thought. Deception is laid bare when one with the strength unsheathes it."

"What happens if I don't have this strength?"

"Then you will die. The sword will kill the unworthy at the first touch." Darkness closed in around Emrys. The campfire winked out of existence. Wind howled in the darkness of empty moorland and carried one last instruction on its wings. "Find the sword, Arthur. Ask your sire."

*

Cold shadows sent gooseflesh over Arthur's sweat soaked body. By his side was the pool of light from summer solstice that moments earlier, had erupted over the altar stone and himself. Internal time sense told him differently. At least one standard time unit had passed for the sun to travel so far. Around the fallen columns, he caught sight of squatting forms of his group. Some looked outward, on guard duty and the rest had their eyes fixed on him, silent, waiting.

Kai flowed to his feet, moving toward Arthur with an almost feline stealth. "What happened?"

"I know why I must find this sword of my dreams." Arthur leaned back against the shaded altar, losing himself in pressing thoughts. *Ask your sire*, Emrys said. Just go up to him and say, *Here I am, your firstborn? Sorry, I'm part fish, not much choice there, but I am your son. So what do you know about this sword I need to find? Give it to me. I know it can save our race. Oh? What from? Well, I can show you if I have the sword.*

"Arthur? Share with me." Kai reached out to grab him by the upper arms just as a raven settled on one of the capstones. The bird looked down on them cawing, sounding amused in its raucous fashion.

"Dragon knows where it is. I have to ask Dragon." Arthur used the Brethren name for his father. It seemed less personal that way.

"By the Seventh Hell, I could see something amiss the moment you came back to yourself. I told you not to trust Emrys."

"He is not a problem. I understand what he did, and why, now." Emrys knew the genome types for the original ruling council had been lost. He knew no one could access the primary console and so release him. That is why he wanted a body, one that matched his own as near as possible. He wanted to engrave his engrams in Arthur's brain, to take over before the dome failed and the water came in. *Then we made the gestalt, my brother and I.* And it worked. Arthur looked up at the bird, wanting to be as free.

"Uther of Tadgehill, the black dragon duke. His name still sends waves of fear through gatherings, I am told." Kai's face lacked any movement, any trace of expression the second his lips stilled.

This alone warned Arthur how seriously Kai opposed any contact.

Waves of disapproval flowed from Kai. "And you think he is the type to hand over a weapon, maybe one he values, to a stranger, who just happens to be half-mutant?"

"My skin doesn't look so obvious now. Not the parts that are suntanned, anyway."

"This is summer, in case you hadn't noticed. Were you also planning on wearing a neck wrap to hide your gill slits? Don't you think he might find someone wearing winter gear right now a bit strange?"

"Fine. You've made your point, Kai."

"Then we go steal some women?" Haystack and Stalker both stood up to moved closer to Kai as if to add their own weight to his question.

"I track down Dragon, ask him, and then we steal some women." Faced with a need from his men for a realistic goal, Arthur could not tell them all he now knew. Kiri Ung grasped the bigger implications from the failure of Avalon. Without Brethren to provide shelter and sustenance, Submariners couldn't survive on land. If Brethren lacked Submariner firepower, Brethren numbers would diminish and those left could not support a useless group of people, especially in the numbers a crumbling city would generate.

"Arthur, let one of us go instead." Haystack leaned against one of the upright stone sentinels. "Or both of us. You risked enough visiting the Archive, or whatever that thing calls itself right now. We heard what it did to you before."

"Dragon used to welcome Brethren at his fort." Stalker moved forward one pace to a level with Haystack. "We might be able to get him drunk. Kai's father could do that."

"Thanks, but it must be me. The sword is dangerous in some way. Emrys, the Archive, said it kills any touching it who shouldn't." Arthur turned towards the west, looking out from between two columns. The scent of wild roses came on the wings of a light breeze. Grasses, just starting to turn golden, swayed as if caught in a ritual dance. Clouds drew shadows on the ground beneath, and the west way led toward darkness. *Why did I think that? West is where the sun sets.* Yet darkness hovered at the fringe of his awareness. A great winged creature of black with a heart of stone.

Chapter 7

A THICK PLUME OF smoke spiraled, twisting toward the night sky into the dark mantle overhead. Arthur poked at a clump of damp seaweed on the top of his fire, willing Dragon to spot his blatant challenge.

The duke must respond to a presence on this, his own private beach, so close to the man's emergency escape route and well stocked supply cache. From his mother's memories, he knew how closely Dragon guarded his bolthole. Arthur tossed aside an empty can from that hoard. The contents had satisfied his hunger and nourished his need for retaliation. He got a small satisfaction at stealing from one who should have been his provider and protector during childhood.

Those thoughts sparked off discomfort for having left his unit stranded on a safer southern beach. Arguments, spoken and silent, had made poor companions as they retraced their path to the submersible. Aware of Dragon's hostility to Brethren, everyone predicted a violent reaction to any incursion into the ruler's territory. They wanted to wait until they had an established base.

During the long hours of that last night with them, Arthur ran through every possible encounter in the silences of his soul. Any show of force would precipitate battle, and that meant casualties he could not afford.

Submariners on the last watch of the night proved easy targets for a sleep suggestion. He felt better about his actions once he unloaded supplies from the vessel for them.

Now alone on Dragon's beach, the submersible buried in soft sand offshore, Arthur faced his fears. What if Dragon didn't come alone? Would the man open the way to this secret place for the eyes of others? He gambled on Dragon's need for an escape route from enemies if forced to take such an action. Enemies with the elements of surprise and planning in place could overrun any fort. Dragon knew he was at risk of being made an Outcast. One slip of the man's iron will to reveal his submerged psi powers . . .

Arthur recalled the session of sensory playback where he had learned Dragon answered a mental summons not directed at him. Riding out after Rowan from High fort, the duke confronted Shadow, and she learned her former mate wanted her dead. So what happened when he found he had a son by the woman he wished to kill? Arthur briefly considered forcing answers from Dragon's mind, but that might awaken the man's latent abilities, and then what; the sentence of an Outcast to remove him from his fort? Arthur could picture Dragon unleashed amongst the Brethren, fitting in with their lifestyle, fighting alongside them, and gaining trust until he found Shadow. He'd kill her.

The calming mantras helped while away empty hours of waiting. Stars crept across the night sky to Arthur's chant. "Ohm mani padme hum." It infused vital energy over and over until dawn kissed night to awaken the silver sky through to a fiery blush.

*

Uther, Duke of Tadgehill, rode his horse out into crisp morning mist after suffering a sleepless night. The smoke had disturbed him. One of the sentries spotted it, and he countermanded a unit going out to investigate when he saw the direction. No one knew the path down to his bolthole, save one. *Was it possible? Could she still be alive?* He knew Brethren possessed a limited lifespan. Most of them vanished after five years at the most, but there were exceptions. That one with flame-colored hair lasted fifteen turns before he dropped out of sight. Then there was the dark-skinned Outcast, still active, by report, after twenty. Those were men though. How could a woman survive the harsh life of a mercenary? She could fight a challenge, but a battle to the death countless times? What if the other Outcasts cared for her? They seemed defensive and protective around her.

He spurred his horse toward the tree-lined path rising upward from Tadgehill and by a waterfall. The way that droplets of moisture clung, weeping, to leaves brought unwanted memories.

How alive she had been that day so long ago, on the horse he had just gifted her. She rode as if one with the beast, clearly demonstrating her skills, his War Maid. The memory of desire clawed at him on the appearance of bleak moorland at the top of the gorge. Riding over those windswept wastes, she had looked so vital when her hair had loosened to fly behind her like a veil of golden silk. Later, on his beach he remembered her prickly reserve crumbling. *By the Harvesters how did she do that to me? How did she make me care so much?*

A kiss, one single kiss and he wore his heart on his sleeve for sake of an untried virgin. Cold rage burned through him at the thought of how she had betrayed him. The priest made sure she paid although he wished the ceremony had been delayed until he returned to his fort.

Uther spotted the gully leading down to his beach. He let his horse have his head on the descent. She knew her life was forfeit. So why did she take this risk, if it was her? Did she think time mellowed him? Was she so old and infirm that she sought death? Was that the reason she signaled, knowing what he would bring? He wondered how she would look. Her golden hair had become a close-cropped helmet last time he saw her.

The descent reached a perilous stage where granite became laced with mica and other rock. That required his concentration in case the horse stumbled on any loose debris. He freed his feet from the stirrups by habit rather than thought. Two more sharp turns by a sheer drop onto rocks below, and then the route began to level out. A final turn and he saw . . .

A figure seated by a dying fire within a few paces of the surf line. Clad in silvery-gray from head to foot, it blended into the mist. He made out a half cloak with a head cowl from the way the fabric billowed in the wind and the faint glimmer of a sword hilt glinting in the growing light. No horse though, and this puzzled him. Something wasn't right. He proceeded cautiously, abandoning the charge he might have considered. The figure rose to face him and pushed back the cowl. Shock numbed Uther. He saw himself wreathed in mist. Surf slapped on the beach, sucking sand to the depth. Crash, grind; over and over, and the likeness stood immobile, watching him.

Without direction, the horse continued toward the figure until Uther hauled back on the reins. The other self-assumed a position of defense, hand on weapon hilt. Uther's flesh crawled as he recognized the grace and precision of a Brethren fighter. A shaft of sunlight bathed the apparition, reflecting off its face. Reflecting? *By the Harvesters, a mutant wearing my features.* He drew his sword, swallowing back the bile that rose in his throat.

The creature stepped one pace back. "I just want to talk." Quiet words.

Uther dismounted. He had no wish to endanger his horse when he could take the creature on foot. He advanced slowly, aiming to get between his opponent and the water. It had to have come by water, so that was its escape route also. This parody of his appearance outraged him. He wanted it dead.

The mutant also drew a sword, backing away some more. One pace to the rear and one side step nearer water. Uther charged, aiming an overhead blow. Swords clashed, ringing, muffled in the mist. He recovered for a sideswipe, again countered, and then the mutant fought back. The screech of metal on metal and the grunts of effort filled his ears. Sand slipped beneath his feet. He saw an opening – took it to meet empty air. A rush of wind warned him too late. Stars exploded in front of his eyes, filling his vision. He hit the ground hard and hurting. His head pounded. A weight landed on his chest and sword arm.

Uther looked into his enemy's eyes as his vision cleared, expecting the deathblow from the man astride him. He didn't understand why his enemy had used the flat of the blade and not the edge. Why stay the moment of death? Sand shifted under his back as he tried to move. The weight pinning him down merely adjusted to compensate. Uther breathed in the salt of ocean and the harsh tang of dried seaweed. There was a clump near his face. Maybe if he threw it at the creature . . . ?

The sword tip altered direction to snag the vegetation and toss it out of reach.

Those eyes . . . deep violet eyes looked at him, anger tightening the corners. Memory hissed through his soul, but the sword now aimed at his neck made him draw one last breath. A seagull launched off its cliff top nest through the clearing haze. Uther wanted to fly with the bird.

The weapon flashed in the growing sunlight on its descent, to stop just short of contact.

"Why? Why do you hate her so much?" The mutant demanded. "What did she ever do to you that she earned banishment?"

Violet eyes glared into his, and then he knew where he had seen them before, but not why this one wore them. What were these mutant creatures that they could mimic the features of others? How did this one know of her – his first wife? What business had a mutant with an Outcast, turned Brethren?

"Too craven to answer? Did she offend your pride?"

"Who are you to know of her? Did she send you?" The words came painfully against the pressure on his chest. The creature standing on him appeared to possess perfect balance.

"Who am I?" The mutant's lips tightened to a thin line. A muscle at his jawline started to tic. "Her son—and yours."

Shock sent a tingle over Uther's skin until a cold, clammy sensation took over. His own face wearing her eyes continued to glare down at him. *By the seventh hell, how could this be?* But the creature claiming to be his son was mutant. His heart stopped pounding its frightened message. *Lies, all lies.*

"Nice . . . try. I can see the . . . scales of your hide . . . and the gills." *Will it kill me now?*

"Fact," a voice so like his own insisted. "Her father was a full mutant." The creature carefully stepped off him, keeping the sword ready. "Not that cruel apology for a sire who lives at Menhill . . . the real one."

"Not possible." Uther rubbed at his sword arm to get back some sensation. He didn't know what to think. This male had features from both of them and knew of Menhill, yet she could have told that story.

"Why do you think Menhill's ruler, Hald, traded her away?" The man flicked at a lock of black hair wind blew across his face. The eyes never wavered though. "What king, or duke, trades a Gold Band lady for a few parcels of ore? Not even full parcels and he didn't take the time to check."

"How, by the seventh hell, do you know?" His former duchess would never betray a fact like that, however low she had sunk. It diminished her too.

"I am her son." The eyes turned a darker shade of violet as if the owner held memories of pain. "I know everything."

"Then why did she play false with me and lay with a Silver Band?" Uther's seagull screeched, flying out to sea. He wished he could fly with it, away from this. He wished he had never seen the smoke in the night. How could he bear to hear the same answer over again from yet another source?

"She didn't." The sword grazed his throat, causing a sharp pain and wetness there. "She has no idea why she earned disgrace."

"But my priest said . . ." Could this be right? Was she innocent? "Then why destroy her life?"

"He lied." The mutant's eyes narrowed. "I have her memories. Memories cannot lie. She lost her way of life because her mutant heritage was emerging. The priest couldn't allow that to happen."

"The Silver Band confessed." Uther knocked the blade aside. He threw himself, rolling right, gaining his feet, to square off against his opponent. He wanted to die standing.

72

"Do you remember an Outcast leader warning you to be good the last time you saw Shadow?" One dark eyebrow quirked up, questioning. "Priests know your thoughts, and can manipulate your mind. Do you want to be free?"

"Go ahead. Kill me." The memory of his last meeting with the one now called Shadow danced before his eyes. He recalled the urgent need to drink water from a certain stream that day. When he arrived, she had been there. He didn't recognize her at first. She had concealed her lovely face with skin dye in hideous patterns, and the way she moved – like them, the Brethren. He wanted to snap her neck then, but the odds of four to one stopped him even trying. "Tell her you have avenged her, or did you want to take her my head?" A sick feeling made him shudder. She was mutant; he had slept with a mutant. "Is she watching?"

"Shadow doesn't know I am here, and I came in peace." The man backed away, toward the waves, sheathing his sword.

"Why? What do you want from me?"

"Answers."

"Then go. I have nothing for you." Uther looked at his son, the son he always wanted and never had. Anger at her and at fate boiled in him. This son could never rule in his stead. If she were normal, then so would be his son. She should have turned a child over to him to raise, but he could see why she didn't. What should have been a reunion shredded his soul.

"I claim but one thing in your power to give." Hunger burned deep in the eyes of his son. "I need a very old sword forged from sky metal that I am told you may have."

Uther laughed. It burst from him unheeded until he remembered that he had never told his former wife about the legend. How had this young man found out? "I don't have it. I don't even know if it exists. My father told me of it as a family story."

"Then I ask for all you know."

His son stood straighter as if this mattered a great deal to him. Somehow, a mantle of authority settled over those young shoulders. Uther caught a glimpse of the man his son had become. Reluctant respect washed away his outrage.

"There is a lake to the south that is said to connect to the ocean by an underground river." Uther looked out to sea, hating the memories surfacing. "That is where I lost your mother's trail when I tracked her. Since you claim to know all she knows, then you will not have a problem finding it. She vanished without a trace. All I found was evidence of a riderless horse heading north from that point. My father said the sword was thrown into that lake, and one day one of us would find it. That was the promise of the luck legend. We were to watch for it when danger threatened."

"And now it does. I thank you." His son started to back away into the waves.

"Wait. What danger?"

"The one you fear. Why else keep your mind locked from other thoughts?" The young man reached into a pocket to produce a shining golden wristband. "Do you wish to be free?"

"I don't understand."

"The band you wear as status symbol lets priests read your thoughts. This one will shield your mind from them." His son took a step toward the shore. "I intended to give it in trade."

"Bands are attached for life." No one could remove a band. Sometimes a Bronze Band tried, and then there was a bloodbath to clean up, although nothing large enough to bury.

"Shadow's wasn't. She is free, as are many others."

To be free to think as he wanted without the fear of being made an Outcast? "Do it."

The young man produced a tubular device from another pocket as he advanced. The tip glowed green and then turned blue as it made contact with the band on Uther's wrist. It snapped open to fall onto sand. The replacement closed into place with a faint click, hardly audible above the noise of breakers.

"You will see things that you must learn to ignore." His son wore a neutral expression as if he gave instructions by rote and not choice. "Your gods are mortal and now visible. They have craft that fly. Look away from any unusual sight." The young man nodded briefly and turned toward the waves, wading out. Surf swelled around his thighs, seeming to welcome him.

"Stop. I don't know your name." Now he wanted to know. This proud young man needed a name. Uther wanted to remember his son as a person.

"Arthur. My name is Arthur." The slow, calculated smile of Brethren lifted familiar features in a chilling way and then he dived. There was a brief flurry of bubbles as the last evidence of passage vanished.

Uther looked out to sea, at the home of his son. He wondered what was down there as he tried not to think about breathing. That was an issue he needed distance from until he found a way of dealing with it.

Chapter 8

FRIGID WATER TRIGGERED Arthur's gill flaps open when he dived. He had worn his boots for the confrontation, needing a good grounding, but elected not to take them off in front of Dragon, his father. Arthur didn't want Dragon to see the membranes poking out between his toes. He lived with the consequences now, not having the extra thrust of fins at his disposal.

This man he had expected to loathe was also a victim. Shadow, his mother, never thought of the possibility that Dragon had been duped by false information. Rage for the Nestines made him want to swear. Not an available relief when his lungs were closed off. Without air, he couldn't vocalize. The need dug into him as he swam deeper into murky waters. His implanted proximity sensor directed his path while his rage boiled.

The sense of loss formed a hard and cold core within him. Arthur knew now why Shadow mourned the loss of this man. Dragon possessed enormous charisma. The man suffered from their separation as much as she had; something made apparent by his father's abrupt change of attitude immediately following the disclosure that Shadow had not betrayed their union. This revealed Dragon's need to vindicate her.

Arthur brushed aside a shoal of pilchards that fled in panic from his path. The flash of their silvery scales from a shaft of sunlight piercing downward brought forth another image; the sword, so near, and yet so inaccessible. Dragon's coordinates pointed toward a huge lake Arthur and his men used as an escape route before their ill-fated visit to Avalon. Had the Nestines tracked his unit there? Would they be watching? Those questions rattled through his brain even as he located the sub-mersible. One touch on the control panels of a beacon made the craft emerge from its sandy tomb. Arthur closed his eyes against particles and used the beacon to locate a round access hatch. Moments later he gained entry.

As water drained away from an entry pod and was replaced by air, he made his decision. Time must pass before any attempts at retrieval of the sword. Nestine interest must be focused elsewhere before any search could be instigated. That meant a pre-emptive strike of some sort. He looked through a transparent port into the cabin where a map of land and a map of underwater were superimposed against a wall. More delay, whatever fort he chose to be a target. And it must be a coastal one to minimize risk to the group, which left few choices.

His gills shut off in synchronism with the flap across his trachea shrinking. Arthur inhaled and began to swear.

*

Stony silence met Arthur when he emerged from the waves to rejoin his group. Kai looked away and began packing supplies. A basilisk of cold stares bored into him.

"Without us?" Stalker's truncated Brethren comment spoke volumes. Submariners joined Kai to make ready for a departure, but all the Outcasts drew into a semi-circle around Arthur.

Haystack, his face devoid of expression, stepped forward.

"Back off," Kai's command rang through the soft sound of wind and breakers. "He had his reasons for what he did."

"And they were?" Stalker half turned toward Kai.

"Dragon is his sire." Kai shifted to edge between Arthur and Stalker. "Hear him out."

Haystack exploded into action, swinging a right hook that landed Arthur on his back in the sand. Bright motes swirled like fireflies in his vision for a few moments, and then he sat up, fingering his bruised chin.

"Did he survive his relationship with a mutant?" Haystack leveled out his words in a flat, incurious tone.

The quiet words cut Arthur more than the name. "I needed to meet the man who wanted my mother dead. He had information." Speech hurt his mouth, and he tasted blood.

"Then Tadgehill is adrift without a leader." Stalker pushed by Kai to stare down at Arthur. "Only a Brethren could take down Dragon. This is known."

"We will be hunted by all," Haystack said. He shook off Stalker's restraining hand. "Was getting him worth putting yourself at risk?"

"I didn't kill him." Arthur stayed down, not wanting to increase the tension by fronting them. "There was a misunderstanding we cleared up. He offered the information without being threatened."

"Arthur, if you awakened his psi factor with a mind probe then he is dead for sure," Kai said, pushing between the two other Brethren.

"I didn't. We talked after fighting a bit. Then he let me re-band him."

"Arthur," Huber joined the angry triad, a nervous tick near his mouth making his scales shine in the starlight. "You have just given him access to every Brethren camp. Any Submariner will let him in when he passes a scan. He will search for Shadow."

"Dragon has laid his vengeance to rest, at least as far as she is concerned. His priest might want to make sure not to walk near any overhanging rocks though, unless he wants to wear one in his head."

Huber tried to stifle a nervous laugh. Kai smiled, and the other two shuffled their feet, looking away. Arthur held out his hand, and Kai hauled him upright.

"What now, brother?" Kai said. Just a hint of stiffness in his tone warned Arthur that Kai hadn't laid the matter to rest, despite what he had told the others.

"We go around to the east coast to make some noise. While the Nestines search for us there, we can find a site for a base elsewhere."

"The sword?" Haystack raised one eyebrow.

"Is in Dozary lake. We can go fishing when the Nestines decide to target another trade route."

Tension dissolved like snow in summer. Haystack, Stalker and Huber turned back to the camp where others stood waiting. Only Kai remained in Arthur's path.

"So what really happened? That story sounds too easy on the ears."

"Dragon tried to kill me." Arthur turned away, looking out at white tipped breakers on the seething blackness. *I wonder if he would have tried harder if he had known of our kinship at the start?* Perhaps that maggot-ridden corpse should be left undisturbed. He felt Kai's hand on his shoulder. "He's good. Almost as good as you."

"My father sparred with both of us in practice sessions." A slight tremor shook Kai's hand. "How did you turn him around?"

"After I took him down I just wanted to get away. He called me back. That's when we talked."

"Show me." Kai jerked him around to make eye contact.

They both knew the risks mind link between them engendered. The blending of minds that so nearly ended both their lives invaded dreams to bring either one of them awake, screaming: the formation of one sentient entity where two should exist. For them, Kai's request expressed the depth of his concern.

Arthur separated the incident into an isolated memory ingram, and then he shared in one brief burst of togetherness.

"Dragon has unexpected worth," Kai's comment summed up the entire experience. "He still loves her."

"The Nestines have a lot to answer for," Arthur agreed. "So we go stir up a swarm."

*

Arthur waded out of the surf to take up his position for a good laz gun shot. Kai and the other Brethren remained in the submersible while each Submariner stood vigil at various beach locations around an eastern coastal fort. They waited for a skyship to begin patrol. By collective choice, they had decided for a swift, teasing attack followed by immediate retreat. Kai with his fey gift, along with the other Brethren, would know who needed to be retrieved first from who stood in greater danger of detection.

He selected an outcrop of rock standing clear of waves for his placement. From above they would look like patches of darkness against the ocean by moonlight and one more solid shape wouldn't be noticed. The position gave him a good range over the cliffs and an immediate water exit once the shot was fired. He settled in for a long and boring wait, confident of his aim with only a gentle neap tide coming in. This still, cloudless night gave him a perfect target zone. His transmitter vibrated, and he brought it to his ear.

"There's a disturbance coming your way." Kai's voice sounded unfamiliar through the electronic distortion.

"Nestines?" Arthur scanned the skies, looking for a telltale light.

"No, a new Outcast hunt." There was a pause. "Or something like one. The target is panicking, and that is a fresh factor."

"A trap for us then?"

"Not that I can sense. I am feeling a time nexus and a Terran with psi powers heading toward it, followed by hostiles. Be prepared to dive."

"Acknowledged." Now more curious than concerned, Arthur scanned the cliff line; aware Kai wouldn't have broken silence without a good cause when the Nestines could pick up on a carrier wave signal. He knew Kai would relocate the craft, but he also need to watch out for skyships.

A faint thudding sound grew louder from the top of the cliffs. A horseman appeared, made a frantic turn, but the ground crumbled beneath thrashing hooves. The horse screamed as it fell; its rider kicked free, falling silently, a cloak whipping up around the ankles in a headfirst dive.

The horse hit rock; a dull thud of flesh crushing and then lay twitching. A splash gave Arthur a trace of hope for the rider. Other thuds sounded from above, and he picked out at least ten riders, who now stared down at the broken carcass for a few moments before melting back into the night.

Arthur dived, striking out for the fallen rider's position. He found a body minutes later, drifting underwater in the current. First, he attached a demagnetizer to the victim's band, waiting until it clicked open. Once the bracelet drifted to the bottom, he towed his burden toward the shore, staying underwater; it didn't matter to the rider any longer. The second his feet found purchase he closed his gill flaps. Holding his breath, he dragged the inert body above breaker line. He dumped the rider face up on the sand and knelt down to lock their mouths, and then he sucked, using his gills to expel water from the rider's lungs. The second he ran out of water he switched to air, breathing for both of them with one hand pinching the rider's nostrils tight shut. Just as he decided to give up, the chest underneath him heaved as the victim began to breathe. This remained the only sign of returning life; something else was very wrong with this person. Looking around, he saw a dark slash in the face of the cliffs ahead – a cave that might be wide enough to shield him from marauding skyships.

The small Terran was light in his arms as he trudged across soft sand to the cave mouth. A faint suspicion surfaced in his mind. Fortunately, sand extended into the rock, a warning that this formation would be underwater in a spring tide. For now, it served his purpose. Arthur laid the light body down, careful to do so slowly. He reached into a pocket in his tunic for a glow globe.

The soft radiance confirmed his guess. She didn't look more than late second decade, seventeen, maybe eighteen summers. Fair hair draped around her, fanning out in strings, like wet seaweed. Her oval face was the most beautiful he had ever seen. Dark lashes brushed her cheeks as if she slept. Under a small, tip-tilted nose, her lips formed a perfect bow. Why would anyone want to harm such a beauty? But he knew the answer already. Hunters chased her because she had become prey. She had emergent psi power, and that was enough to condemn her.

A large bruise near her temple explained why she hadn't stirred. Faint tremors shook through her slight body. Her sodden clothes chilled her, and he risked losing her if she took a fever. Arthur knew he wanted to keep her in that moment. They had talked of a settlement and women; well here was one for the taking. A raid or two to get some more companions would give them a chance for the future. What woman wouldn't want to escape the drudgery of fort life where she had to be submissive to all males of her ranking? He knew the Brethren women lived how they chose, without any man to naysay them. They took a partner or a series of lovers as they wished, as by right. Submariner women held equal rank to men also. Not one male in his group would overstep those imperatives. From outside and in the sky came a faint whistling hiss that announced a skyship's quiet engines. Arthur killed his light. Now he was stuck until daybreak at least. The Nestines would want to make sure the bracelet they tracked remained static. His skin tingled as he remembered how removing the girl's band had come as an afterthought. They might also scan the general area for any type of metal she wore. He stripped off her jerkin, hands clumsy in the dark, and then her riding pants with their copper eyelet closures. It took endless moments to sprint down to the surf and throw them in. Time seemed to stand still, holding him captive for the attention of whoever might be concerned.

Once back in the cave mouth, he watched the vessel where it hovered in the same spot. A cry from behind him sent Arthur groping into darkness. He had to keep the girl quiet at all costs now he knew how keen Nestine hearing really was.

She whimpered once more before he found her curled into an almost fetal position. His touch sent her flying into his arms, trembling. Any second and she could start crying. He risked a light scan into her mind and found what she thought she fled from. Her father had arranged a marriage for her with an older ruler, so she decided to run to other kinfolk while he thought through his decision again. She didn't understand why the hunters fired arrows at her, and she thought they must have been wearing false uniforms to disguise a kidnap attempt, or to hurt him by killing her.

The whistling whine retreated to begin a grid search pattern. Now they could talk if but in whispers.

"Steady now, be very quiet, the ones who hunt are still searching," he warned.

"You will hide me?" Her voice sounded like a smooth bite of midnight, low and rich.

"Until they are gone. Then you decide what you want to do." Arthur calculated dawn to be breaking in less than an hour. He didn't think the Nestines would stay out to wait for it since daylight missions took far more psychic energy to maintain their concealment from Terrans.

"I hit the water." A faint waver betrayed her uncertainty and her fear. "Did you save me?"

"I happened to be passing by when I heard the splash."

"Then there must be a reward." Her hands grabbed his hair, pulling his face down to hers.

Not averse to light recreation, Arthur obliged with a kiss, not his best, but the one meant to convey 'I am flattered, but you are not who I want to be with.' Again he sent out a light probe into her thoughts. Her head hurt from the bruise, and her thoughts jangled in confusion, reduced to one objective and the need to forget all else that frightened her. She wanted a lover before she went to the old man. She didn't care who it was; she just wanted to revenge herself on her father and his choice.

Now was not the time to begin telling her the real reason for the hunt, not when he needed her quiet, and she couldn't think clearly. She didn't ask so big a price, and he had been celibate for a while now. Arthur got into the spirit of her invitation. Several times she moaned when he touched a bruised part when taking off the rest of her clothes, but she aided him where she could.

Terran skin felt very different from Submariner, more like the difference between smooth, shiny fabric and the petals of a flower, both pleasant if worlds apart. He explored, aware the girl appeared to be a novice at this delightful sport, although he didn't want to probe too deeply into her mind to confirm his guess. That would mean explaining, and he wanted to continue loving her. She learned kissing quickly and then the rest followed until he pierced her, bringing a muffled cry from her lips.

Arthur almost stopped then. He hadn't been prepared for a virgin, but she made no further protest and seemed to relax again. He continued, gaining rhythm as the first rays of sun shone through to bathe them both. Her body responded around his shaft, and he prepared to lower his body temperature even as she opened tight shut eyes to look at him.

And then she screamed and fought. Stunned, Arthur lost control, collapsing against her as he tried to hold her fingernails from his eyes. He couldn't stop his seed flowing, nor could he withdraw. He used his only option to quieten her noise. He sent her mind deep into sleep.

Chapter 9

PINK TINGED CLOUDS smeared an azure sky as if shamed to emerge. *A few more minutes of darkness . . . I could've talked to her, explained.* Her scream echoed in his mind, blending with the sound of surf crashing onto shingles. He couldn't think beyond a need to make matters right.

Clothes, he must retrieve the rest of her clothes. The need sent him diving to stay below until he found all of her discarded belongings and the Nestine band. He buried that beneath rocks on the seabed to stop their scans detecting any trace of a signal. In a few days without neuro-stimulation from a wearer, it would fade to become another useless scrap of flotsam. The girl must be safe though, and for that he needed to erase all memory of their encounter.

Arthur struggled to dress her in her wet leather clothing. He managed the tunic, but the pants, without her conscious cooperation, took time. She fought against his sleep suggestion all the while, making the job more difficult with her twitching and sudden thrashing spasms. Thank the stars they all kept false wristbands, just in case of encounters with new Outcasts. He programmed his spare to match her former band of gold. Still, she thrashed, but he dared not increase his level of control on her mind, not with the purple bruise on her temple. If any area of weakness existed as a result of her fall, then having her fight for control might kill her. At the finish, her resistance forced him to release his restraint.

Her eyelashes fluttered, and then her eyes snapped open. Her gaze wasn't the deep Brethren stare that so discomforted others;

it was worse, as if he resembled some lower life form that had come to her attention because it smelled bad.

"How are you feeling?" Arthur wanted her talking. His opening enquiry sent the corners of her mouth down in a moue of distaste.

"Look, you needed a male, and you got one," he reasoned. "It didn't matter who a while back."

The girl lost focus to look right through him as if he didn't exist. Her face shifted until it settled into harsh lines with narrowed eyes and thin lips compressed by loathing. She looked now as she might in later life – a bitter woman with a score to settle.

Arthur took a deep breath and tried again. "Lady, I can't change what happened, but I can remove all memory of it. Will you allow me to do that for you?" A tentative mind touch bounced off her resolve. "There could be a child of our union. I could stop a pregnancy."

"If one does happen . . ." Her voice rasped like a blade being sharpened. "I will be forever free of men. What mate would choose a woman who births mutants?"

The fierce note of triumph sent cold chills to his soul. She looked directly at him, letting her eyes rest upon those differences all Submariners bore. "And I will still be free, should the child look normal. I would raise such a child to wage war against filth like you. Think on that."

"Vengeance gives a hollow victory. It leaves emptiness and despair as a bitter aftertaste. Consider living as you were before our encounter."

"Leave." Her tone carried no trace of emotion. It was final.

"Know that touching one of us will open your eyes to sights you could not see before. Enjoy the experience." Arthur regretted the lie he told, yet he could not share the truth with an enemy, and she would hurt him if she could. He turned away, not looking back as he marched down to the waves. His one consolation was that she hadn't got a clear memory of his

86

features in the dim light of the cave. Her mind contained images of gills and the silvery sheen on his face. He hoped priests would cull any child conceived of their union at birth. A kinder fate than being raised by such a mother.

Arthur dived for the bottom to swim in cool currents. After harsh sunlight, green hues soothed his eyes, and the cold bathed wounds that none could see. Wounds he might carry for the rest of his life. He settled in a large clump of kelp to wait for retrieval.

*

"Why did you leave her?" Stalker voiced the question for all of them.

The last to board the submersible, Arthur endured every eye turned on him. "Because she used me." Truth cut sharper and deeper than any knife. "This girl didn't want a mate. She wanted to remain a War Maid for life." They knew everything except that from his first explanation. The words echoed around the cabin, bouncing off lighted controls, to mock him.

"We are better off without a hater of men," Kai said.

"The girl makes a hard bed for herself." Huber shrugged his shoulders as if shelving the matter.

"I think I know of this War Maid." Haystack looked up from honing a gutting knife. "She is the oldest girl child of Cedric, Earl of Soothwold. I heard he wanted to marry her off to Grimes ruler. Lief is too decent a man for a bitch like Morgaise.

"She didn't say her name," Arthur said.

"No need." Haystack slid his knife into his belt sheath. "She has the beauty you described and the black heart to match it. This girl torments Brethren with her charms just because she knows it is death for one of us to make a play for her. She has three notches on her belt from her 'games' already."

"What if there is a child?" Linden, the youngest Brethren asked, his face creasing with worry lines. "Haven't you avoided producing before?"

87

Arthur looked out of a porthole into the cool green expanse of lighted water. A flatfish flapped away, panicked by the shadow of their vessel. He didn't want to think of what happened, yet he must. "The chance is that any product will be destroyed after birth. Her psi factor condemned her once and couple that to what it gets from me . . . ?"

"Enough gloom," Kai said. "Huber scored a direct hit on a skyship. It crashed into rocks and was vaporized by a backup flight. I guess there were no survivors." His mouth quirked up at one corner, and then he continued, "Now the Nestines are focused here, what is our next move?"

"South coast," Arthur decided. "I think taking the underground channel to Dozary lake might be premature, since we don't know if Dragon reintegrated into his fort yet. Also, until skyships pull back from that trade route, it is off limits to us."

"I agree." Kai turned back to his controls for a moment to adjust the course heading. "South is a good location for a camp. I can think of a bolthole along a river valley not so far from High fort. It gives us a quick escape if we are discovered, and access to major trade routes as well as the fort."

Huber walked over to lean against a bulkhead where he could watch Kai. "On land?" The Submariner narrowed his eyes, waiting.

"A cavern," Arthur said, picking up the direction of his brother's thoughts."Big enough for all of us and any stolen horses.

He saw the place in his mind's eye, a Brethren refuge until the old High King, Alsar, took a dislike to Outcasts. Two caverns, rather than one, and a waterfall flowing from a small aperture above to create a mist that disguised smoke from any fire lit. Daved's rule meant that High fort opened to mercenaries once more, and his group would not look out of place if sighted in the open.

"Why haven't I heard of this place?" Huber frowned, his eyes swinging to Arthur.

Kai looked out into the ocean with an expression that spoke of time and hurt. "It was one of my father's safe places."

"Copper believed in keeping each safe location known to a few, in case a Brethren got taken by Nestines." Arthur tried to put aside the image of a fire burning in that cavern, the place where the self-styled King of the Outcasts won through Shadow's defenses to snare her heart. He saw Kai's eyes on him. A faint tic in his brother's cheek showed the only sign of life in a face carved from living rock. Arthur held his left hand down to move his thumb and forefinger in a slight gesture Kai spotted. In Brethren sign language, it meant silence. What happened in that cavern did not concern others.

"Rowan doesn't keep secrets." Linden walked over to a map displayed to the right of Kai's control panel. His comment on the official Outcast leader brought the eyes of older Brethren to focus on Kai, Copper's son and presumed heir.

"And he loses ground by reversing good policies just for the sake of being different." Arthur didn't want politics to interfere with tactics. Rowan made a good lure to draw the Nestine's attention from his group. The man's blunders also provided willing recruits. Now if he could snag some Submariners from Rowan's group . . .

*

Kiri Ung surveyed the reports on his desk with interest rather than rage. The loss of a ship bothered him, but where it crashed and why, compelled attention. Brethren, even with Submariners in a fighting group, attacked from land not water. Rocks sheltered against laser fire, but water did not.

This attack from the shoreline seemed to be an invitation. The humans instigating such an attack appeared easy targets; too easy. He leaned back in his chair, enjoying the softness of the cured human skin covering, letting his gaze sink into the slick grayness of a metallic ceiling. So why risk death when the same attack on land could be made in comparative safety? *What else is*

89

happening here? What am I looking for? He let his memory take him over the landmass from a high altitude, and then compared the fort concerned with neighbors. *If the attack force intends to win this fort, then they are under the command or a moron . . . or a genius.* The fort held no particular strategic value to either side, and it could be reacquired without much effort should Brethren overrun the place. *Supposing I am just expected to look? So I look here and what happens?* Nothing, for over a week. Not an unexpected tactic, but Kiri Ung had a bone-deep feeling this time a second attack wouldn't come.

His thoughts went to the half-breed he wanted. Now that one could have some obscure motive for an apparently senseless and dangerous attack. *What doesn't he want me to see? Where am I expected to look away from?*

Kiri Ung read through the reports once again. His attention caught on a small passage relating to the culling of a human female registering as telepathic. The thoughts of those prey beasts diverted to hunt her were identical. The female died when her horse fell off a cliff. That fort registered as clear from higher mind functions, so she must have been the only one. Was that why Arthur, the half-breed, ordered that attack? To save the female? KiriUng then saw the time frame from discovering the female with powers to her death. All much too quick for any rescue. Not the female then, something else more important.

If I wore his body, then I would want a base on land so that I could recruit. Now where would I choose? He opened a top drawer in his metal desk, frowning at a slight scraping noise. The pads on the drawer runners needed renewal, but that could wait until he thought through this intriguing maneuver. Kiri Ung withdrew a large rolled map of the northern inhabited landmass. It had black markers for each place of a positive sighting of Arthur. His eyes went from a lake in the west, to north of a fort by the Brethren stronghold and then returned east to the crash site. Somewhere in that triangle and it had to have a water source close for the mutants. But Brethren were troglodytes by choice.

So, I am looking for a cave by water, and they will need fires in winter. We don't have long to wait. His crest pumped into full erection as he contemplated bringing Arthur alive to the Moon Base.

*

From his position by the surf line, Uther, Duke of Tadghill, leaned against a large rock as people scurried about their business in the outside compound. It helped if he couldn't hear their voices well enough to pick out words. He knew they whispered about his moody temper that remained at flare point. Since he returned from what he'd told everyone was a fall from his horse, he tried to keep to himself.

A new priest began morning prayers for the children, who stood in a semicircle facing east. Uther wondered how many other new priests waited for a chance to see the world outside priest quarters. Would this matter to men such as these? The old one took time to die after Uther dropped a rock on his head. There must have been pain, and yet the man made no outcry.

How right of Arthur to warn of strange sights. The impossible happened following the priest's death, when a huge disk emerged from a hole to the left of his fort. The faces in the round windows of that disk . . . he didn't want to think of those; they gave him nightmares. And now he saw one of those creatures emerge from his fort. Not one soul paid any attention to the beast, for it was a beast. Around seven feet tall, he reckoned, and covered in thick brown fur except for a crest of rosy flesh stretching from what would be a forehead in a man, to the area between his shoulder blades. The jaw jutted; a great wedge of importance in a noseless face. The tusks spoke for the diet of the creature.

What would happen if he killed it? The thought felt good until he remembered that every other person in his fort was slave to this creature's slightest whim. Uther had seen it redirect a water bearer to bring a drink, and witnessed the mindless expression

91

wash over the man's face during the episode. He thought about killing those who had hunted down his duchess, but then the water bearer's face came to haunt him.

Uther spotted one of the men he suspected, his captain of the guard. Aleric's cheery expression froze to one of rigid attention when he saw who looked at him.

This had to stop. If he pushed too hard he would have a revolt. For a moment, the thought brought relief. Life as an Outcast meant he could find her, his first duchess. But his second lady swelled with his babe. He couldn't leave her defenseless, nor would he leave a child without a father.

The scene around him faded to the crash and suck of waves. He saw his son, Arthur, poised to fight on the beach, wearing hard lines of suffering about his face. What a ruler that son would have made. Bitter laughter burst from Uther. The duke that never was. Deep within him the wound festered. A man should have the right to claim his son. He wanted to see Arthur again. The wish became a decision carved from rock.

Ashira? Where have you hidden our son? Uther thought back to the two occasions he caught a glimpse of her since her sentencing as an Outcast. He thought her not yet a Brethren on the first sighting, for she'd run from them too. Only later, just outside of High fort, did she look the part. High fort, both times, and she went to ground as if swallowed by the earth. Brethren must have had a secret camp nearby.

One unpleasant task remained before he organized a trip to his chosen location. The gentle girl bearing his child must be told. If he left within the next few days, then he could return with a few weeks to spare before she delivered.

*

Arthur, alone with Haystack, Linden and Stalker stayed silent and still in the cover of trees on the higher side of a river valley as a patrol from High fort rode by. He regretted sending Kai and the Submariners back to the submersible, buried off the south coast, but Nestine skyships swarmed overhead. They should be concentrated in the east, not engaged in a sweep and search pattern here.

Kai sensed increased threat and wanted to make a second strike at the original battleground. The tension flowed away from his brother the second that decision became a task. In those moments, Arthur wondered if another mind attempted to second guess his motives.

The ships here meant a token force in the east. Arthur reckoned Kai's unit could stir up trouble by second nightfall.

"Arthur, there is a skyship heading our way again," Haystack said, looking north over the heads of the distant patrol.

"Are they searching for us?" Linden's voice warbled into tenor for a few syllables before it settled into bass. A flush colored his face. Arthur knew how the boy loathed these lapses caused by puberty. Not one of them made fun of Linden's temporary affliction. This Brethren wore maturity beyond his years through suffering.

"Seems like they will be disappointed," Arthur said as the skyship turned west to begin another sweep. "Our new earrings work well."

"We need to hunt for meat." The ever practical Stalker pulled a catapult from his belt. "Field rations could become useful if we need to stay out of sight."

"What if Nestines send fort patrols to search for stray Brethren?" Haystack put in. "Daved's policy of welcoming us is a two-edged sword."

Arthur distrusted the new High King's switch of tactics. By giving Brethren work and welcome in all forts, Daved made evasion from acceptance stand out as suspect. Sooner or later . . .

"We hunt," he decided. "Don't clean any kills. Let's not leave clues to our presence. Spread out, and regroup here by moonrise with whatever you catch."

Three rabbits, one hare and a pheasant later, the group moved by moonlight in the path of Arthur's borrowed memory.

Red tints of dawn sent long shadows by the time they reached a rocky outcrop with a split for an entrance to their new base. Bone weary, the men stumbled past a narrow fissure, pausing to light glowglobes before entering the first cavern. Not a trace of habitation violated the dry and dusty ground. Arthur led them through to the main cavern to the sound of falling water.

At the left of pooling, splashing water, a hole in the ground gave access to an underground river channel. Not big enough for a Submariner to squeeze though, it offered a way to eliminate wastes without betraying any sign of occupations. Such a resource also preserved the purity of the water supply to the cavern by nature of its flow. Here, all of them dressed their kills. Meat must not be left to spoil; every Brethren knew this. Feathers and hides formed neat heaps to be dealt with after they rested.

Arthur took first watch, making sure all of his men settled for sleep before he took up position in the entrance to the first cavern. It looked to be a glorious fall day about to unfold.

*

Kai led Submariners overland toward their new camp. The skies above during the previous night eased his feeling of threat, by now centering east. Merrick winged a skyship from the beach Arthur had occupied on his fateful vigil. That hit gave them the attention they needed followed by a swift retreat.

He felt the nearness of his brother and searched ahead in time for a safe path, almost missing the rider bearing down on them. Swift hand signals sent all of his men diving for cover. The rider stopped in the middle of a sun dappled glade to dismount and throw his sword and dagger to one side.

"I know you are here," the rider called. "I am alone. I can't be tracked by the creatures controlling others."

Kai stood up. He faced a man like an older version of Arthur but for one detail. He looked into the blue eyes of the dragon duke.

Chapter 10

AROMAS OF COOKING, and the smoke from curing meat warred with each other to tear eyes and activate saliva. Arthur turned a spit, his stomach churning in anticipation. Every eye watched his moves; waiting hungry. They had field rations from Avalon, but all of them wanted to bite into fresh meat to feel the juices running.

Underlying hunger, the worry of Kai's absence clawed at Arthur. He didn't expect to hear from Kai until nightfall, but it disturbed him to have their group split up.

Dusk dwindled down outside, to cast long shadows over tree-lines and rolling hills. Stalker, just back from sentry duty, reported no movement apart from a few airborne saurians. Kai had drawn the Nestines away but for how long?

"This is a good place to make a permanent camp," Stalker said, poking the fire to send sparks flying. "I could get used to a waterfall if it means our cooking fires are hidden."

"Wind blowing through this valley drives any smoke into the water mist and the canopy of trees." Arthur pictured the ancient, leafy shield stretching over the river that supplied the waterfall. The entry hole was so narrow that smoke seemed to absorb into fine droplets of water.

Haystack came rushing into their midst from outside. His face wore a controlled look as if he prepared for conflict. "We have company. I heard a horse."

"Just one?" Maybe one of Rowan's forces had stumbled on the place? That could be a big problem.

95

"Yes and the horse is nervous." Haystack dumped his cloak near his bedroll and extracted his gutting knife from the bundle. "Foot troops also, but they are quiet. Too quiet."

Swords appeared in every hand. Laz guns stacked near the entrance way. Laz guns brought Nestines like flies to a corpse. Arthur added his own to the heap. No one spoke. They held the battle discipline of silence, filing out to take cover among trees and rock formations outside. He checked positions as he scaled a tree. Each man remained in eye distance of another. They would wait to see who came.

The cry of a screech owl pierced through silence; an unnatural sound in daylight, if not so at dusk. Arthur relaxed. That sound was a prearranged signal. Kai approached and wanted caution. He didn't come alone.

A single rider appeared at the head of a deer path. He rode blind, with a cloth tied over his eyes and his hands behind his back. Huber held the reins, guiding the animal. Fanned out in a semi-circle came the rest, with Kai at the rear. Something about that black horse stirred Arthur's memory. He swung down from his position on a branch.

Kai moved forward, halting the rider and signing to Arthur, *He wants to see you.*

That confirmed his guess, but why did Dragon seek out a half-mutant son? About to sign to Kai, his hands froze at Dragon's shout.

"I want to speak to Arthur." Somehow, the duke knew that he had reached his destination.

Arthur signed for Brethren to remain hidden. He didn't want Dragon to know the size of his group, not until he knew what the man wanted.

"Bring him closer," Arthur called. Kai took over the reins, signing for Submariners to take cover as he did so. The brothers hauled Dragon off his horse to set him on his feet. Kai removed the blindfold, taking up position behind the man, now facing due west, in the path of a setting sun.

Dragon squinted, turning his head as if to search for others. "I'm not here as a spy."

"Maybe not." Arthur stood with his back to the sun, watching for minute changes in the man who was his father. Dragon appeared relaxed, but that might not be a good sign being Brethren trained in fighting skills. "There is a way to know for sure. Now you will learn information that will cost your life should you prove false."

"Ashira is here?" Uther started forward. The movement halted when Kai's blade touched the back of his neck.

"Be still. I need to scan your thoughts. If you fight me, you will be hurt." With this warning Arthur speared into Dragon's mind. An instant of shock registered before wonder, then acceptance tinged with pride. A huge sense of rage, disgust and longing throbbed through Uther's consciousness. The thoughts centered on Shadow and Nestines in equal proportions. He wanted to destroy invaders infiltrating his territory, and he needed to see Shadow. Part of him could not let go of her. Arthur withdrew, satisfied.

"She isn't here." His statement created an expression on Dragon's face very similar to one on Brethren in killing mode.

"Neither is that flame-haired Outcast, though I see one who looks just like him." Dragon glanced over his shoulder at Kai.

"You speak of my half-brother. Our mother reclaimed her life." Arthur saw the duke's jaw clench, and then his shoulders drooped.

"She is safe and happy?"

"Both." Now was not the time to tell a jealous male that the object of his attention had lost her second mate and resided with a third.

"How . . . ?" Dragon cleared his throat. "How do I get those creatures out of my fort? I will not lose another child, or another innocent woman."

"The price might be beyond your willingness to pay. If we flush those vermin, then your territory will become a battle zone."

"We don't have enough fighters," Kai said. "Are there people you don't trust among your own?"

"But?" the duke looked at Arthur.

"Those beasts, Nestines, pluck thoughts from all who wear their original band. I can't pick through fort dweller's minds without leaving a trace." Arthur tried to keep the excitement from his voice. Gaining Tadgehill gave him a strong base and access to Dozary lake. "You will need to lead out small groups to be re-banded."

"Those controlled by Nestines can't be allowed to survive," Kai said, moving round to face Dragon.

"I want my fort and my people free." The duke's shoulders straightened as if he had come to a decision. "Any who bow to animals are yours, with one stipulation. If you find among them the men responsible for your mother's fate, then they are mine."

*

Kiri Ung stood at an observation window, looking at a distant ball of blue and white in the heavens. For the third time, he made a conscious effort to deflate his crest and retract his claws. *Another ship lost.* The thought angered him, even as it imprisoned his attention. He tried to picture that unseen enemy, the one called Arthur.

Skyships patrolled in swarms over the eastern coast of one tiny landmass, and they reported normal activity levels for Terrans. Not a trace of any rebel band. Had they gone to ground again, or maybe water?

Te Krull, Planetary Governor, ducked as he entered the small room. Kiri Ung made a snap decision to call a meeting with a member of implant development. How many more centuries must pass while they were forced to crouch through doorways? Perhaps a modified implant for Terrans might generate a team of metal workers, capable of operating above level of drones while still being under full mind control. He glared at Te Krull.

"How long am I to continue a worthless search?" the younger Nestine demanded, inclining his head a fraction less low than Kiri Ung's rank demanded.

"Until I order otherwise. Have you scanned for underwater energy patterns?"

"Yes, but they bury craft under sand, where we can't detect them. They can flood their vessel with water and continue to breathe."

"Yes, what?" Kiri Ung made no attempt to repress his crest. He felt it rise to full extension with a certain degree of satisfaction.

"Yes, Queen's Mate."

"I believe I might have mentioned this is a crew containing Terrans and mutants. I am astonished that this vital detail escaped your attention. Dismissed."

The stale odor of fear contaminated the air. Kiri Ung almost forgot to duck on his way back to his office. Once there, he activated a holo display of the territory in question.

So you intended a blind draw to divert my attention. You strike again at the same location, and it is still not a good target area from your point of view. Kiri Ung let his eyes wander north over the map as he settled into the smooth texture of his chair. He wondered how many skins it had taken to cover his favorite piece of furniture. Maybe a skin-covered desk surface would feel good, too.

Reports from infiltrators indicated Arthur and his force as conspicuous by their absence in that direction. West drew like a fly to rotting meat, but that was too obvious. The rebels must have a base between east and west in the southern section. Not in water, though. Landing mutants placed the team at a disadvantage. High fort attracted his attention. Yes, the Terran members could blend in if they had an outlying base.

Kiri Ung typed out a new set of instructions for airborne reconnaissance; aware Te Krull would have already given out orders to remain on the eastern coast to his flyers and would lose face by changing orders. He decided to put in a call for a light snack.

*

Arthur led his men over the shingles of Dragon's private beach to his father's safe cave. The Brethren stumbled, not quite recovered from stasis, but able to function in an acceptable manner. They adjusted quicker with each timeout. That was a plus point.

Having Dragon's emergency stash at their disposal made a big difference too. They wouldn't have to forage so they could keep out of sight until the fun began.

Dragon's suggestion of re-banding all his outlying groups first represented a master stroke of battle tactics. Without reinforcements, the fort was a ripe fruit ready for plucking.

Arthur activated a glow globe on entering the narrow fissure. It looked like a normal cave with a sand floor and dried seaweed clinging to jagged walls. He knew that there was a secondary chamber fit for habitation, and about the water line from a recent visit. To the back of this cave, another narrow gap led into a much larger cavern, with tiered beds for twenty against one wall. Shelving containing canned and dried provisions, as well as primitive Terran weapons and clothing. A fire pit nestled against a third inner wall, and the entrance wall held a good selection of barricades, suspended from pegs and ropes.

"Who gets the lower bunks?" Haystack asked.

"Brethren. "Not a hard, or an unfair choice, given their slowed reaction times after stasis, Arthur reckoned. No one objected.

Huber broke out travel rations, handing them to each man as he found a bed. Arthur took his own and started to climb three bunks to a top one. A hot meal would've been nice, but fire smoke looked less noticeable in daylight.

Arthur saw no need to set a watch here, not with his angry father returned to Tadgehill. Not one fort person would risk Dragon's wrath by venturing forth at night. Even so, Arthur couldn't risk a night fire in case Nestines overflew the area. He had noticed swarms of ships converging on High fort the night after they broke camp.

Who is the one who guesses so well? The thought worried at him until exhaustion took its toll and sleep carved away his consciousness.

*

A woman's shrill scream and sounds of scuffles tumbled every sleeper out of bed. Kai had a slight form pinned to the floor except for her feet kicking at his legs. A wild mass of black hair mingled with Kai's deep red locks. His hand closed around her wrist, banging it hard down to dislodge a wicked looking knife from her hand. It clattered when it hit a rock at Arthur's feet. Another flurry of fighting and a pair of ice blue eyes looked into his. The girl's mouth dropped open in shock. Kai followed her gaze.

"Shit! She's seen you." Kai twisted to one side to avoid a head butt.

Arthur sent an immediate sleep command to the girl's mind. The strength of her resistance surprised him, and he felt her psi power stir, a psi power no Terran should possess. Even as she lost consciousness Arthur knew he had a big problem. He couldn't remove memories from someone with the gift.

"By the deeps, she's a fiery one," Kai remarked, getting up. "A sense of threat awakened me and then I found her creeping around."

The intruder was a beauty. Dressed in figure hugging War Maid clothing of tight leather pants and a hip-length tunic, her curves and her petite frame belied her calling. Fine black brows arched over the now closed big blue eyes. He wondered at finding a warrior princess so near Tadgehill.

The others grouped around her, their faces a mixture of expressions. Huber looked worried while Haystack and Stalker openly appraised the girl. All the Brethren came to a sudden alert. Arthur heard a clatter of metal on rock.

"Harvesters! What have you done to my daughter?" Dragon burst through the entrance, falling to his knees by the sleeping girl. He gathered her against his chest, glaring up at Arthur even as he checked her pulse with his free hand.

"She will recover." Arthur squatted down by Dragon, waving the others away. He needed a space around his sire before the man started to feel threatened. "But we have a big problem. She saw me, and I couldn't remove that image from her mind."

"What are you going to do with her?" Dragon's face assumed a flat expression, but his eyes bored into Arthur's.

"She is a complication." Arthur pushed down his own sense of shock. The girl, Dragon's daughter, looked around seventeen. Not then the child of the young wife his father claimed and this girl wore a Gold Band. That meant she had to be the product of a legitimate union. So he'd taken another mate just a few short years after he lost Arthur's mother. The thought hurt as did the care his father gave to the girl. "You didn't mourn my mother overlong."

"I had no choice." Dragon looked from Arthur to Kai to the girl and back again, one brow raised in question. "Unlike your mother, I was left in a weak position after her removal from my fort. Scandals spread on the whisper of a breeze. Alsar, the old High King, ordered me to take his kinswoman as wife to protect my position as a ruler."

"How convenient." Arthur couldn't keep the sneer out of his voice. A memory of his mother grieving for her lost love chased away caution.

"No. Not for either of us. She was too old for child-bearing, but Alsar demanded a productive union because he wanted her established." Dragon closed his eyes, his hand absently stroking the girl's hair. "Ranoa died birthing Avriel. I raised her the only way I knew how, as a War Maid."

Uther used Ashira as a role model for his daughter. Why else would she have her sire chasing after her, fearing she disobeyed his orders and finding the worst already happened? Arthur had to re-band his sister, yet that brought another set of complications into play.

"I love her, Arthur. You'll have to kill me to take her from me."

Arthur looked up at Kai. His brother signed the word 'nexus'. Whatever they decided would have a huge future impact.

"If I release her to you, I require you to guard her at all times. She cannot be let out of your sight." He caught a glimpse of Haystack moving forward and then a large hand touched to his shoulder in warning.

Silence, a blanket of silence, and waiting permeated through the cavern as if everyone held his breath. The faint sound of surf sucking at the sands of time pushed for a decision.

"She will have to be re-banded, and you will be the one to walk her through what she is going to now see. If you think she will react to the sight of Nestines roaming through Tadgehill, then you will leave her here."

"Are you threatening me?" Dragon released his sleeping daughter to ease up with his hand hovering over his sword hilt.

"Avriel is threatened by what she is becoming." Arthur also stood, facing his father, unsure how to proceed. "When I sent her to sleep a part of her mind awakened. She will be at the same risk as Ashira from Nestines for the same reasons. Choose her fate."

Chapter 11

ARTHUR'S ULTIMATUM ECHOED around the cavern. Uther bristled under the flat stares from all the black-dressed men. Each one of them, whether Brethren or mutant, bore the same alert but relaxed expression common to Outcasts before battle. Avriel moaned in his arms as if fighting to regain her senses. He needed her safe.

Silence intensified to the faint sound of surf breaking. The smack of water on shingles followed by the suck of an undertow grating the small pebbles together marked time. Uther looked up at his son, trying to penetrate through the bland mask. Then their reasoning hit him. Arthur knew he wouldn't risk her. Grudging respect followed by a warm glow of pride filled him. His son was a leader. Disappointment and rage rode on the heels of that thought. Arthur could never take over Tadgehill as duke because of his mixed heritage, despite being the first legitimate son.

Still his decision for his daughter hurt because he knew how much Avriel would fight his judgment. She hadn't followed his orders excluding her from this retreat. What if she attacked a Harvester? What if she failed to keep her thoughts in a simple mode when in Tadgehill? Uther knew how much practice that took from his own experiences since his last meeting with Ashira. The pain of her loss clawed a hole in his gut; to see her as the Outcast known as Shadow. The call his banished duchess sent, not even aimed at his mind, had propelled him to spiral into another level of awareness. Not until Arthur re-banded him and gave his mind the barrier of privacy had he regained a measure of peace. Thoughts reflected on expression through and in body language. Avriel's face betrayed her moods.

"Avriel stays here under guard. She will resist remaining." Uther looked down upon his sleeping daughter dressed in her War Maid leathers, aware of how difficult a task he set these men.

"How will you explain her absence?" Arthur's quiet question cut through the stillness of tension in the cavern. Those words created their own pocket of silence, in which the sounds of dripping water and the slough of surf boomed.

"We ran into a trading party returning to Menhill, and I sent her with them to ascertain their possible barter needs from us, as well as to re-establish friendly relations." A convenient and plausible lie.

"Has she performed any diplomatic tasks in the past?" Kai questioned. The depth of perception in that observation caused the duke to remember Kai's sire, the Outcast King, Copper. Now there was a leader of men. His son took after him. Also a son of Ashira's. How much of her went into this individual? The thought of her with another man hurt.

"Avriel is of an age to serve. None will question my decision as I have no apparent son. A War Maid may also be an ambassador if she has no female siblings to protect at home."

"Kai caught her. He will be her guardian," Arthur decided. A faint tightening of his jawline betrayed the hurt.

Uther felt his son's pain. They were brother and sister. She would reject him, and he knew it.

"What if she resists?" A blond Brethren objected. "Kai can't control her mind."

"Haystack, my brother has a way with the ladies." A rumble of male humor greeted this remark from Arthur. "He will know when he has to call for help."

"Am I missing something here?" Uther didn't like the sound of this.

"Some Brethren, like Kai, have a gift of sensing danger ahead of time." Arthur glanced at Kai. "He will not hurt her."

"I have your word on that?"

"Given." The commitment held a ring of authority.

Uther looked over at Copper's red-haired son and wondered if Avriel would withstand his strong masculine appeal. Misgivings aside, he had no choice. He knew how his daughter would react to sighting a Harvester. Having her alive outweighed any other consideration.

"Do you want to tell Avriel she is to stay here by your will, or did you want her to think rescue might be coming?" Arthur looked back at him, a faint half-smile lifting his lips. "She might not resist with the same intensity if she has hope."

Again the precise, cutting logic shocked him. First Kai and now Arthur voicing statements more appropriate from graybeards. How they came to acquire the wisdom of old age sent a chill to his bones. Had these brothers ever experienced the freedom from care that came with childhood? The slow smile of the Brethren that each of them produced on occasion spoke otherwise, though neither had been in a position to earn the harsh sentence. His anger against Harvesters grew in that moment to surpass any battle rage he had ever experienced. What would be a way to kill such a creature slowly?

Uther let out his breath and his temper. "Tell her nothing of my visit."

*

Kai witnessed Arthur's expression as the dragon duke departed, catching a faint clenching of jaw from his brother. He felt sorry for those two who wanted to like each other and stood at a distance through circumstance. His own father, Copper's firm guidance and approval, meant much to the child he had been. The deep wound of sudden loss for his sire ached within.

106

"I might need to discipline Avriel if she behaves badly," he said. "She's your kin, not mine. Shall we fight over this should it become necessary?"

"Do whatever you must to keep her under control and alive." Arthur stared into the distance.

"I want a long chain attached between her wristband and mine." He thought for a second. "And I also want a shielded latrine for her use. I'd not antagonize her by offending her dignity."

"You volunteering to empty it?" Huber said, looking amused.

"No. That comes under the banner of Avriel's dignity. She'd have to come with me." He looked each one of them in the eyes. "Since I get the pain of her company, then you can all share the lesser task."

Mulberry rummaged in his kit sack to produce a length of fine chain and two locks. The young Brethren tucked a strand of brown hair behind his ear as he glanced at his peers with an innocent, wide-eyed expression. "I stole these from the last fort I visited. Nobody seemed to miss them."

Laughter greeted the remark as Kai secured himself to Avriel. A laughter that jarred his sense of rightness. No lad of Mulberry's age should possess a need to steal, let alone deliver the goods in a mocking manner. It said a lot for the way all of them gouged a handhold in their fight for survival.

"Wake her up please," Kai said. "We may as well get the shrieking and crying part over with now."

A sudden flurry of activity directed all of the others into necessary tasks to take them out of range. Avriel stirred. Her eyes snapped open to look at him, and then at her chained hand. She followed the links to his imprisoned bracelet.

"You shouldn't have come here," he said. "Now you've seen things that we can't allow you to report."

Still Arthur kept his face averted. Kai couldn't fault his brother for trying to postpone the unpleasantness.

"Why am I still alive? To be your pet?" The words came out of her mouth like shafts of frozen arrows.

Kai opted for an immediate fight. "Now there is a thought. As long as you are volunteering for the position . . . ?"

Avriel grabbed a slack link of chain from the ground beside her to whip at his face, but Kai jumped back, jerking her forward into a slouch with her hair dusting the ground.

"Try that again, and I'll shorten the links," he warned, releasing his hold. "Should make sleep time interesting." Avriel's face flared crimson.

"My father's men will rescue me before that happens." She wriggled into a more dignified sitting position. "Don't think your plan to replace him with that one will work." She glared a hole in Arthur's back. "The likeness isn't good enough to fool anyone."

"Avriel?" Kai enjoyed watching her blue eyes widen in shock at being named. "Meet your brother."

"I refuse to acknowledge some chance by-blow bastard as kin." Her chin jutted, and her mouth became a thin line.

"Kai!" Arthur's startled objection came too late. "She knows too much already."

"Deeper drinking from the same cup might waken her to what is really happening." He preferred truth rather than a series of complex lies that he must commit to memory. The girl hadn't started shrieking yet. A good sign as far as he was concerned. "Avriel, Arthur is the legitimate son of your father's first wife."

"A union dissolved on her sentencing."

"Yes, but the product of their union belongs to the surviving parent if conception occurred before sentencing. It did." He noted Avriel's complexion turn a pasty white.

"Then I was right. You are going to kill my father."

"No." Arthur moved closer, squatting down to be on a level with his sister. "I don't challenge his rule. We come on another mission."

Avriel's eyes flew around to assess all the Submariners. She looked Arthur up and down. "You have a look of the mutants. I don't believe this tale of make-believe."

Arthur gave a slow smile before he walked away. Kai suppressed a groan. Now he had two hurting people to tread softly around.

"Fine. Believe what you will." He gave a gentle tug to her chain. "It's my turn to cook breakfast. I'm not a good cook so if you are so skilled I would like help." He caught a look of rebellion from her. "Or you can watch and not enjoy the result."

*

Arthur sat on a rock looking out to sea, cursing his mixed heritage. Before coming to dwell on the surface his skin allowed him to blend with Submariner's without comment, but now? Sunlight made him almost Terran, yet not quite enough to pass for one. Maybe a few more years of exposure might make a difference. He didn't have years, not with his sister.

If only he had looked Terran then Shadow could've found him as an infant. The thought rolled around in his mind like seaweed on the surf line, to and fro in endless repetition. And then what? Would he have even come under consideration as a substitute body for the Archive entity if he looked Terran as a child? He thought not. The entity he now knew as Emrys possessed a hard, practical side that didn't evaluate compassion for a victim when pursuing the greater good. Emrys would have discarded a useless implement, and without the entity's protection his survival became unlikely. At that moment, Arthur envied Kai for being Terran in a Terran environment, an ugly thought that he dismissed for what it was.

Kai seemed to have a good handle on Avriel. The girl burned with anger, but she didn't lapse into hysteria at her predicament. Perhaps she would come around to a more approachable position. Arthur hoped so for Kai's sake. In the meantime, he needed to organize a separate latrine and then some sleeping arrangements for the conjoined pair.

*

Uther fought against the sick fury raging through his soul as he rode over bleak moorland to his fort. He slowed his mount as he came to a ravine leading down to Tadgehill, stopping halfway down at a waterfall. The splashing eased him with the familiarity of home noises. He needed calm before he caught sight of another Harvester and was tempted to disembowel it on the spot. How far could he trust Arthur with Avriel? Uther made an effort to refocus his thoughts, aware that his expression might betray him even if the Harvesters could no longer read his mind.

The sword. Arthur wanted the sword. Maybe something from another generation, hidden in a heap of discards in some storage room might give a better lead to the weapon. A half remembered thought slid across his mind like a spider skittering across gossamer webs. He seemed to recall an old map. Symbols he didn't understand; scratchings that looked like ants crawling on a narrow bridge.

Chapter 12

S ITTING BY THE cook-fire with his back resting against a smooth rock wall, Kai enjoyed a certain satisfaction as Avriel added seasoning to a stew she prepared for the midday meal. His deliberate sabotage of breakfast had gained the desired result. The stink of burnt flesh swirled like an evil miasma in the air of the inner cave. The moment when she had pushed him aside before he burnt more food played in his memory.

An impatient yank on their chain brought him to his feet. He dusted down his clothing just to irritate her for disturbing his pleasant thoughts. Now what did she want?

"We need to gather more crabs to make this meal stretch," Avriel said, looking him over as if he were a roof bug that had fallen at her feet on purpose. "Can you at least manage to catch food?"

"No problem." Kai ignored smirks from his comrades lounging around the cavern playing dice. They had all played their part well during breakfast, and he could use some relief from the sets of eyes following his every move near his very attractive, if unwelcome appendage.

"Then I can go outside?" Her comment came couched as a sneer.

Kai didn't like the way her mouth turned down. He wanted to shake her into being halfway human, but she had a right to be angry. More than anything, he wanted to tell her the truth of why she was a prisoner.

"Just as long as you don't try screaming for help. I would hate to chastise a lady." He gave her the slow Brethren smile that

111

would have sent most ordinary people running for cover if they hadn't been chained to him.

*

Kiri Ung reviewed the last report from Planetary Governor Te Krull, who now stood before him with eyes lowered. His subordinate's body language showed he expected a reprimand for lack of result, yet Kiri Ung held back. Several reports on the subject called Arthur sat on his desk in precise alignment. He leaned back in his chair, resting his eyes on the dull gray of the ceiling, letting Te Krull suffer in the absence of another seat.

Arthur's renegade band hadn't chosen a base around High fort. He wondered why not? Kiri Ung's thoughts returned to the immediate when he caught the sour scent of fear on the air from Te Krull. Amused, he dismissed it, preferring the interesting game of speculation instigated by this remarkable mutant telepath. That strike against skyships in the east stunk of a diversion, yet if not to set up a base at High fort, then where? Kiri Ung punched a sequence on his console to activate a map on the view screen. The lower half of an island land mass condensed into relief.

A report from a subverted Submariner in Avalon indicated Arthur as the son of a Terran ruler in the far west. He remembered the ruler mentioned in another report from High fort for being a regular guest. Kiri Ung connected the location dots on his map. It didn't make sense unless Arthur had a way to read Nestine minds. Why would a gifted renegade choose such an isolated fort to settle near? There had to be a reason.

Another waft of liquid fear on the air made his eyes water. Kiri Ung made his decision. "Te Krull, you will station three ships above Tadgehill fort. I want an additional twenty personnel to assist resident Nestines in that location, and I want the Terran ruler taken."

"The strike leader there is one of my best operatives." Te Krull swallowed before he continued, shuffling his feet on another

112

prized possession, a hair rug. "And he doesn't need help to make one feeble Terran an Outcast."

"Did I say I wanted this target altered by that procedure?" Kiri Ung raised one brow ridge, letting the implication sink in. He noted Te Krull's crest struggle not to erect.

Te Krull lifted his chin. "We always alter a cull."

"Not this time. I think I would like to know how far our security is compromised in that fort." Kiri Ung ran his hand over the so-soft hide covering his favorite chair. "If I am correct, you will need extra personnel to effect this capture, unless you have acquired a taste for failure?"

"Taking a ruler will disrupt the efficiency of that fort." Te Krull's crest pumped into full erection, reflecting off the surface of the silver-colored door to give a multidirectional image.

"Patience is the mark of an effective leader." Kiri Ung began to enjoy himself. "I was about to order you to take one of the modified Terrans with you. Have him infused with the thought processes from our victim. A telepathic illusion will serve our purposes just as well as the real person in the eyes of his people."

"The procedure is not field-tested." Te Krull's claws extended from their protective finger sheaths.

"That is why this mission is the prime opportunity. Tadgehill is not an important fort. We can eradicate it if the field trial fails." Kiri Ung slowly extended his own claws, one finger at a time while he let his crest pump into full erection by stages. Once more the stink of fear sliced into his orbits.

"What do you wish done with this ruler, Queen's Mate?"

The use of his personal honorific at this late stage was not lost on Kiri Ung. A warm glow of satisfaction spread through him. Arthur gave rise to many enjoyable experiences just by existing.

"Bring him to me, intact and conscious." And then he would find out what Arthur wanted from his sire, one way or another.

*

When Kai reached the opening giving beach access, a cool sea breeze whipped back his hair. Avriel pushed past him, dragging him forward by their common link. He followed, not sensing any danger from outside, almost running into her. She turned, eyes blazing.

"Where is my horse?"

"Moved to a safe place where it will not cause comment." Kai blessed Dragon's attention to detail in that moment.

"You lie! She has unusual coloring."

"I give you my word that you will ride her again." Some feeling of unrest disturbed him. He looked up at the clifftop, only partially listening to her. Nothing, and yet his fey sense stirred. Perhaps the girl caused a vortex in time by her presence. He turned back to her.

"Then where is she?" Those big blue eyes filled with tears.

"Out of your reach. Save the little girl crying act. That won't work on me."

Avriel turned to stomp to the nearest rock pool. Kai kept pace, interested to see her next tactic. He joined her to squat down, looking into the watery depths. Two crabs edged near each other, vying for territory amid tendrils of seaweed. Avriel made to grab, but Kai caught her hand, wanting to see what these tiny warriors would do in their own world. Much posturing followed until one asserted dominance to catch the other in a death grip. The victim responded with a similar pinch. Now locked, the two thrust against each other in a test of strength. Kai plunged his hand into their world, grabbing both. The crabs looked a size to make up for any shortfall in a stew. He started up when Avriel, sucking in air; round-eyed, warned him. She looked at a red sail from a fishing boat out at sea. Sound carried well over water. He dropped his catch, covering her mouth with his hand to stop the scream she started to form.

Avriel tried a punch into his groin, but he barred her with his hip, not breaking his grip. He groaned when she kicked his shins, holding on still and now beginning to enjoy their contact, despite her painful counters. She smelt as good as she looked, and he began to wonder what she tasted like.

The ship now bobbed on the horizon like a piece of flotsam, well out of earshot. Kai took his hand away from her mouth but continued to hold her tight. Her soft curves began to focus his thoughts in a more personal direction.

"Let me go, and you can do whatever you want." She burrowed against his chest, pushing her body against his.

"Offers of sex won't work any better than tears." Kai pushed her away with a firm hand. Disappointment bled a hole in his heart. "I won't release you, but you can continue the persuasion."

Avriel stiffened as if he had slapped her. "Get the crabs before lunch is ruined."

Kai reacquired his catch and made a mental note to ask Arthur about finding a replacement jailor as soon as the girl went to sleep.

*

Uther entered his fort in a foul mood after spotting a Harvester feeding from a full catch his fishermen had just landed. This creature, who contributed nothing, ingested vast amounts of food to deprive those who did. He schooled his features into indifference on his passage through stables into the living area. His first priority lay with his wife. He had to inform her of Avriel's absence lest that gentle lady started an early delivery from worry. He found her in her quarters working on very small garments.

"Irene, I have a seamstress who can make baby clothes."

"It is my joy to work on garments for our child. Will you deny me this small pleasure?" She looked up from a side table where she stitched by the light of a candle. Her chestnut eyes looked into his with calm acceptance. He could deny nothing to one who asked for so little. Uther squatted to examine each tiny work of art so lovingly created, aware her face lit with happiness as he did so.

"Uther, you are not really interested in baby clothes." She looked down at the garment, frowning in concentration as her needle flew in and out of the cloth. "Why are you humoring me?"

"Can't I just want to be with you?" He tried to immerse himself in her attempts to make this room her own. Her stitched covering on what had been a plain wall filled the room with bright color.

"Sometimes, but not just now." She laid down her work to face him. "You are angry."

"Not with you, Irene."

"But I am involved, or you would not be here."

Her quiet comment pierced his soul. For all her youth, she saw through his motives. How many times had he compared her gentle dignity with Ashira's fire? How many times had she guessed he rated her second best? Still she stitched tiny garments to welcome his child with love. Uther found he didn't like himself much. He couldn't find an easy way to give his news, so he just spat it out.

"Avriel won't be assisting in your delivery."

"But we were becoming friends. I thought . . ." Her chestnut eyes filled with unshed tears.

Uther thought his heart might crack. "We were out riding and ran into a group from Menhill. They were interested in trading." The lie stuck in his throat, trying to choke him. "I sent her with them to improve relations. They are our nearest neighbors."

"Of course. I understand." Irene's softly spoken words lacerated him. He wanted to tell her the truth in that moment, yet he dreaded frightening her.

"I will make sure you have the best of birthing women, even if Avriel isn't there to give encouragement."

"The priest will do."

"No!" Uther saw the shock in her eyes. He wanted to gather her up in his arms and run far away from any priest, but he

116

couldn't. "I want no males around when my duchess delivers." Guilt ate at him. She knew a priest would help her birthing pains, but he couldn't risk either her or his future child in the hands of a Harvester servant.

"Your wish, my lord." Irene picked up her sewing, looking at him as if waiting for permission to continue.

Again her quiet acceptance and personal brand of courage shamed him. He found he couldn't meet her eyes as he took his leave of her.

Somehow his fort looked lifeless as he walked toward storage areas. People he encountered seemed mindless. This is not the way it was meant to be. He wanted them free, and if what Arthur wanted would guarantee his son's help, then the weapon would be found.

*

Kai endured Avriel's silence until bedtime. He hauled her in the direction of his bunk, intent on getting some rest before his watch. She suddenly became a dead weight at the end of their chain. He turned to find her sitting on the floor to the obvious amusement of all. "I am not sharing a bed with an Outcast." Her mouth set in firm lines.

"Fine. Sleep on the ground."

Kai dragged on the chain until he could settle into a lower bunk. He stretched to reach one of the two blankets and tossed it at her. Avriel arranged her bedding on the sandy floor as if it were the most comfortable bed she had ever slept in.

Tired of her tricks, Kai turned on his side to face the wall, willing sleep. He started to drift when a warm presence joined him.

"Move over, you great lump."

Kai obliged, smiling in the semi-gloom. Maybe this duty wouldn't be so bad after all? He muffled a groan when she kicked his legs out of her way. Perhaps not.

Much later an urgent sense of wrongness shattered layers of sleep. Kai opened his eyes, listening. No shouts came from outside where those on duty watched. Avriel breathed deeply by his side, but the feeling intensified. He shook her until she roused.

"What is it?"

She sounded sleepy and cross. Not good signs, but he didn't have the luxury of caring.

"I need to go outside."

"Couldn't you have used the latrine before?"

"Not a nature call. Listen, something unpleasant is coming." He felt her tense up. "It is not a rescue for you. If I release you when we get out, I need you to stay close to Arthur. He will protect you as no other can."

"What do you mean?" Her voice rose.

"Hush. I might be wrong. No need to disturb the others if I am."

Kai's estimation for War Maids increased over the next few minutes. She moved on silent feet and without complaint until they joined the two on guard.

"What's the problem? I felt nothing . . . no, wait." Haystack moved away from the shelter of the cliffs to look east. He ducked back under cover. "Nestine ships. Three of them."

"Rouse everyone," Kai ordered. "We may be on the move."

"What are Nestines?" Avriel whispered, looking worried.

"Look up. In the sky." The three ships came into view to settle in a hovering pattern over the position of Tadgehill. "Avriel, your father is in grave danger. Are you with us or against us?"

Arthur emerged from the caves, his hair mussed by sleep. He pushed past them to glance up. "This is not good. Huber, I want our people evacuated to the submersible right now."

"Kai? My father?"

Arthur turned to face his sister. "I don't know. The creatures who man those ships are not friendly to us. I mean all of us. I have never seen three skyships over a fort before."

"What does it mean?" The wail in Avriel's voice couldn't be ignored.

"Bad things." Kai refused to lie to the girl any longer. "Those creatures might be after us since they appear to follow us, or they may want Dragon as a way to get to us. Either case won't be good for him."

Arthur whirled to confront him. "Kai!"

"She has a right to know. I don't want to be the one explaining later."

"Put her in stasis. You and I will go to Tadgehill. Maybe we can get him out before they land their troops."

"What is stasis? I want to go with you. I know Tadgehill."

"She has a point." Kai saw the commitment on Avriel's face. She looked battle-ready to defend her home.

"Avriel," Arthur put one arm around his sister's shoulders, "These creatures are not like us. They are what you worship as gods and call Harvesters. I've always wondered if they have a sense of humor because that is what they do, harvest humans for food. Forts are the farms and wristbands are the means of keeping you all docile."

"How come I have never seen any of them?" Avriel yanked free of Arthur's comfort. "Why should I believe you? What if they are gods and you are lying to hide from the shame of your sins?"

Kai grabbed Avriel's arm to bring her around to face him. "We have never been a part of society to be expelled. You can see those circles of light in the sky, and that means you will also face your 'gods' if we take you with us." He spat to one side. "Be a good girl and go to sleep while we go get your father out of danger."

"My father's wife is about to give birth. He won't leave her."

Arthur hissed out a lungful of air. "If the Nestines are interested in Dragon, the babe doesn't stand a chance. We'll have to get all of them or risk having the woman held as a hostage."

119

Avriel squared her shoulders and compressed her lips, firming up into a warrior in front of Kai. "You're serious about my family being in danger, aren't you? Irene is very gentle, and I don't think she has ever been outside the women's quarters since she arrived in Tadgehill. That is where my father will go if he thinks there is danger, but why should he? If we couldn't see the creatures before, then what is to stop them doing whatever they want with him?"

Kai glanced at Arthur, who nodded permission. He took a deep breath. "Arthur altered Dragon's band so it didn't interfere with his ability to see the creatures. He has been pretending not to see them for a goodly time now."

"Is that why he has been so moody?" She pulled away from Kai to face Arthur. "I can help find my family quickly, and I know every corridor and passage in Tadgehill."

Kai's doubts about her motives vanished. "Let her come."

Arthur made eye contact, his doubts showing in his expression. He turned to face Avriel. "Open your mind to me. I want to show you what they look like. I can't let you go with us if you scream at the sight of them."

Kai fingered a stasis disk in his pocket as Avriel stiffened and then her shoulders slumped.

"I will not scream." Her chin came up, challenging. "May I kill them? Can I have my knife back?"

"You can have a sword if you can handle one." Arthur grinned . . . a feral smile in moonlight. "No killing, unless I give the order though. I want to go in, get our kin and get out before any are aware. Is that clear?"

"Yes."

"Good girl." Arthur turned to a passing Brethren. "Mulberry, your sword."

Kai unlocked both of them from the chain. He pocketed it, not wanting to leave more evidence of their presence in this place than necessary. He had a bad feeling about this rescue mission. The odds stacked against them.

Arthur strode toward the surf-line with the last of their party to call the submersible. Kai looked at the girl he had guarded.

"Avriel, we might not live through this."

She shrugged, looking in the direction of her home.

"Dragon knows you are with us. He left you here for your protection." Now he had her full attention. Her eyes seemed sliver orbs in moonlight.

"There is no hope?" She didn't waver. Her chin came, challenging.

"Slim, but no more."

"Then I am sorry for some of the harsh things I said. I didn't mean all of them."

"And I am sorry for baiting you. If we come through this, maybe we can start over."

She looked up at him through her lashes with the hint of a smile tugging at her lips. Kai got a feeling the war between them had just jumped to a whole new level.

Chapter 13

"COME ON, YOU two," Arthur called to them through the sound of surf crashing on shingles.

Kai broke off from their kiss with the tastes of honey and spice in his mouth. He imagined he might be called on to pay for the privilege he had just enjoyed if her father got wind of what had happened.

"But I thought we were going to Tadgehill?" Avriel backed away from him, her eyes accusing.

"So we are. By the fastest route." Kai made a grab for her arm, marching her to the surf line where Submariners, as well as Arthur, waited. So much for a temporary truce. "They have sky power; we have water power. Trust me and don't argue."

"I can't see any boat."

"It is submerged. Where do you think all the others have gone?" He looked over at Arthur and the remaining Submariner standing just beyond wave break in the swell.

"I can't swim." She stopped, looking at the water in horror.

"We will both go to sleep while Arthur and Huber take us where we need to be." He hoped she wasn't going to fight.

*

Kai woke on a wooden deck under gentle moonlight to the sound of Avriel heaving out her guts. His own stomach lurched after stasis, but he had become used to the sensation. Arthur hunkered down between them, his hands extended.

"No. You need all of your strength," Kai objected, guessing his brother's intent. Too late. Energy flowed into his body. Avriel looked more alert.

"I need both of you ready for action." Arthur looked back at the fort once. A dark stain on the sky with pits of midnight for eyes. "We have one hour to get in and out. After that, our transport will leave without us."

"Avriel, take us to your kin," Kai said.

*

Uther pushed aside a large collection of his grandfather's stored personal possessions in frustration. A mirror shattered on impact, giving him a cleaning chore to aggravate his annoyance. He thought he remembered a voice from the past talking about a sword. Not just any sword, but a family treasure. Grabbing a box, he began to pick up shards and reached for the now worthless frame when he saw what silvered glass had hidden. Resting against the backing was a map. As he reached for it, a huge feeling of threat washed through him. He tore the paper free, thrusting it in his tunic, even as he started to run to the quarters of his lady.

Heart pounding minutes later, he found her sleeping like a babe. Something wasn't right. He hadn't felt this way since . . . since Ashira mind-called a Brethren forth from High fort, and he answered her sending uninvited. Arthur? Did his son call? The feeling intensified until sweat broke out on his brow. Irene–he had to get her to safety. He shook Irene awake.

"Uther?" Her sleepy smile of welcome did things to his heart.

"Get up. We have to leave right now."

"What do you mean?" Irene struggled into a sitting position, hindered by her gravid belly.

"I have a place that is out of danger." Thinking of the caves on his private beach, he put his arm around her to haul her upright, despite her sleep soaked state. "Don't argue. We haven't got the time."

"But Uther?"

The door to their chamber crashed open. Uther released his lady to reach for his sword. He faced Arthur, Avriel and Copper's son.

"So I was right? We need to leave?" He guessed they came to him because they sensed danger too.

"Yes," Arthur said. "We have a way out of here for you. Do you need help with her?"

"He's . . ." Irene turned white as she stared at Arthur. She crumpled like a broken flower.

"Form a hand link under her," Arthur ordered, extending his hands.

"No, not you." Kai pushed him aside. "Let me. You need to stay focused on getting us past trouble."

Uther joined Kai to carry Irene while Arthur peered into the corridor. He motioned them forward while Avriel followed.

Not expecting to see any retainers at this late hour he itched to have his sword arm free when Arthur signaled for a sudden halt. A picture formed in his mind of Harvesters roaming through the next corridor. He caught Arthur's eye, and his son nodded once to confirm the image was from him. Using mind link came as easy as learning to fly, Uther found as he tried to form a picture of Irene to send, without success.

Kai nudged him, looking at an alcove. A good place to stow Irene in a fight. He hoped this didn't happen, not with her near, as much as he wanted to destroy the invaders to his fort. They tucked Irene inside in a comfortable looking position.

The farthest end of the corridor ahead called to Uther with a silent, menacing intent. All of them watched, waiting for the faintest sound. Kai flowed into Brethren fighting stance, his feet apart, knees bent just a little and one foot in front of the other. Uther slid his sword free from the leather scabbard. The blade withdrew, noiseless and gleaming, a tongue to lick sweet death.

A few mumbled words drifted, senseless and yet dreadful from the non-human throats making those sounds. Two voices receded. There were three. What happened to the third? Then a shadow darkened flooring, followed by a scaled biped, patched by scant, light brown fur in places. It looked up, sniffing, almost tasting the air. A great crest running from forehead to mid back flushed into full rigidity.

Kai drew a knife, throwing it as if by instinct alone. The point struck left of central in the midsection. A gasp of whistling air came from the creature while both its paws grabbed at the knife. Arthur and Kai rushed it, knocking it to the ground. Uther couldn't see what they did then; he didn't need to. The flash of knives sang a familiar song.

Time to go. Uther scooped Irene into his arms and used her limp legs to push at Avriel; the shocked Avriel. Didn't they warn her what to expect?

Arthur looked back as he stood up. He motioned them forward. Kai grabbed Avriel's arm to half drag her into a shambling run. Uther followed, aware of Arthur behind him, acting rearguard. They ran to the dock, but he couldn't see a boat.

Shapes emerged from the black slickness of water. Shouts sounded behind; the choice no longer existed. Uther leapt into the water with Irene held against him. Water closed over his head. He kicked for the surface, but a hand clawed him under. Irene's body wrenched away from his in this blind place. His lungs burned, bursting with the need for air. His hair pulled tight, caught in a savage grip. A cold mouth latched onto his.

Relax and suck air from me, Huber's amused thought suggested to Uther's mind along with an image of the two of them locked together, swimming for the submerged ship.

Uther opened his mouth to breath. He locked his arms around Huber's chest to continue this strange kiss. *Irene? Where is Irene?*

We put the ladies to sleep, Huber related. *Arthur imagined you might want to discuss their fate without hysterics happening in the background.*

Can you hear my thoughts? Uther wasn't sure if Huber just made a lucky guess or if the man rifled through his mind. He noticed a change of direction.

Keep relaxed, we are nearly there. And yes, I can, but we restrict ourselves to the surface layer of thoughts as a courtesy.

That helped, if not much. Uther still wondered what alternatives Arthur could offer for his family. Did displaced dukes have any use? What of Irene and the babe? And Avriel? Was she to become an Outcast warrior like Ashira? He didn't want that to happen.

We will sort something out for all of you, Huber supplied, a flavor of concern coloring those thoughts. *I need you to take a deep breath now and hold it. I am going to push you into the access tube. There will be air at the top.*

Uther did so, releasing his grip on Huber at the same time. He felt hands propelling him to a faint light. Once again his lungs strained. He broke surface gasping, to see Arthur extending a hand.

The room, he saw, constituted a wealth in metal. Every wall, even the ceiling, seemed to be made out of the stuff. Not copper or tin either, but more like iron. And lights studded walls inset in metal to glow in a way beyond his understanding.

"Welcome to my world," Arthur said.

"What is this . . . ?" words failed him.

"Try to think of it as riding inside a horse. Quickly now, Huber is waiting, and he is the last." Arthur firmed his grip, hauling Uther out. "We want to be elsewhere right about now."

"Irene and Avriel?" Uther looked around in this metal tomb. It seemed a box with no outlets.

"In the cabin, and as comfortable as we can make them." Arthur turned toward a wall, which slid aside to show another room. Uther edged through the aperture, not knowing if it would suddenly shut to cut him in two. Beyond was a larger area with some seating mostly occupied by Arthur's men. Avriel and Irene lay prone and unmoving on a floor space. He rushed over to an ice-white Irene, whose chest wasn't moving.

"Calm down." Arthur's hand rested on his shoulder. "Both of them will be revived when it is necessary."

"They're not breathing." Was this what he bought for his family? An easy death?

"They will awaken when we remove the silver disks from their foreheads."

"And the unborn child?" Was this stranger son telling the truth?

"Will be as safe as they are." Arthur firmed his grip on Uther. "We use the device with all Brethren if we need to disembark when submerged."

Uther turned to his son, his mutant son. "What happens to us now? A refuge in Brethren Haven?"

Arthur's face closed of all expression as if the light within him died. "That choice is not a good one. We think Harvester's might have a foothold there."

"Where then?" With Irene about to deliver their child, he didn't want her dragged around with a band of renegades. Uther became aware of every eye upon Arthur and a breathless silence.

"This ship is going home." Arthur's voice came flat and hard. "None of my unit are permitted landing, but Avalon might take in refugees. Prepare yourself to meet my mother."

*

Arthur left his father keeping vigil over the ladies. He joined Kai at the controls.

"How is he taking it?" Kai said, not looking up.

"He's quiet enough." Arthur took a seat on the co-pilot's chair. "He doesn't know the risks."

Neither of them spoke. Kai headed their craft out to deep water while Arthur watched a disturbed dogfish fluking away from them, seeking safety in darkness ever out of reach until the craft overshot it.

A safe haven for a fish meant a niche in kelp or rocks. What would he give for a place called home? Circe laughing; Circe crying, comforting him, exciting him. Her absence created a void inside him.

Circe, you started my steps on this path. Why couldn't I accept my life, our lives as they were? The answer came to him. Because it could not last, except as a brief escape from reality.

"Arthur?" Kai cleared his throat, keeping his eyes on the instrument panel. "I have to make a call to Avalon, or they will attack our ship."

Kai's discomfort equaled his own. *By the deeps, how do I explain our refugees to Mother?* Would she turn them away? Kai knew her as he did not. "Call Elite headquarters. Ask for Ector. We'll try for his approval."

"Now that is a smart tactical move." Kai looked up, his smile betraying his relief.

"Ector's very diplomatic," Arthur agreed, grinning back.

"I knew I could rely on you to make a sound decision." Kai activated a transmitter signal. The response came within a minute.

"Elite command to rogue vessel. You are not authorized to navigate within three thousand haemesters of Avalon."

"Avalon submersible to Elite command," Kai leaned back, putting his hands behind his head to assume a relaxed posture for the view screen. The slow Brethren smile lighted his features with a touch of pure mischief. "We have passengers the Nestines are eager to acquire. Should we oblige them, or are you interested?"

The blank console screen flickered into life. Ector appeared ruffled. "Kai? You better have a very good set of reasons for breaking banishment."

"I have three, with a fourth about to become a new person." Kai pushed against his seat to get a more comfortable position, seeming to enjoy Ector's discomfort at their blatant violation.

"Arthur? Are you there too?" Ector's brows drew together. "Stop playing games. Weapons are trained on you."

They were being warned off? Arthur took his time to get into a position where the com eye could detect both of them. "Nice to see you too, Ector," he offered, aware of the result of his sneer by the man's reaction. "We sort of elected you to be our spokesperson, and we are not asking to disembark anyone except our passengers."

"Why am I not going to like the outcome of this request, as innocent as you two make it sound?"

"We didn't plan for this to happen." Kai's face now wore an open smirk.

"We were at the right place, at the right time." Arthur watched for Ector to break. He needed this man's cooperation.

"Hit me." Ector assumed a patient expression.

"The Nestines decided to acquire Dragon and his new family." Arthur let the shock of his words settle before he continued, "Didn't think that would've been a good idea, so we took them instead. We can't let them loose in any Brethren safehold, can we?"

Ector's mouth dropped open. He took a deep breath and squared his shoulders. "I knew I wasn't going to like this. Give me the rest."

"My sister is a War Maid; we had to take her too." Arthur began to enjoy himself as Ector's eyes bulged. "And then the duchess, who we have in stasis, is about to give birth."

"And Dragon? What am I going to do with him?"

"We could give him back, I suppose," Arthur paused as if he seriously contemplated this action. "Or we could work out a compromise. Did you want him in Nestine clutches?"

"Permission to dock is granted. None of you will disembark." Ector glared at them. "I will attempt to explain the situation to your mother."

The screen went blank. Kai heaved a sigh of relief that Arthur echoed.

Huber rushed forward, looking worried. "Our passenger is going into labor."

"She's in stasis," Kai objected.

"Stasis slows life signs, Kai. It doesn't stop them." Huber looked at Arthur. "If we don't revive her right now, we lose both her and the babe."

Chapter 14

I RENE LAY ON blankets in the vessel's aisle, her long Terran skirts giving her an unreal appearance among the metal walls and flashing instrumentation. Ripples convulsed her belly in gentle waves. Dragon knelt beside her, holding her hand, oblivious to all around him.

"Does anyone know how the birthing process goes?" Arthur asked with a sinking feeling. Not a head lifted. "What about Avriel?" He had to shake Uther and repeat his question.

"She preferred learning battle skills to women's concerns, but she has helped on occasion." Hard lines settled into Dragon's face. Age and grief settled on him in those few moments.

"Revive them both." Helpless frustration seared through Arthur. He glanced over Dragon's head at Kai to catch a bleak look on his brother's face. His Submariner recruits tended not to form relationships because of the danger of their work. Brethren, unless part of Rowan's group at Haven, didn't have access to available women. He hoped Avriel carried an idea of the care a birth entailed.

A deep, suppressed groan heralded the lady's return to reality. Her face tightened as she looked about in a strange place filled with mutants and Outcasts. Irene's golden brown eyes seemed to plead with Dragon for help beyond his capacity to grant. Avriel roused from stasis looking sick, but she knelt by Irene's other side to clasp her clenched fist.

"Irene, we were attacked." Dragon's voice sounded calm and confident. "These warriors are taking us to a place of safety."

"The baby . . . ?" Her words cut off as another massive contraction clawed at her body. Beads of sweat glistened on her face,

131

and her teeth clamped down on her lower lip. A trickle of blood began to flow there. Avriel slid another blanket under Irene's legs.

"Our child doesn't wish to wait." Dragon mopped her brow with his kerchief. New droplets formed. His hand crushed the fragment of cloth out of her sight. "Tell us what must be done."

"Get those men out of my way." Avriel glared at her father. "Can't you see she needs privacy?"

Uther looked up with helpless, trapped expression. Warriors shuffled to the prow of the craft like a collective groan of embarrassment, leaving the lady alone, but for himself, Avriel and Arthur.

Avriel's sapphire eyes sent shards of ice toward Arthur. "You too."

He stood his ground before his small sister, aware of Irene's pleading looks at Dragon. He moved around to her head, giving her as much privacy as he could.

"Arthur?" Dragon's question held elements of both censure and fear.

"I can give her help to ease the pain." He didn't want to see her suffering. Part of him carried a sense of guilt for the agony a brief moment of passion meant for a woman.

"Irene, he has my trust." Dragon drew a deep breath, waiting out another contraction. "He is part mutant, but he is also my firstborn son."

Irene's hand wrenched free to cover her convulsing belly. A protective gesture confirmed by the terror freezing her expression into a wide-eyed stare.

"Lady, the fort is lost." Arthur grabbed at a few thin threads of logic; aware she didn't have time for long explanations. "There is no reason for you to fear my motives if the child is male. Let me help you."

"How . . ." Once more her voice failed her as she fought her battle. The soft whirr of engines marked time passing.

"Let me take the pain." He saw Avriel moving down to Irene's lower body to arrange her legs. Knowing nothing about birth, he guessed the agony tensed muscles that needed to relax. Dragon's second Lady, Avriel's mother had died birthing her. His father's face wore a gray tone of shock and deep hurt.

The lady bit her lip, sending a stream of blood over her chin to run in crimson trickles onto her white neck. Avriel grabbed a bundle of shirts Huber had left within reach. She began to shred them with a frenzy that spoke of desperation. Engine sounds increased with the growing momentum.

"Do whatever you must." Avriel's chin raised in direct appeal.

Arthur reached up to one of the overhead storage units. He detached a med kit and rummaged through it to find what he wanted. Not a soporific, but a relaxant. The applicator had an easy load mechanism. One dose now and maybe one in reserve, he reckoned.

The duchess sent one look at Dragon before she closed her eyes. Arthur pushed the medicator against her neck, triggering a release. Just touching her opened a slew of her thoughts into his mind. Fear and pain hit him like a session in the Hakara chamber. The primeval need of life emergent shook him to his core. Then he felt the frail failing spark of life that was his brother. Time was running out for both mother and child. The craft gave a faint shudder as it reached maximum velocity, and lights dimmed with the drain on power, as time dragged by to the sound of Irene's ragged breathing.

Medication reached muscle tissue; the birth began in an accelerated fashion. Still Irene held back screams, and fresh blood ran down her neck, seeping into her damp white gown.

"Avriel?" Arthur brushed the sweat from the lady's face and mopped some of the blood from her bitten lip; a wound of courage. "This is sucking out her life force. Do something." He poured some of his own strength into Irene as his sister worked against time. The contractions quickened.

133

A baby's thin wail of outrage cut through the silence of held breath much later.

"The blood. There is so much." Avriel's shocked cry sounded like a sword thrust. One very small individual wailed his woe from a hastily torn off portion of Dragon's cloak. She tied and cut the cord, then cleaned the child before passing him to his stunned father while she attended to the mother.

"Irene, we have a son." Dragon's face wore a look of incredulous wonder mixed with guarded worry as he gently showed the angry bundle to his wife. She closed her eyes, hardly breathing, her skin turning gray. Avriel worked with sick-faced intensity.

Arthur joined his men in the prow, needing space from what had just happened. Mother and child needed attention at once. Would they get this? Would Avalon grant them entry?

*

"Avalon to submersible." Static made Ector's voice crackle. Lights dimmed another lumen level. Fuel indicators dipped below an urgent marker.

"About time," Kai said, looking across at Arthur. All the many months of careful conservation of fuel cells, and now one desperate run pushing the ship beyond limits meant a one-way trip.

"Landing is granted to your female casualty only."

Arthur leaned over Kai to allow Ector to see him. "The child must be included. He needs attention. His breathing doesn't sound right." They could argue over landing for the rest of them later. No power meant no air and no heat.

Ector's mouth tightened into a thin line. "We don't have a neonatal unit in Barracks, but we can't guarantee his safety elsewhere either." There came a pause as if Ector re-evaluated. "Dragon can also land for two days if he agrees to all restrictions I choose to impose."

"He isn't going to like that," Kai suggested, hands clenched on his control bar.

"Evegena swept through Sanctuary like a bad dose of the runs." Ector shrugged. "She might not have caught all the drones yet, but she has decimated the numbers of Seers. That leaves a gap in ranks. So, unless Dragon volunteers to be neutered?"

"Can't you arrange protection?" Arthur didn't consider Ector's alternative suggestion as serious. It sounded more like an excuse.

"I could, but how long before he resists confinement? What happens if the baby dies? Dragon has no defense against Seers, and he carries part of your genome, Arthur. He might as well wave a banner reading 'come get me'."

Arthur knew Dragon would not be content with the compromise, not with his family so ill. "Fifteen days? That way he gets to see what happens to his wife and son first hand."

"Four days," Ector countered, looking concerned as he checked a series of instrument readings to one side.

"Ten," Arthur bargained. Ten would force Avalon to let them all land.

"Six and that is my final offer." Ector looked out from the screen at him. "How long could I contain you within Barracks?" The parallel touched a raw spot; Arthur remembering all the times he had escaped from the confines of the Seer's Sanctuary at will. "Six days stretches the limits of patience for any man, particularly if we get a good outcome, and he gets bored."

"Agreed then." Arthur hoped he could fast-talk Dragon. "You have medi-techs ready to meet us?"

Ector gave a brisk nod, adding, "I will order supplies for your craft, and I will have a guard set to ensure no other landings. It's not as if I don't trust you . . ."

"You're just going through the motions," Arthur finished for him. "We understand."

*

Uther wrapped one of the shirts around his new son, aware of the ragged nature of Irene's breathing, and the flutterings of his child's tiny chest. Looking down on the boy, Uther didn't want to think of all Irene's wasted time stitching garments their child now lacked.

"Where do we journey?" Irene's voice came weak, as if from a great distance. "Who will take us in?" She glanced around at this metal tomb lit with pieces of star shine as if she couldn't believe what she saw.

Avriel squeezed her hand, but his daughter also betrayed unease from the way her eyes darted around, never resting on one person or one thing for long.

Questions he didn't want to face, yet for her, he must. "I think we travel to a mutant base."

"There is more." Irene stated this as a fact, looking at him from eyes beyond tired. Harsh lighting, even at a lower level, made her exhaustion apparent.

"Arthur is the son of my first wife, not the result of a casual encounter." He paused, pushing down the waves of pain remembering activated. "Ashira did not sin. She became an Outcast because she wasn't entirely human. She didn't know—none of us did." *Where was Arthur born? In some dank cave with only Outcasts to help his mother?*

"A mutant?" Irene reached toward her child, shielding him from the unknown.

Avriel just stared at him, her lips drawn in a thin line.

"She looked normal and had a pedigree. Irene, she can't have been more than sixteen summers when she fled from Tadgehill, one pace in front of hunters, and carrying the spark of life that became Arthur."

"Ashira is a mutant. She will be at this base." Quiet acceptance colored Irene's fading voice. Her eyes broke contact with his. The engines throbbed with life in the silence between them.

"Yes." Uther struggled with truth, unsure now what was real and what an unfulfilled dream. "Know that I tried to kill her at our last meeting. When I saw her with Outcasts as a fledged

Brethren, I wanted to give her peace." *Her deliverance, or an ease to my wounded pride?* He wasn't sure.

Irene made a motion to touch her son. Her hand fell short. "How can she be both Brethren and mutant? Is this a trap?"

"I trust Arthur." *To a point,* a small voice inside him suggested. Arthur had an agenda. He'd made contact for that reason alone.

"Do I hear my name?" The deep tones of his grown son's voice sounded from behind. "I came to see how my new brother thrives."

Uther moved aside, watching Arthur reach out with one gentle finger to stroke the dark fuzz on the baby's head. As if aware of the attention the child stirred, his blue eyes focused on his elder sibling. A tiny fist flailed, to grab a calloused finger. Uther witnessed a swift look of pain cross Arthur's face like a spoiled wish.

"Irene questions our welcome at a mutant base."

"I have the word of a member of their ruling council." Arthur kept his eyes on the baby. "I need to discuss medical needs, and I think mother and son could use some rest." He looked toward the other warriors, cramped as far away from the family as possible to give some privacy. "Will you join me in the prow?"

Something warned Uther that he wasn't going to like what Arthur needed to say out of Irene's hearing. He edged past bodies in Arthur's wake until they stood just behind Kai at the controls of this strange vessel. An enormous eel undulated into light cast by the ship, adding to the nightmare aspect of this whole experience. The massive body glided through deep water with more grace than any aerial saurian.

"The problem is?" Uther wanted straight answers. He wanted to break something, in particular, a Harvester's head. Irene needed help. Avriel did the best she could, but he recognized the beginnings of panic in his daughter.

"Avalon will take Irene and the babe." Arthur looked at Kai, who met his glance, and then back again. "I got them to agree a six-day visit for you. None of the rest of us are permitted to land."

"That's monstrous." Pain in his hands, and then wetness, made Uther relax his fists, now aware he had drawn blood from clenching. He couldn't leave her alone with strangers, but she must have help. He could play this game for her. He'd agree for now.

"We were banished for our own protection while they fixed an infiltration problem," Kai offered, glancing at Arthur.

"He needs to know all of it." Arthur's jaw set in a hard line. "One faction, the Seers, have a breeding program to enhance their mind gifts."

"Spit it out man." By all that was dear to him, this was like extracting teeth. Both young men failed to make eye contact. This must be bad. Arthur possessed an eerie ability and Seers also? This sounded like stock management with people. Waves of disgust threatened to choke him.

"Arthur . . ." Kai cleared his throat, "Arthur is the best Seer they ever caught. They wanted him to breed them more, and he declined."

Uther's breath went out with a whoosh. That look of pain in Arthur's face when he touched the baby wasn't jealousy, but regret. His son lived in this hell? His son survived a place out of nightmares, and now they expected him to leave Irene and the babe there?

"Kai has the fey gift of some Brethren," Arthur continued. "He can sense events ahead of time. They want him too, only . . ."

"They are terrified of us." Kai locked glances with Arthur. "We combined our gifts once. The outcome brought Avalon to its knees. Now the Seers have less power, but they are still a danger to any of those with special talents."

"How does this affect me?" Uther tried to push aside disgust. He knew of the fey gift and had seen it in action. How could these two combine talents? What had they done?

"Your seed is valuable." Now Arthur faced him. "They can't try for us, or our mother. You though are as helpless as the babe Irene just bore."

"Ector can't guarantee your safety." Kai also made eye contact. "He thinks you couldn't be 'restricted' for an extended time."

"What does restricted mean?" *This must be a nightmare. I will wake up in my own bed with Irene beside me. They want to breed me? Could they? Could they send my mind to sleep? I'll kill the first one to try.*

"Confined to Barracks with no constructive occupation."

"And my son? Irene?" Did this mind-sick threat include them?

"They will be safe since Irene is not used to much freedom of movement." Arthur's voice had an edge. "We hope to reacquire Tadgehill before your son's presence in Avalon becomes a problem."

"And my fate?" Six days and then what? Scraping against his skin, from an inside pocket of his tunic, Uther touched the edge of a parchment map. Arthur wanted the sword, and this was a map of its location. A bargaining chip he was going to use for Irene's benefit.

"Join us," Kai suggested, shrugging as if they already decided it.

Fuming, Uther accepted his sentence for the moment. Not an Outcast, but near enough to make no difference. How was he going to tell Irene? What should he tell her? Years of separation from his family faced him. He had no illusion of that after witnessing the ease of his eviction from Tadgehill. *Yet we are alive, and there is hope.* That fragile thread turned into a white-hot need for retribution.

Chapter 15

Kɪʀɪ Uɴɢ sᴛᴜᴅɪᴇᴅ his longest claw, listening to a series of lame excuses from Te Krull via his console connection to a skyship. A mote of dust fell from above, swirling, caught as a dancer in the flames, to land on the sharpened tip. He wondered how long he could balance it there while the voice of misfortune droned and whined in the background. *The duke and his mate cannot be found. Ce Lak is dead, discovered alone with multiple stab wounds.* Those words echoed in his mind as rage built.

"Our substitute ruler?" Kiri Ung hesitated to ask, given the miserable performance so far admitted. How could one man and a breeding female overcome a Nestine enforcer to disappear as though they had dissolved? He closed his hand around a metal cup, crushing it as he wanted to crush Te Krull at that moment. Fortunately for him, Te Krull had elected to give his report from a distance.

"Is installed and functioning. Memories of other Terrans in that location have undergone adjustment to eradicate any trace of those missing."

A small comfort. Yet not all failure remained negative. The fort functioned in another way now. Kiri Ung suspected Arthur's hand in the duke's removal. That meant a return strike sooner or later.

"Keep those extra enforcers in place. Hold Tadgehill on full alert and maintain aerial surveillance until further notice." He caught an expression of relief on Te Krull's face just before visual contact ceased.

Fury sent the spoilt drinking vessel at a far wall with every ounce of his strength behind it. The cup caught against a light fixture, smashing it in passing and deflecting against another wall. It rebounded at an angle to smack into Kiri Ung's foot. He roared his pain, poking his console for a server.

A Terran drone scuttled into the office in response to Kiri Ung's command. After the creature had bandaged his foot, he ate it, slowly.

*

A musty smell of Avalon air rushed into the cabin seconds after docking. Heads lifted, inhaling, and Arthur moved forward to watch the view screen as Kai activated the device. They saw Shadow with Ector, standing in the forefront of Elite troopers. Somehow he thought she would stay away knowing Dragon traveled with them. Now he faced the task of explaining her relationship with Ector to his father. Not a job he anticipated with enjoyment.

A slight whisper of air warned him. Dragon stood at his shoulder.

"She hasn't aged." Those quiet words from his father betrayed wonder rather than hurt.

"Part of the difference caused by mutation. We don't age at the same pace." Arthur waited for the storm to break.

"You too?"

"See the fair-haired male next to her?" He wanted to get all the shocks aired now. "He is mother's mate. They have a child together."

"That one is a mutant." Horror cracked Dragon's voice. "Where's Copper?"

"My father died in battle," Kai said, his shoulders tensing in betrayal of his inner stress.

"Ector saved her from despair. She is still alive because of him." A picture formed in Arthur's mind of Shadow just after Copper's death. Brethren to the bone in the worst way.

"Is she happy?"

"She can live with her past and take joy in those moments any of us can snatch in war," Arthur replied, aware of the effect Dragon had on her.

Docking clamps unsealed to permit exit. Arthur waited for the next move, unsure of how to proceed with Shadow present.

"We are sending medi-techs through to get the casualties," Ector's voice instructed over the com system. "We will revoke landing rights to Dragon if he resists."

"I won't let my wife and son go alone," Dragon stated, squaring his shoulders.

Ector appeared to study the image he had in a hand-held unit. "Disarm and we have an agreement."

Uther unbuckled his sword belt and removed various knives from a number of places. He twisted two buttons on his tunic to detach a concealed garrote wire, surprising Arthur.

"He is barehanded," Kai reported as Uther turned to rejoin Irene.

Footsteps sounded in the umbilical link. A stretcher party eased through the crush of men to their goal. Dragon, Irene and the baby departed to leave Arthur and Kai staring at the screen.

Shadow locked glances with Uther for long seconds, and then she went to Irene's side with a smile of welcome.

*

Bright light with a cold greenish cast lay at the end of a structure Uther thought resembled the inside of a giant worm. Out before him, Irene's gasp faded to a formless whisper even as one of the mutants dived to catch his son. The babe slipped from her limp arm into the male's waiting hands. Uther found the newborn thrust at him while the mutant ran an oval box over Irene.

"Ector, we need to move her right now," the attendant called. Both stretcher bearers increased pace to what looked like a low sided room on wheels. Uther began to doubt his sanity when the 'thing' swallowed Irene and her bearers. The thready wail of his son prevented him from following after to free her. An arm on his shoulder steered him to a set of seats in another room on wheels, but this one had no roof. And then she sat near him . . . Ashira.

Her eyes drew him from madness into a single pearl of sanity where only they existed. Those violet windows to a soul of darkness and light glittered as though with unshed tears. Innocence didn't mar the expression on a face that appeared no older than nineteen summers, nor did the pain of trust betrayed cloud her flawless features. Violet depths radiated maturity at war with apparent youth. Uther saw their son in her eyes. *What crucible of suffering tempered Arthur that he bears the same scars as his mother?*

Vibration thrummed in his bones. The half room hurtled forward at a sickening speed. Uther folded his body over the baby, trying to block out images of squared rock formations with windows and doors that rushed past. He gasped at the smell of ozone mingled with an aroma almost like fresh blood.

*

Ector tucked Morgan into bed, kissing his daughter goodnight while he wondered at Shadow's absence. She liked to share this evening ritual with him. Morgan fussed, wanting her mother, and then Shadow rushed in to hug the child.

One extended bedtime story later, with Morgan now sound asleep, they adjourned to their own bedroom. Ector dreaded this moment after witnessing Shadow's guarded reaction to Dragon.

"Did you get our guests settled into Barracks?" Ector tried to keep his tone casual.

"I made sure secure quarters of a suitable size were prepared and arranged for medical attention." She looked into an unseen distance. "I assume you debriefed Dragon?"

Relief washed over him. "No, I talked with Arthur and Kai over the com link. Dragon was clamped tighter to his woman than a starving leech."

"Have him watched. The reaction will come when he knows she is safe." Still, that distant place called to her. She went through the motions of preparing for bed.

A sick feeling crawled over his flesh. Twice before, he had witnessed Shadow slipping into a half-life. First when Seers stole Arthur as a babe, and then when Copper died. Each time she'd sunk deeper than before into a Brethren place. He grabbed her as she walked past, spinning her around to face him. Her eyes focused on his.

"Ector?"

"Talk to me. Don't shut me out." To his amazement, she nestled against his chest.

"You thought . . ." She hugged him. "I was remembering in an attempt to find an answer. The pattern is repeating too close for comfort."

"What pattern?" Ector wondered if she spoke of a lost lover. *Has she resolved her feelings for Dragon or not?*

"Maybe I clutch at a swirling current and will emerge empty handed." She leaned back to look up at him. "Tadgehill, and the pattern repeating there. I conceived a child perhaps hours before becoming an Outcast. Uther lost his heir, and I lost that life. Now another attack with his mate and unborn babe very involved."

"I see your point." All of them regarded Shadow as the target, thinking the emerging mutant abilities to be the reason for her abrupt ejection from Terran society. What if this revolved around Dragon? Was there some reason the man could not be permitted a male child? He sent a thought pattern to the mind of Ambrose for an extra security detail. The exchange complete and measures underway, Ector focused on Shadow once more.

"Ector, someone has to question Dragon."

"I will at wake time. You visit with Kai and Arthur." He got the reward of a happy smile.

*

Uther stirred from a soldier's doze at the sound of movement. Two medi-techs maneuvered a cot into Irene's room. They set it up while a third brought covers.

"We understand you wish to stay with her, though we need to keep her sleeping," the tallest mutant said.

"Where is my son?"

"In a . . . special box that will help him breathe," the same male said. "Tarvi is tending to him. I can take you there."

"No. I will not leave my lady." Uther turned back to Irene, ignoring them as he ignored his surroundings. None of those devices looked real. He didn't understand how 'things' worked, or why Irene slept so sound. No silver disk marred her face, and her breathing seemed deep and regular. He wished for Arthur, but that wasn't allowed either. He heard them leave and another one arrive, but wanted to be left alone to dream of the life now gone.

"Dragon? You have questions?"

The name chilled him. This title set him outside civilization as he knew it. Only the Brethren called him so. "None of you give me straight answers, so what is the point of voicing more questions?" He did not bother looking at this new intruder.

"I'm Tarvi. I care for your son as I tended Shadow when she needed aid."

That got Uther's attention. He swiveled around on his chair to face a tall blond mutant with close-cropped hair. This male looked older than the others if any age could be fixed on these people. All he'd seen looked between twenty and thirty summers. Something about the eyes of Tarvi gave an impression of more years.

"Aiding Shadow can't have overtaxed your skills. She healed faster than most others I saw wounded." Uther tried not to think of his small son, alone in this nightmare place. That the child had not been returned scared him.

"A venomous saurian bite enabled us to find her, but saving her was not easy." Tarvi walked over to Irene, checking the 'things'

145

attached to her. "None of us knew she shared our heritage until it tried to emerge without the essential pathways in place. Again, we almost lost her. Does that answer you?"

"My son?"

"Which one?" Tarvi squared off against him, fists balled. "I delivered Arthur at a stage of development not capable of sustaining life in your world. Do you question my care of your infant?"

"I didn't know." Guilt ran through him. He'd imagined Arthur as a strong baby, not a half-fledged hatchling thrust untimely from his nest.

"Seers stole that faint whisper of life from us because of what he is." The fists unclenched and fingers flexed. "You had a part in making him, and that is why you can't stay."

"How safe is my boy?" The worm of fear gnawed at Uther. He didn't trust these people. Everything here defied his control.

"Arthur was stolen from a civilian care facility. The baby is guarded well in Barracks, where no Seers are permitted entry as of his arrival."

"Irene?"

"Your mate recovers from an early birth. Sleep is now the best cure. She will waken in six hours after we move her into more natural quarters. The baby will be returned at that time if he is stronger." Tarvi finished poking at strange looking boxes. Seeming to be satisfied, he left Uther in the company of two Elite guarding the door.

What if the baby dies? Would any of this have happened if he hadn't gone looking for Arthur? He buried the name set aside for this new son, wanting Irene to have a say. How could these people imagine he intended to leave her and the child? Abandon them? First they needed to gain strength, and then he'd make some alterations to those high-handed arrangements. With that thought, Uther settled on the cot to sleep.

*

Kai listened to the sounds of tapping from the outside hull, aware an extra skin of metal now enclosed their submersible. Submariner maintenance crew worked in this depressurized buffer zone, almost weightless in the water. The noise they made unnerved him, made him feel trapped.

Some Brethren played dice, but the Submariners looked out at Avalon. Arthur lay curled on a row of seats, seeming in a deep sleep, yet Kai wagered his brother to be engaged on a mind quest. Perhaps Circe still cared enough to share in a mental reunion? Kai didn't know enough about the rules of Sanctuary to speculate on Arthur's success there.

He sneaked a look at Avriel. She sat on the floor near an aft bulkhead with her arms wrapped around her knees looking frightened and lost. She might start a fight from pure reaction if he went over, but he didn't have any other plans. She didn't look at him as he sat next to her.

"Waiting is hard." Kai wished that she had chosen to sulk on a padded chair. While he had comforts, he liked to use them.

"What then? What happens when my father returns? Why am I not allowed to be with Irene?"

"She's sick. You're not." He wanted to bite off his tongue the second the words left his mouth.

"No, I am a useless appendage. Why don't you just put me back in stasis so I don't use up air and food?"

"Self-pity isn't productive." He resigned himself to an argument at that point.

"Who are you to judge me? Did anyone bother to consider me? Have I a role to play?"

A well-aimed spear. Kai couldn't recollect anyone considering Avriel. He gathered his thoughts into speculation mode. "Avalon is off-limits to you because you are Dragon's daughter and of an age to breed." Her face registered shock, but he continued, "Our family has special abilities that Seers covet. Did you want to become a brood mother?"

"That's disgusting." She moved a few inches away from him.

"That's why you are here and not with Irene. Dragon has greater experience fighting, and he is mature. Much more capable of withstanding an attempted abduction. Besides, one is easier to guard than two."

"I need to defend Irene." Avriel rounded on him, her eyes narrowed.

"She isn't in any danger. Nor the babe, who will not be viable for many years."

"I can't leave her alone with these . . ."

"People," Kai finished her thought in a more diplomatic way. "Irene is not a War Maid. She will not resent seclusion as would you."

"Tell me where am I going to be dumped?"

So this was what she feared. Kai began to feel more comfortable. "You're a warrior already. We will watch out for you until you come up to our standard."

"Why you . . ." she aimed a punch at his face that Kai blocked, catching her hand and holding it in a firm grip.

"Am much faster than you," Kai finished, aware he irritated her more. "Both Brethren and Submariners are trained to fight in ways you must learn."

Avriel tried to free her hand, but he held tight. She made a futile attempt to pry loose his fingers, one by one.

"I'm a duke's daughter."

"And I'm a king's son twice over." Kai saw her mystified expression. "My father would have been a fort king. Instead, he became King of the Outcasts. I have a score to settle, too."

Her big blue eyes filled with tears. Kai drew her into his arms as the storm broke. He wished he could spare her the fight to come. Despite her status, she didn't belong with an itinerant group of renegades, but what other choice did she have?

Chapter 16

FEATHERED WINGS OF sleep clouded Circe's mind when Arthur invaded her thoughts. He'd wanted a waking connection, but perhaps this served better since their last meeting ended in angry words and a threat on his part. Still, he missed her.

She dreamed of their last lovemaking as if it were not the illusion he created to evade capture by the entity then trapped within Archives. He'd given her the viable seed she craved in that reality. Circe's deep sense of fulfillment suffused Arthur, bringing with it a joy of creation that made him long for inclusion.

Emrys, why am I different? Why can't I enjoy the simple pleasures of a family? His questions fell into black nothingness devoid of the sense of presence. Arthur wondered about Morgaise. What if that one carried his child? The child he had denied Circe.

Sudden waves of mindless panic thrilled through the sleeping girl. Dreams of love turned to anguish beyond endurance. Someone came to steal away her dream baby. A cowled figure swaying forward with a gait he recognized as Evegena's.

Circe tried to scream in her sleep. Her hands twitched at the hovering nightmare. Arthur couldn't bear her terror. He forced her mind into consciousness. Her thoughts flew in all directions, and yes, someone did stalk her in Sanctuary.

Arthur? I can feel you near. I'm frightened.

He pushed down rage to answer. *I'm coming.*

You're not allowed. Wake Evegena.

Thoughts of him disobeying his restrictions outweighed her need for protection. Arthur ignored her concerns. *Has anyone occupied my former room?*

No, but . . .

Go there now. I'll try to hold off whoever comes.

Arthur built am image of himself in the minds of those still awake on the submersible. Aware that those who guarded watched with their mind's eye, he trusted that they would see what they were meant to see as he left the sleeping illusion of himself. Guards at the exit received an impression of moving air as he passed them. Arthur now broadcast the appearance of a full Seer, robed and cowled, as he ran toward Sanctuary.

A sense of sliding inside his head shocked him. A time of uncertainty approached as if he had walked into a fog. Realization almost destroyed careful illusions. This was how Kai saw into the future. How much from one brother crossed bridges into the other when they had joined powers to defeat the Archive? Danger hovered over the fleeing Circe like a raptor bent on feeding.

Sanctuary towers loomed ahead; twin shards of dark against bright lights of endless day. This must be their sleep time. Arthur adjusted the illusion he carried to blend with the uniform gray of Sanctuary walls even as he entered. He stalked through deserted corridors and jumped onto a continuous series of platforms rising up a shaft.

His room on the seventh level lay at the end of a corridor down a left-hand intersection. He felt her panic, and then nothing. White-hot killing rage gave wings to his feet. He crashed through the door into a waking nightmare.

She lay like a broken toy in a tumble of sheets with a Seer reaching for a bleeding wound in her neck. That Seer's hand held a small cylindrical device Arthur didn't recognize. He sent it spinning with a blow to the man's wrist.

The dead eyes of a Nestine drone confronted him. The few seconds that one took to gain new instructions saved him. He dodged a shaft of blue light aimed at his head to launch himself at the creature. Blows rained down on him. Some he parried, but others struck home. The pair of them fell, rolling on the floor, crashing into furniture, hitting, kicking and gouging. The creature grabbed at his weapon, but the edge of it caught against a storage chest and went flying. The drone twisted free in an attempt to reach the device. Arthur caught his head in passing, giving one violent twist. A gentle click sounded, almost drowned out by harsh breathing, and then the body fell like a lightning struck tree.

Alarms shrilled through Sanctuary. Arthur didn't resume his illusion, he just stalked over to Circe, picking up the cylinder intended for her neck on the way. She was in his arms when the first guards burst in. He faced their weapons smiling.

*

Shadow came awake to the thrumming of a mind call. She turned to face an equally disturbed Ector.

Get to Sanctuary at once. Evegena commanded. *Arthur has broken parole, and he has Circe. He's forcing his way out by will-power, and he's left guards convulsing in his wake.*

Arthur gave his word. Shadow couldn't believe her son violated their trust.

Why? Ector's harsh thought slashed into the exchange.

He killed a Seer. Evegena's tone held shadings of terror.

We're on our way, Ector advised. He added a laz gun to his belt as they threw on clothes, but he didn't look at her, giving Shadow more reason to worry.

"That is not needed." She looked at the weapon. "I can control him."

"Can you? Can any of us? You heard Evegena." Ector faced her, worry etching lines on his face. "We don't know what happened to him on the surface world. We do know he can destroy Avalon."

She didn't want to believe her fears because that meant Kai too. *This isn't a ruse. My son is not a Nestine drone. I felt his thoughts.*

151

The journey in their groundrunner passed in a haze. They came to a halt in front of Sanctuary. A crowd of Seers had cornered Arthur, with Circe drooping in his arms, against the front wall. Even as Shadow watched, her son gathered his will to begin forcing them backward. She jumped out to the vehicle to run toward him.

"Arthur. No!"

"Make them stand down before they get hurt," Arthur said. His cold tone sent shudders through her. Waves of his anger lashed at her mind. Ector caught her arm.

"Keep back. He has a killing rage on him."

She tore free to push aside Seers. "Arthur, why are you doing this? What have you done to Circe?"

A hard laugh answered her and then he threw a small cylinder at her feet. "I did nothing. Tell me why this thing was about to be put into her neck? Explain why a 'Seer' has access to Nestine weaponry?"

Ector retrieved the object. "Where do you want to take Circe?"

"Back to my ship."

"All Seers stand down." Ector's voice echoed around the plaza. "Let him return to his chosen confinement."

"Ector, we have a dead Seer." Evegena emerged from the cover of a doorway.

"And serious allegations to investigate." Ector held up the small object Arthur had thrown at Shadow. "Go do some housecleaning Evegena. Seems rather more pressing a chore than fighting me for authority."

Elite guards swarmed into the plaza with weapons trained on Seers. "As you see," Ector continued, "I contacted Ambrose. I want all Seers confined to Sanctuary while we investigate this incident."

Arthur began his march, and Shadow started forward to join him but Ector held her back.

"Give him room. We don't know what else might happen yet. Don't get in his way." Bruises showed on Arthur's face, yet he seemed oblivious to hurt as he marched. Blood dripped from the wound on Circe's neck, staining her fair hair with each step.

Ector drew his laz gun and signaled for a unit of Elite guard to follow. Moments dragged into years during the journey. Shadow relaxed when Arthur entered the submersible.

*

Arthur laid Circe down on a row of seats. Blood stained her white robe. Blood trickled down her pale neck. He knew she still lived, or she wouldn't bleed, yet she looked empty, lifeless, crushed by an uncaring foot. He wanted to smash something, anything, into atoms, and he didn't care what it was. A hand on his shoulder radiated calm. He looked around.

"Will you let me tend to her now?" Shadow's eyes held a depth of compassion Arthur had never before witnessed. He moved aside.

Shadow put her hand on the gaping wound while her brows drew together in concentration. Her quietness of person shocked him into the present.

"What have I done? Please don't let her die. Emrys, help her." No presence lightened his despair. The sound of Circe's ragged breathing echoed around the metallic wall of her tomb. He felt the awareness of others trying to touch his mind in sympathy, but he didn't want them near. He wanted Circe.

"She's lost so much blood." Shadow touched his hand. "Feed me energy, or we will lose her."

His mind flickered into a dark place. He couldn't concentrate. He heard Shadow call for Kai and Ector. His brother's touch ignited fire. A fire so hot and so bright Arthur couldn't bear to feel it.

"Shadow. Back off!" Ector pulled her away. "They're joining."

The sense of self vanished. Calm and power beyond comprehension filled the void. Two became one and that one focused

153

on Circe. Energy flowed into her broken body. The rasp of death became the regular breathing of healing sleep. Light intensified, to break into crystalline splinters, peeling away like a discarded snakeskin. And then there was nothing. A darkness so intense no light penetrated. Weightless, soundless, floating nothingness.

Sighing wind on a starless night pushed the combined entity forward, over rocks, over grass, toward flames. Emrys sat at his fire, waiting.

Coal black eyes raised. "Find the sword. Time runs out." Vivid images flashed in the mind of the two that were one.

Dark shards shattered to spiral into oblivion beyond conscious thought. One divided into two. Light returned. Circe healed. Arthur looked into his brother's eyes. As one, they turned to Shadow.

"We must leave now," Arthur said.

Kai faced his mother. "Get Dragon here."

"Hold on." Ector thrust himself between them. "Circe needs medical attention. We need to find out what happened back there."

"Circe is recovering. She will stay with me." Arthur looked at Shadow. "Emrys told us we are out of time. Either get Dragon or arrange to contain him. We can't wait."

"Settle down." Ector squared up to Arthur. "Restocking your submersible will take time, and you bargained for days Dragon needs to spend with his wife and child."

"No, Ector." Shadow placed a restraining hand on his arm. "Whatever it was they saw needs dealing with at once. I'll cope with Dragon. Arthur, give me one hour to get him here, or you can leave without him."

"Power packs are replenished, but we are still manufacturing food and weapons." Ector spun Arthur around to face his team. "You have six months' supplies of either if you are careful. Another three hours will see you restocked for five years."

"We don't have five years." Kai stepped in front of Ector. "Every second counts."

"What is so important that you can't wait to restock?" Ector's face now carried the harsh lines of a decision made.

"Avalon has less than fifty years of life." Arthur looked into his mother's eyes. "This is set in stone. If we fail, then there is no future."

"But this is a self-regenerating . . ." Ector began.

"Disaster in the making," Kai finished. "Run scans on the substructure. Without surface resources, you are doomed. Even if we win a base with access to raw materials, you have a finite time line. You cannot replace the dome. No one knows how to recreate it."

*

Avriel rubbed her eyes, trying to dissolve the whirling specks of darkness from her vision. One moment she had seen Arthur and Kai standing together and the next moment a sphere of light so bright it blinded her. Now her sight cleared, they appeared to be arguing with Avalon representatives. She didn't understand what the fuss was about. Arthur had brought back some scantily clad woman who now appeared to be sleeping from what she could see. *Why cut short my father's time with Irene?* She turned to Haystack. "Who is that woman?"

"Circe is a Breeding Mistress for the Seers. She and Arthur go back a long way."

"Are you telling me my brother is involved with a slut?"

"Circe is a whole lot more than that." Haystack looked away. "She breeds high psi rate children for the Seers. At least that was her job until now."

"Arthur broke parole to steal a slut?" Avriel didn't want to believe her brother capable of such a self-seeking act. "One who resisted his intentions by all appearances?" Stories of Brethren stealing women circulated around forts, but none really believed them. That rumor kept fort women away from the mercenaries. Yet looking over at the mutant woman, Avriel began to doubt. What did she know of how he had been raised?

She jumped when Kai grabbed her shoulder, not having been aware of his approach. "Don't judge others by your own narrow standards when you have no idea why Arthur acted as he did. He would never force Circe to come here against her will."

"Oh? And I wasn't forced to remain your prisoner?" Haystack backed away to Avriel's annoyance. She had intended to use him to support her statement.

"That was different." Kai's amethyst eyes narrowed. "You disobeyed your father, and we endured the result. Grow up and hush up."

Avriel tingled with shock. Her shoulder retained the impression of Kai's fingers after he left her to hover over that woman as if he cared about someone of light morals. *How could he? I hate him.*

*

Kiri Ung surveyed the disorder in Tadgehill's ruler quarters. For a species that required coverings over their flesh, nothing looked missing. He held up a tiny, well-crafted garment for an infant as yet undelivered. Why didn't the female take garments for her offspring? Every sign indicated an immediate decision to leave and yet this garment lay within reach of the bed.

Witnesses reported the duke rooting through a storage area. What did he seek that was so important that a handcrafted covering for his child lay forgotten? Te Krull stomped into the chamber, disturbing his thoughts.

"They can't be far. No riding beasts are missing."

Kiri Ung shredded the exquisite garment with his claws. It dropped, in fragments, to lay unheeded. "Gravid herd beasts do not ride." The longing to shred a Terran filled him.

"But we have searched the warren." Te Krull glared defiance, his crest rising.

"You have searched this warren, *what?*" Kiri Ung's own crest pumped up to full expansion. His claws extended again.

"Queen's Mate." Te Krull looked down.

"Never forget the courtesies with me again. I would not support a Planetary Governor who reduced us to the level of animals by his lack of propriety." Stupidity made him want to howl.

"They must be near," Te Krull offered, still looking down.

"The duke and his mate have evaded us." Kiri Ung gathered himself to deliver a simple lesson with extreme patience. "Check the dock for DNA traces. I would be astonished if you don't find a match for one of the aquatic species, even if there is none for our quarry."

"Mutants have them?" Te Krull looked up, his facial expression going through disbelief into doubt.

"Of course they have them. Why else would a Terran bitch about to whelp leave coverings for her pup behind?" Kiri Ung took a deep breath. "These females are feeble-minded. If she saw a mutant how would she react?"

Te Krull's eyes opened wide. "Females lose consciousness unless controlled. A deplorable weakness that inhibits the joy of feeding on them."

For a moment, Kiri Ung pictured Te Krull dying slowly under his hand. The image brought enough calm to continue.

"Just supposing you wanted the female alive and not shrieking, so you could get her out of this place?" He found he couldn't even look at the other Nestine. "Would it not be more convenient if she were unconscious? Would you not be able to exit without undue attention?"

"They left with mutants? I'll alert my skyships to scan."

"No. You will not pursue ineptitude with futility. Arthur removed these creatures. This is not the first time he has struck in this area." Kiri Ung stared a hole in the nearest wall as he collected his thoughts. "That one wants something in this area, and the ruler had access to it. Forget the duke. He is lost to us now. Arthur has gained something from this warren that he needed. He will be back."

Chapter 17

UTHER WOULD FIGHT leaving Irene. Mind-numb, Shadow set controls on her groundrunner for the last place she wanted to visit, Barracks. A man used to giving orders was not open to directives conflicting with his wishes.

How would she get him on that submersible? She could lie, concoct some excuse, but that left Arthur and Kai with a mess to unravel. No, she'd not trick him. The decision coincided with her arrival, and she made her way through gray metal corridors to the quarters designated for Uther and his family.

A final set of doors opened at her approach to reveal Uther sitting on the bed watching Irene suckle their son. His smile betrayed his inner joy at the sight. Pain cut through Shadow deeper than a sword thrust.

Where was he when Arthur needed him, or her? Their son grew hooked up to machinery for the first year of his life. Why did it have to be like that? The dark fuzz of the feeding baby's head made her wonder what Arthur had looked like – something she could never know.

"Ashira?" Uther stood to give her a formal half bow.

"She has been dead for twenty years." Shadow wanted to turn around and leave this happy family in peace, but she couldn't spare them the pain she brought with her news for their own sake. "My Brethren name is Shadow."

"Ashi . . . Shadow?" Uther's shoulders tensed. "There is a problem? I would prefer not to disturb Irene. Can we discuss this elsewhere?"

How well he knew her. Shadow braced herself for the battle. "Since this concerns Irene I will not exclude her."

The new mother's head wrenched away from a peaceful contemplation of her son. Her eyes widened and her bottom lip quivered.

Pointless details rushed into Shadow's mind. She recognized the effort Ector had made to make this a home for them, and how far short that effort came to Terran expectations. How could a holo projection of marine life on a wall compare with the richness of a handcrafted tapestry? Furniture made from plastisteel and fiber lacked the subtle feel of wood and the hint of life captured in an aroma.

"Bad news is always best delivered quickly." Uther's hand went out to touch Irene's shoulder. He faced Shadow, daring her to speak.

"A Nestine drone managed to lure Arthur into Avalon." She took a deep breath, stilling the threat of tears from her voice.

"One of those creatures is here? My son? He is hurt?" Questions fired like arrows of molten lead from the duke. His face looked even more like Arthur in those moments, the non-human child they shared.

"Arthur executed the attacker. He is fine, but this wasn't an attack from the surface. They subverted one of the Seers in the same way as they control Terran priests. His mind was not his own."

Uther moved before she could react. He clasped her to him, offering comfort and also empathy. Shadow pushed him away, shaken.

"What more?" Those words fell from Uther's lips like a death sentence.

"Failing to get our son, any remaining drones will try for a lesser target." Shadow caught a glimpse of understanding from Irene. The Terran woman hugged her newborn. *Nothing but the truth now.* "I am not on their list of acquisitions or they would have made an attempt before now. Irene is not at risk, and your babe is an unknown factor."

"Which leaves me." Uther looked at his son just once. His face set in hard lines.

"Think back on our history together, how we were forced together and then separated. Every unnatural action compelled from a Terran by a Nestine betrays a driving need. Nestine need, whatever it is, must be denied." A shoal of holo fish swam in peaceful union on the wall above Irene's head. Shadow wanted to lose herself in their midst. Ector's debriefing of Arthur and Kai; the Nestines stalking both her sons, superimposed over the scene. Arthur remained one jump ahead but for how long? "You must leave Avalon at once."

"Uther. No!" Irene clutched at him, tears swelling in her eyes. "Who are these Nestines? Why should you leave? What is to become of us?"

Uther locked gazes with Shadow. "If I refuse?"

"Then you become a bad luck charm for Arthur. What if you are the next victim? What of your wife and son then?"

Uther bent to embrace Irene and the baby. He kissed the baby's dark fuzz and ran a finger over Irene's quivering lips. "I have to go now. What name do you wish for our son?"

Irene's face paled, and her lips set into a thin line. "Vortigen, after my father. A steadfast man."

"So be it." Uther detached himself, but his eyes bored into Shadow. "Stand in my stead. Care for them."

Uther's request came with an unspoken expectation of death. Shadow caught the nuances that he would never voice before Irene. This warrior went out to face unknown dangers and an uncertain future. His sacrifice forced her hand.

"Irene is family. She will not lack for my friendship or help."

*

Avriel's hostile stare drilled a hole in Kai's back. If he turned to look at her she looked away, yet he knew she watched. It unnerved him to be confined inside a submersible with this angry girl. *What, by the deeps, have I done to offend her now?* He

160

gave up on futile speculation. Women thought differently – they must. No man in his right mind would behave the way she did toward him. Baffled, he decided to help Haystack load charged lasers into a cargo bin.

"She's looking at you," Haystack said as he worked. A whimsical smile lit the blond Brethren's face.

"I'd noticed." Kai handed over another armful.

"She also looks like she's swallowed a stomach full of seawater every time she glances at Circe." The smile died.

"Avriel is unreasonable. Why is she angry with Circe?"

"Well Circe is sort of—not a type Avriel is used to meeting." A crimson flush colored Haystack's cheeks.

"Then she needs to grow up. Circe didn't ask for her vocation."

"No, but by all accounts, she was good at it."

"Enough." Kai put down his load. "Circe isn't a Breeding Mistress any longer. That girl is as free to choose how she lives as if she were a new Brethren Outcast we rescued."

"But she is not though, is she?" Haystack looked across the cabin at Arthur hovering over Circe sleeping across a row of seats. "Those two have a history. Avriel isn't going to like Arthur's interest in someone like Circe."

A surreptitious glance around all the crew informed Kai that they all waited for trouble. He suppressed a sigh, resigned to doing damage control. The last place he wanted to be near was anywhere around Avriel, and that was just where he must go for the sake of a tenuous peace.

*

Uther engraved his last sight of Irene and Vortigen on his soul. His thoughts flew over incidents of near misses. First, losing Ashira and then being a fugitive from Tadgehill as a result of his encounters with Arthur. *What is it that these beasts want with us?* Threat from a Seer level was something tangible, but he didn't understand this new menace.

161

A slight change in the groundrunner's angle shifted his tunic and something inside scratched against his chest . . . the parchment map of the location of that old sword. Probably useless now, after getting wet. Irritated by the discomfort, he opened his tunic to yank it out. No point in taking waste on a trip.

Part of him remained curious. He opened the scroll. By some quirk of fate, it looked blurred but not ruined. Maybe Arthur could use this after all? Perhaps searching for a useless relic would give them a purpose in this madness? He stowed it out of sight.

"A territory map?" Shadow turned her eyes back to the route.

"Maybe once. Arthur wanted an old family legend." Uther decided the thing was probably worthless. "This might be a location."

"Make sure he sees it." She slowed the horrendous monstrosity in which they rode to avoid a walker. "Arthur needs all the help he can get."

"Those words don't sound like a vote of confidence in his leadership."

"Avalon is doomed." Shadow's lips thinned. "If he doesn't find a way to win this war, then our fate is set in stone."

"That is an unfair burden to place on any man, let alone our son."

"Uther . . . there was an entity trapped in the . . . system that ran Avalon." The pauses in her words told of how Shadow struggled to find words. "This entity, a life force, imprisoned for countless years, wanted to be free. That is why I exist. I am part of a breeding program to get the best possible host body."

Horror vibrated down to his heel bones. He swiveled around in his strange, unnaturally soft seat to look at her. "You are talking of a god who would do this. There are no gods."

"No, not anymore, but he was a god once. He wanted to be free." They sailed past the twin towers of Sanctuary. Shadow made a course correction. "Avalon's stock didn't have all the raw material needed, so this being manipulated my conception. I think our union further enhanced his plan."

"You expect me to believe . . . ?"

"Arthur does. He has contact with Emrys, the entity. You see Emrys planned for Arthur, but not Kai and then the boys worked together, freeing him in a different way than he imagined. Whatever chance Submariners have for survival hangs on a thread of reluctant help."

"Why does Arthur need an old sword?" Uther's question caused a momentary deviation in course as Shadow swerved.

"Emrys told him to find it."

"Our son expects to save Submariners by getting his hand on what is probably a lump of rusted metal? Now you are pushing the limits of belief."

"When no hope exists, perhaps a leap of faith is the way forward." Shadow edged the groundrunner up to the wharf entry. Elite guards saluted her from their position by the huge wormlike entry umbilicus. "Uther, our son wasn't meant to exist. He was created for a purpose. That purpose has now changed. He needs all the help we can give him."

"I agreed to leave Avalon for the protection of Irene and Vortigen." Uther looked over at the twin towers of Sanctuary, black against artificial daylight.

Shadow followed his gaze. "Arthur grew up in that place. I know, from Ector, the horrors Acolytes endure. My upbringing in Menhill, under the authority of a stepfather who resented each breath I took, was easy by comparison."

*

Watching Circe's chest rise and fall with a regular pattern Arthur began to appreciate the simple act of breathing as never before. Guilt clawed at him, bringing hurtful images of all those might-have-beens. What if he had given her a child? Would she now be an exile from Avalon, from the only life she knew? If he had supplied viable seed, what of their child? Would Emrys have claimed that innocent life? So many possible outcomes to a

163

scenario with no winners. *She looks so helpless. What have I done to her?*

Circe liked her creature comforts, but none existed on the path he caused her feet to follow. Never, in his planning, had he envisaged recruiting a Submariner Breeding Mistress. By the deeps, how could a girl like Circe adjust to the life of a surface dwelling renegade?

Guilt forced Arthur to consider Avriel, another hostage to fate. Avriel had War Maid training and could adapt if pushed, despite her youth. This train of thought brought him back to Circe, having noted the hostile looks from Avriel. Kai sat on one of the bench seats in a huddle with his sister talking fast, not a good sign. He'd expected Avriel to have some compassion for a victim of Nestines, yet the strong overtones of hostility for Circe permeated through the submersible and it emanated from her.

Kai shifted his shoulders the way he always did when he felt trapped. Bracing himself, Arthur walked over to Avriel, who glared up at him.

"I broke parole because Circe was in danger." Arthur squatted down to face his sister. "I know what my action has cost our father, but I also know that if I hadn't acted as I did, Circe would now be a slave of the creatures who drove you from Tadgehill. Circe put her safety at risk for me when I most needed help. Should I have acted any differently?"

"Naturally you would run to protect your bedmate." Avriel's eyes bored into his soul like frozen shards of ice.

"She is a person, not a function. Shall I put you off this vessel because you are an untried warrior? Should I make this call because you might endanger us with your inexperience?"

"That has nothing to do with bringing a prostitute along for personal pleasure."

"Avriel!" Shock raised Kai's voice. Heads turned in their direction.

"Circe did not have a choice in her assigned task. She is now free to make her own decisions."

"Which will involve justifying her keep by loose behavior?" Avriel's mouth turned down as she delivered her triumphant epitaph. "Or are you about to suggest she will become camp cook instead?"

Arthur glanced at Kai, who shrugged. Both of them knew Circe expected appetizing food to be placed in front of her, presented regularly, in an attractive manner. He executed a short, formal bow to Avriel and left her to Kai.

*

"I note neither of you jumped to your pet prostitute's defense." Ariel took out her belt knife and honing stone, intent on driving home her own usefulness.

"Arthur is unused to being around those with a childlike mentality." Kai met the stares of all those men party to the argument. One by one, the warriors turned away. "He has more manners than I, although this point would be lost on one like you, who commands none."

Avriel muffled a cry when her hand slipped, earning her a painful nick from her blade. She sucked at the wound, hating him. She refused to rise to his baiting.

"Try to place yourself in Circe's shoes for a moment." Kai slipped on a patient smile that sat ill with his narrowed eyes. "She is a Seer in her own right and so on level with a Gold Band lady in a fort. As such, she has enjoyed a privileged life. Now she is about to enter a world primitive beyond her worst nightmares. If you can't make an effort to be nice, then at least try to remember that you are also supposed to be a lady."

Avriel didn't think, she just aimed her knife at his heart with as much strength as she could put behind the blow. Her target moved with eye blurring speed. Her knife banged against a bulkhead, jarring her bones. A solid mass hit her, knocking her to the floor on her back. Kai's amethyst eyes bored into hers while she fought for breath under his crushing weight. He twisted her wrist, making her drop the weapon. She struggled to dislodge him, wildly looking around for help. Her eyes met her father's.

"Help me."

"Kai, my apologies," Uther said. "I thought my daughter had more discipline. Chastisement for this attack is at your discretion."

"But he . . ."

"Defended himself." Her father ignored nervous laughter to walk across to them. The Outcast, that woman who was Kai's and Arthur's mother, matched paces with him. "Allies resolve differences in a civilized fashion. Children are punished for unacceptable behavior. If you can't give me your word that you will uphold our family dignity then I will have you stay with Irene, after Kai has enacted whatever discipline he sees fit."

"I give it." Horror forced the words through numb lips. "Make him get off me."

"I suggest you begin peace negotiations. Fix your own mess."

Her father moved away, taking that woman in tow. *This can't be happening.* Laughter echoed around the vessel. A hot wave of shame flooded Avriel's face. Kai pressed his body tighter to her.

"I beg your pardon." The admission fouled her mouth.

"Not given. Forgiveness is earned by humility, not suppressed arrogance." Kai flowed to his feet, a fluid motion so coordinated that it shocked her.

He hauled her standing by his hold on her tunic. She struggled to find her feet, aware of more laughter.

"I think punishment will be deferred until we reach the surface." Kai's expression remained distant as if he saw her in the form of a bug to be crushed. "I would not want to disturb my companions with your wails of woe."

"Don't you dare lay a hand on me. My father . . ."

"Gave me the right to do as I see fit. He will not interfere in a matter of internal discipline." Kai let his lips stretch in a slow Brethren smile. The tips of white teeth showed. "When you beg my pardon you will mean every word you say."

166

Chapter 18

UTHER STEELED HIMSELF not to become involved in the threatening exchange of pleasantries going on behind him as he walked away. Avriel deserved her punishment, and he trusted Kai not to make it too harsh.

"Shall I arrange to have her contained with Irene?" Shadow had worry lines scored between her eyes.

He hesitated, half wanting to accept. Did he want a spoilt and bored child creating trouble for Irene? No. The surface was where Avriel belonged. She must adapt. "Kai won't hurt her. They are interested in each other."

"And you will allow this to progress?"

The doubt in Shadow's tone made him face the circumstances. "A week ago, I would have fought him to the death for looking at her in that way." Uther collected his jumbled thoughts. "Avriel is becoming aware of males. Shall I leave her in Avalon to pursue those interests as her boredom directs?"

"Then you risk a relationship forming. My son was raised as Brethren. Be aware that Outcast society holds different standards than any fort."

"I admired Kai's father." He sucked in his pride. "Avriel is as good as an Outcast now. She could do a lot worse."

"You support a match between them?" Shadow glanced back to the angry pair.

"I propose to let them rule their own lives. Every circumstance I considered fixed has become unraveled, starting with us. Shall I stand in the place of your cruel father and give her to a stranger for the sake of a few parcels of copper?"

"Hald wasn't my father." Shadow's voice trembled. It hurt him to hear it.

"He filled a father's place." Uther put his arm around Shadow's waist, intending the gesture to be one of comfort. The charge of empathy between them that surfaced on contact shocked him. He'd thought them safe from the attractions of sex. She pulled away first.

"Ashira, I love my daughter. I will not dictate her life or her loves." He looked away, unable to bear her steady gaze. What was it with violet eyes? Copper had them, as did Arthur and Kai.

Shadow cleared her throat. "What if this attachment doesn't work out?"

He considered. "Then Avriel and I will live with the consequences. How will she learn to fly if I don't let her try her wings?"

"I wish . . . no matter." Shadow's incredible eyes betrayed a lifetime of unanswered questions. "Uther, don't let them destroy each other. Promise me you will level down the fights."

"I will. For them and . . . for you." For one instant the barriers dropped. He saw his War Maid again with her simple courage and her faith intact. Uther recalled their last perfect day together, racing on horses through the breakers on his private beach. Each of them daring fate; confident of their life and their love. Something in her expression told him she remembered too. He wanted to lose himself in those violet eyes, but that cup had passed from his lips.

*

Kiri Ung observed Tadgehill's substitute duke perform his duties. Te Krull had worked hard with that drone to integrate it. No flavor of doubt clouded the minds of fort Terrans. They accepted this duke as a bachelor who had never formed any unions. Some of them even hoped he would someday, to ensure the succession.

Te Krull exuded confidence by his side as they watched the ceremony. Such confidence began to cause feelings of disquiet in Kiri Ung. A Planetary Governor could demand an audience with Shi Nom. *What if she is impressed? What if she sees him as a mate?*

Kiri Ung shuffled uncomfortably. Shi Nom expected Arthur, and the half-breed wasn't in sight of capture. Te Krull could claim precedence since his troops had secured Tadgehill. He began to feel the Queen's mandible closing around his neck in a death grip.

"Make a ship available to me. I need to survey this area from an aerial location."

"Why?" Te Krull's question carried all the implication of a challenge. "Here is just as good. You said Arthur must return."

The Queen's Mate didn't miss the absent honorific in Te Krull's reply. He began a mental review of Te Krull's immediate subordinates for a possible successor. Now was not the time for open challenge, however.

"I trust you to maintain watch in this place. I wish to pursue a less certain objective."

"Then a ship and its crew will be at your disposal, Queen's Mate."

Now the correct form of address is given, when he thinks I make a mistake he can profit from. Kiri Ug suppressed his thoughts even as he felt Te Krull give the mental command to a skyship captain. He had a plan.

*

Arthur sat beside Kai to pilot the submersible. He'd called Kai over to co-pilot because he wanted to get his brother away from Avriel after the knife incident. Strange that those two fought when he could have sworn they were beginning to like each other. Arthur couldn't imagine fighting with Circe. They'd disagreed on occasions, to the point where she might use sex as a weapon and then he either conceded or stood his ground.

The word weapon caught and held in his mind. Were the girls really so dissimilar? If alike, then what prompted Avriel's attack?

"Kai, what started the argument?"

"She made cruel remarks about Circe." Kai's lips compressed. "Avriel is prejudged without any idea of the circumstances."

"I suppose you called her childish?"

"What if I did? We can't afford tantrums where we are going."

"I agree. Just remember how young she is when you decide on a punishment."

"She will be more mature and have a kinder outlook to others by the time I'm through." Kai glanced back at Avriel. A slow Brethren smile curved his lips.

"What did you think about the way our mother and Dragon seemed overfriendly?" Arthur said, wanting to change the subject. Kai's reply made him uneasy for Avriel.

"She made him dance to her tune, and I don't think he minded all that much."

"Trouble ahead, you guess?"

"No. My point about maturity."

Arthur repressed the urge to squeeze the full answer out of Kai. Sometimes the Brethren tendency to be cryptic, expecting others to guess their thoughts, went too far.

"They still care about each other, but they accept that they can't reverse time. Dragon has Irene and mother has Ector. I think they might avoid each other from conscious choice."

A statement Arthur tended to accept, given the way his parents behaved to each other. He'd picked up on the respect and the careful maneuvering around each other's feelings.

"Heading? I have a final course correction to make soon." Kai activated a holo map of the approaching land mass.

"I think we need time to become a unified fighting force." Arthur studied the map with a plan in mind. "Our original home base will give us the peace we need to make this so." He pointed to the position of the cave near High fort.

"Submariners aren't going to like that after enjoying a cave by the sea," Kai said.

"I know they won't like the land trek, but I want us at a distance from Tadgehill." Arthur resisted the urge to look at his father. "What if his fort is under attack?"

"Good point. He'd want to go running."

"Exactly."

"Going to be tough on Circe." Kai looked over at the girl.

Arthur sighed. "If she is going to be a problem, then I want to know why and how before it becomes an issue."

*

Night air carried the dying heat of a summer's day as the small group traveled inland. Arthur felt the misgivings about their journey from the thoughts of others leaking out and then they began their complaint in earnest. Kai and Haystack swore they felt no threat in the vicinity of Tadgehill when they cast their minds into fey mode. Huber pointed out fishing was easier than hunting and staying near the submersible made sense. Dragon wanted access to all the goods and weapons he had stored in his cache and Arthur guessed his father might have private plans to hunt down every Nestine in Tadgehill.

The dry grass caught at his clothing when they started out across a series of rolling hills added to his disquiet. He didn't like the collected resentment aimed at him for choosing their camp near High fort. None of them really listened to his reasoning that they all needed quiet time to become a tight fighting unit. He stilled an oath as a huge cloud meandered across the face of the moon, making walking more of a chore.

The lonely howl of a dog fox echoed into darkness. Rustles sounded in the underbrush. A branch caught in Arthur's cloak. He paused to detach it, wary of leaving any threads to announce their passing. A muffled cry from behind sounded. Circe's voice; something in the tone of it caught his attention.

She hadn't uttered a complaint during their three-hour trek. He picked out her slight figure against darker shades of tree trunks. A formless shadow, she stumbled and then continued forward with over-careful steps. Just then, a shaft of moonlight pierced through cloud, and he saw her face.

Light caught in the pearls of tears streaming from her eyes. Arthur hated to see a woman cry like that. No screwing up of the feature, or sobbing, just silent tears that speared his soul.

Too exhausted to fight his mind probe, the source of Circe's woe was laid bare. Her shoes had shredded, and her feet bled. He scooped her into his arms as others filed past, following in Haystack's path. She was tiny, lighter than he remembered, but then he had grown into manhood during his absence from Avalon.

Arthur? Her thought unfolded in his mind. *Put me down. I can manage.*

We have a way to go before we make camp. Tomorrow we will sort out some decent footwear for you.

I don't wish to be a burden. She started to struggle.

Circe, stop that or I will send you to sleep. He stepped over a fallen branch in his path.

The trail opened out onto moorland. Easier to travel, but more exposed. Arthur picked up his pace to match the others. A dark smudge on the horizon signaled their goal this night. Maybe another two hours before they made camp. He didn't want to risk them being spotted by patrols from High fort after dawn.

Circe stiffened in his arms. She pointed, her hand shaking. "Saurians?"

"Just deer." He sent her an image of what deer looked like in daytime, aware that such beasts would seem strange to her. A stag with a full rack of antlers trailed the herd, marking the change of seasons. Fall rut approached. That thought set off alarm bells.

"Circe? Do you have any special needs?" He didn't feel comfortable asking her outright. The time between them as a couple seemed an age.

"I will adjust."

Embarrassed now, he tried to find the right words. Time passed, and the dark smudge of their destination drew closer without any tactful way of framing his question. Steeling himself, Arthur blurted it out. "Are you with child?"

Her merry tinkle of laughter turned the nearest heads for a moment. "Oh, you thought . . . ?" Giggles consumed her.

"Well?"

"After you left I decided to become an Acolyte instead." Her face registered wonder when the ghostly shape of an owl flew across their path.

"But you tried for me when I came back for the first time." Arthur's heart skipped. She'd given up being a Breeding Mistress? And yet she reverted for him?

"I wanted your child. Evegena's order gave me one last chance." She snuggled against his chest.

Relief mingled with sorrow. Away from the influence of Seers he could raise a child and yet outside of all that she had known, Circe could not bear one, not in these primitive conditions. He didn't know how she was going to endure the surface.

"Don't be sad. Maybe one day, when you have vanquished all the Nestines, then we can live as we choose."

Her lighthearted retort sent his mental barriers into a higher stage. He did not want her to know his pain. "Yes, when all are gone."

*

Avriel marched behind Kai, determined not to let the ache in her calves show in her stride. She wasn't going to let herself become a spectacle like that pale worm Arthur carried. *How selfish she is. How can she drain him like that?* She turned to glare, missed her step and fell, catching her foot in a burrow. White-hot pain raced up her ankle. A sob caught in her throat.

Kai turned at the sound. She tried to stand, but the pain wouldn't let her. It closed around her, crushing out stars. Strong arms caught her, lifted her onto shoulders as if she were a sack of grain.

"That was very clumsy of you," Kai advised. "Looking where you are walking is usually the best plan."

Furious, Avriel wanted to kick him, but the mere motion of being carried brought jolts of agony. *I am not going to cry. I am not going to cry.* Repeating that didn't help, but anger might.

She chose to challenge Kai. "How can anyone see in the dark?"

"By looking at the ground for patches that don't seem even. If you look with the corners of your eyes, instead of trying to focus, then you might see the rabbit hole everyone else stepped over."

Now that was too much. She thumped her fist in his back. Shafts of pain shot up her leg. Tears started.

"I imagine that hurt you far more than it did me. Was it worth the effort?"

"I hate you."

"That's fine. How would you like to crawl? Maybe you might reach our camp before we set out again." He paused as if enjoying her agony. "That is, if a saurian doesn't decide to make you a pre-breakfast snack. Most of them hunt at dawn."

"You're the most detestable man I have ever met."

"Should be all the more interesting for both of us when you beg my pardon then, won't it?"

*

Silver streaks in the night sky heralded dawn. Uther forced his aching legs into one final push to a copse ahead. Used to riding, he found walking stretched tendons and muscles unused to such punishment.

Thickets of gorse gave way to saplings springing from a bed of ferns, all drained of color in the twilight. High pitched tweets of stirring birds began with the first pink glimmer of morning. Spider webs glistened, heavy with dew, catching the light. Uther inhaled damp air smelling of loam. He couldn't remember being so free before. Marching with these young men made him feel as if the years fell from his shoulders. No planning for others, no listening to disputes, no trading trips to organize, no territory to defend – this freedom coursed through him.

Had Shadow experienced this in her years as an Outcast? He thought she might, for when everything else is lost except freedom, then the small wonders of nature give pleasure.

As he approached a massive pine tree, he noticed a squirrel busy cropping cones from above. They fell to the ground, crashing into leaf litter to be grabbed by an opportunist of the same species. When the industrious one descended, he spied the thief, screamed his rage and set off in pursuit. An angry scuffle sounded out of sight as the pair fought.

Haystack led them into a clearing concealed from above by a leafy canopy. The unit began to make camp in a half circle of brambles. Not a place where a flying predator could make a strike from above and only one side to guard from a ground attack. He approved. Moss and leaf litter on the ground, rather than bracken, would hide their passing from outriders. His respect for the woodcraft skills this group displayed grew with each passing second.

Arthur settled Circe gently on a thick patch of leaf litter near the back of the briar patch. His son, who must be exhausted from carrying her, then peeled off the shreds of her shoes to tend to her bloody feet.

Kai walked past him to dump Avriel down not so gently on a carpet of moss. Her hiss of pain cut through the quiet sounds of morning. Uther didn't blame Kai. He'd caught the look from the light of a moonbeam that Avriel directed at Circe just before tripping. If he hadn't promised Kai the privilege, he would have wanted to punish her himself for her lack of discipline. Despite her War Maid training, she acted like a spoiled child.

Uther intercepted a glance from Kai. That young man winced as a tirade of complaints streamed from Avriel. Sighing, Uther went over to them.

"Father, did you see the way he dropped me? I'm hurt. Make him build me a litter for tomorrow night."

"You're lucky Kai carried you this far." Uther gathered his courage. "I would have left you after what I saw. I suggest you make some attempt to be agreeable to him, or he might not waste his energy carrying you when we leave. Are you skilled at hopping?" Uther left her to fume. It would do her more good than sympathy, which she did not deserve.

*

Kai glared down at a red-faced Avriel. Something Dragon said had touched a raw bone with her. *What did he mean, what he saw?*

"Don't just stand there like an oaf. My ankle needs attention."

"Say please."

"Excuse me?"

"I said say please."

"How can I travel if I don't get help now? Are you so stupid you don't know how to fix an injury?"

"Skilled at hopping are you?" Kai smiled a slow smile that held no warmth. He turned away.

"Please."

He continued to walk toward Huber, who carried the med pack. Yes, she had to have aid, but he would be damned to the seventh hell before he danced to her tune.

"Please Kai. It hurts." A muffled sob sounded from behind him. "I'm sorry."

Sorry because it pleases your purpose. But he snagged the pack to take over to her.

Avriel shrieked when he tried to cut the boot off her swollen foot. Kai had to call for Arthur to send her into a deep sleep before he could continue. *Circe never uttered a single cry when Arthur tended her. This one needs to grow up.*

The damage wasn't as bad as he'd feared. She had a sprain, not a break. Kai bandaged the swollen area to give it support, but he knew she wouldn't be walking on it anytime soon.

Chapter 19

CIRCE SHUT HER eyes against bright spears of sunlight. Noise crushed against her. Flying things in trees shrieked, but even worse was the hum of bugs. Those that crept over debris in a silent stalk sent her flesh creeping. She knew an ugly black bug lurked in one corner of delicate, dew-covered gossamer. She wanted the muted tones of Avalon's light and her own quiet room. How could she live in this terrible place?

Sounds of men making camp added to her unreal dream sense. After Seers, these warriors, with their brash camaraderie isolated her in a background of Avriel's complaints to the scorn from the men. Arthur would help if she asked, but that would weaken him as a leader.

A many-legged something skittered over her hand. She flicked it off, pushing down the scream in her throat and her mind. A creak of leather and a slight change in the air warned her she had company.

"Arthur?"

"No, Haystack. Arthur's sleeping."

Ah yes, Arthur's watcher. Had he come to guard her now? Did they think she might give way to hysterics? Anger stirred from a sleeping coil within her core.

"You should sleep too," he said.

Sounds of cutting leather came from his direction. Circe opened her eyes a fraction, to catch sight of him sitting cross-legged, fashioning a rough pair of shoes from an old tunic. He had the remnants of her shoes lined up for a size match. The light made her eyes water.

"Submariners have a fear of bugs, don't they?" The cutting sounds stopped.

"I'm fine." Never would she admit to weakness in front of one of Arthur's men.

"Huber can't stand ants. Those tiny crawling things that appear in groups. He thinks they will crawl up his nose while he is sleeping." Haystack chuckled. "That's why he stuffs fragments of cloth up his nostrils before he sleeps, and that's what makes him snore."

She could hear the low snorts not so far from them. A picture formed in her mind, bringing her lips into a smile she didn't intend.

"That's better." The sound of cutting resumed. "Leeches give me the shudders. They live in water. Creep into a man's clothes and dig into his skin. When they swell with the blood they have stolen, that turns my stomach."

"How can you bear this?" *By the deeps, what other horrors live in this surface world?*

"Feeding leeches won't kill me any more than ants will want to crawl up Huber's nose. Little creatures can't harm us unless we turn them into nightmares to sap our courage."

Somehow, having a warrior share her fears helped. Her feeling of uselessness persisted though.

"Arthur said you had started Acolyte training." Haystack sounded conversational now as if this were an ordinary morning. "Does that mean you can do mind tricks?"

"I can bring sleep, and I think I can hasten healing." Not like Arthur. No one had his strength.

"That's good. Sometimes we divide into two groups. Having another Seer is going to be a bonus."

The kindness behind Haystack's words shook her. Brethren didn't have a kind bone in their bodies, did they? But he must know how useless she was in this strange world. Did he think she could adjust? Somehow, she must.

*

179

Circe awoke from a deep, dreamless sleep to the sounds of movement. A red-tinged sky drew her breath away. Never before had she seen such beauty, the way the sky seemed to boil with light. By her side lay a pair of fur lined leather shoes crafted by one who should have been sleeping. Her notion of Brethren motives underwent a subtle readjustment.

Arthur came over to offer a flat biscuit. It was gray and looked unappealing.

"Field rations. We can't make fires out in the open to cook." He smiled in a quirky way with an almost comical regret. "Smoke attracts all kinds of unwelcome attention."

Her first bite of the dry lump wasn't so bad. The flavor didn't resemble anything she could recall, but it wasn't unpleasant.

Avriel's angry voice sounded, demanding a litter. Circe saw Dragon heading out of his daughter's sight. Kai, not so fast, reluctantly heard her out. A low muttering came from him before he too, made his retreat.

"Arthur, you're not going to leave her?" Circe couldn't believe any of them capable of such callousness.

"Hush." He looked toward Avriel, his mouth compressing into a thin, angry line. "She needs to think we will."

"That's cruel."

"Avriel needs to learn she is not the center of attention. She will not have any help from me until she accepts that others have feelings, too."

Circe's feet felt better, and a swift look revealed the pink of healing skin. Not a natural healing, yet how much strength had it cost Arthur? In that moment, she understood why all followed his lead.

"I think I can walk tonight."

"Part of the way." He glanced at her bare feet. "Stamina is acquired by stages."

"I will not sap your energy."

"No. We will take it in turn for you and Avriel both."

Relief washed over her. She feared Arthur had become hard, like the Brethren. Even the Submariner Elite with the group projected the same implacable indifference, yet it screened a gentle side not one of them would show by choice.

Arthur ran a light finger over her frown, moving it down to touch her lips. She held her breath, wishing they were back in Avalon, before the troubles. Yet she found she wouldn't trade the man he had become for the boy he was then. Somehow, he had taken on a mantle of power; one well hidden, but ever present. Circe recognized that she would do his bidding in future. He was out of her control.

"Deep thoughts?" A whimsical smile lit his face, making her insides do somersaults.

"I wondered what motivates men."

"*You* ask this?" He cupped her face, looking deeply into her eyes.

"Don't." Circe pushed his hands away. "Avriel is staring."

"Ignore her."

"And create more arguments?" She wasn't sure how much Arthur would tolerate from his sister. While he didn't intend to implement drastic punishment, he could make life very unpleasant.

"This is what I think of Avriel's opinion."

Arthur's swift action caught her by surprise. His lips just touched to hers, caressing, exciting, yet not intrusive. Not a maneuver she had taught him, but one so erotic it left her tingling. When he broke contact, she recognized the face of a lover. Something else too – iron control.

"You shouldn't have done that."

"Maybe not." Again his whimsical smile destroyed her. "Perhaps I wanted a taste of what might be if we win."

He flowed to his feet, a movement of grace and strength combined. Executing a short, formal bow that had nothing in common with manners, yet exuded a challenge, Arthur rejoined his men. Hearing his easy banter with them made her want to call him back. Those days of her sexual power over him lay in the dust of wishful thinking. Arthur had made his point in a way she acknowledged.

*

Night sharpened all senses. Once, Circe caught the musky smell of saurian on the air, a scent she recognized from the projected thoughts of Submariners, comparing memories with each other. Everyone froze, waiting until some invisible factor convinced Brethren that danger was past.

Moonlight cast intricate patterns of light through foliage. Circe inhaled wonderful scents of crushed underbrush. Sounds of things scurrying through cover thrilled her. She wanted to see them, but she wasn't fast enough.

Avriel began to moan from near the end of their column, where Merrick carried her over his shoulder. The Submariners took turns sharing the burden of her presence. Circe wondered why no Brethren helped. Even Dragon distanced himself.

For a horseman, the duke bore walking well. Twice Circe noticed Arthur helping him with a touch supplying stamina. Each time Dragon seemed to get another burst of energy. While she wondered how much strength Arthur had to give, Kai dropped back to walk alongside her.

"How are you feeling?"

"I'm good for a while yet," she lied.

"Not what Arthur says." He made a sudden grab and then she was in his arms.

"Please. I can manage."

"Not much further now. You're a lightweight."

"At least carry me like Avriel is being carried." Circe didn't want more trouble. "This way strains your arms."

"Someone will take over when I am done." His lips curved up in a shadowed smile.

"Kai. It's not fair."

"Life isn't. Get used to it."

Relief from walking and tiredness lulled her with each step. Sometime later she became aware of being transferred to another set of arms. The way those arms held her told her who now carried her. She slept.

*

"We must have transport." Dragon's voice echoed around a vast space. On waking, the sound of water splashing seemed strange to Circe.

The light and warmth of a fire sent shadows dancing on rock surfaces. A damp, earthy smell permeated the air. Dragon stood with his back to a cascade of water falling from a hole near the ceiling of the cavern. He had his arms crossed against his chest.

"Theft will be noticed." Kai glowered from the fire he fed. "Stealing stock from High fort would bring unwelcome attention."

"There are wild horses." Arthur tossed a pebble into the torrent. "Taking a number of them won't be noticed. We have wounded, so we have time to catch and break all the mounts we need."

"Time wasted. What is happening to Tadgehill while we play horse trainers?" Dragon started pacing.

"Let's get one point clear." Arthur squared up against Dragon, seemingly relaxed, except Circe detected his inner tension. "Tadgehill is not a target. Nestines will expect a counterstrike, so that is not what we are going to do."

Dragon fished inside his tunic, bringing out a battered scroll of parchment. He thrust it under Arthur's nose. "This says we will. You wanted an old sword. Here is a map to its location."

All movement ceased. Every head turned toward Arthur and Dragon. Liquid waves of antagonism coming from both men hit Circe.

Taking the scroll, Arthur unrolled it with painstaking slowness that must have tested him to the limits. He looked at the thing and returned it to Dragon as if it was of small interest. Kai tensed.

Circe guessed Arthur had transmitted the image for Kai to store. *So, Arthur values this map, but he doesn't want to let Dragon use it as a lever over him.*

"Nestines will run out of patience if we ignore them long enough." Arthur looked over at Kai. "We will know when the odds have shifted in our favor for a retrieval attempt."

"How?" The parchment crackled as Dragon crushed it in his hand. The duke's voice decreased in volume, reminding Circe of Arthur in a temper.

"Brethren fey gift. They sense danger from future actions."

"I'll go get the sword myself if that is what it takes to get your aid for Tadgehill." Dragon thrust the map back into his tunic.

"How?" Arthur smiled the slow Brethren smile, sending chills over Circe's flesh. "Will you wander around the shores of a large lake calling to it?"

"Dragon, the threat level for you had increased," Kai warned. "Arthur's right. Let's wait until Avriel is fit to travel, at least. I'll scan ahead again when she is fit to march."

"Don't you put blame on me." Avriel sat up, white-faced with fury. "I say we retake Tadgehill. My ankle will be better by the time we get there."

Dragon's mouth tightened into a thin line. He turned to look at his daughter. "Your say is not worth the air you used to utter it. When you have earned the right to pass judgment on battle tactics, you may voice an opinion."

"I'm a War Maid. I've studied."

Her father shut his eyes and took a deep breath. He looked over her head to Kai. "I recall that chastisement for ill-disciplined behavior was granted to you. Would you be so kind?"

"Anything goes?" Kai raised an eyebrow, ignoring Avriel's gasp.

"Short of strangulation. Try not to break any bones. I've grown weary of her complaints."

Kai flowed to his feet, scooping up Avriel in the process. He marched out of the caverns with his shrieking victim to the sound of laughter.

Dragon squatted to tend the fire, and Arthur came over to Circe, sitting next to her. The sound of Avriel's distress ceased abruptly.

"Don't look so worried. Neither of them meant any of that. Kai won't hurt her, and Dragon wouldn't let her out of his sight if he didn't trust Kai."

"But he is going to punish her." Circe shivered, aware of how hard Brethren could be.

"Avriel needs to learn manners." Arthur put his arm around her shoulders. "I've an idea what it is he has in mind. Dragon won't approve, but then I don't think Avriel will want to discuss what Kai does to her."

Chapter 20

AIR WENT OUT in a painful whoosh as she struck the ground. Avriel couldn't even gasp. Nothing mattered but the fight to breathe. Black spots danced inside her eyes. Her chest heaved and filled. Minutes passed before her breathing returned to normal.

Kai stood leaning against a tree trunk looking unconcerned. He had a thin branch in his hand and was shearing off all the twigs. Just the end tassel of leaves remained.

"Don't you dare!" Horrified, Avriel met his hard gaze.

He raised one eyebrow. "Thought you might need a switch for the bugs. They tend to gather in swarms near open water."

"What do you mean?" Relief that Kai didn't intend to beat her gave way to suspicion.

"Big predators don't come out until dusk. That includes most saurians. You should be safe enough." He tossed her the switch, executed a formal half bow and turned to the caves.

"Kai? You can't leave me here!"

He arrested mid-stride, turning to face her with a polite, if distant smile. "I can and I have. Your behavior is offensive. Until you learn to respect others, you will be on your own."

Avriel looked down at her only weapon, a useless stick. The sun already dipped with the promise of evening. He wasn't serious. He couldn't be, but his face wore a studied indifference in his very lack of expression. For the first time, she saw him as pure Brethren. Something about his slight shift in stance warned her he prepared to move.

Panicked, Avriel tried a desperate gamble. "Is this the part where I am supposed to grovel? To offer you sexual favors for forgiveness?"

A short laugh burst from Kai. He ran his eyes over her, evaluating her as if she were a mare. "Virgins aren't all that interesting. Bad-tempered ones even less so." He gave a polite neck bow. "Have a nice night."

Avriel held onto the shreds of her pride until he reached the edge of the clearing. Panic demolished her control.

"Kai, please." Her voice broke in a sob. "I'll do anything if you will take me back inside."

Again he retraced his steps to face her. No trace of kindness lighted his expression.

"Anything?" The word was soft spoken.

Avriel shuddered and then nodded, helpless.

"I require the Kiss of Peace."

Shock sent gooseflesh over her. Once given, such a vow held her to cease hostilities, but he had no right to demand this.

"That only holds between equals," she objected.

"Yes, I am making a special concession." He looked down on her. "I was the son of a two-times King. You are only the daughter of a former duke."

"You're an Outcast."

"Brethren, yes. Outcast, no. For that, I would have to pass through the hands of a priest. As must you, girl." The corners of his lips lifted, but no warmth reached his eyes. He glanced at the lengthening shadows.

"Agreed." After all, what did it matter if she promised not to harm him? She hadn't intended to really stab him.

Kai hauled her upright into a tight embrace. He lowered his head. "Fair enough. On my lips."

Such a vow committed her to defending his life. Caught, she touched her lips to his firmly closed ones. Memories of that other kiss on the beach humiliated her further. Hot waves of

187

shame coursed over her face and neck. His face remained cold when she broke off.

"See that you mind your manners as befits a former duke's daughter." His violet eyes narrowed. "I might decide on a Kiss of Peace from you for all of our party." With that, he swept her into his arms and headed for the caves.

Hot tears spilled over. Avriel didn't want to go inside now. She didn't want to face anyone, least of all Circe. All she wanted was a quiet spot to die. Kai dumped her, none too gently, right by the fire in full view of all. Adding to her misery, he went over to sit by Circe. Avriel could only imagine how much fun he gained from her misfortune by the way laughter came from that corner. Sobbing, she dragged herself to her bedding against a wall.

*

Excited voices echoed around the cavern, coming from a group lounging by Circe. Merrick and Linden were out exaggerating each other in stories about the size of bugs in their respective homes. Arthur knew Avalon didn't generate a roach the size of a man's fist. He was also certain the surface didn't contain spiders the size of dinner plates, but it made for entertainment.

Huber had out his pack of cards for an ongoing lesson to Brethren in ways to cheat. From the cries of outrage, Kai and Haystack had improved, but Stalker remained too honest.

Mulberry took a turn by the fire, adjusting the spit holding their sizzling roast. Dragon sat, cross-legged by the heat to hone the blade on his sword. All of them focused on ordinary pastimes.

Arthur constructed an image of himself sleeping to insert into their minds. He wanted a time of quiet to think through strategy. A small part of him missed the hours of solitary contemplation every Acolyte enjoyed in Sanctuary.

Weak autumn sunshine gave gentle warmth to the outside. He noticed some of the trees around had begun to change – that one last burst of color to lighten hearts before bleak winter. An overripe smell of fruit on the breeze wafted down from the valley sides. He sat with his back to a tree, just enjoying peace. A twig snapping brought him to full alert, his senses reaching out – Dragon. The duke crept from the cave behind him.

"Shadow would have your hide for that misstep. Did you have a reason for sneaking up on me, Father?" Arthur sensed the sudden shock radiating from his sire.

"I wanted to see if I could." Uther circled around into view, his eyes a touch wider than normal.

"Why?" Arthur wanted most to know how Dragon saw beyond the illusion. That could wait, unless the duke chose to raise the subject.

Uther hunkered down next to a raised bank of dirt, facing him. "Tactics. I like to know every strength of those I fight alongside." A quirky smile lit the duke's face. "You might consider leaving your image asleep further from a fire the next time you want to vanish. A large spark passed straight through your face while I watched."

"Good point." Arthur brushed an ant from his hand. He hoped he wasn't sitting near an anthill as he guessed Uther wanted to continue their argument.

A falcon soared above them in lazy circles, ascending on a thermal. The screech of a tiercel challenged filtered down.

"You came out here to plan." Dragon picked up a twig, poking at a loose hillock of dirt. "I would."

Arthur followed the path of the bird plummeting to ground at a breathtaking speed. A high-pitched scream of captured prey sounded.

"We need a base in the west." Would Dragon rekindle his argument?

"My cave is off-limits. Why?"

"Tactics. The Nestines have a smart strategist who targets me. My opponent is only a few paces behind." Arthur smacked an ant off his leg.

189

"Explain."

A promising start. Arthur condensed his thoughts. "We created a reasonable amount of havoc for the Nestines until this spring. That is when they discovered a way to trace us to our earrings." He looked up. "You know about them?"

"Thought they were a fashion statement—something girly to make you all look more threatening by contrast."

Arthur shook his head. "Earrings free up speech in 'made' Brethren; a property of the blue-banded stones in each of them. Black wristbands are replaced by fakes as soon as new victims meet with veterans so Nestines couldn't use those to locate Brethren anymore."

"They targeted the baubles?" Uther rammed his stick into the mound.

"Avalon fixed the problem for my group." Arthur slapped another ant from his leg. "We are invisible to them, and yet they seem to know where we are."

"You sure? Seems to me that Nestines had drone spies planted in the city." Uther stabbed the mound again.

"True, but the point is they always show up. Take Tadgehill for instance. We had just attacked an east coast fort, regrouped here and then we moved to your cave. They swarmed over the skies here just after we moved out." Arthur shook an ant off his hand. It stung him. "That swarm took Tadgehill."

Uther ground his stick into the loose dirt. "Because I sheltered Outcasts in the past? That is a long shot."

"A specialty of my opposite." Another ant crawled over his boot. Arthur brushed it off. "I wish you would leave that anthill alone."

"Oh. Sorry." Uther dropped his stick. "They will come here?"

"When they run out of patience waiting for a counterstrike at your fort." He gave up the losing battle with an army of ants, brushing off his clothing to reseat himself on top of a boulder.

Dragon started batting at his legs. He too moved a few paces before squatting again.

"We need mounts to blend in with other Brethren bands. On foot, we are suspect."

"Training wild horses is going to take time." Dragon frowned, looking into the underbrush without focusing.

"Not done my way." Arthur began to enjoy bouncing ideas off this seasoned warrior.

"Fine, so we abandon the ship?" Dragon raised an eyebrow, doubt written on his face.

"How about splitting into two groups? You, me and the Submariners take our submersible around to the west coast. Kai, Avriel and the Brethren ride overland." Arthur held his breath, waiting for the fight to start.

"I agree the selection as Avriel isn't fit to walk."

Trying to keep his face neutral, Arthur felt his respect for Uther increase. "I want a cave, or caves on the south of the peninsular. I know that is in the Bad Lands, and that's why Nestines won't look for us there."

"No forts in the area mean no Nestines." Uther smiled, a feral expression. "Those mutant weapons will keep off saurians?"

Having fun now, Arthur matched his father's wicked grin. "Given. And we will be near that lake of yours."

Dragon dug out his crumpled map, spreading it on the ground. He anchored each corner with a rock and then they studied it.

"Here," he said, jabbing a finger at an indent in the coastline. "I had to rescue some of my fisherfolk after a shipwreck. The currents and rocks were too bad to risk another vessel. We went overland." Uther looked up. "That area is crawling with saurians."

"Good. It gives us an extra line of defense." Arthur thought for a moment. "Any ornisaurs?"

"The trees are too stunted for roosts. They need height for takeoff."

One last problem remained. Arthur didn't want to deal with it, but he had to resolve this remaining glitch. "You'll tell Avriel?"

Dragon stiffened. A tick twitched beside his mouth. "No. I think Kai can do the honors. You might want to tell him not to inform her until we are ready to leave though."

Chapter 21

DRY, RECYCLED AIR irritated Kiri Ung's throat, and the sky-ship's acceleration unsettled him. Traveling planet-side upset his digestion, unlike the smooth trip in artificial gravity through space. He hated being dependent on the two pilots and the navigator, all busy in front of their glistening array of instrumentation. His own digits twitched at each maneuver, aching to take over, but he must maintain a superior position.

The dull gray of his view-screen portrayed an outline of the underlying topography. Blue circles indicated Gold Band slaves, but none of those appeared. Not one purple circle of a Black Band either. This fifth quadrant searched proved as empty as the preceding ones.

Kiri Ung tried to hope for success as the ship began a search and sweep of the sixth. He'd already given up on the byzatrone emitter. That brilliant device failed miserably to detect any ear ornament from Arthur's assault force in Tadgehill. The resident Nestine should have been alerted to their approach. Alarms failed to trigger. Records from view-screens remained unscathed by the brilliant red lights indicating those with earrings. Once again outwitted by Arthur.

If not on land, then Arthur must be underwater, but in all the years of conflict with aquatic mutants, not one vessel had ever surfaced. Kiri Ung knew the mutants transported Terrans in a death trance. He had to admire the concept – dead lungs didn't draw in water. That fact failed to help his dilemma. How to catch Arthur?

"Flight Leader, start searching the quadrant to the seaward side of Tadgehill." At least Kiri Ung wanted the satisfaction of knowing where Arthur lurked.

"Queen's Mate, I need to re-polarize the Herrison drive." The sky pilot turned to face him while the space pilot nodded agreement. "If I have to switch to atomics, then we can't use the thought-wave resonator. Terrans will be able to see the ship."

Kiri Ung made a conscious effort to control his crest. "Why didn't you tell me this before?"

"We thought we would land after the fifth quadrant since meal time is past due." The pilot lowered his eyes.

Kiri Ung didn't want to return to Tadgehill. Not with Te Krull there waiting to gloat. He was also aware of the strain on resources that a fort with three Nestine ships suffered.

"Is there enough charge to get us to High fort?"

"If we fly high and slow . . . maybe." The sky pilot glanced at his colleague, who shrugged.

"Make it so and I'll arrange for juvenile meat."

A low thrum of pleasure sounded from the flight crew.

*

Avriel sat in the shade of a large tree while Brethren selected mounts. She didn't understand why a herd of wild horses stood so quiet in the glade. Stalker said it was because Arthur called them, but she didn't believe him. No one could do that. Perhaps the grass the animals cropped was sweeter here? She found it more entertaining to watch each Brethren bond with his chosen beast. Now that was real magic.

Kai had the chestnut stallion and blew into the animal's nose, rubbing his hands over the face and neck. It quivered when he slipped a rope halter over its head, but it remained still. Kai's strength and grace when he leapt onto its back took her breath away. She nursed a private satisfaction that Circe had missed this by choosing to stay inside. The mutant woman faced a long trek by foot that night and claimed a need to sleep. Avriel, knowing someone would carry her, contemplated Circe suffering. At least being carried wouldn't be as uncomfortable as riding bareback.

She looked over at Arthur, sitting against a sunbaked rock, his eyes closed. *Arthur is asleep. He isn't responsible for the herd. What nonsense.* But something impossible was occurring. One by one, the unwanted animals wandered away from the herd. Each mare with a foal and all pregnant mares disappeared into forest cover without a flicker of protest from the stallion. By rights, he should be rounding them up.

The Brethren, now all mounted, walked their chosen beasts in a tight circle. Gradually the pace increased. Each rider and mount continued to bond in a way that should have taken weeks.

"Interesting skill." Her father settled beside her to watch.

"Why aren't Brethren used to break mounts in forts?" Avriel could see the advantages.

"That isn't them, it's Arthur."

She caught a half-smile lighting her father's face. The way he looked at Arthur . . .

"I'm told his mother had this control over horseflesh. I heard she managed a breeding stallion with a broken mouth as if he were a lap dog." His eyes became unfocused, and his smile matured.

Overhead a crow flapped to roost. It ruffled its features and let out a raucous caw as Avriel wondered about Shadow. *What sort of hold does Arthur's mother possess over my father? Where does this leave Irene? What of my mother?* A ghost walked over her grave.

Huber ambled over to them bearing a cup of something that sent a faint vapor trail. He squatted down beside Avriel.

"Reckon this might numb your ankle a bit for the journey." He handed her the beverage.

Avriel sipped. It tasted of herbs, but it warmed her. She didn't want to let her injury hold up the walking party.

The crow cawed once more as if mocking her. Warmth crept over her like a woolen wrap. Her eyes grew heavy, and the bird call came from a great distance.

*

Uther caught his daughter before she toppled over. He laid her on her side in a patch of sunlight. She would be angry, but she wouldn't want to lose face. He nodded to Huber and got up, brushing the dried leaves from his clothes.

"I wouldn't want to be around when she wakes up," Huber said, looking at Kai, who was putting his horse through its paces.

"I have a feeling my daughter is in for a rude awakening on the subject of manners." Uther eased a kink out of his neck. "Perhaps she will grow more mature during her journey."

"Don't think she will get much choice." Huber grinned. "Brethren don't carry excess baggage."

Arthur stirred from his trance, stretching. Strain evident in the young man's face worried Uther. From what he understood, Arthur didn't possess the future sight of Brethren. This trip promised to be trying.

Linden emerged from the cavern weighed down with travel packs. He dumped one at Arthur's feet and tossed a second to Uther, shouldering his own.

"Is the fire out?" Arthur looked at the trail, his shoulders straightening under the weight of his load.

"Smothered and we left firewood inside to dry," Linden said.

"We're ready then." Arthur waved farewell to Kai. "Let's get started."

*

Avriel floated on a wave of discomfort. Her tailbone hurt. Rhythmic jolting continued, and there was a band of iron around her waist. Her head flopped around on her chest. Her

196

first sight was of a faint outline of horse's ears in the starlight. She pushed at the constricting band.

"Steady. Don't spook our ride," Kai's deep voice advised from behind her.

"What?"

"You're with us. Less of a burden that way."

Avriel hated him then more than she had ever hated another living being. "I didn't choose to go with you."

"Adapt, or I'll let you down right now."

The quiet, cool way he uttered his ultimatum shocked Avriel. He didn't value her former status, or her War Maid skills. Kai had made it plain he didn't find her interesting enough on a personal level to want to keep her around. None of the Brethren did nor the Submariners. Yet all of them rushed to assist Circe. Why?

Circe hadn't slept with any of the men: Avril had to admit this fact. Not even Arthur, though she could see the attraction between those two. Circe hadn't uttered a complaint on the march to the cave, despite her feet bleeding. Avriel began to review her own behavior.

"Kai? I'm never going to go back to being a true Gold Band, am I?"

His arm tightened just a fraction. "I can't see an arranged marriage with a fort ruler in your future."

"Really?" a certain relief washed over her. She dreaded the thought of being given to a stranger. If Kai couldn't see it happening with his fey gift, then she didn't mind as much as she thought she would.

Kai urged the stallion into a faster pace to lead the others over a barren area. They slowed on entering trees once more.

"That is just a reasonable guess," he said, continuing the conversation. "I can't see the future in terms of life."

"But it won't happen, will it?"

"Not unless all Nestines suddenly catch a real bad case of dead."

Her tailbone hurt even more now. She tried to think of other things, to distance herself from the discomfort. The jolt of a sudden stop brought tears to her eyes. About to complain, she swallowed her words on feeling the tension ripple thought Kai. Behind them, other riders stopped as if frozen in time.

"What is happening?"

"Hush." His warm breath touched her neck.

The distant tone in his voice held her rigid. The horse didn't seem spooked, but a swift glance around showed her each shadowy rider still sitting immobile. Kai urged his stallion under the cover of trees. All of them grouped together, waiting.

Avriel strained to listen in the dark. Wind sloughed through trees. The cry of a dog fox sounded in the night air. A ghostly owl glided through the glade on silent wings. Lifetimes passed in waiting.

As suddenly as the unseen crisis started, so it ceased. Brethren dismounted to begin forming a camp. Kai slid off the back of his stallion and handed the halter to another. He then eased Avriel to the ground. She clung to him, frightened.

"Easy. It's over now." He clasped her to his chest as the horse was led off.

"What happened?"

"Someone else's misfortune might be our gain come daylight."

"Kai?"

"Saurians hunted. There were many people."

The way he spoke of people scared her. Images of the giant reptiles rending flesh flooded her mind. She buried her face in his tunic.

"They will feed until sated, and then come back for more carrion." He cupped her chin in his calloused hand, making her look at him. "Learn now how Brethren gain equipment."

"Those people . . ."

"Are dead and don't care anymore. We need saddles and bridles."

"We must give them a decent burial." She didn't want to think of bodies left untended.

"Not possible. Do you want to be next on the lunch list when saurians find their kill gone?" His tone dipped down into deep sorrow laced with resolve.

Chapter 22

AVRIEL SHIVERED, HER body growing cold after the heat Kai and the stallion generated. Chill crept through her bones from the damp ground. At least it numbed her bruised buttocks. She bit back on a complaint, aware the men must be sore too from the stiff way they seemed to move in the moonlight.

Two of them hunkered down by a collection of wood that failed to brighten into flames. A low grumbling terminated in muttered cursing. Avriel thought she recognized Kai coming into the clearing. She knew he had gone to picket their mounts, but wasn't sure if one of the dark shapes returning had been him. At least he had set her down with her back to a tree for some sort of windbreak.

"Here, let me try." Haystack joined the group, distinctive with his blond hair that looked bone white in the darkness.

"Good luck," Mulberry said. "There is not a shred of dry tinder."

"Could someone give me a knife?" Her voice sounded unnaturally high and loud to her ears, but at least a group of pale faces turned in her direction.

"Avriel, you're not in danger." Kai straightened to come over to her. "We're trying to get a fire going. Don't start being difficult."

"You need tinder." She tried to sound bright, hating the choice she had just made. "I have the most hair."

He handed her a blade, hilt first, his eyes shining in the pale glow from moonbeams. Avriel hacked off a thick clump, passing it and the knife back. He didn't thank her, but he did raise the lock to his nose, seeming to inhale before he took his trophy to the others.

A sharp smell of singeing hair stung her heart. Tongues of yellow flames caught twigs and grew. Smoke spiraled up, growing thicker as branches added to the pyre of vanity. Sweet smells of burning dead-fall masked other odors.

Linden rummaged in his pack to break out rations. He served her first, handing her a strip of smoke-dried meat. Chewing on the leathery lump, Avriel began to list the utensils she hoped to find during the carrion picking of the morrow.

People dead in numbers meant a trading party. Those travelers would have cooking equipment. Brethren needed to eat decent meals. She tried not to think of blood and body parts.

Kai sat down beside her, too close, yet she didn't move away. Heat from any source made a difference. Avriel added bedrolls to her wish list. Her own wasn't warm enough for her liking.

"Hair grows back." Kai gave her a quick hug. "I'll level the rest in daylight. It won't look bad. I promise."

"We have fire." Avriel was proud that her voice didn't betray her sick fear of looking repulsive.

"Aye and the smell of it will keep predators at bay while we sleep."

"I need to find an extra bedroll tomorrow. Every day gets colder." She hoped for one untainted by blood.

"We share when one is in need. Will you sleep with me this night?" His arm snaked around her waist, remaining in place.

Blood rushed Avriel's to face. *Surely he doesn't intend . . . ?* Hints and whispers flooded through her mind. Heat now burned her.

"Will you behave?" She wanted him close, but she feared the rest. He said virgins didn't interest him. Was he truthful?

"Behave as what?" His arm tightened around her until she nestled against his chest.

"Kai! You know what I mean." She didn't pull away. He smelled good, of leather and horses, with a musky male under-scent.

"Maybe I will and maybe I won't. That depends, doesn't it?"

Half-shocked and secretly pleased, Avriel recognized the sexual banter that she had seen Circe inspire. Looking around to see how private their conversation was, she saw others begin to curl up in their bedrolls. Haystack fed the fire, his back to them.

"Depends on what?" She wanted to sound like Circe.

Kai pushed her away, and she died inside. He groaned as he stood, rubbing his tailbone before he walked away.

Pride kept her lips sealed, but he returned with his bedroll. Panic formed a hard pit in her stomach when he set it out beside her, scooped her into the folds and joined her.

"Depends on whether you are playing games." He leaned over her; his weight braced on his arms. His face hovered over hers, shutting out the starlight. "Brethren respect women."

Firm lips closed over hers, gentle yet questing. His breath came hot on her cheek together with the faint prickle of whiskers on his chin and the warm fall of his hair on her neck. He rolled to one side, breaking contact to unfasten the ties on her tunic.

Avriel caught his hand. His strength and size scared her, and the thought of being in his power unnerved her.

"Yes, or no?" Kai's whisper was more of a strained hiss.

"Kai, please . . ."She wanted him. She hurt from wanting him, but she needed time. This had got out of control.

"Please continue, or please stop?"

"It's not how . . . I want . . ."

"You want a formal wedding with the usual celebrations of a fort. That is something I can never give you." His voice in the dark seemed to come from a great distance. Kai removed his hand from under hers and shifted over onto his back.

Black hatred against the Nestines burned a hole in her soul. *Not for me the wedding rites, the new home to raise children. Not his fault he can't offer these luxuries because of them.* His harsh breathing began to settle into sleep tones. Avriel felt the need to pray, then it hit her, she had no gods. Harvesters were Nestines. Nestines were beasts, not gods. The desolation of abandonment seared through her soul.

*

A sense of unease made Arthur look back over his shoulder at the night sky. One star traveled at a steady rate in the direction of High fort. A point of light moving high and slow. Not a star. Had they left just in time? Was this coincidence or a lucky guess from his opposite?

Chills brought gooseflesh to his skin. *Did Kai escape?* He couldn't feel a disconnection, but then would he? Kai wasn't telepathic. Arthur sent gratitude to Emrys that he had thought to download the location of their new camp to every Brethren. Whatever happened, someone would get through. If attacked, they would separate in the Brethren way. He hoped for a miracle.

"Trouble?" Dragon expressed concern.

"Possibly. Now you know why we must keep moving."

"Avriel?" The question came from a worried father.

"Takes her chances with Brethren. Not one of them will abandon her." The boom of a saurian challenge lacerated the stillness of night, startling Arthur. He froze for a moment and then continued moving. The sound was a long way behind them.

"I should have left her with Irene."

"Where she would have lived a half-life." Arthur crushed a slight pang of guilt. "Wishful thinking doesn't win wars. If she is now dead, then at least she had her freedom to grow."

Dragon's hand caught his shoulder, spinning him around. "This is your half-sister, for the love of light!"

"And I care what happens to her." Arthur brushed off the hand. "I can't turn time around to run backward. Like you, I have to hope she will arrive at our meeting place."

"I will not lose another to the Nestines." Dragon's words grated through stiff lips.

"Then you had better send a prayer to Emrys that it doesn't happen. No other deity will care." Not the god of Brethren, Herne. That one wallowed in blood and battle. Arthur sent his own prayer to Emrys for both Kai and Avriel. He could only hope Emrys listened.

*

Kiri Ung surveyed the distribution of deactivated wristbands from his ship view-screen. Forty dead Terrans on the surface – a scene of carnage. He barked out an order to hover.

"Queen's Mate, we must refuel," the sky pilot pleaded.

"Hover, mark location and instigate a thermal scan with a five terraclick area." He sensed the hostility level rising from the crew's masked thought patterns. This find outranked their hunger. He needed answers. "Proceed to High fort once you have the data. We will return at first light."

"Your will, Queen's Mate." The pilot turned back to his instruments, his extended claws clicking on the controls.

"Shall I load the carrion, Queen's Mate?" The navigator's paws hovered over the scoop collectors.

"What is your name?" Kiri Ung swiveled in his seat to inspect the instigator of an independent thought.

"Na Pan, Queen's Mate." The male seemed to be trying to shrivel into his station.

"Not tonight, Na Pan. We dine on juvenile flesh still throbbing with life." Kiri Ung observed a certain return of confidence. He made a mental note to elevate this male. "The carrion could prove enticing bait."

Na Pan ran his tongue over his tusk bases. "The quarry?"

"State your logic for this conclusion?" *One to mark, indeed.*

"Our renegade prey is on foot. They will need riding beasts if any remain alive . . . also supplies." The male paused, looking almost blind for a moment. "Black Bands always seem to know the location of carrion."

"Do you prefer male or female meat?" Kiri Ung set his reward at a value to distance Na Pan from shipmates.

*

Kai inhaled the soft fragrance of female as he awoke. An instant physical reaction to Avriel's proximity sent him into meditation. The process became more of a challenge each time she excited him, but he needed control. Avriel was such a child still, and Kai refused to frighten her.

Avriel stirred when he tried to untangle himself from her. She smiled up at him, undoing all his efforts. He hunched over in a sitting position, embarrassed by his growing erection. *Damn, caught like a boy with his first crush. Concentrate.* Control established once more.

Her face froze, taking on a mole-blind look that was closely followed by fear.

"I won't hurt you." Kai stifled an oath unfit for her ears as blood rushed up to color his face.

"Where we are going—I can see it. I can feel the direction." Her eyes widened. "I've never been to that place. How can I know these things?"

Relieved that this was the reason for her unease, Kai still felt the need to punch his absent brother. "Arthur gave you these images, the same as he did for us, only delayed in your case."

"Inside my mind?" Her voice rose. "He went into my thoughts? That's not possible."

"Isn't it?" Kai began to enjoy the upper hand. Now fit to stand, he did so. The day looked to be fine and clear from the rosy tints of dawn. Bird call shrilled around him, signifying the absence of saurians, which would eat anything that moved. He stretched, easing out the kinks of sleeping on a tree root.

Haystack ambled back from a dense thicket, adjusting his clothing. Linden and Mulberry headed off out of Avriel's sight. Kai felt his own need, and then considered the girl who couldn't walk on her own. He set out with two tasks in mind. The first, soon accomplished, he found a deadfall branch with a crotch. It looked just about the right height for a walking aid and should fit under her arm.

Avriel hadn't moved except to sit up when he returned. She watched Stalker wander out of sight, and sighed.

"Want a privacy break?" He tried to make it seem ordinary, aware now of how much she had resisted drinking since her injury. Her face flushed red. He braced himself to bear her temper.

"Oh Harvesters, I must." She averted her eyes.

"Then let's try an extra leg." He hauled her to her feet, fitting his aid under her arm. "Try a step with your weight on this."

Avriel stumbled once. He caught her, but she pushed him away to begin again, setting off in a determined lurch to a thicket.

Kai joined Haystack to retrieve the mounts while the others struck camp. Avriel returned shortly, looking happier, and he walked his stallion over to her, scooping up their bedrolls on the way. She clasped her stick in a very possessive manner when he hoisted her up, holding it away from the animal's side to set it across her lap. He vaulted behind her with the halter in one hand.

"We need cooking pots," she said. "I can't cook a decent meal without them. Any unspoiled supplies, too."

"Yes, Princess."

*

Avriel tried not to think of bodies. They were dead people who weren't there anymore. Empty shells. She tried to focus on what she wanted to acquire, but it was difficult. *Once this part is over, then I can forget. One step at a time.*

Her thoughts returned to the safe zone of Brethren. Used to male dominance, she found their care of her feelings a new experience – one she liked. Men turned aside whenever outside to pass water. Brethren, the Outcasts made themselves scarce for nature calls.

Autumn mists swirled on the ground, bathed by lazy fall sunshine. The buzz of drowsy insects mixed with shrill bird call. Dew pearled spider webs to make them sparkle with light. The sharp tang of rotting fruit heralded an end to summer, and a light breeze ruffled dying leaves.

Avriel recalled the scent of sea; it brought other, intrusive memories to her attention. *How did Arthur put those images in my mind?* While she skirted around the subject, she couldn't deny he had when the directions were so clear. Then the reason for his actions came to her. *He makes sure we can all regroup if we get separated.* The enormity of that concept shocked her.

Thoughts of Arthur turned to more interesting ones of Kai. Not her brother, but Arthur's. Kai's method of dealing with her privacy issues overwhelmed her. She began to review her behavior with him, not liking how she had acted. But he wasn't like other men. He expected her to consider the feelings of others. Someone else had always taken control of her life without considering how she felt, until now. And she'd tried to stab him in a fit of temper.

"Kai?"

"Yes, Princess."

"Stop calling me that." She didn't want to be superior, only equal. And he did it to aggravate her.

"Yes, Your Highness."

"Kai, I beg your pardon." *Please let him be nice.*

"For what?" His arm around her tightened.

"Attacking you, and the rest."

"It's a start." His lips grazed her neck.

Chapter 23

UTHER RUBBED HIS aching calf muscles as he sucked in the warmth of a blazing fire. Smoke sent a pall into the night sky, but the smell of it deterred predators. He looked across at the small Submariner woman also engaged in relieving sore legs. In this light she looked almost human, her soft blonde curls cascading down over her shoulders.

While Circe didn't position herself next to Arthur, she cast looks at him through her lashes when she thought him too busy to notice. Uther tried to imagine her as his son's wife. The thought sat ill with him. Somewhere along the timeline he had stopped thinking of Arthur as a mutant.

The boy wouldn't pass for human, so why did he have a problem with Circe? A snowy owl feathered on silent wings overhead, bright eyes intent on any rodents disturbed by the travelers. It quartered the clearing, impressing him by the economy of its movements. Was that how Submariners glided through water? He recalled the sight of Huber's webbing snap back into place between the man's fingers. Arthur's children wouldn't be human. Again, the thought disturbed him.

A slight movement caught his attention. The tail end of a snake disappeared under Circe's skirt. Her eyes expanded into dark pools of horror.

"Stay still, girl," Uther called, forcing his tired muscles into action. He was at her side in moments, grabbing her under the arms to whisk her high off the ground. The reptile struck inches short of her foot. Shudders rocked the girl while Arthur grabbed the snake just behind its head. His son marched out of camp. Seconds later two loud thwacks sounded.

"It's dead now. Nothing to fear." Uther held the trembling girl even as his mind raced back through time to another incident. Shadow, who had a terror of snakes, woke to find one in her bedding. He hadn't comforted her. He berated her for screaming. Guilt did nasty things to his innards. That had been a harmless garter snake while Circe had encountered a horned viper. Guilt persisted. He handed Circe over to Arthur, watching as she wrapped her arms around his son, trying to hide from a world she didn't understand.

Over the girl's head, Arthur raised one eyebrow in question, his face taut with worry. Uther shook his head in negation, guessing his son feared a venomous bite.

Slowly, Arthur sank to his knees, lowering Circe without releasing her. He held her in his arms as if he never intended to let her go.

"The creature won't come back," Arthur murmured into her hair. He stroked the flowing locks almost in reflex. "What if I sleep on one side of you and Dragon sleeps on the other?"

Circe took a deep breath and clenched her fists. Still, she didn't cry. Her quiet courage shook him. The surface world groaned with the presence of creatures she must fear, and yet it took a near fatal encounter to shake her.

Arthur's sons, his grandsons, filled with the courage and endurance of this delicate looking girl. Suddenly, he didn't care how different Circe was. In that instant, he stopped looking for differences in any of the Submariners. They became people with alternative skills.

*

Circe fought inner demons. Things with smooth scales that slithered, warm against her legs. Creatures that propelled Arthur's exhausted Terran sire to instant action. She longed for her rooms in Sanctuary, but they weren't safe either. Somehow, repeating a mantra helped stop the shuddering. The cold hard core of terror remained like a leaden weight on her soul.

"Circe?" Dragon's deep voice so like Arthur's penetrated her core of darkness. "Arthur's mother had a huge fear of snakes, too. She screamed where you did not. That was well done."

His words helped. Shadow, the Outcast feared nothing, or almost nothing. Circe felt the love for Shadow hidden in Dragon's words. Empathy also told her that Dragon wanted to help where he had shut her out before. A hint of acceptance colored his emanations. Guilt, anger, and fear came from Arthur, overlaid with an overpowering need to protect.

They knew this world, both of them. They would shield her until she learned to accept this place.

"Don't leave me alone." The cry burst from her lips. Shame at her weakness stained her cheeks in a hot flush.

"Someone will be with you always." Arthur agreed, hugging her tight.

"No. You or Dragon." She felt, rather than saw the silent agreement between father and son. An aura of protection came from both of them. The nightmare zone began to retreat.

"Arthur, would you like to give me a history of Avalon?" Dragon's voice contained relaxing soothants.

Circe doubted Dragon knew he had this skill, rare even amongst telepaths. She began to see the building blocks of Arthur's power. Dragon's simple request sent a tense hardening through Arthur's muscles. He hid something. Even as the thought came to her, she sensed his decision.

"Gather around, all of you," Arthur said. Those Submariners trying not to intrude now gathered close. "Emrys said a time would come when I must share information. That time is now."

Every face assumed a rapture except Dragon and Arthur. While Circe knew of the new Emrys religious cult, she hadn't paid attention to it.

"Submariners were Terrans in distant history." Arthur seemed to be collecting his thought. "When the surface world became overcrowded, incredible as that now seems, the ruling planetary council developed two plans. The masses knew of a scheme to seed other worlds with people. What they didn't know was that technology failed them."

"What other worlds?" Dragon interrupted.

"Every star in the sky might have worlds circling around it. They are too distant to reach in a lifetime. That is why Nestines came into being, as a species created from animals and then humans. They were meant to be the crews of starships."

A snowy owl dived with talons outstretched. A single shrill scream punctuated silence. The bird flapped for lift with a limp corpse dangling.

"The alternative plan of underwater cities continued in secret. When the first plan failed, the project leader took his Nestines to a moon base. From there he destroyed all life on the surface of this world in a fit of madness." Arthur looked into the night with a look of blind horror Circe had never seen on his face before. A cloud passed over the moon. The fire crackled, spitting sparks. "Nestines restocked the surface for their own hunting grounds. Terrans head the menu."

Dragon buried his head in his hands, uttering curses.

"Submariners survived, adapting to their new environment until now. Avalon is dying. In fifty years, maybe less, it will not be able to support life. Without Avalon's backing, those of us on the surface cannot win the war we fight."

"Emrys will help us," Huber put in, his face shining with devotion.

"Emrys told me to find the Sword. Forged from sky metal, it will reveal the truth of Nestines to fort dwelling slaves. That must be our goal."

Circe sensed the finality in Arthur's words. Shock radiated from every listener. In her heart, she knew he held back other horrendous details. She felt the tension in his limbs. At that moment in time, their ages reversed. He became the eldest. The sense of countless years flowed off him.

His pain threatened to drown her. Endless strings of life and death hovered over him, creating a blue aura she had never encountered before. Circe's own psi factor stirred, expanding in a way she hadn't felt since puberty. She responded in the only way she knew, with love directed at him.

"I was ultimately created by that filth?" Dragon's voice vibrated with outrage.

"Repopulation came from awakened sleepers aboard generation ships." Arthur reached out to clasp Dragon's clenched fist.

"Payback is long overdue." Dragon sat straighter. He glared into firelight as if it were the furnace of the seventh hell. "We get the sword."

You have them now, Circe sent to Arthur's mind.

At what cost? Were they ready for this? His return thought contained deep regret.

None of us are ready to face the unacceptable. We must fight or die in the attempt. They are ready to die for a just cause. Keys to the kingdom, my love.

His doubt came through with his thought into her mind. *Men will fight and die for a cause that will be taken up by the next generation. There are no successors for us.*

Then we exist in this moment. We will live until we die, win or lose.

I love you. I always have. Arthur's transmitted thought encased her.

As I love you. This is our time. If there is to be no more remember, as will I, when the final moment comes. His arms pulled her tighter to him. She inhaled the musky odor of pure male, glorying in it.

*

Kiri Ung emerged from a cleansing unit satisfied. No trace of prey lingered on his hide after feeding. Shi nom despised the odor of spoiled food on her males, and he hoped to stand in her presence soon. *If my guess is right . . . if Arthur has cut across land for a centralized base, I will have my prize.*

He noted the navigator, Na Pan, already curled on a sleeping platform. Despite the banquet both pilots still enjoyed in the killing room, Na Pan had limited his appetite. That bespoke control and foresight. Kiri Ung's respect for this male grew. Na Pan would be alert, rather than bloated and sluggish at first light.

For a moment, Kiri Ung regretted letting the crew glut, but he needed their loyalty more than instant reflexes. And he had Na Pan. An alert scoop controller was worth two slower pilots any day.

Kiri Ung viewed the communal sleeping pad with distaste. Raised three feet above ground, it sported the pelts of dead animals rank with the acrid aroma of tanning. His hide already itched with anticipation of the parasites such coverings might contain. A longing for his own quarters on Moon Base made this primitive excuse for sleeping arrangements repulsive. The silken, gossamer spinning of insect's manufacture on his couch gave no acrid aroma.

At least the Nestine underling in charge of this fort would not join them. Having suffered that male's unclean odor, he'd ordered him to immediate night surveillance in High fort's skyship. Kiri Ung wanted to make sure Arthur hadn't traveled to that east coast attack point in the underwater craft.

The area of this room was big, but other unclean scents wafted although it contained nothing except the sleeping pad. Fighting his disgust, Kiri Ung gingerly lowered his bulk onto the furry surface near Na Pan.

The other Nestine stirred. "Queen's Mate?"

"Yes, Na Pan."

Na Pan rolled over to face him, holding out a small bottle of liquid.

"This only stinks for the first few moments. Rub it all over and the hoppers will not then disturb your rest."

Kiri Ung accepted the surprise gift. Angry for the need, yet wanting to remain clean, he smeared the evil-smelling substance over his hide. The stink made his eyes water, but it soon dissipated.

Grunting in thanks, Kiri Ung returned the bottle. He willed day to come quickly.

*

Kai enjoyed the sensations of morning freshness while he could, aware of what lay ahead of them all. The smell of damp loam curled up on a mist caressed by dawn. Bird song trilled in ecstasy from trees glowing with fall colors. The lazy buzz of stirring bugs sounded as a gentle undercurrent. Reaching out with his other sense, Kai found no threat lurking in a future moment. Satisfied, he urged his stallion to a faster walk.

Avriel half turned in his arms, pointing to a squirrel gathering nuts. Kai smiled, happy that she seemed content. While he enjoyed her entrancing girl scent, he waited for the complaints to start. He didn't understand why Dragon had entrusted Avriel to him. He'd expected the girl to go with Arthur on the easy route. Maybe Dragon and Arthur wanted peace from the tension between the girls?

She hadn't whined though, and he found her growing more interesting by the moment. While his sexual banter with her hadn't started out as serious on his part, he had to concede it now was. She stirred him in a way that was beginning to cause problems. He'd intended a straightforward seduction to mature her, but now he wanted more. Her shorter hair thrilled him. He'd seen how much the sacrifice had cost her.

Kai didn't hold out any hope that Dragon would be receptive to his daughter engaging in a casual liaison, and he found he didn't want that anymore. Caught, he began to look ahead to a future as Arthur envisioned, where Brethren maintained numbers in a stable base. He wondered what his children with her would look like, aware of his mutant genes.

"You're quiet." Her voice slashed through his thoughts.

"Just enjoying the morning," he lied.

"I won't cause a problem."

"I know." He didn't think she would, despite the carnage he expected to find. Somehow, she had found courage to step outside of reality. His other senses confirmed this for a fact. He wanted time to work out a way for them, but here and now wasn't a constant. It never had been, not for him or his father. *Live for the moment and be damned to the consequences.*

"About last night . . .

"Not an issue. I'll enjoy the moment more for having a longer chase."

She glanced around, her eyes wide, vulnerable.

A throbbing urgency started in his loins. *Damn. Not now.* He began a mantra to calm his urges.

A bird with iridescent wings and body flashed past his line of sight. A kingfisher. Flowing water must be near. Kai's stallion snorted, pulling to the right. He reined the animal in.

Trees began to thin out. A lighter area loomed ahead with patches of sky showing. A feeling of unease disturbed Kai's fey sense for a few seconds to pass as swiftly as it began. Part of him wanted to hand Avriel over to another while he scouted alone. She was quiet with him. Would she behave with one of the others? He thought not. How would she react to the carnage? Doubts flared through his concentration. They needed equipment. He wished this mess were months old.

Rolling grassland replaced trees. It swayed and rippled in the wind. In the distance, one covered wagon stood upright, but four others lay on their sides. A lazy spiral of crows circled overhead. Kai caught a sickly sweet taint of blood on the air, mixed with the aroma of things he preferred not to think about.

"What's that smell?" Avriel held her hand over her nose.

"The killing fields." His stomach churned. "Try not to look at the bodies. They're dead. They don't care how pretty they are anymore."

From her profile, he saw Avriel's face drain of color, but she nodded. They passed by a severed leg, half eaten.

"Kai, I'm getting mixed feelings about this," Haystack called.

Kai scanned ahead. "So am I. No increase in the threat level though. Keep your eyes open."

A stream of entrails, buzzing with flies now lay across their path. The stench turned his stomach. Avriel gagged once, and her muscles became rigid. Now he wished for Arthur's gift – to be able to slide into the mind of another and alter perceptions. By the seventh hell, no girl should see the gore they both witnessed. To the right, the partially crushed head of a young male wore a rictus of horror. Avriel started crying quietly. He didn't blame her. This was enough to make the stars weep.

They moved near a downed saurian. Urgent warnings clawed from his fey senses. Kai reined in, raising a hand to halt the party. Threat sense diminished as quickly as it started. He urged his mount past the creature. Kai looked back at the others. They searched around the area, at full alert.

Another few paces forward brought the sight of many bodies, both men and horses. Saurians lay, recumbent in the bloody remains. Horrified, Kai saw the rising of rib cages. *They live! Shit. Oh Shit.*

One of the mares whinnied in fear. The beasts stirred. All hell broke loose.

Chapter 24

Kiri Ung viewed the scene below with considerable distaste. Prey body parts lay scattered in untidy disarray. What a waste of food. All of it was sure to be crawling with maggots.

A blip on his screen showed the advance of a party of Black Bands with one Gold Band at the forefront. The ruler of Tadgehill and Arthur? His crest pumped into full erection. Could he get so lucky?

"Get the scoop ready." He pinned Na Pan with a stern glance. "We want live prey this time. Don't make any mistakes."

Kiri Ung switched over to infra-red screening. Seven saurians slept in the midst of their kill, and the prey moved toward them. His crest deflated so fast it felt like someone had cut it off. When the saurians activated, the roar that burst from his throat made both pilots and Na Pan leap out of their chairs.

"Protect those Terrans!" His chest constricted. He fought against pain. "Kill the saurians."

"But Queen's Mate . . ." the sky pilot started to object.

"Do-it-now." The words came out in a controlled hiss. Arthur couldn't die.

*

"Scatter!" Kai roared, kicking his panicked mount. It didn't need his urging to bolt. Screams sounded behind him. He couldn't stop. He couldn't control the headlong gallop. All he could do was hold tight to Avriel and try to keep them both on a fear-crazed horse with no saddle.

Grasslands flew beneath them in a blur. Avriel threw herself forward onto the stallion's neck, hanging tight. He clung to her belt, determined that if they fell they would be together.

Kai lost track of time in the mad race. Every bone in his body screamed for respite. His legs began to feel numb. The stallion lathered in sweat made the effort of staying astride near impossible. Kai began to look for a soft landing place for them when it slowed to a walk, spent. He kept it headed west to find a place to stop, but not one tree violated the flat moorland. Toward dusk, an outcrop of rocks loomed ahead. The stallion came to a rest in the shadows of boulders. Kai dismounted, pulling a terrified Avriel into his arms.

He set her on a flat rock and turned his attention to the horse. Ignoring his shaking legs, he fixed the rope halter to a tree stump. The animal stood trembling, its head down. Their bedding, water canteen and one cooking pan still remained attached by a rope to its back. Kai released the knots. At least he had water to give the poor beast.

Avril was another problem. She had curled her arms around her legs in a tight fetal position. Her body shuddered, uncontrollably. Time for a wake-up call. He fought against guilt to do what was necessary.

"You're alive and unharmed. Stop feeling sorry for yourself."

Her head snapped up, eyes wide, filled with the bleak horror of a child in the face of desolation beyond her concept. He'd seen that look once before on the face of an innocent – hoped never to see it again.

"Avriel, we can't know for certain who . . ." He bit back the word 'died'.

"If we'd stayed to fight . . ." Tears welled in sapphire depths, spilling over like glistening pearls on cheeks of apple blossom.

"Then our casualty factor would be severe." He tried to keep his voice gentle. "No one fights a herd of saurians. All of us know where to meet Arthur. It is possible that we will rejoin some of them along the way."

Kai left her to get the bedding rolls. He didn't bother with field rations. The thought of food sickened him, then he imagined her to be in a like case.

He returned to an empty scene. She was gone. Wind blew around rocks; grasses swayed, rustling. His heart contracted. A sickness soured his mouth. Kai reached out with his fey sense. No threat! What in the hells was wrong with him? Why couldn't he sense danger? Why didn't she scream? Red mists of rage swirled over his vision.

He inhaled, fists clenched as the bedding fell to dirt. No saurian musk. No predator spore. The ground looked uncrushed. An ornisaur? No, he would have heard the wings flapping. Not Nestines? Please don't let it have been Nestines. The night sky twinkled with stationary stars. No lights moved in the heavens. His heartbeat drowned out sound, pounding in his chest. An extra thump sounded.

Space . . . thump. Space . . . thump. A shape formed in the darkness, moving nearer. Space . . . thump. The shadow lurched, tripped and swore. A girl's soft voice blasphemed like an Outcast.

Relief gave wings to his feet as he leapt over rocks to reach her. Kai scooped her up in his arms, stick and all, to hold her tight to his chest.

"Where in the hells did you go?" He buried his face in her hair, wanting to keep her safe, never out of his sight again.

"I had a call of nature, all right?" Her voice came in a high tone laced with embarrassment.

"A call of nature? By the deeps, I thought . . ." He wanted to scold her, to shout to release the horror. A laugh bubbled up through him bursting from his lips. *She's alive. I haven't lost her.*

"You thought?" A second later she started to giggle.

Waves of laughter rocked both of them. Kai staggered back to their bedding on weak knees. He dumped her still giggling on her rock, making a bed for both of them on a mound of swift gathered grasses. This night he didn't care that he left evidence of their passage. If a bed of hay was all he had to offer her, then so be it.

"Kai?" A new, sober note colored her tone. "We shouldn't be laughing."

"'Tis the Brethren way." He caught a glimpse of her body tensing under starlight. "Laugh, for tomorrow we may die."

"But the others . . ." She jumped at a saurian boom from the far distance.

Kai joined her, pulling bedding rolls over both of them. "This is survival time. When we reach safety there will be a head count. Then we mourn."

"Live for the moment, you mean?" She snuggled against him.

"No. Live in the moment." Her face was a blur of paleness under him. He kissed her as he dreamed of kissing her every single night. On her cheeks, her eyelids, her lips. Lips as sweet as honey opened for him, shy, yet quivering with desire. He searched under her tunic for the buds of springtime. His hand cupped over her breast. Her nipple hardened under his caress. Her heartbeat throbbed through him.

Kai paused, releasing her mouth, asking a question without words. His loins ached with a need, yet he held back, wanting her willing consent.

Avriel's hand locked in his hair, drawing him down. "Tomorrow is a moment that might not come." She tasted his lips, his mouth, his soul.

He hesitated at the fastening to her tunic. *Does the sleeper awake?* Her hands joined his, helping him with her clothes and then his. Kai lost himself in the sweet delights of love. She gasped once, a tiny sound that speared his soul as he speared her body. They moved together.

*

The warmth of skin against Avriel brought a blush to sear her face when she woke. An aching below her waist stirred memories of the night. What had she done? How could she face him after what happened? What was he going to think of her?

She tried to stir; only he lay with his head on her breast and one leg draped over her, pinning her down. He had disturbed the covers during the night. Sunshine picked out flame-tinged streaks in his hair. Powerful shoulders, a warrior's shoulders, tapered to narrow hips and a tight pair of buttocks. Well-shaped, muscular legs disappeared from her line of sight.

Live in the moment, he'd said. Laying in dawn sunshine, Avriel felt an inner peace wash over her. In that moment she understood Brethren even as she joined their ranks.

She ran her fingers through that dark mane of fire, thrilling to the heat of it. The scent of him, that male aroma did things to her insides.

He stirred, a lazy movement to suck at her nipple. More strange sensations disturbed her. He looked up, a question in his eyes. Those eyes destroyed her thoughts. Violet irises contracted with desire.

"I'm sorry, Sweeting. I should have been more careful." His eyes transfixed her. She didn't understand or care.

"The moment was more than I ever dreamed." Avriel let her hand run over his mouth, feeling the curves, the moisture.

"I can control my body." He shut his glorious eyes, an expression of pain flittered across his features. "Arthur taught me how. I've no excuse."

Horror speared her soul. He regretted being with her. "What has Arthur to do with us?" Avriel heard her voice sounding like that of a stranger – high and brittle with unshed tears. He'd not see her cry.

Kai moved, hovering over her. "I might have planted fertile seed in you last night." His mouth formed a thin line. "I didn't intend to do that."

Shock and relief coursed through her. He did want her, but what if? She began counting back. Another two weeks before she knew for certain. He could've stopped it? How?

"Avriel?"

The pain in his voice, in his eyes, cut into her being. War Maids made marriage alliances, but she wasn't one anymore. She'd never have to submit to a man she didn't want, not now. The thought of bearing a child to him clawed at her. She tried to imagine a mixture of them both.

"Look, I've said I'm sorry." Kai rested on one arm to cup her chin with his free hand. "If there is a babe, then I'll want a father's role . . . and that of a mate, if you'll let me?"

She drowned in those incredible violet orbs. Part of her longed for his seed to find fertile ground. Another part, that cold voice of reason, said this was not the time or the place.

"I have no regrets." And she found she didn't. "Just be more careful next time."

His eyes went dark in a heartbeat. A smile transfigured his face. Not the slow Brethren smile, but one that came from the depths of his soul to light his eyes. His lips burned against hers, his arousal thrusting at her, filling her. His light, teasing touch thrilled her. The moment consumed her.

*

Kai woke to a burning sensation on his back. Sunlight heated skin not normally exposed. His butt hurt most. He eased himself off Avriel, noting her reddened shoulders. Damn. Now they would both pay for their fun. He eased bedding over her, reluctant to shut out the sight of delights, but aware of the burning.

Clothing rasped against tight skin. Damn. The thought of riding, of sitting on that burned area made him wish for a cool stream to soak his dignity. They had to keep moving though. Saurians had the bloodlust, and what of Nestines? He had to get Avriel to a safe place.

"Ow." She stirred, opening her eyes. Her hands went to her shoulders.

"Sunburn." He winced as movement caught fabric against inflamed skin. "We slept overlong."

"Kai, can we go back to the caravan?" Her face set in lines of maturity. "We still need tack, and we should do a head count."

He noted she didn't suggest a burial detail. His fey sense warned of danger from that direction. Could he trust it? He wasn't taking chances with her along. No. Never look back. Hell waits for those who linger.

He knew hell. Hell for him was a place where she didn't exist. He wouldn't go there again.

Avriel paused, in the process of dressing. "Then break out field rations to eat while we travel. Has the horse been watered?"

"Yes, Princess. I'll get right to that." The morning seemed brighter. Where he'd expected complaints, she proved positive. He glimpsed a new persona emerging – one that captured his full attention.

"Is there any remedy for sunburn?"

Kai and his butt wished there were. "Not until we get a dose of Arthur's healing."

Her eyebrows rose. "You too?"

He attended to his chores, not prepared to discuss his infirmity. He had the sneaking suspicion that she would laugh.

Midday sun warmed through clothing as they rode. Kai began to wish for a winter blizzard. He could feel Avriel's pain through her stiffness against him.

Moorland rolled ahead. High grass whispered in the wind. A curlew flew overhead. Threat bore down on Kai. He ignored it. Uncertain about his fey sense after the saurian disaster, he didn't see anything wrong and spurred the horse to a trot.

The buzz of late autumn insects throbbed through the air. Sunlight bounced off dry grass, rustling to light zephyrs. A glint of water showed in the distance, mere flickering through grass and shrub. Kai headed for it, relieved that he could water the horse properly. An urgent sense of unease coursed through him. Why was he getting warnings now and not when there was danger? Maybe Arthur would have some answers.

"I want to bathe," Avriel announced.

So did he, urgently. The sense of wrongness pressed down on him. "Not yet. Let's water the horse first." He waited for argument in vain. A warm feeling permeated his soul. She was learning.

Kai dismounted at the stream, heading the thirsty horse forward to drink. He caught a flash of movement. One brief glance of a huge shape charging. He just had time to turn the horse's head, let go the halter and fill his mind with an image of Avriel. And then time ran out.

Chapter 25

THE CAVES UTHER had suggested were dry and above the waterline. Arthur found a small stream of fresh water trickled through the larger one, forming a pool at the back that overflowed in a runnel down to the sea. Ideal for a stable and they could haul water to their living quarters. He liked the two good accesses to the headland from the beach. Too small for a saurian, they were defensible, and one could be rigged to block with a few boulders half-tipped with levers.

"See what I mean about this cove?" Uther called from the beach. "No enemy can land a sortie from a ship. The current is too fierce."

Arthur just waved. That was the sticking point. The same current that stopped a sea attack also made a rough passage for Submariners trying to haul Terrans to the surface. It had taken two of them to manhandle Uther.

"You look pensive." Uther joined him at the cave mouth.

"Just thinking about getting a large group of air breathers on the Submersible in a hurry." Arthur looked out at the angry swell.

"What's the problem?" Uther sat on a rock to remove a pebble from inside his boot. "Your craft isn't going to be swept on the rocks like mine was."

"Swimming in strong currents isn't . . ." Arthur broke off. A sense of dread thrummed through to his bones. Not a Submariner mind call – something else. He scanned the sky.

Uther looked up, his hand shielding his eyes. "I don't see anything." A faint tic at the side of his mouth started.

"What did you feel?" Arthur's words dropped like rocks into a chasm, bouncing, falling, out of control. He didn't want an answer. He didn't want to hear, yet he must.

"A sense of sliding coming from inland." The tic matured into a twitch. Uther's hands clenched, the white bone of his knuckles showing. "I thought of Kai and also Nestines. There is a sense of ending."

Seagulls screamed overhead, making a rhapsody of their own against the shushing suck of waves. The ebb and flow of time, Kai said when he spoke about his fey sense. Stick a rock in that flow and the course altered. A new channel formed. Did the Wild Hunt ride tonight? How many of Arthur's kin and comrades would join?

"Arthur?" Uther's voice barely registered above a suppressed hiss of anger.

"Change of plans." Arthur wanted to smash his fist in a Nestine muzzle. He wanted to see blood spurt, brains and bone fly. "I downloaded our location into the minds of all the other party. If even one of them is captured alive, then we are all at risk."

Circe's happy laughter carried from the shoreline where she vied with Huber in a fishing contest. Her sleek blonde head disappeared as she dived under the waves.

"What of any survivors?" Dragon's shoulders slumped. "I see the need to evacuate this place."

"You get your wish. The craft goes to your private cove near Tadgehill. You and I will stay here to wait if you wish to remain."

Circe emerged, struggling to hold a big fish, just as Huber broke through the waves roaring theft. Merrick dived to join them in the game.

"There is a tree-covered hill not far from here." Uther's lips compressed. "We could watch the paths to this beach under cover."

"You go tell my Submariners to take the craft." Arthur saw Circe emerge again, her clothing slick to her body. He'd wanted

226

a safe place for her, and he'd let her down again. "They are not to surface when they arrive. If we don't make contact in two weeks, then they are to return to Avalon."

*

Trying to keep the semi-conscious youngster from falling, Haystack held Linden tight against him as they rode. He'd cauterized the stump of the boy's wrist before shocked-shut arteries began to pump out lifeblood. The pain of that created their present problems.

Cold seeped into his bones. Visions of Mulberry being torn apart danced before his eyes. At least Mulberry died quick. Haystack shuddered, thinking of Stalker's fate. *Why did they take him alive?* Nestines sucked mangled shreds into their ships – he'd seen them. Stalker floated upward, screaming all the way.

Fey sense kicked into play the second he'd set the horse's head at their meeting place. That threat increased with every passing league. Unsure of whether it was true or not after the attack, he had to risk it. Linden couldn't survive without his hand, not on the surface. Arthur would send the lad to Avalon.

Perhaps Kai and Avriel would be there ahead of him? He knew they'd won clear of saurians. He hoped they hadn't suffered Stalker's fate.

*

Avriel kept a light rein on her mount. She knew the beast would smell saurians first. The ache in her tailbone and thighs remained a faint whisper of discomfort compared to the pain in her chest. She called up an image of a Nestine in her mind, scanning the body for weak spots. How to kill one slowly? The leg structure looked similar to humans. Hamstring one first? Maybe cut the tendons of the upper arms too?

A crow circled overhead, cawing. Carrion eaters. Were there more? She searched the sky. Pink-tinged clouds cried the death

227

of daylight. Rest time soon, but not sleep. She didn't think she'd ever sleep again. Last night she'd dreamed of Kai, of the saurians' death charge. Live in the moment. No more sleep.

The stallion stumbled. She headed him at a stand of trees. He needed to rest and fed. The place suited as it had a pool. Water for the horse and her. Slime green verdigris covered the brackish pond, and frogs chirruped in the dying light. Avriel went through the motions of making camp. Another chunk of her hair served as tinder for a fire.

*

Roasting fish popped and spat over the flames. Uther turned the spit more from the need to do something, anything, than from any sense of hunger. He wanted to have an offering for Arthur when his son returned from watch up a tall tree. A pile of traps, made from greenwood stood ready for the morning. They needed meat after this last fish. Rabbit burrows littered the hill.

A rustle from above heralded Arthur's descent. An angry squirrel screamed rage at the intrusion into its domain. Uther didn't bother to ask if any dust trails violated the landscape. They'd waited five days and would stay three more. Nestine skyships had flown the night sky above for the last two in a search pattern that drew ever closer to their position. Uther tried to think of another vantage point to watch, but his mind kept returning to his daughter.

Deep in his heart he accepted Avriel's death. A girl, even a War Maid, couldn't survive where hardened Brethren fell. Hope, that fragile ray of light, died hard.

"That fish smells bad." Nose wrinkled, Arthur hunkered down beside him.

"Take your chances." Uther reached out to drag his berry-ladened cloak towards them. "This is the alternative. I'd say they have equal chance of turning our guts to water."

"Perhaps one will cancel out the other." Arthur reached for some berries. "Might be an idea for whoever's on the ground not to stray too far from the lookout tree. Just how fast can you climb down with a fire in your belly?"

"Point taken." Uther served out the food in plas-glass serving containers. At least those washed easy.

A moving light shone through the tree canopy. Nestines! Too close this time. He kicked the fire with dirt from the fire pit, smothering it.

"Maybe Nestines save us from fire belly," Arthur quipped, a feral smile turning up his lips in the dying light. "They hunt early. I suppose a bath wouldn't hurt either of us."

Uther guessed his son's intentions. He'd seen the river shining in sunlight on the far side of the hill. If they made it back to the submersible, he was going to get himself a Submariner outfit. His clothes stank of rot from constant wetting without proper care afterward.

They set off at a dead run, flitting from tree to tree, halting to wait out a sweep. One mad dash for water. Uther dived, the icy water closing over him. Hands grabbed at him. He fought against the need to breathe, to surface. Arthur's lips locked onto his. Air flowed. He let his body go limp, the need to breathe overriding all else. Arthur couldn't breathe for him if he wasn't still. He fought against his need to gasp in air after his run. Dull sounds of movement bubbled against his eardrums. He let his mind drift into a happy place. Irene holding their son for the first time; the look Ashira gave him when he woke the morning after their lovemaking; Avriel laughing as she rode with him on patrol.

You're doing fine, Arthur's thought intruded. *I need you to think about time sliding. Tell me when you think it's safe to surface.*

Something slimy touched his cheek. He felt a burrowing. A leech? Every instinct screamed to break for the surface.

Hold still. I'm going to make a slight change in you that will make it lose interest.

Uther experienced a tingling in his body. The burrowing stopped, withdrew. He tried to calm his breathing.

You taste nasty now, like me. It won't come back. Start thinking about sliding time.

Uther tried. He thought back to that moment by the caves and the sensations that had come to him. Nothing happened.

Relax and let your thoughts drift around our camp. We can stay submerged for another hour if need be.

The vague sense of wrongness disturbed him. A feeling of sliding with no ground underneath. He knew there was threat near without knowing how he knew.

That's good. Keep focused. Nestines will lose patience long before we need to surface. They don't know for sure that we are here.

*

After a night spent shivering, without a fire, Uther wondered if he was ever going to warm. When they emerged from the river full darkness cloaked the land. Neither wanted a stray spark spiraling into the sky to wave at a searching skyship. He climbed up the lookout tree to take first watch. Having witnessed what Arthur did to tame their mounts, he didn't want to think about how his son was going to catch breakfast.

Sitting in the fork of a branch, he enjoyed the breeze that took away the stink of his damp clothing. Weak autumn sunshine made a pathetic attempt to pierce the leafy canopy overhead and heat his bones. Hungry, Uther reached out to pick a handful of beechnuts. He looked inland through a gap in the greenery, watching the shadows shorten by degrees as he made periodic sweeps.

Neither of them had brought up the subject of abandoning hope. That wasn't necessary after the Nestine overflight. Hope died and with it, communication. Uther had seen his son's expression shift into a bleak cast that morning.

He didn't blame Arthur for what had happened. Splitting the group to gain mounts while keeping the craft had been a good plan. One that should have worked. Damn Nestines to the seventh hell.

A faint movement caught his eye. Arthur calling for horses? No! The beast had a rider. No, two! Hope flared into life. Avriel rode double with Kai. He crashed out of the tree, skinning his hands in his rapid descent.

"Arthur!" The silence shattered with his bellow.

I hear you. I'm coming.

Sounds of running, a dead-fall snapping. Arthur didn't make a noise when he moves. Uther drew his sword. His son cannoned into sight, skidding to a halt, his face ablaze with hope.

Riders. Two on one horse.

Arthur focused in that strange way of outreaching thoughts. The joy drained from his eyes from one heartbeat to the next. "Haystack is riding double with Linden. The boy's been injured."

Numb, Uther struggled to find some motivation for the both. "Did you catch any rabbits?"

"Two. I'll go get them."

Uther knelt by the ashes of their campfire. He stacked wood and made a pocket of shelter for the tinder. A spark caught from his flint stone, and a few tongues of flame stirred into life. Dead inside, he forced himself to put on more fuel.

Arthur returned with his cleaned and skinned kill. "I called Haystack in."

Both of them worked to get the carcasses on spits. Now larger logs had caught, the fire gave off a decent heat.

"I shouldn't have split our group." Arthur poked at the blaze, misery apparent in his every move.

"In your place, I would've done the same." *And felt just as guilty.*

Hoof beats sounded on hard ground until the beast encountered leaf litter. Arthur concentrated. A few moments later the stray pair came into camp.

Uther reached up to take Linden from Haystack and placed him by the fire. The charred end of the boy's wrist killed his appetite. By the time Arthur had finished the healing process his face was waxen, and the boy's stump a healthy pink color.

Burning flesh reminded him of cooking. Uther turned the spits, aware when Haystack finished seeing to the animal and joined them, but not wanting to look at a survivor.

"What happened?" Arthur's words dropped like rocks into a stagnant pool, sending ripples of disquiet through all of them.

"Our fey sense stopped working." Haystack hunkered down by the fire, warming his hands. His expression took on the Brethren mask of indifference. "We didn't feel a threat when we found a trading group massacred by saurians. We thought we could get supplies. None of us had warning that the saurians we saw lying down were sleeping and not dead."

"Who did we lose?" Arthur's tone remained mild, but the volume of his utterance decreased almost to a whisper.

"Mulberry, for sure." Haystack squinted as a sudden shaft of sunlight caught his face. "Stalker got caught in a Nestine beam." He looked at Arthur, his fists white-knuckled. "How, in the name of all the hells, did we miss sensing Nestines?"

"Continue."

Uther heard death in Arthur's mild command. His son wanted answers.

Haystack shrugged. "We all scattered. I grabbed Linden in passing."

"Kai and Avriel?" Arthur's tone remained mild.

"Won clear. Didn't see any signs of them coming here, though."

Uther's hope flared into life. He didn't want to think about alternatives.

Sounds of another horse bearing down on their position sent his heart thudding. A lone rider emerged from greenery – Avriel. His smile of relief froze when he saw her face. The child he remembered had matured into something else. Not a woman, for no trace of softness remained in her features. Uther started forward to help her down, but a hard hand caught his arm.

"Don't." Arthur warned. "I've seen that look before. She's Brethren to the exclusion of all else."

Uther shook off Arthur's hand. "She's in pain. She's my daughter, damn it." Then he remembered Kai and met Arthur's hard eyes.

"Give her space, or she might make a suicide run on Tadgehill." Arthur's face could have been carved from marble for all the expression evident. "I need to know what happened to Kai."

"Ask her, or I will." Uther started toward Avriel, but Arthur spun him around.

"You don't understand. She's beyond authority."

Avriel dismounted with care for her foot. She eased a forked stick under her armpit to lead the animal to a tether alongside Haystack's mare.

Uther returned to the fire to start serving out food, handing Haystack a plate while Arthur poured water into cups. Avriel limped over to join them, accepting food and drink in silence.

Chapter 26

AVRIEL FINISHED HER meal and used the last dregs of her water to clean the plate. Arthur waited, boiling inside with questions. His sister wore the expression he'd seen on Shadow's face after Copper died. No emotion, no life, just the sort of stare that looked through stone. He reached out a hand for the plate she passed in his general direction. Their eyes met.

"Kai's dead." Her words echoed, flat, in a glade rustling with life.

Insects buzzed. A songbird shrilled. Leaves rustled in the breeze. "How?" Arthur bit off the rest of what he wanted to say.

"He'd dismounted. A saurian attacked."

"Did you see him die?" Hope, a fragile flower, refused to wither in the frost of her certainty. Arthur needed to nurture hope. A frail ray of sunshine pierced the leafy canopy overhead.

"It ran at him. There wasn't any cover, and he had a river at his back. The horse bolted." Having answered, Avriel lay down facing the fire. She closed her eyes.

Arthur tried to maintain a possibility that Kai might have survived, but the petals of that blossom withered and turned brown. Their years of friendship, of family, flashed by his eyes as the pain mounted. He didn't have any reason to linger here.

"We need to rest the horses, and then we head for Tadgehill."

*

Rain lashed down on the travelers for a third day. Everyone was soaked through, miserable and longing for a hot meal by a fire. Arthur sneezed as he ran, startling Haystack's mount. At least

234

most of them got a chance to warm up with the riding roster he'd set. Haystack doubled with Linden, holding the boy in place. Uther rode with Avriel. Haystack had drawn the middle straw in their pick that morning, so he'd take a turn at running when Arthur was spent.

High moorland made travel easy, except for the wind and driving rain. Gray clouds boiled overhead, discouraging any bird. Tall spears of grass drooped under a water burden, soaking Arthur's legs even more. His spirits lifted at the faint taint of salt in the air. Uther reined in.

"We're getting close," he called. "Keep watch for outriders. I'll get us past sentry points if the new ruler follows the same sweep patterns."

"Made a guess on your rival?" Haystack said.

Dragon half-turned to glower. "Alvic was my father's eldest bastard. I inherited him as my second-in-command."

"You'll know his actions, then." Arthur said, huffing up to join them, his chest heaving.

"He'll copy my plans." Dragon grinned, his teeth showing. "This is the third quadrant so outriders will sweep mid-afternoon. There is a small stand of trees in a gully where we can wait them out."

Haystack looked down at Arthur. "Your turn to ride. The boy's passed out. You'll need to rouse him to swap places with me."

"Leave him be." Arthur straightened, letting the heat of his run flow through his body. "I'm not done yet."

Once more they set forward into a sheet of falling water. The ground became increasingly uneven, dropping into a sharp valley. In the distance, a thick stand of trees loomed ahead. Uther stopped suddenly, holding up one arm for caution. He walked the horse forward a few paces and then gestured for the rest to join him. The rotting carcass of a cow lay at the side of the trail. Maggots dripped from the remains of a predator feast.

"We're not that hungry." Arthur's gut contracted.

"You don't understand." Uther looked back, his mouth set in a tight line. "This is days old. The carcass hasn't been cleansed."

Arthur jogged forward to look at the stinking mess. "Cleansed?"

Avriel turned dead blue eyes on him. "Alvic isn't ruling. We burned predator kills if there was any flesh left, or poisoned the remains."

"Whichever was most practical," Uther said, looking startled by Avriel's sudden participation after her former silence.

"This means?" Haystack urged his mare closer.

"Whoever runs Tadgehill doesn't have any idea how to manage a fort." Uther's teeth showed in a cruel grin. "We have a clear run to my cave."

Haystack looked west, a searching expression clouding his face. "The odds, if I can trust them, are good. I can't sense any threat."

"Then we push for home?" Uther looked at Arthur.

"Aye, it's past time for comfort."

"Trade with me," Uther said. "I could use a warm up." He slid off the stallion, bending to cup his hands for his son to mount.

Arthur set a slower pace. While he needed rest, he also wanted Uther to scout while running. Fey sense couldn't be trusted anymore after what had happened. The land dipped down and then rose once more into bleak headlands. Linden groaned, coming awake. Arthur called a halt to trigger the release of endorphins into the boy's mind.

"Hey, Dragon?" Haystack called. "Trade places with me. I want to get warm too."

Arthur moved his mount close so he could steady Linden while they transferred.

Uther took the lead once more. He guided them to a rocky pass at the head of a high cliff. "The path is steep. Let your mount find his own way. It's a dangerous descent, and that is why my beach is still private."

Arthur found out how much he didn't like heights in the minutes that followed. By the time they reached the beach sweat battled with rainwater in his clothes. Once down, he sent out a call to the submersible to stand by while he checked out the cave for a trap. *Either we have a home or I'm going to have to make a hard choice who I am taking with me.* Not Linden, since the boy was wounded, but that left his father, his sister and his companion to choose from if he had to dive.

His father had a wife and a newborn who relied on him. Avriel was at the beginning of her life, but she had become Brethren. Haystack knew how to keep alive against the odds. It had to be his father. *Please don't make me have to choose, Emrys.*

Uther halted, inspecting the sand for tracks. Satisfied, he urged his mount around a shallow surf break. The dark opening of a cave mouth yawned at them. Uther disappeared in the gloom.

Avriel kicked their mount forward to Arthur's surprise. He dismounted inside the entrance to find torches. Haystack pushed past with a glow globe already shining in one hand and a sword in the other. Arthur followed. The inner cave was just as they had left it.

"Fey sense seems to be holding true," Arthur said.

"I feel like I lost both legs." Haystack looked around the cave. "How, in the name of all the hells, can a thing go missing and then return as if nothing happened?"

"There's a reason for everything." Arthur shrugged for Haystack's benefit. The sense of wrongness terrified him. "Now we have a chance to review what happened. Let's get this settled."

Arthur sent another call to the submersible. This time he caught Circe's mind. Her joy at his safety thrilled through him, along with sorrow for Kai's loss. He found he had an urgent need to be with her.

Avriel limped toward him on her crutch. Her expression remained colder than death. "Could I get healing?"

"You could have asked before." *So why hadn't she?*

"Not without straining you." She eased into a sitting position on the sandy floor, sighing with relief.

Arthur concentrated on her ankle. He gave her all the strength he had to spare. At the finish he wanted to sleep without interruptions for a few hours.

"Thanks. I'll take first watch." Avriel stood up to test her ankle. She took a step without her crutch and then she jumped, testing the healing. "I give my word I won't sneak out to Tadgehill for vengeance." Her mouth lifted in a smile that failed to light her eyes. "The retribution I want is going to be lasting."

"I think you might have to stand in line when we hand out punishment." Arthur matched her dead smile with one of his own, remembering Kai.

*

Circe surfaced to the gentle patter of rain on her face. The sensation disturbed her, being neither wet nor dry, but somewhere in the middle. A gray overcast sky brought a memory of Avalon's deep blue hemisphere in an unhappy comparison. A sky that cried cast a pall on her relief at rejoining Arthur. His grief at Kai's loss made her want to take him far away from this dreadful place, only he wouldn't heed her. He'd committed himself to a cause more important to him than all he cherished.

She passed by the basilisk stare of Avriel on sentry duty at the cave mouth, on through the outer cave with horses tethered, to the inner cave, where Dragon had a fire started. Linden lay by it, his face as white as breaking surf, with a bandage on a shortened arm. Haystack hung wet cloaks over a framework of sticks that leaned against one wall. Circe reached out with her thought to the others she'd expected.

Arthur hovered on the verge of sleep, but she couldn't find a trace of Mulberry or Stalker. Her heart contracted. They must be riding sentry duty on the headland. That accounted for the lack of beasts. Haystack wouldn't meet her eyes.

"We are diminished." Dragon's quiet statement echoed in the cavern, seeming to mock life.

In that moment, her legs turned to wet seaweed. She sat on a wooden chest, thankful to have something solid under her. "How?" Words forced out through numb lips.

"Fey sense went wrong." Haystack shrugged and hunkered down, drawing his sword to begin taking the notches out of his blade with a whetstone. Steel shrieked in protest.

"Wrong for all of you?" She felt the black waves of exclusion coming from him, yet she didn't want to believe . . . not this.

Haystack leveled his gaze at her, through her, through rock. Now she shivered with fear for the first time in the presence of a Brethren. She broke eye contact.

"Does Arthur know why?"

"Losing Kai . . ." Dragon jabbed at the fire with more of a sword thrust than a poke.

Circe forced herself to look at Haystack. "Let me in your mind. I might be able to help find a cause."

"Girls can't stand bloodshed." Haystack glared at her.

"Shadow could," Uther rumbled, his tone hard with challenge.

"She's Brethren." Haystack resumed his sharpening, watching her, daring her to speak.

"I'm a Seer." Circe tried not to wilt under his frozen blue stare. "I ask as a courtesy, where I could raid your mind."

"New earring." His lips curved up, cruel in victory.

A flame of anger flickered into existence inside Circe. She'd forgotten about Evegena's gift to these Brethren. The fire built, mounting into fury. *Take it off.*

Haystack ran the stone along his blade by touch alone, his eyes glaring defiance.

Circe channeled her rage into thought, her thought into metal. The molecules forming the earring began to move. Haystack groaned. She increased the intensity of heat.

"Enough!" He took the bauble off, dropping it to rub his ear.

239

Raiding, she saw through his eyes and his mind. The sense of threat flowed and ebbed. Dead, maggoty corpses; the stench of decay, and saurian musk overlaying all. Haystack finding a supply wagon. His feeling of triumph. The saurians not dead but sleeping off a meal. Shock. Horror. Mulberry's head flying through the air. Linden screaming, bleeding. A Nestine skyship overhead. Panic. A blue beam striking Stalker, lifting him intact, struggling, into the bowels of the enemy vessel. Haystack riding over dead bodies to grab Linden. Hooves pounding. Saurians booming. The whine of the blue shaft of death.

More images of a previous close call. The blue light shredding victims into gobbets of flesh. Returning to Stalker rising through the beam intact this time. Arthur telling him that Nestines ate people. Haystack's sick fear that Stalker had been eaten alive. She broke contact, gasping, gagging.

Haystack snatched his earring to stumble from the cave like a drunkard.

"Satisfied?" Dragon said.

Circe buried her face in her hands. She wanted to vomit. Her mouth filled with saliva almost faster than she could swallow. Seer training kicked into play. Circe made a conscious choice to adjust her body chemistry. The nausea retreated. She wiped cold sweat off her brow.

"Haystack didn't want to share. You made an ill choice."

She let Dragon's scolding flow over her head as the internal adjustments continued. Cold logic locked into place. Fact – no threat presented as definite when threat existed. Fact – saurians and Nestines attacked the group. Fact – the Nestine scoop took Stalker alive. Her awareness entered a higher level. Pieces slotted into place with the neat click of a lock opened.

"Bait." The whole picture formed in perfect detail.

"What?"

"Brethren walked into a trap."

"Circe?" Arthur's voice came from behind her.

"The Nestines either caused saurians to massacre that caravan, or chanced on the result by accident." She turned to face him, hating what she must tell him. "They wanted you. That is why they hunted."

"Our group is causing them grief." Arthur squatted down beside her. He took her hands. "Killing us must be high on their wish list."

"Remember Avalon?" Circe drew his hands to her heart. "You broke parole because Nestines turned some Seers into drones. Would you have violated a trust if those drones hadn't attacked me?"

"Arthur stopped them putting something into your neck." Dragon stood up, his expression hard. "It was small and metallic. I saw it after."

Logic caught her thoughts. "Would that have turned me into a drone? Were you my intended target?"

"You're overreacting."

"I think not." Dragon joined them. He gripped Arthur's shoulders, shaking him. "Think, boy. Why was my fort targeted? Why pick me, if not to draw you out? Nestines know your bloodlines through subverted Seers."

Arthur's face turned into a stiff mask of horror. His thought patterns blanked out, excluding her. A tremor ran through him. Circe continued, "Fey sense didn't warn Brethren because the Nestines wanted you alive."

"They know we're cut off from supplies," Dragon said. "They guessed a raid on a slaughter site for what we needed." He paused, a distant expression on his face. "Their looking devices can't have been that good, or they would've spotted living saurians. I'll bet that the Nestines would've taken all our Brethren if the saurians hadn't snarled their plan."

Arthur broke free to pace the cave. He looked as if he wanted to smash his fist into something.

Dragon stood in his path. "How good is that improved earring at blocking mind raids? Circe just forced Haystack to take his off."

Arthur froze, mid-stride. "How?"

"She heated it up somehow. She now wishes she'd failed on her attempt."

"Linden needs a new hand." Arthur sidestepped Dragon to resume his pacing. He ignored Dragon's look of incredulity. "That boy must have medical attention to survive in this world. We can't provide it. Neither can we stay here. The Nestines will break Stalker if they have to cut off his ear to do so."

"We go to Avalon?" Dragon's face lit with hope.

"Huber can pilot the submersible and Merrick is a trained medi-tech. They'll take both of you. Avriel should leave too. Haystack can make his own decision. I'm going to search out the sword."

"I'm not going home." Circe couldn't believe Arthur didn't offer her a choice. She wasn't going to desert him. This dank cave with him was better than a meaningless life without him.

"I want you safe." Arthur strode over to her. He knelt, taking her into his arms. "Without me, you will have the life you were meant to live. Nestines won't target you if I'm not there."

"I don't want to exist. I want to live." Circe pushed him away. Will you disable me against my will? That is what has to happen to make me leave."

"I'm not going, either." Dragon put his arm around Circe. "How can I look Vortigen in the eyes and tell him he has no future? Avalon is dying."

"Don't leave me out," Haystack said from the cave entrance. "I was listening. Stalker and I go back a long way."

Arthur looked at each one of them in turn. "Fine, I'll go tell Avriel."

"No." Circe stood up. She had her man. Avriel had lost Kai. The girl's face and emanations betrayed how much he'd meant to her. She headed for the entrance before any of them could object.

Chapter 27

AN ONSHORE BREEZE ruffled Avriel's shortened black hair into ragged tendrils. Circe walked over to her wondering if the girl was lost in thoughts, or if she would hear footsteps over the sound of crashing waves. Brethren seemed to have the ability to detect a feather falling.

The younger girl glanced around, skewering her with a frigid blue stare. There was no hatred in that look, nothing warm; nothing living. Circe recalled Avriel's expression when Kai was near. The difference almost made her back away.

She met that ice-colored appraisal, while she collected her courage. "Arthur is going to make a run for the sword. He is intent on leaving behind all those he can." The layers of chill intensified, but Circe continued. "You're one of them."

"Why tell this?" Avriel's voice blended with the break of waves, a sound of nature so familiar that it bled into a background of insignificance.

"Because I thought you would prefer to choose your fate." Circe took a step backward. There was that about Arthur's sister that reminded her of Haystack in Brethren mode.

Avriel nodded, "Thanks. Tell him he doesn't get the stallion unless I go too." She turned to face the sea.

"Is there anything I can do to help you?" Circe made the offer for Kai's sake. She knew he had feelings for the girl.

"Forgive me." The words came low and calm. "For I have sinned against you in my thoughts. I would carry no burden on my shoulders when we leave this place."

Circe shivered. Death rode on the heels of Avriel's comments. A mature Brethren personae had replaced the spoiled child. The

Wild Hunt might boast a new member if she couldn't turn the girl from thoughts of ending.

"I will, but would Kai? Think of him before you waste your life." Circe turned to head back into the caves. High above, the scream of gulls swooping and diving, seemed to mock her.

*

"Got one!" Na Pan wrestled with a series of controls. "He's breaking the cohesion. I need help."

Kiri Ung activated a containment field in the ship's hold. A prey marker for one of the surface Terrans went gray even as his paws flew over the controls. *One dead.*

"Queen's Mate, we're going to lose the rest." The space pilot spun around from the flickering lights on his console, eyes wide. "They haven't got a chance."

"Use laz cannons. Target the saurians." Kiri Ung looked at Na Pan. "On my mark. Transfer the captive to me . . . now." He didn't have time to check for an identity on the captured male. The life signs of one more Terran on the surface dipped into a danger zone.

"Two Terrans are escaping," the sky pilot yelled. The ship altered course to pursue a pair mounted on one riding beast.

"Let them go!" Kiri Ung clung to a strut, hanging. His bellow resulted in a violent course change. "Get a path cleared for those other Terrans. One more casualty and I'll have you all guarding prey on Moon Base."

The craft leveled, hovering. Both pilots now worked laz cannons. Another pair on one beast broke free from the ring of death. Rage sent tremors down his back. *Their consoles are set to infra-red, so why didn't my pilots detect live saurians long before I called warning? If they have cost me my prize . . . if Arthur died . . .*

"Saurians destroyed," Na Pan reported, his voice hushed.

Both of the pairs of escaping Terrans headed off in different directions. Kiri Ung wanted to howl. He had to know who died.

Lack of direction from the fleeing prey screamed of the loss of a leader to him. Was Arthur on board, or was he lost permanently?

"Queen's Mate, our Terran is damaging the containment force field." Na Pan fought with controls, trying to stabilize an angry red winking on his console.

"You're with me." Kiri Ung threw himself toward the hatch. "He's not to be hurt." Gripping the rails, his feet on the outer tread cases, he slid down into the hold. Na Pan's bulk obscured the bridge deck by the time he had cleared the rail.

A crackling roar sounded. Blue light snuffed out as cohesion dissipated. Red running lights flickered. The screech of a sword being drawn echoed. Kiri Ung whirled around to see the Terran attempting to turn the blade on himself. He launched, crashing into the creature. They fell, both fighting for the blade. Kiri Ung closed his paw over the male's wrist, holding it still. The Terran heaved up and to the side, bringing his free wrist down hard on the blade. Blood fountained in an angry series of spurts.

Na Pan grabbed the Terran's injured arm, holding a firm pressure against the wound. Blood ran down, dripping, pooling on the deck. The Terran thrashed for freedom.

"Let him leak some more," he ordered Na Pan. Blood squirted high, covering them all in red splotches. The Terran's struggles became weaker. "Enough."

An angry pair of brown eyes glared at him. Red running lights made them look feral. *By the last egg of Shi Nom, he sees us.* Harsh breathing from all of them echoed around the empty hold.

"I might let you go free if you cooperate." Kiri Ung ignored Na Pan's hiss of displeasure. He watched this prey's face for signs of weakness while he tried to suppress disappointment. Not Arthur. The pheromones told him that much.

"Go . . . freeze in the . . . seventh hell."

Kiri Ung noted the weakness, the pallor. "I want a yes, or a no. Did Arthur die? Was the casualty your leader?"

"Keys to the kingdom." The male's eyes dulled, the lids closing. His head fell to the side.

Rolling off, Kiri Ung scrambled up to head for a close medi-kit. He broke open an orange colored box attached to a bulkhead to grab the sealant stick he wanted. Activating the rod, a short blue beam expanded from the tip. He ran back to aim the instrument as Na Pan released his hold on the wound. Nerves, tendons, muscle and skin knitted together without a trace of a scar.

Kiri Ung glanced at Na Pan. "Strip him. Tie each wrist to the matching ankles and then thread both wrists to each other. Not tight, just enough to prevent him standing."

"He's dangerous, Queen's Mate. He should be trussed."

"I want him comfortable. Able to imagine pain. Give him water if he wakes and treat him as if he were one of us."

"Queen's Mate!"

"He needs to be thinking about pain, not experiencing it. This one is outside our control and I want the reasons why." *I want answers. Where is Arthur? I am finished if he died.* He imagined the Queen's mandibles closing over his neck. "I'll navigate."

The smell of blood churned his stomach. Na Pan must be feeling the same need to eat. Kiri Ung had to get the Terran to a base fast. He headed for the flight deck, using scaling rungs on ascent. The sight of risen crests on both pilots greeted him. They'd smelled the blood too. He took Na Pan's position to plot a course for High fort. No way was Te Krull going to learn of this disaster.

"Queen's Mate. The nearest fort is Tadgehill," the sky pilot said.

Both males looked at him. "High is central. My target will not go west."

*

Merrick helped Arthur and Circe manhandle Linden into the craft. He carried the boy to a bunk and then turned, his expression set in lines of anger as Huber secured Linden for travel.

"I want to go with you." Merrick's eyes narrowed. "I'm not a pilot like Huber. Three Terrans need three of us."

Arthur faced the man. He didn't want this argument with someone who could fit back into Avalon. "Our chances of returning from this quest aren't good."

"Avalon is dying." Merrick squared his shoulders. "This is my chosen path. I want the right to defend my people—to give them a chance for a new home. Who are you to deny me the right to spend my life?"

"Get your last messages sent to your family." Arthur looked across at Circe. "You too. Think about living. This is the last chance either of you will have to back out."

Merrick marched to a communications port to begin his voice recording. Circe crossed to the opposite side of the craft with similar intentions. Having finished with Linden, Huber joined Arthur.

"I know I've drawn the easy job." Huber looked at Linden and sighed. "Where do you want me to wait once I've delivered him?"

Where to regroup if they had that grace? Arthur tried to put himself in his enemies' place. After they broke Stalker, they would go to Uther's new cave base. They'd find no signs of habitation. *If I were them, I'd come to father's bolthole next.* Stalker didn't know the location of the sword, except that it was in a lake. Nestines might patrol that particular lake, since it was the biggest. Would Stalker's mind be picked clean? Would they find out Dozary had an underground channel to the sea? A plan began to form.

"Wait for us at the outlet to Dozary. If we survive, we'll take the water route."

"How long?"

"Seven days to get there." Arthur added an extra two for sharing the horses between six people. "Another three days to search. He stopped, caught in the germination of an idea. "Make that five. If Nestines show up, we can dive with the Terran's in stasis. They can't catch us if we're not on the surface."

"Another day to the exit point makes eleven." Huber frowned. "If you don't find this object in that time then bring me the Terrans. I can wait while you complete the search. It won't be easy finding an object buried in mud."

"Good point." Arthur stretched, aware of inner tensions. "Bring me a metal detector when you return."

"That'll draw the Nestines like crabs to a carcass. You know they can detect our technology."

Circe joined them, her face a picture of worry. "Arthur that is too great a risk."

"One I'll take alone." He folded her into his arms. "We have this single chance to carve out a future. Too many lives hang in the balance for any individual to matter."

Circe raised a stricken face to his. Tears pearled her cheeks like dewdrops. "I'm going with you. Huber, bring two detectors."

"Make that three." Merrick replaced the voice recorder. "I've just committed myself to a life partnership. I'd like my future children to have a future. I plan on returning to Avalon.

*

The captive Terran choked and gagged on a funnel of directed water. Helpless, lashed down on a sleeping pallet, naked and spread-eagle, he fought against the hand that tortured him.

"What are you trying to do? Drown him?" Kiri Ung thrust High fort's Nestine away. "Leave."

"But you ordered him watered."

Kiri Ung pointed to the exit, not trusting himself in the presence of imbecility. This wasn't what he'd ordered. Now he'd have to do damage control on a subject already hostile. He waited until the culprit slithered out of his sight. Now he was alone with the Terran in priest drone quarters. At least the moron who moved him hadn't chosen an observation room filled with controls that a prey beast shouldn't see.

As he waited out the Terran's coughing fit, Kiri Ung tried to see this creature as a sentient being rather than food. The well-muscled male bore evidence of battle on his white flesh. Kiri Ung tried not to think of the taste of flesh. He viewed a long scar down the Terran's right thigh muscle with some revulsion. Outcasts didn't receive priest healing to prevent such a marring of the muscle fibers. That created a gristly knot in the texture of the meat. Maybe he should rescind that order? But they lived outside, so perhaps that might be a pointless exercise.

He touched another angry scar on the Terran's chest, pulling back, surprised when the male began a frantic fight to break his bonds. The rank stench of fear flavored the air.

"What is your name?" Kiri Ung watched eyes widen and the mouth flaps turn down. He projected his will at the male. *What's this? A barrier? I can't see into his mind!* Shock rippled over his hide, chilling him. Something, some spark of pure defiance in the creature's eyes told Kiri Ung that this male knew he couldn't be picked clean of thoughts.

"You have found a way to evade a mind probe." He saw the male's fist clench. "Interesting." Pouring water into a drinking vessel, he approached the Terran again. "You're thirsty and I have water. Stay quiet." He slid his arm under the creature's neck. Muscles there tensed. Presenting the vessel in a civilized fashion, he helped his captive drink, easing the head back down after.

The male's brown eyes narrowed even as a pink tongue licked the last dregs from mouth flaps. Those eyes now studied him.

This male can see me and evade mind probes. He is one of Arthur's. Adrenaline coursed through his system, leaving him breathless, shivering. Kiri Ung sent out a thought command for a Terran food. He needed this creature less hostile.

"Hungry?" A growl from digestive organs answered him. "Food is coming." He hunkered down, returning the Terran's stare.

250

A priest drone glided in with a covered dish that smelled of roasted fowl. Kiri Ung took the offering even as he sent a thought command to leave in the drone's mind. He stood to place the platter on the sleep pad and removed the lid.

"Smells good. Like some?"

The Terran's eyes narrowed. Jaw muscles worked. The throat made a swallowing motion. Now hunger entered this battle of wills.

"Your name?" Kiri Ung reached over to release the captive's hands, noting the eyes widen and breathing rate increase. He tore off a chicken leg to hold within range.

"Stalker." The name came out with a hiss of fury behind it.

Stalker devoured the morsel, throwing aside bones in his frenzy. Impressed, Kiri Ung ripped free half a breast for his entertaining new captive.

Chapter 28

WATER SWIRLED OVER Merrick's dark curls as he descended into the ocean through one of the exit ports. Arthur caught an expression of resignation from Circe as she watched. Her shoulders drooped, and her generous lips formed a tighter line.

"Your family isn't happy with your choice." His guess was confirmed by the way her head snapped around.

"They are disappointed that I am swimming in the wake of a renegade shark."

The brightness pearling Circe's long lashes said to Arthur that 'disappointed' was an understatement. She'd changed her career from a Breeding Mistress to a Seer because of him, and now he caused her to risk her life.

"Why not wait for us in Avalon? You're not a warrior."

"Three for three." Her eyes narrowed. "One of us for each air-breather, or you'll be making hard choices. I wish . . ." She shrugged, turning to begin her descent.

Arthur took the second port. He emerged in time to witness Circe's skirts swirling in the current. The sight of her long, shapely legs thrilled him. He powered his strokes to catch her, wrapping her in his arms so that they both tumbled in the water, sinking until they began to use their feet to stabilize. He didn't know if making love underwater was possible, but he intended to find out. He grabbed a handful of skirt fabric to yank it above her waist.

Arthur! What are you doing?

Granting a wish. He closed his lips over hers, gently prizing them apart. His tongue brushed against her pearly teeth and then she opened to him. They sank deeper, nearer to the bottom.

I love you. I won't withhold viability. I won't leave you empty and grieving like Kai left Avriel.

A shudder ran through her body. *Don't think of death.* She pushed against him, breaking his kiss. Her eyes mirrored her soul. *Why now?*

Keys to the kingdom, my love. His foot struck sand. *A man will fight to the end for only one reason. If he leaves the trust of another generation with a woman who loves him enough to raise their child alone.*

Her hands were at his clothing even as they drifted on a current to a soft bed. They moved together in languorous abandon, at the mercy of their element, yet at home. Locked together, both in mind and body, their loving took on the slow ebb and flow of raw nature.

*

A dark shadow fell across his line of sight. Haystack looked around from the pile of supplies he sorted from Dragon's hoard. Avriel's bleak expression greeted him.

"Come to get armed?" He dismissed her knife as useless in combat. The girl wasn't strong enough to win a fight with her short reach. He doubted her stamina with a sword, also, and Dragon wasn't around to ask.

"Found anything my size?"

Her tone told him she'd take whatever. Haystack recognized death in her voice. "Ever notched a bow?"

"I've hunted." She shrugged, looking at a rack of blades.

"Forget those." He reached for a long bow and a quiver. "You're too short for a swordsman. An archer is as much advantage in battle. Have you made a kill?"

Avriel stared a hole through him.

"Dump the attitude with me." He met her dull eyes. "Kai died clean. My love didn't. I hear her screams in my nightmares."

"How can you bear to go on living?"

"I celebrate her life." Memories of a laughing girl with hair the color of smoked hickory filled his mind. He held that image as a shield against other visions. "I fight for all the other lads and lasses who will live out happy lives if I win."

Avriel took the bow from his hand, testing it. She strapped on the quiver and began to gather stacks of arrows neatly tied in bundles. Something about the tension of her shoulders told Haystack he had made his point.

"Is living for the benefit of others enough?" Avriel added a tinderbox to her possessions. "I thought priest-made Brethren were washed clean of memories at the time of sentence."

"We are, mostly." That terrible period of nullity he had missed sent shudders down his back. He didn't want to recall what caused him to miss the renascent stage. "We remember in time. Once that happens we're cursed with total recall."

Her back quivered and then heaved with a silent sob. Her hands continued to reach for survival items. She added a whetstone to her store.

"Avriel, for the sake of Kai's memory let the grief out." Haystack placed his hand on her shoulder. "Kai was Brethren from birth. He knew the odds."

The girl's chest heaved. A suppressed sob burst from her lips.

"We all sensed the attraction between you two. Did you find a moment to share your love as man and woman?"

Quiet sobs filled the inner cavern. She whirled around to bury her tear-drenched face on his shoulder.

"I'll take that for a yes." He stroked her midnight locks, trying not to think of lighter hair. "Treasure the memory of your time together. He would've done if he'd been the survivor."

Her control dissolved in heart-churning grief. Over the top of her head, he saw Dragon poised on the threshold. The duke gestured at Avriel, asking an unspoken question. Haystack nodded, answering. Dragon backed out, an expression of relief on his face.

*

A crackle of blue sparks ended with Stalker twitching on the floor of his cage. Kiri Ung viewed the reddened result on white flesh with displeasure. His captive persisted in attempts at self-termination.

"Stalker. The settings are at a level to produce pain, not death." An angry pair of brown eyes met his in a glare of pure defiance. "You are hurting yourself for no purpose."

"Rot in the seventh hell."

"A meaningless insult, since we invented your religion." He noted the dilated nostrils and the rapid breathing. "Would you like coverings? I've noted your species tends to prefer concealment."

The captive staggered to his feet to begin mindless pacing on the cold, smooth rock surface. Water dripped from a crack in the cave wall, adding to a dank, wet smell.

"I'll tell you nothing."

"I could order the removal of your wristband and ear ornament." The pacing hiccupped for a microsecond. "I'd get every question answered at that point, wouldn't I?"

"What's stopping you?" Stalker halted, turning to face him, fists clenched.

"Perhaps ennui." The smell of this miserable hole offended Kiri Ung. He detected urea, sweat and feces. Not all of them came from the Terran. "The information I can squeeze from you is already useless. I'll find a deserted base with evidence of a rushed departure."

"Why keep me alive?"

Kiri Ung scooped a parasite-infested fur from the floor with extreme distaste. He fingered the vial of repellent nestled in his belt. Stalker's flesh puckered from cold.

"Amusement." The statement caused an immediate tension in firm muscles. "Sit, and I'll lower the force-field long enough to give you this. There is no penalty involved."

Stalker hunkered down. Kiri Ung waited, fingering the pelt. The captive glared, settling into a sitting position. Only then did he trigger the release with a thought.

He extended the gift. "It is crawling with parasites—biting insects." A shudder rippled over his hide. "Is this offensive to you? I have a deterrent if you will tell me the name of the one who died."

"Find out for yourself." Stalker eyed the pelt.

"That would take time. Do you enjoy being bitten?"

Stalker shrugged. "Mulberry. Satisfied?"

Kiri Ung dropped the fur near Stalker more from relief than conscious choice. He reached for the vial in his belt. "Rub the contents of this all over." Tossing the ointment, he noted Stalker's swift reflex.

A sudden flash of inspiration sent a chill through him. *We didn't do a head count of those Terran's.* He thought back to the slaughter. *Our Avalon drones reported a much larger group before contact terminated.*

"Arthur is going to be disappointed when you don't meet him at the regroup point." Kiri Ung noted Stalker's hand freeze for a second in the application of the repellent. *I'm right! Arthur split them. He's alive!*

Finished, Stalker hurled the jar at his head. Kiri Ung caught it, aware the missile had been launched to test his own reaction time.

"Go fish in another sea." Stalker yanked the fur around himself. "You'll get no free information."

I just have. My Terran pet is far more entertaining than Te Krull's cat. And he doesn't need sanitation training.

"I'm not telling you." Stalker's brown eyes narrowed. "Why are you still here?"

Kiri Ung saw tremors masked by anger. "I am going to search for your leader at first light." He considered leaving Stalker, but he didn't trust the fort Nestine. *What if my pet gets mistaken for food? They all look so alike.*

"He'll be gone." Stalker bared his teeth in the semblance of a smile containing no warmth.

Water dripped, puddling in a dank pool. A trace of smoke wisped on the air to mix with unclean odors. Kiri Ung repressed a shudder at the thought of spending one more night in this disgusting hole in the ground.

"Stalker, if you give me your parole not to fight me, I'll agree not to ask direct questions about Arthur's location." A rodent scuttled across the floor near Kiri Ung's foot. He stamped on it. The prickle of bones on his sole, and the slimy feel of intestines made him yearn for the ship's cleansing unit.

"Why?" Stalker's shoulder's tensed.

Kiri Ung shrugged; aware truth might win him respite from discomfort, but not willing to admit weakness. The sight of that fur, now covering his pet, swayed him. He could almost see the hoppers swarming within hair follicles.

"I would prefer to sleep on a skyship. It's clean, and there are proper couches." He met a hostile stare. "I can't leave you, or you might appear on the breakfast menu."

Stalker swallowed, his eyes bulged and flickered from side to side as if searching for an escape.

"Terran meat is our primary food source." Kiri Ung let that gobbet of information sink in for a few moments, aware Stalker was near to breaking into action from the pheromones on the air. "You are mine and are safe while with me."

"Are you trying to tell me you've turned into a plant eater?" Stalker's muscles popped with tension. His legs moved to enable an instant launch.

Kiri Ung laughed. He tried to dispel a picture of himself forcing down vegetation, but the image was too powerful. He fought to regain dignity, aware Stalker's eyes were wide and on him. The pheromone level, indicating threat, dropped. *Why did I never consider a Terran pet before? This one is so stimulating.*

"What's so funny?"

"The idea of eating plants." Kiri Ung leveled the concept down to basics for this primitive. "My skyship has no hoppers and smells good. Your parole?"

"Given, for the rest of this day."

"Then lose that hopper home. I'll find other coverings, your own, aboard ship."

*

Rain oozed its way under Avriel's collar. Icy fingers dripped down her back. She looked out at heaving water in the cove, unwilling to join the others in a warm and dry series of caves. Witnessing Arthur and Circe emerge from the waves firmed her resolve. Their body language told her they had been together. She began to speculate on how aquatics made love, only that thought brought memories of Kai. *Why him? Why didn't he sense the threat?*

Her mouth flooded with saliva. She swallowed again and again, but it kept forming. Her stomach contracted. Cold sweat pearled on her forehead. Avriel lost her last meal.

Unaccountably, she felt better except for a sour taste in her mouth.

Lightning cracked across the sky, followed by a distant rumble of thunder. Spears of water streaked toward ground. She ran for the caves.

Haystack looked up as she burst into the outer cave, a supply of arrows in his hand.

"Trouble?" He dumped his load by a longbow.

"A storm. We won't be going anywhere until it's over." At his raised eyebrows, she continued, "Water cascades over the pass down to this beach. Our mounts need good purchase for the ascent."

"Go change into something dry. Dragon has a stash of clothes here and Circe is cutting down soldiers' gear for both of you."

"I'm not that wet." Avriel didn't want ill-fitting garments that chafed.

"You're as pale as a fresh-hatched maggot." Haystack caught her arm in a firm grip. "You'll be a burden to Arthur if you get sick."

"Sorry. I didn't think." She shook off his hand. "And I will take the bow. Some instruction for hitting the target would be nice. I'd like to bead an eye at one hundred paces."

Haystack grinned. "You will be by the time I'm through teaching you. Knife fighting, too."

Avriel shivered, cold beyond personal discomfort. "What about Circe? All of us should know defense at least."

His jaw firmed and his eyes narrowed. "Circe has Seer skills. Stay close to her if we fight."

The way Haystack looked when he spoke of Circe puzzled Avriel. Used to the easy banter between them, she sensed a withdrawing from him. What were Seer skills? She squelched into the inner cavern. Why was he guarded against her?

Circe sat on a rock cutting down the length of arms and legs on uniforms. Merrick glanced up from his task of packing field rations in saddlebags. Tack for two mounts lay in neat heaps beside him. Arthur and her father picked through an assortment of swords and knives. Arthur also fingered a long piece of wire with the ends wound round pieces of metal.

"A garrote might work with Nestines." Arthur argued. "At least we should all carry one."

The two men looked up at her entrance. Their eyes traveled over her dripping clothes.

"How bad is it out there?" Her father asked.

"Too wet for the horses." She didn't need to explain to him. Arthur's eyes widened.

"So we can use the back door if we must, and sacrifice our rides, or we have the sea option still?

Arthur shook his head and turned to Uther. "Huber's gone. I don't want to lose our mounts. You and I will ride up the pass when the rain stops and the others can climb through tunnels to the cliff top. If we divide the load of supplies then we have an even chance."

"I should be a rider. I know the route as well as my father." Avriel resented being overlooked when she could do this.

"Good point, but neither of you can link to another's mind." Arthur's mouth quirked up in a lopsided smile. "Go get some dry clothes."

*

Kiri Ung viewed the weather report with irritation from his navigator's console on the skyship bridge. He was aware Stalker watched from an inset bunk closed by a force field.

"What's the matter? Got a problem?"

Any question voiced in that insulting tone would have earned a Nestine instant reprimand. Kiri Ung chose to be amused at his pet's courage.

"Flying in a storm we don't control is unwise." Generating a storm was easy, but controlling a natural one wasn't possible. "Arthur will be pinned down too, if he's where I think."

"Ever guess wrong?"

Kiri Ung turned to observe Stalker's expression before he answered. "The former duke had a bolt hole close to Tadgehill. Arthur will regroup at that location. He'll not risk the meeting point he told you."

Stalker's hands flexed. His expression didn't alter, but that one reaction betrayed him. A flex instead of a clench denoted good control. Kiri Ung liked this game.

Chapter 29

SHAFTS OF AGONY shot through every part of him. Chill water lapped around his mouth as he floated. Black birds circled overhead. *They wait for carrion. Me.*

Kai tried to think through the gray fog in his mind. He remembered the saurian's charge, but the beast seemed to be wading through liquid mud. That last instant when it turned to attack the bolting stallion, the impact of its tail sending him flying through the air. Another pain-filled crash – splintering . . . something.

I'm in water. I can see branches. Broken branches. Why don't I sink? He couldn't put the thoughts together, and the cold eased his pain. Sleep began to reclaim him, a comforting dark presence.

No, I can't go there. I have to move. I have to stay awake. He tried to raise his hand. Something sharp stuck in his chest. Sparkling lights danced in his vision. Through brilliant star-bursts he saw the birds spiral lower. Their harsh calls sounded so close.

Emrys, let me die now. Don't let them peck out my eyes while I live. Wings fluttered over his head. Branches rustled. A pounding sounded.

"Over here!" A man's voice called.

"I see it. Not worth the effort."

"We might find weapons."

A harsh squawk came from too close. Kai tried to move. Blackness enveloped him.

*

Consciousness returned with waves of pain. Hot needles of agony laced through Kai. He tried to turn away from the pain.

"Stay still."

261

A bottle neck touched his lips. He drank and choked. Hard liquor. Kai forced open his eyes.

Two men hunkered down at his side. A rugged brown-haired man with a homely face held a bottle. On his other side, a wiry man with dark blond hair held rags and a straight tree limb.

Where is Arthur?

"He's coming round. Harvester's balls, why now?" The skinny man hawked and spat.

"Leave off, Willow. He's one of ours."

The man with the plain face put his hand under Kai's neck to raise his head for another pull on the bottle. "Drink as much as you can, lad. We have to set the bone before we can move you." A gush of fiery liquid hit his throat. He swallowed.

"More," his tormentor urged.

A hand came to pinch his nose shut. More liquid fire entered his belly. Sounds became a vague hiss. Images blurred. Voices and then movement. Instant agony descended into night.

*

Cool soothing wetness bathed his burning face. It stopped, and Kai groaned in protest. Liquid dribbled on his parched lips. Water gushed around his teeth. He swallowed, only then aware of a hand under his neck. The pain seemed wrapped in blankets of fog.

"Wake up, lad."

Kai opened heavy lids to see the stocky man kneeling by his side. He squinted from a haze of sunlight coming from a cloudless sky.

Brown, wide-set eyes looked into his. "I'm called Goat because I look like one. You chose a name yet?"

"Where am I?" Kai's fey sense thrilled through his body warning him not to give truth.

"Hey, Willow?" Goat called to his companion. "You're right. He's a new-made brother. What about a naming?"

"How about Copper?" The wiry man bent down to flick hair out of Kai's eyes.

"Rowan wouldn't like that." Goat's eyes narrowed. "Copper was King of the Outcasts before him. Best not to give this lad a bad luck name."

A crow caw sounded close. The bird balanced on top of a scraggy bush, watching him.

"Hey, look at his ear." Willow held Kai's chin to keep his head still. "Someone already clipped an earring on him."

"Not recently, either." Goat knocked Willow's hand aside. "The flesh has healed. Who clipped you, boy?"

Kai met the hard brown eyes with a stare of his own. He felt a shift in future possibilities in that second. Threat level increased.

"Don't know," he lied. "We got split up after a saurian attack." Pain throbbed through his leg. Beads of sweat pearled on his brow. He shut his eyes.

"Goat, he's trouble. I can feel a shift in the odds."

"We'll let Rowan deal with Darkfire, here." Goat slopped another wet rag over Kai's forehead. "If he survives the trip."

The cool wetness brought relief of a kind. Kai drifted down into sleep.

*

Days and nights congealed into a pain filled blur. Fever raged through his body. Lashed down aboard a jolting sled behind a horse, he couldn't even cast off his covering for relief.

In his lucid moments, Kai dreaded meeting Rowan again. His thoughts centered around their last confrontation, when Rowan had turned both his mother and himself out of Haven. Shadow's incredible quietness of person at that eviction still impressed him. *She could've taken him in a duel, but she didn't. Was it because of me? She'd have had to fight off challengers if she won.*

He recalled those years spent digging in ruins, his mother teaching him survival skills, interspersed with the return to

263

Avalon. She needed replacement power packs for the arm that was not.

What was Rowan going to do with him? Those bitter parting words sat like drops of acid in his mind.

The horse pulling his sled lifted its tail and dumped. Fresh scents of feces now coated the underside of his conveyance. The terrain dipped lower to become a softer passage. Mist swirled around Kai along with the brackish stink of stagnant water.

"Hold." Goat called.

The painful jolting stopped.

"Why?" Willow's voice came from nearer.

"Last time we crossed this place you almost served us up as a free meal."

"I can't sense any activity." Willow sounded irritated.

"That's what you said before." Goat's tone dripped with distrust. "Darkfire is a sitting target on a hurdle. He needs to be with one of us."

Willow dismounted to free Kai from protective restraints. "You heard that, Darkfire?"

Kai skewered the Brethren with a hard stare. "I'll fight if you throw me across the saddle like a sack of grain. I want to see where I'm going." Kai didn't like the feel of this place, the rotting vegetation and another sour odor overlaid all. *Vortei! Stars, we're at the Blanket Bogs.* His fey sense activated, warning of a lurking presence.

Willow hauled him upright. Dark flecks swirled in his vision – a mad dance accompanied by agony. Kai fought to stay awake, aware of movement and being lifted. At the last moment, he found the strength to swing his good leg over the horse's back. Hissing sounded in his ears.

"Stay with me, lad." Willow's arms closed around his waist. "If you fall, you're dead."

Kai didn't need urging. He remembered the gigantic, blind snakes from riding through this place with his parents. He'd seen them from a distance. A glimpse of those white forms was enough.

"Goat, I'm moving out," Willow called. "Stay in my shadow." He urged his mount to a slow walk into the brackish water. Hummocks of sick-looking vegetation protruded from the surface like warts on a diseased skin. Layers of mist boiled and swirled to blanket the terrain in gloom unpierced by any chance shaft of sunlight.

"Darkfire, not one moan out of you," Willow whispered. "Sound brings the Vortei. One of them could swallow us whole."

Kai bit his tongue to prevent curses pouring out. *Is he mad? Can't he feel the threat level increase because of his needless babble?*

"Willow, there's an eddy up ahead," Goat hissed from behind.

"I said quiet," Willow turned to his companion.

A creamy dome emerged, dripping, from black waters. It quested, the blind forepart cracking open to allow an enormous jaw to gape for scent markers.

Kai grabbed the reins, kicking the horse with his good foot, lost to everything except his fey sense.

Willow snatched them back, but Kai was at one with the horse. An impossible connection to the animal's mind sent it leaping to his commands. Right, and then left to slide to a halt. Four heart beats . . . another four, and they headed off at a dead run, to swerve left, leaping over a hummock. Extra speed, Vortei thrashing all around, and then hard ground with a bank looming into view. The horse leapt for safety. Kai lost his battle to stay in the light.

*

A cool wave of effervescence flowed through his body bringing relief from hot, grinding pain. Kai sighed, aware of a firm bed under his back and covers over his naked body.

"Wake him up," a deep voice ordered. "I don't care how smashed up he is."

"He needs healing, and he's lost a lot of blood," a light tenor answered.

The crack of a fist on flesh sounded, followed by a grunt of pain and a thud. "Now do as I say."

Kai opened his tired eyes. Rowan, a fat and grizzled Rowan, stood over a slight Submariner nursing a bloody lip. Rowan's foot rose for a kick.

"No!" Kai managed to lift his head. The effort cost him too much; he couldn't continue and sank back to his pillow.

Rowan turned, his fat jowls spoiling the symmetry of his ebony face. He smiled, sending ripples of fat into action. "Nice of you to join us."

"You underwhelm me with your concern." Kai recognized a standard living alcove for Brethren. A bed, stool, and clothes chest partitioned off from the commons with a leather curtain. *He's put me among warriors? Why not an isolated cave? What is his game?*

"I banished you and your mutant dam." Rowan swiveled to deliver the kick anyway. The Submariner started to crawl under the leather curtain.

"Does it look like I wanted to return?" Kai fought down a need to smash that grin off Rowan's face.

"You're here. I want supplies." Rowan glared at the man slithering out of sight. "Avalon is being difficult."

Kai imagined why. *I'm a hostage. He's the same power hungry monster I remember. Shit! I've got to play on his ego.*

"Shadow won't like your holding me for supplies."

"She'll give me what I demand for the continued life of her only whelp."

"Just how did my father get caught in crossfire? He rode out on a routine surveillance mission." Kai chanced his hand, aware he had nothing left to lose. Rowan had no intention of handing him over.

"Learn about my power, worm." Rowan smirked. "I caused the capture of an Outcast, and knew that Copper would be attacked when that man's mind was picked clean. You will beg your foul dam for supplies, or I'll start delivering pieces of your body to her agents."

Kai made his eyes drop. His weak body obligingly shuddered. "What do you need?" Rage burned through his soul. He wanted to kill Rowan slowly, but he had to be strong to stand a chance, guessing that the Outcast King gained fast reaction times from artificial means. How else could a man that age stay in office? *I'll play the weak son for now. Then I'll roast you alive, you sick bastard.*

*

Darkfire? Darkfire, can you hear me?

The unfamiliar name jarred his mind as it sounded in his thoughts. Faint snores came from beyond Kai's alcove. Night time and late at that. The intruder in his head tried to delve deeper, but he knew how to stop a raid.

My name is Kai. Those other thoughts snapped out of range, leaving the sensation of the seeker's shock. Minutes past.

Shadow's son? Is that what Rowan meant?

Kai caught the flavor of loathing from that other mind. He didn't trust his night companion, speculating a trap.

Are you alone? I can bring healing.

At what price? Kai tried to move. His ribs ached, and his leg sent a shaft of agony through him. He could see a faint outline of light from under his leather door curtain.

Freedom. Willow told Goat you guided them through the Vortai. That was before Rowan had Willow flogged senseless.

Now that didn't add up. *Why punish Willow?*

Because his fey gift won't grow.

Kai peered into the gloom, listening for breathing of a watcher. Beyond snores, none stirred. His fey sense remained at a steady alert.

I'm alone. Come with a searching mind. Kai hoped this Submariner possessed more skill in the head department than Willow. He wanted healing not just to kill Rowan; that route

267

held too much mercy. He wanted the man to scream out his life in a Hakara chamber. For that to happen Kai needed allies.

The curtain eased to one side like a thief's dream. A shadowy figure skittered inside. In that brief ray of light, Kai recognized the Submariner, who had wakened him. A purple contusion marked one side of the man's face.

Peace. I'm here to help. Held in the man's hand was a diagnostic unit.

Your name?

Call me Ix. The unit began to glow under the Submariner's hand as he made a sweep.

The flavor of the lie toned the name. Kai wondered what sort of hierarchy generated this massive distrust.

One based on terror, Ix supplied.

You raided my thoughts!

I survive because of a lack of Avalon protocol. Ix bent over the light of the unit. *You have a compound fracture of your left femur, five broken ribs, extensive internal bruising and infection from the wounds. You're lucky to be alive.*

Got any good news? Kai wanted to smash something – anything.

Anger won't help. Ix's thoughts contained an overtone of sympathy. *I can make genetic enhancements to accelerate healing.*

No! That's forbidden.

Rowan has frequent adjustments. It prolongs his life. There's no risk.

I'll take natural healing, or I'll tell him you helped me. Warned now, Kai set a barrier in his thoughts. He wondered how human Rowan still was as a result of 'help'.

Are you mad? How can you get us free unless you become his equal?

I'm Shadow's son by Copper. Get us out of this hell and I'll bring my brother to help me. You don't want to see Arthur and I go into battle together. The few who have still suffer nightmares.

Chapter 30

PINK-TINGED CLOUDS HOVERED, almost touching swirling tendrils of mist that bled off the water of Dozary lake. Standing alone on the shore, Arthur enjoyed this moment of quiet renewal. The rich aroma of dew-drenched vegetation mixed with earthy smells of wet clay.

A distant memory revived Avalon's sterile air and bone old scent. *This lake is the place of my dreams. Here is where my soul returns after each death. Do I stand with the shades of comrades, hidden from my mortal eyes? Kai? Are you caught in this place of waiting?*

"Arthur, Dragon wants to know if we can make a fire?" Circe emerged from waist-high ferns. She moved with abandon in her warrior's clothing.

"Is someone cold?" He caught her in his arms to swing her high. Her squeal of joyful surprise thrilled him. Laughing, he crushed her against his chest to rain light kisses on her upturned face.

She pulled away, her face turning to one side. "Have you discovered the sword while the rest of us slept?"

"I found a moment of joy to cherish with you." He gazed over her head into the mists, where the faces of the fallen might watch. "My brother taught me how to laugh and I'll honor his gift by sharing it with you, who opened my heart to love."

Circe reached up to touch his lips with her slender fingers. "The capacity to love and to laugh is in all of us. I miss him, too."

Arthur caught her hand to plant a kiss on her palm. "You don't feel cold to me. Why a fire?"

"Avriel didn't want dried meat and berries. I thought she might like fish if we caught some."

"Good thought, but she'd resent being singled out." He sighed, aware Avriel seemed off her food. "Haystack is watching out for her. She's identifying with Brethren because Kai was one."

A loud squawking set them scanning for intruders. Mist parted around a duck lumbering into air followed by a red-brown body, launched in a determined, but futile leap. The fox landed, glaring balefully at its departing prey.

"Time races to catch the laggard." Arthur slid his arm around Circe's waist. "We need to start this search."

*

Te Krull paced restlessly while Kiri Ung lounged on a fur-covered couch in the priest quarters of Tadgehill with Stalker sitting on the floor by his feet. He had ceased listening to Tadgehill's Nestine commander some time back and was now attempting to interject intelligent sounding grunts every time the voice paused. He fed Stalker slices of apple while he waited out the diatribe of failure, aware his actions were infuriating Te Krull. Stalker, on the other hand, although not hungry, obligingly ate the snacks just to add to the irritation factor.

Te Krull joined the fort commander to face Kiri Ung, neither one of them able to occupy the other two couches unless he gave leave. He chose not to accommodate them as he passed another slice of apple to his seated pet.

That Stalker was unchained seemed to aggravate Te Krull even more. *My pet is smart enough to know he can't leave my side in the presence of my kind.* He felt a warm glow inside. *I do believe he is enjoying upsetting them as much as I am.*

"Queen's Mate, why are we wasting time pursuing an insignificant band of renegades?" Te Krull's crest rose.

"Would you care to explain your reasoning to Shi Nom?" Kiri Ung watched that crest deflate like an eviscerated intestine. "Our Queen has small patience with failures."

"Then make that lounging Terran disclose their location."

Kiri Ung shielded Stalker from the instant thought probe. He didn't want Te Krull to find his pet's mind impervious to attack.

"You're protecting him!"

"Because his information isn't current." Kiri Ung sliced another segment of apple for Stalker, who accepted it with an expression of relish. "He will prove his worth when the time is right."

"What worth?" Te Krull's mouth flaps raised in a snarl.

"How much useful information do you glean from your pet cat? Is it able to provide useful bargaining details? Is its information relevant to our needs?"

Te Krull looked down.

"Leave us." Kiri Ung yawned, bored with the conversation. "Maintain a search pattern over Tadgehill."

Te Krull stormed out with the fort Nestine one pace behind.

"That one wants to kill you," Stalker observed, looking amused.

Kiri Ung studied his claws. "They all do."

Spitting out a pip, Stalker asked, "For power?"

"That and the chance to mate."

Stalker looked him over, eyes narrowed. "You're stopping them? That's got to create tension."

"Shi Nom, our Queen, chooses one of us to be her consort for the rest of his life." A sigh escaped.

"What about other females?" Stalker stood up to begin the stretching exercises of a warrior.

"There is only Shi Nom."

His pet paused, doubt oozing from his entire body. "Then you're safe as long as you watch your back?"

"Or until another male catches her attention."

271

"But you said a consort position was for life." Stalker resumed his exercise.

"It is. Should I fail her I will become her next meal."

A gasp turned into a fit of coughing as his pet tried to hide astonishment. Brown eyes wide, Stalker stared at him.

*

Flickers of light sidled under Kai's door curtain, but the bearers didn't stop. Muted conversations seemed strained in tone. *I'm going to get you, Rowan. You'll pay with your life for killing my father, but you're going to suffer for destroying Haven.*

A tankard of water and a moldy looking oatcake lay on a table by the side of his bed. Right underneath it, someone had left a not too clean piss-pot. He shivered, naked and cold under a single coarse blanket. Pain carved an angry path up his leg and across his ribs. The sharp dig of a crude splint pushed against tender flesh.

Two faces formed in his mind's eye; his mother's deep violet eyes framed by short blonde curls and Avriel's sapphire orbs, offset by long jet tresses. He couldn't let Rowan use him as a hostage. He might have a chance to make a strike if he could distance the pain of his injuries, but where did that leave Avriel?

Rowan's guards will shred me after I kill him. They must, or acknowledge me as leader. They'll not allow an outsider to rule. If he followed this plan to spare Shadow, then Avriel might be left to rear a child alone. His negligence came back to haunt him.

Swift movement on the floor caught his attention. A large brown rat snatched the oatcake to drag it toward a crack in the wall. Kai closed his eyes. He needed to take Rowan down in a fair duel. If the rules of the Brethren still held, then that would make him King of the Outcasts. With Haven as a base, he'd have a home to offer Avriel and a staging post for Arthur. An impossible dream, given his injuries.

Shrill squeaking turned his attention to the rat. The beast lay on its back convulsing among the crumbs of the meal intended for him. Its paws stretched, stiff from its arching body, one last time before life fled.

Not enough poison to kill a man, but sufficient to weaken him unto death. Cold rage built inside Kai. He needed healing of the sort Arthur supplied. *Why did my brother get that gift? Dragon only has a touch of the fey abilities that blossomed in my sire.* Did the gift come from the sire of the dam? Kai began to wonder. He thought back to his melding with Arthur when they bonded spirits to free Emrys. Without the gestalt, he would've died from the injuries sustained before they began their attempt.

Arthur converted energy into matter to heal. On that occasion, his brother drew energy from all the people around them who possessed psi power. *What if fey sense and psi power are part of the same gift? What do I have to lose by trying?* Kai focused inward as he'd seen Arthur do when healing. He concentrated on a small cut on his arm, aware he hadn't the energy needed for massive regeneration.

Cuts ripped through skin. Skin was three layers deep. He started with the deepest, trying to imagine the flesh knitting into scar tissue. Water dripping from the roof distracted him. People passing by his door curtain with their lights clawed at his attention. Time sped as he continued his inner battle. At one point, Kai became aware of someone bringing a meal from the smell of hot vegetable soup. He forced his awareness on that small cut and the heat beginning to build in its depths.

Warmth spread from his core to reach over his entire body closely followed by exhaustion. Kai stopped fighting. Beaten, he glared down at his arm. But the cut had healed! One small white line marked its site. He wanted to shout his victory aloud. Instead, he gripped the tankard of water with a shaky hand. They'd not try to poison water and show their hand by any bitter aftertaste. Kai drank deeply.

*

273

Kiri Ung urged Na Pan to plot a course through a dust storm in the firmament. He could see Te Krull's ship streaking toward the Moon Base from his position at the observation port. Now he thanked fate that he had overindulged the crew of this ship because he wouldn't have had warning of Te Krull's betrayal without them. A groan from his pet distracted him.

Stalker heaved into a waste unit, looking green from space sickness. Kiri Ung dismissed the illness, aware his pet's fate rested with the crew. He couldn't keep Stalker with him when they landed. If his crew decided to snack in his absence, he couldn't risk offending them with his wrath.

"Queen's Mate, what if Te Krull has captured our prize Terran?" Na Pan glanced up from his instruments.

That possibility had goaded Kiri Ung from the moment he learned of Te Krull's scramble for Moon Base. "Stalker?"

"What?"

His pet's terse reply in front of other Nestines annoyed him into extending his claws. He marched over to a high storage unit and extracted a metered slap-shot for space sickness. Irritation at the impertinence peaked as he grabbed the Terran's long head pelt and delivered the curative into neck muscle in one swift motion, ignoring Stalker's yelp of surprise.

"Did you hear the question, or were you too busy wasting nutrition?"

"What have you done to me?" Angry brown eyes glared up at him.

"Fixed your problem." Kiri Ung released his grip on the mane fast enough to elicit another cry. "Did you?"

"Yes, but I'm not telling you where Arthur is."

A collective hiss from all the other Nestines echoed around the flight deck.

"That's not the question." Kiri Ung smothered anger, aware Stalker didn't respond to threats. "Te Krull was at Tadgehill. In your opinion, is it possible Arthur would have gone there to set up a base nearby?"

Stalker backed away, his muscles tensing.

"We aren't trying to catch your leader right now." Out of the corner of his eye, Kiri Ung noticed every Nestine looking at them. "It's very important that Te Krull doesn't have him. What are the chances?"

"Don't know. Depends on whether any others of my group survived."

"Four of them. Two sets headed of in different directions." Kiri Ung saw the relief in Stalker's expression. "We were occupied destroying saurians so we didn't follow either pair."

Stalker frowned, and he shuffled from one foot to the other. "There was a regroup point." He looked at the deck, shoulders hunched. "Arthur wouldn't linger there once he knew what had happened. If any survivors from my group saw me taken captive, then he'd not set up a base near Tadgehill, either."

"So he wouldn't go there?" Kiri Ung held his breath.

"We needed supplies. The duke had a cache stored in a cave. If he thought you knew of that place, then he'd go there to collect on the guess that you'd think he wouldn't."

Yes, this rings true. A sick feeling made Kiri Ung long for a slap-shot to dispel fear. "Would he set up base?"

"He'd get what we needed and then head out." Stalker's head was down as if he carried a heavy load.

"Are you sure?" The beginnings of hope began to germinate.

"Arthur doesn't stay anywhere he thinks your kind overfly."

Vindication. I was right to let him keep his mind intact. The crew must see how important he is now. "I want my Terran protected when we arrive."

Not one crest raised. All the crew turned back to their consoles.

*

Circe handed out field rations to the group. She ignored the expressions of distaste, aware no one had time to go fishing or hunting. Dragon drew a large grid of the lake in a patch of sun-baked clay, ignoring his portion while Haystack shoved food in his mouth as he prepared to post watch. Avriel regarded the waybread as if it were a three day old summer corpse.

"It's not that bad," Circe urged. "Won't you try to get something down?"

"Not hungry." Her lips stretched in the skeleton of a smile. "Thanks for caring."

Avriel's eyes were ringed with circles, and now that Circe looked closely she could see how much weight Avriel had lost. She was sick and hiding it.

Although her Seer training disallowed invading the mind of another person without their consent or knowledge Circe followed her instincts and raided.

Crushing sorrow and fierce hatred of the cause of her loss seethed through Avriel. The girl blamed Nestines for Kai's death and waited out her chance to strike back, uncaring for her own survival. Circe expected this, but not the panic caused by nausea from aromas. Food smells in particular made Avriel abstain, even though she craved sustenance. Circe probed deeper.

"Get out of my mind!"

Startled by a Terran aware of being raided, Circe withdrew.

"I think we need to take time out to clip an earring on you," she suggested.

"Feeling guilty?" Blue eyes as cold as deep ocean stared at Circe.

"I have those in my kit." Circe extended her hand to Avriel. "Arthur will raid your mind if he spots you heaving. He's far stronger than me. We need to talk."

Looking puzzled, Avriel accepted the helping hand up. She followed Circe, first to the baggage and then away from the others into a tangled mess of bushes.

"Am I dying? Is that why we're moved apart?" An angry hope sharpened Avriel's features.

Circle sat down in a swath of rich ferns as she put together the words and the offer that had to be delivered. Stiff with tension Avriel hunkered down beside her.

"You loved Kai deeply."

"Going to tell my father? Is this a session of, 'Do as I say, or I'll tell that you slept with him'?"

"No." Circe considered a gentle approach and then dismissed it. Avriel wasn't capable of listening in her current state of mind. "I want your thoughts private because you need to decide your own fate without the opinions of others interfering." She took a deep breath. "Can we seal your mind right now? I really think you will betray the problem if we don't."

Seconds passed. A lark spiraled overhead, rising on a thermal with a joyous call. Wind whispered through the ferns that surrounded them.

"Lean forward. The next part is going to hurt."

Avriel blinked twice as the earring anchors scrunched through gristle to become a part of her. She looked at Circe. "Now tell me the truth. I want a chance at revenge before I die."

"You're bearing Kai's child." Circe watched the girl's eyes widen in first horror and then wonder that wasn't displaced even by a family of grouse rushing through the underbrush. Each chick following their mother in eager pursuit as if she alone existed in their world.

"I can stop the fetus growing and make you expel it if that is your choice. This conversation will remain private between the two of us."

Avriel put her hands over her eyes. She rocked back and forth for a time and then she stilled to face Circe.

"You'd do this for me?"

"If that is what you truly want."

"No one will ever know?"

"You have my word." Circe steeled herself to a hard task. She didn't want to snuff out a potential life, but she wasn't prepared to let Avriel suffer.

"My father is going to be very angry." Avriel looked into the distance with blind eyes. Wind whispered through the ferns, blowing back Avriel's dark locks. Her face appeared frozen until resolve hardened her expression. She straightened her shoulders. "I know you aren't a warrior so this gesture is doubly appreciated. I won't deny the product of my love for Kai."

"There is time to change your mind." Relief surged over Circe, but she had to make certain the decision stood. "I can still stop a baby for the next two weeks."

"If I can't have Kai, then I'll have a living reminder of him." Avriel's lips turned upward in the promise of a smile. Her eyes glistened with unshed tears. "Keys to the kingdom. A woman who loves a warrior enough will raise his child alone to continue fighting for the cause for which that warrior gave his life."

Thank you, Emrys. I didn't want to destroy Kai's child. Tight bands of tension around Circe's heart relaxed. Tears prickled against her eyelids. "If you will let me into your mind, I can stop the sickness."

"Please." Tears rolled down Avriel's cheeks. "I don't want to tell my father yet. I need time."

Circe opened her arms. Avriel leaned into them, sobbing. She stroked those midnight locks, trying to give what comfort she could. In the distance, a dog fox howled a warning over his territory.

Chapter 31

A SMALL SIP OF water that tasted sour swirled around Kai's mouth. His fey sense screamed threat, but his new skill took his awareness to a deeper level. *Rowan knows I'm fasting, so he poisons my water to weaken me.*

An image of the molecules leapt into Kai's mind. Having no other challenge to relieve his pain and boredom he directed his newfound sense at the image, trying to get those with an angry green aura realigned. The inner picture changed to show a swirling mass of chaos.

Time passed to the footfalls and muted conversation of others in the passage outside. A spider slid from the rough ceiling on a thread of shining gossamer. A huge web stretched across one corner that had flakes of debris and dried carcasses. Water dripped from a fissure in the roof near his bed. Green verdigris colored the opening. Kai blocked out all the images to try a series of adjustments. Sweat trickled into his closed eyes, stinging them. One more pattern before he spat out this muck. The image shifted through colors into a clear cerulean blue. The sense of threat diminished. Kai swallowed what he hoped his body could now handle. How long did the poison take to work?

Marching feet, accompanied by the rasp of weapons unsheathed gave Kai an answer soon after. Trusting to fate, he decided to feign a clouded mind and opened his eyes in a drowsy manner.

His curtain swept to one side. Two Brethren warriors rushed in to secure his arms and good leg. Rowan followed, thrusting Ix at him. The Submariner struggled to keep his balance and maintain a grip on medical equipment.

Gross overkill. Kai caught Ix's look of sudden inner concentration just as his message arrived. *Is all Brethren subtlety destroyed by this man's strong grasp on power?*

Kai? Did you drink any of that water?

The urgent overtones of Ix's thoughts answered many questions. *What should I be feeling if I had?*

Sleepy and very suggestible. Did you?

No, Kai lied. He didn't trust Ix not to switch sides. The Submariner valued his own skin too much.

Fake it. Do whatever Rowan wants.

"Well Worm? Is this mutant filth ready?"

Kai managed a glassy stare as instruments whined. He spotted a transmitter dangling from Rowan's meaty fist. The shock almost threw him out of his role. *He'd violate Haven's security to contact Avalon? Doesn't he know Nestines can triangulate any transmission?*

Rowan needs supplies. Ix's thoughts radiated spite. *He doesn't care about the future cost. Brethren are starting to question his rule.* "He's under. He'll do whatever you want."

"Give him a shot of the pure compound." Rowan dumped the transmitter on Kai's stool to bring the device online.

"Rowan, he's injured," the black-haired Brethren holding Kai's leg objected. He started to straighten. "Full strength left Willow an idiot after he'd done convulsing. We need those supplies."

Rowan's fist connected with flesh. The Brethren smashed against a wall, to slide down in a silent heap. "Do as I say, or you'll be next." He fixed his eyes on Ix.

The Submariner obeyed. Kai felt the sting of a sub-dermal delivery unit discharging drugs into his neck. Numbing cold flushed through his veins to be met by heat.

"Bitch's whelp. Did this fish scum help you?" Rowan's fat jowls wobbled into Kai's line of vision.

"Help . . . how?" Kai slurred his words. He caught sight of the shadow of someone who listened out of Rowan's line of vision in the passageway beyond. *They don't trust him. There's hope for me yet.*

You shouldn't be able to think. Ix's shocked thought intruded.

I'm my mother's son. Trust me.

Rowan's deep voice echoed around the alcove in velvet tones of death as he contacted Avalon. Within moments, Shadow's voice replied.

"You want proof that your mongrel whelp survived? I'll give it." Rowan thrust the speaker module in Kai's face. "Say hello to your dam."

"I'm . . . sorry." Kai considered his next words with care. "Don't . . . abandon . . . your only son."

Rowan withdrew the communicator. "Satisfied? Now I want those items delivered at our established pickup point in three days."

"Not enough time." Shadow's voice quavered with concern. "The medical components and equipment you demand must be made. Even with our plants running without pause it will take ten days to fill your needs."

"Make it six, bitch, unless you want your whelp to start losing body parts."

"We'll give you everything we've got in six days with the rest to follow?"

This is your mother? Panic surged through Ix's thoughts. *What is she doing?*

Following my orders to buy time. Through half closed lids, Kai saw Rowan's indecision.

"Which body part would you like first?" Rowan's eyes traveled down Kai to rest on the approximation of his genitals.

"I'll give you all we have on hand." Shadows voice took on a touch of granite. "Lay a hand on Kai and your supply dries up permanently. Your choice."

The hard stare from the remaining Brethren appeared to decide Rowan. "Trade agreed. Your son's life for my supplies." He stabbed a fat finger at the off button.

Ix? Can you get closer? I need energy.
That's Seer stuff. You're not a Seer.
Want to take a bet on that?

Ix inched closer until he could touch Kai as Rowan turned aside to pick up the communicator. They established contact. Life-force energy transferred.

*

Dragon sat on a boulder looking out over mist rising from Dozary lake. He jumped when Arthur touched his shoulder.

"Deep thoughts?"

"I tracked your mother here after her re-banding." Creases deepened by Dragon's mouth. "We found her mare along the way. I knew she couldn't escape me. I'd had one of its shoes cast in a distinctive pattern so I could keep a watch on her."

"You didn't trust her?" A coldness settled around Arthur's heart. He withdrew his hand.

"She was very young and headstrong. I knew she liked to ride alone sometimes, and I wanted a way to track her without clipping her wings." He sighed. "I guessed she would disobey my orders sooner or later."

On the far side of the lake, a small herd of deer edged toward water. Adults stood watch while fawns drank their fill. Some cropped dew-drenched grass.

"You followed her to kill her." The words slipped off Arthur's tongue like drops of acid.

"My priest said she'd betrayed me." Dragon crushed a bug underfoot. He ground it into the grass. "I didn't want to believe, but she'd been made an Outcast. I loved her so much . . ."

Arthur scooped up a stone to hurl at a crow pecking at something small and tattered by a fallen tree. It flew off cawing outrage. "You wanted her dead."

"I didn't want that life for her." He turned to face Arthur, fists clenched. "She was just sixteen and a beauty. Despite her War Maid training, she couldn't have survived in the wilds. I know how Outcasts, the male ones, are treated in forts. Visions of mass rapes forced my choice for her."

Circe emerged from the bushes surrounding their camp followed by the others. The group started pointing at the lake and drawing with sticks on wet mud.

Bless her, she must know I want privacy. "A mercy killing then. What did you find here?"

"Faint impressions of many footsteps leading into the water. I thought she'd run into Brethren." Dragon looked at shimmering water once more. "One of their tricks is to fool our hounds by wading through water. I saw her with them at High fort later that year. She dived into an underground river trying to run from me." A tremor ran through him. "When she didn't surface . . . I mourned her while I rejoiced at her release."

In the distance, Circe stripped down to her skin-tight Submariner undergarments. She might as well have been naked. Ripples marked the place when she shallow-dived.

"Copper must have guessed her true nature." Dragon picked up a flat stone to send it skipping across the water. "He pulled out all his uncommitted mercenaries that night while I was getting blind drunk. When I saw her with them the next year I almost didn't recognize her under the face-dye they'd all started to wear." He threw another flat rock. It skipped some distance from the shore. "She'd become full Brethren by that time. I never knew she'd had our son until I saw you."

Circe's head bobbed out of the water. She called to the others, who shifted positions as they marked her progress.

"And now?" Arthur watched Circe make a graceful flip to dive.

"We made our peace." Again, Dragon sighed. "I have my firstborn son with me. Both a pleasure and a tormenting agony. All those wasted years . . ."

Arthur wondered if Circe carried his child. He hadn't asked.

"Vortigon is safe for the present. If he's to have any future, then the Nestines must be defeated."

Dragon withdrew a pouch from his tunic. He held up a tiny clump of fine black hair. "Once again I must abandon a son because of them. Is this all I am to have of him?" Bitter lines etched his face.

The crow returned to its grisly feast. Arthur hurled another rock, one that hit the scavenger. It flapped skyward screeching.

"Am I going to get a life with my chosen mate?" Arthur spied Circe's wet blonde head breaching surface. "Maybe, if we get the sword."

Dragon followed his gaze. "She's swimming too far out." He stood up to stretch. "I recall being told it was thrown in the water. One of our ancestors got the notion that it caused bad luck."

"His size and strength at the time?" Arthur began to unfasten the lacing of his tunic.

"Probably about mine."

"Care to try your hand at sword throwing?"

*

Shadow turned away from her console with death in her heart. Ector held out his arms to her, and she stumbled, sobbing, into them.

"He's still alive, and he's told you Arthur isn't with him," Ector whispered into her hair. "We don't know how he fell into Rowan's hands."

"My boys . . ." *Kai lived but what of Arthur? Did Kai mean Arthur was dead?*

The console began to bleep with another incoming signal directed at control command. A control light blinked like a baleful red eye, to be reflected off the smooth gray metallic walls

"Let me take this call." Ector eased her into a chair in front of his desk. He moved around to sit at his screen.

"Avalon to incoming vessel. Identify yourself."

"Huber speaking. I have a casualty needing urgent treatment. Can I dock?"

Shadow launched from her chair to view the screen. Huber looked drained. Bile rose in her throat.

"Who's the casualty?" Ector glanced at her.

"It's Linden. He lost a hand in a saurian attack."

"And the others?"

"Kai and Mulberry died. Stalker was captured by the Nestines." Huber looked away for the vid-camera. "The others are heading for Dozary lake to find the artifact Arthur wants. I'm to bring our submersible to the coastal outlet once I've helped Linden. Will you take him?"

"Affirmative." Ector snaked an arm around Shadow's waist. "Dock at port five. A team will be on hand to collect him." The screen went blank.

"Now we know part of it." He stood pulling her into his arms, his eyes wide with concern. "Arthur is alive. Kai needs help, but he's not in bad shape, or he wouldn't have sent us that cryptic message."

"He's hurt! I saw the bandages."

"Kai's Brethren. He's his father's son." Ector hugged her. "If I've got a take on that young man, then Rowan is in deep water."

The room seemed to fold around Shadow. Consoles blinked, and the desks did a crazy dance. Gray, uniform walls blackened to swirls with specks of brightness.

"Stay with me." Ector's eyes bored into her. "The boys are alive. We need to get working on Rowan's demands." He gave her a gentle shake. "Kai is in a dangerous and interesting position. However badly hurt he is, he will be using his gifts."

Releasing her, Ector sat to run his fingers over the keyboard to execute swift orders. "Yes, I know we can't satisfy Rowan's demands. That's why I will be ordering a unit to track the pickup."

Shadow sat on the edge of his desk, trying to make her numb mind work. "They can't get by the blanket bogs without a gifted Brethren." A frightening image of a Vortai's blind white head questing for vibrations sent her guts into a knot.

"Then perhaps it is time to de-populate this area of a nuisance." Ector frowned over the display he'd generated on his console.

"That would leave them defenseless against fort attacks."

"Do we care?" Turning to face her, he raised one eyebrow.

"If . . . our alliance with Brethren is over . . ." Kai at Rowan's mercy made her want to scream 'no'. *What of Submariners trapped at Haven? What of Brethren bereft of a base?* Through the corridors of time, she heard Copper's laugh ring at a practical joke one of that fearsome band of warriors had played on another. *That was their place to be alive. Copper made it so. Has Rowan turned Haven into a prison?* "We have to find a way in without destroying their defense."

Ector's expression hardened. He gazed at his console, his fingers flying over controls. "Command lock to my retina pattern."

"What have you done?" A sick premonition chilled her.

His eyes met hers in the reflection of the now blank console screen. "Ensured no craft will operate with you on board."

"I wasn't thinking of going to . . ." The lie froze on her tongue.

"Rowan knows you can force a passage wide enough for an army to pass through the Vortai." He spun around to face her, his hands white-knuckled, gripping his arm rests. "He has Kai for a lure. Why else threaten to mutilate him?"

"That's why I have to go with those supplies." *He's made me a prisoner. How could he?*

"What we are going to do instead is use our wild card." His eyes narrowed. "Rowan doesn't know much about Arthur except that some renegade is setting up a complimentary operation that steals away a few of his men."

"We don't know exactly where Arthur is," Shadow argued.

"Huber does."

Chapter 32

Kiri Ung paused on the threshold of the Queen's cavern to suck in air over the roof of his mouth. Te Krull's pheromones were fresh. His rival had an audience and lived still, for he couldn't detect the scent of blood.

Come and join us, Kiri Ung. Shi Nom's thought patterns lashed through his mind.

His crest twitched, limp as a floundering fish on his head. *May his fangs crumble and his claws split. What lies has he told her?* Now shielding his thoughts he let his rage build into a fighting fury. If Te Krull challenged him they would battle until one lay dead. Blood rushed in to erect his crest to its full glory. He marched forward into her magnificent presence, to almost stumble at the shock of her altered appearance.

Shiny black chitin had dulled into a matte gray. Her eyes looked as if a milky film clouded each facet, and she lay on the ground of her wallow with her legs curled under her.

He halted next to Te Krull, not sparing him a glance. *Is she in molt?* He couldn't detect any trace of a split in her armor. Heart pounding, he knelt to give her homage.

Te Krull jerked as if struck by a fist of iron. He staggered, backing out of the chamber.

Sensors indicate a male Terran in your craft. One antenna fluttered like a dying fly.

Trickles of moisture flowed from his eyes. His heart told him that his mate neared death. He wanted to cradle her head in his arms, to comfort her, but she'd never liked any touching except during mating. He wanted to please her, but he couldn't offer her less than the truth, not now.

I have one of Arthur's men. Arthur wasn't amongst the group when I found them. He bowed his head, baring his neck for the crush of her mandibles.

Does he live?

Surprised at a question instead of a death grip, he looked up. Her single fluttering antennae wilted to join its twin, dangling, lifeless. More moisture trickled from his eyes.

Yes, my Queen. Kiri Ung guessed which Terran she meant. *My captive believes his leader is safe.*

I guard the last batch of eggs I will ever lay. Tones of sadness flavored her thought message. *As long as I live, no human alleles will be injected to complete the chain of life you and I have formed. I must have new Queens. The fate of our race depends on your success.*

Shi Nom don't leave us. The trickle of moisture became twin runnels down his face, dripping onto his chest. The vast blackness of the cavern pressed down on him with images of this place without her, the first and only Queen. They had no way to measure her life-span stretching back millennia and now it dwindled.

I wasn't the only Queen. She picked up on his grieving thought. *In the early days we had a compatible Terran, but I didn't want to share my realm. I killed the egg and the Terran, thinking there would be others.*

His crest dropped like a wet rag. *How long do you have?*

When I send you forth, I have enough strength to weave a seal on this place. Waves of exhaustion extruded from her. *Your blood is the catalyst to open a way through. You will reign as regent until you succeed in your quest. Now leave me.*

A humming croon started as he stumbled, blinded by his own tears, to the exit with the dry rustle of her legs moving behind him, but he couldn't bear to see her so diminished. Numb with grief, Kiri Ung blundered through passageways to an elevator and up to the flight bays.

The doors slid open to reveal Te Krull with a charged weapon.

"Say farewell, Kiri Ung." Te Krull's crest rippled. He aimed.

288

"Say farewell, Te Krull." Na Pan's voice echoed around the gloomy shadow-filled cavern, a sound that betrayed no direction. "Kill him and you'll join him in death."

Te Krull whirled to fire off a short burst of laz-beams into a dark corner. Answering fire barely missed his running form. He dived behind the nearest skyship. The sound of his feet pounding on a metal grid echoed.

Na Pan stepped from behind a water tank with both pilots and Stalker at his heels. "Your pet has interesting abilities," he said, jerking his head back at the Terran.

Sounds of a ship firing engines boomed, and the ground shook. The blue haze of a power seal flashed as it permitted an exit. Kiri Ung raised his head, roaring his rage. *He's gone to claim the planet. How can I honor Shi Nom's last wishes now?* He wondered why he was still alive.

"How did you know I was in danger?"

"Your Terran told us." Na Pan yanked a battered looking Stalker forward. "When we ignored him, he started throwing things at us. That's when we decided he'd make a useful snack, but he still kept insisting you were in trouble."

Kiri Ung wiped his eyes to really look at his pet. Stalker's clothes were tattered and bloodstained. The Terran exhibited a relaxed stance that betrayed his readiness to fight. The sky pilot's left eye was swollen closed, and the star pilot favored one leg. Na Pan's gun paw bore a bloody crescent of teeth marks.

"Back to our ship, all of you." He caught and held each different glare in turn until the owner looked away. "We are at war with Te Krull. I'll explain on the way."

*

Flashing steel flipped end over end to land with a splash. Ripples spread in widening circles from the point of entry. Stripped to his underpants, Arthur dived, trying not to take in the delightful image of Circe's bare legs where she marked position on the

289

surface. Sunlight filtered from above to give a green glow. A shoal of minnows made a series of erratic turns to evade his intrusion.

Holding his breath to maintain buoyancy his trachea constricted, and the subtle shift of muscles in his neck opened his gill flaps. All digits spread wide to unfurl webbing. He powered to the depths, enjoying the sensation for the first time.

Why didn't Sanctuary include swimming in my program? I never thought it could be this much fun. He'd utilized his skills for transport and survival since leaving Avalon. Now Arthur experimented, fluking as he dived. *Why am I the only son to be aquatic? Why didn't Kai get this inheritance?* Thoughts of Kai fronting a saurian with a river at his back soured the experience. The dead weight of loss filled him with an empty rage. Arthur scanned the bottom, just twitching his hands and feet to hover.

The silver glimmer of Dragon's sword sparkled from a light layer of mud over rocks. Arthur turned hard right to parallel the shoreline for three body lengths. He then quartered the section to repeat the procedure on the left of his marker. *Nothing. Why did the moron who threw away the talisman have to pick such a damn great lake?*

Midday came and with it a change in shifts. Circe now dived the quadrants and Haystack hurled the sword while Merrick marked position on the surface. Arthur lay in the sun, a carpet of grass tickling against his back. His throat ached from gill action, a dull throb.

Enticing aromas of cooking fish that he'd snagged on his final dive made his stomach grumble. He raised his head to watch Avriel turn his catch on spits over their fire. The glint of an earring drew his eyes.

How deep was she going to submerge herself in the Brethren doctrines? And who in the hells clipped an earring on her? He could've shielded her. Now she'd always bear the stigma. He noticed her inhaling the aroma as if it were the sweetest scent in life. Now that was new. She's been off her food. His relief tinged with guilt at her first steps toward life. *I'm so sorry, little sister.*

Why did I think those damned horses were important? We should've stayed together. I could have called mounts to us here. Why didn't I think?

Arthur grabbed his clothes, shucking them on to go help Avriel. She jumped when he hunkered down beside her to take a turn.

"Cooking is women's work." Frosty blue eyes challenged him, and her mouth formed a hard line.

"Everyone who wants to eat gets to take a turn."

She smacked his hand away from the spit he had almost grasped. "I'm not that useful yet. Leave this task to me."

The jet hue of her now exposed band chilled through his soul. He grabbed her wrist. "Who changed your bracelet and clipped your ear with a Brethren bauble?"

"Does it matter?" Avriel's hand trembled.

"Yes, I believe it does." He viewed the band with distaste. "I clipped our father because he is eccentric enough to get away with wearing the Brethren stigma. He's also capable of dueling any objector."

"The same applies to me." The words shot out like frozen arrows.

"You wouldn't win a duel with another Gold Band, and you're not old enough to have established personality quirks." He settled down cross-legged to endure a battle of wills.

Avriel poked at the fire to expose more glowing embers underneath the cooking fish. "I'm not a prize to be traded away to another fort in marriage any longer." Sounds of laughter from the lake distracted her attention for a moment. Her expression settled into a bland mask. "Even if we win back Tadgehill, I'll never accept an arranged union. And who would offer for a renegade house?"

"Kai's gone." A sudden fit of shivering made Arthur wonder if Kai's shade watched them. For an instant, he'd felt his brother's presence. "He wouldn't want you wasting your life wearing the willow wreath for him."

High above them a crow screeched, diving to the cover of trees with a hawk in hot pursuit. Black feathers drifted downward on the breeze.

"He's with me every waking moment." A smile that lit her eyes transformed her for a brief second. "I can hear the echo of his thoughts. I smell the essence of him. I can recall his every expression. He'll live as long as I draw breath."

She removed the cooked fish from spits to deposit them into a basket woven from fern fronds. With deft fingers, she skewered two more of his catch to place them over the blaze. "Could you call our father? You two get to eat first since you started work first."

Routed and dismissed, Arthur did as she'd bidden him. He sent a thought command to Dragon, on watch in a tree top.

*

Kai tested his leg by tensing his muscles and pressing down with his heel. Despite the splint, he could feel an improvement since he'd stolen energy from the woman who had left his poisoned lunch. The aroma of rabbit stew permeated his cubicle, almost disguising a hard metallic tang. *How long before Rowan realizes I am not going to eat? Could I alter food as I did water?* Part of him wanted to try, but logic stopped him. Water was simple, unlike complex proteins. He jumped when his curtain twitched aside, having heard no noise of footsteps outside. Goat entered with a chunk of smoked meat in his hand. The Brethren wore a dead look that all of them usually reserved for fort people. He extended his gift to Kai.

"Willow died. This is his meal. It's safe."

Kai took the offering in wonder. Somehow his tiny alcove looked brighter, but a worm of caution ate at him. "You know what Rowan does to me? How do I know this isn't a trick?"

Goat looked away to the door curtain, listening. "Willow and me go back a long ways. His fey sense never faltered, except around Haven. Rowan scared him shitless."

Still, Kai hesitated. "I'm the cause of Willow's death. Why feed me?"

"I've heard tell about how it was when Copper ruled." Goat locked eyes with Kai. "This used to be our place. We get treated better when we're working for a fort, now."

Sounds from the corridor held both of them transfixed. Footsteps came and went. Goat edged toward the door on silent feet.

"Copper was my sire. I remember those days." Kai eased up into a sitting position, aware that he betrayed his growing strength. "What do you want from me?"

Those words echoed around the tiny room, bouncing off faded pictures on rock. Kai reached out to Avriel with all his heart, longing to be with her instead of this grim prison.

Goat ran narrowed eyes over Kai. "If you were fit, could you challenge Rowan? Would you?"

For a single heartbeat Kai got a picture in his mind of a fire. Avriel's slim hand turned cooking fish. *I'm day dreaming. Avriel never helped cook, except for that time by the cave near Tadgehill.* He met this Brethren's hard stare.

"Do you speak for yourself, or are there others wanting Rowan gone?"

Goat glanced at the curtain and back again. "Six more that I'm sure of. Willow's friends, all."

Kai's fey sense activated of its own accord. He got a feeling of inclusion from Goat. This man had committed. "I can accelerate my healing if I can have a willing gift of life-force." *Now what will he do?*

Goat frowned. "I give up my life to help you?"

"No. Just a little energy." Kai's heart pounded. *Will he help?*

"You're Shadow's son, too. She had strange powers." Goat shuffled.

"As do I and my brother."

"Copper only had one son." Goat took a backward step toward the curtain.

"Arthur is my elder brother from her first mating." Kai watched the shock set in with a sense of satisfaction. "Rowan doesn't know of him. Are you going to tell?"

Goat's eyes bulged. He walked, stiff-legged to Kai's side. "Two of you? He has the fey gift?"

"Arthur is gifted in other ways." Kai smiled, thinking of his brother. "Imagine the most powerful Submariner you have ever seen and then increase his gift tenfold."

The Brethren hunkered down by Kai, his face alight with wonder. "What must I do?"

"Give me your hand and don't fight when I suck out energy."

Chapter 33

HAYSTACK RAN INTO camp just as Arthur swallowed his last mouthful of fish. The Brethren skidded to a halt, panting.

"Huber's back. He's swimming to shore." Haystack gulped down air. "He's supposed to wait off-shore, isn't he?"

Oh shit. What now? Arthur scrambled to his feet. "Any Nestine sightings?"

"The sky's clear." Haystack ignored the food Avriel thrust at him until she kicked his shins. Grunting, he accepted it without taking his eyes off Arthur.

"I'll go see what made him surface." Arthur made his face radiate warmth even while his gut contracted. "Eat. Maybe he's bringing us good news."

Arthur didn't start running until he was out of sight. Huber never disobeyed orders. He arrived in time to see Huber walking out of the lake. Water slid off those Submariner clothes to leave them almost dry.

"How's Linden?" The words forced through lips stiff with dread. Guilt strangled Arthur's guts.

"Stable." Huber looked around, his brows drawn together. "Where's Avriel?"

"Just over that rise behind me, cooking a meal."

Circe and Merrick joined them. A sense of foreboding continued to blossom in Arthur. Huber stared at a bank of ferns with a mole-blind gaze.

"I've good news and bad," he paused, meeting Arthur's eyes. "Kai's alive."

"He's at Avalon?" Circe's laugh of relief lifted her voice.

"How did he get a transport?" Merrick demanded.

Huber held up his hands for quiet. Arthur rammed a cap on his joy, waiting for the bad news.

"Haven has him. He's hurt, and they're using him as a hostage for supplies Avalon doesn't have."

"Where is my mother?" Dread numbed Arthur. He pictured Shadow heading a rescue mission.

"Fuming in Avalon." A slight grin lifted Huber's lips. "Ector coded all the airlocks to his retina pattern. She's trapped."

"There is more?" Arthur guessed at bad news.

"Kai got a message through that Rowan didn't know about any brother." Huber glanced over the rise toward their campsite at Haystack striding through the ferns. "Avalon is sending all they can muster of Rowan's demands, but they want us to breach Haven by the back door if one exists. Otherwise we're to find a way to get a fighting unit past the Vortei."

"Arthur, my fey sense tells me we need to leave this place now." Haystack nodded to Huber in agreement, having heard the last words. He looked out over the shimmering lake, blinking.

Arthur guessed the Brethren used his eidetic memory to capture the location of areas already covered in their search. He completed his own scan, aware of a decision made by all present from the look on their faces.

If Rowan breaks the treaty with Avalon, then we will be fair quarry. We can't fight a war on two fronts. The sword will keep. Kai won't. A cloud meandered across the sun to cast a shadow on lake waters. "This is a good place to leave our horses. We'll take the submersible around by the sea route."

Haystack stiffened, looking skyward. "Arthur, danger is getting closer." He turned to run to their tethered mounts. Saddles lay near a fallen tree, and now he removed reins from the beasts to free them.

"Circe, start swimming." Arthur caught her in a quick hug. "We'll catch up with you."

"Avriel needs to be told." Circe clutched at his tunic, her eyes pleading.

"Later." He pushed her gently to arm's length. "When we are safe and have time to deal with her."

She didn't look happy, but she ran to the shore to dive. A small ripple marked her passage.

"Huber, take Haystack." Arthur didn't want any questions from Dragon and Avriel. His own emotions swung from joy to despair in an uneasy jerk. He had to get his group safe.

Sunlight reflected off an approaching metal disk in the sky. Arthur broke into a run with Merrick hard on his heels. He didn't dare mind call with Nestines so close. They burst into camp, each of them grabbing a Terran from a sitting position to haul the surprised pair into a running start. The whine of engines grew closer. Arthur wrenched a stasis disk from his tunic pocket. He crashed into the water with Avriel held tight against him. A swift twist of his arm locked the device on her forehead. She went limp. He kicked for deep water and the passage to sea, aware of a flurry of bubbles to his right that was Merrick and Dragon.

*

Moon base faded from view from the observation port. Kiri Ung looked at each questioning face. Shi Nom filled his thoughts. By now she'd have sealed herself in her cavern for the last time. His heart pounded until he thought it might burst. He wanted to be with her to comfort her, but she wanted her final orders obeyed.

"Shi Nom has laid a Queen egg." The crew looked so happy Kiri Ung wanted to smash something rather than tell them the rest. "She has tasked us with finding Arthur." Stalker's face wore a mutinous expression now. "Te Krull also searches. If he wins the race, then he will become the next Queen's Mate."

"She has opened mating?" Na Pans voice wavered.

"Our Queen is dying." Moisture flowed from his eyes. Kiri Ung didn't care that they saw his weakness.

"She can't die." The sky pilot rose from his seat, disbelief written plain on his face.

Na Pan's crest rose. "She's molting. She's done it before."

"Shi Nom feels her ending." He choked on his words, struggling for control over his voice. "I am ordered to bring Arthur. Only my blood will release her web to permit access to the egg chamber."

"Good luck finding him." Stalker took up a fighting stance, backing against an angle of the flight deck.

"What if Te Krull finds him first?" Na Pan glared at Stalker and bared his fangs.

"I will permit him to enter. Our survival as a race demands no less."

"Am I hearing this right?" Stalker interrupted. "Te Krull controls the planet, and you are leader of the Moon Base?"

The sky pilot slumped back into his seat, his crest deflating. "This means Moon Base is cut off from our main food source. Kiri Ung, all of us, including you, Terran, are dead meat unless we grab the prize first."

The space pilot looked up from his instruments for a brief moment. "There are the space arks. We took all the Terrans off already to repopulate the planet, but there are animal species we could revivify."

Kiri Ung heaved a sigh of relief. He'd forgotten about those antique vessels. "Good thoughts. Your name?"

"Sha Gru, Queen's Mate."

"Then, Sha Gru, put that plan into motion." Kiri Ung turned to confront Stalker. "I have fewer ships than Te Krull. Your race won't survive a conflict between us. Give me Arthur's location now."

"No deal." Stalker backed as far into his corner as he could get. "What's a space ark?"

Na Pan flowed to his feet to begin zeroing in on Stalker. Kiri Ung halted the hunt with a curt gesture. *Why is Stalker playing for time? He responds to data with data.* "Our race was created to care for yours while your ancestors traveled in stasis aboard a generation starship bound for a new planet. These space arks contain everything needed to terraform . . ." Kiri Ung dug for words his pet might understand better. "To alter a new planet to make it look like home."

Stalker frowned. "Those arks still work?"

"We have them maintained." He wondered what train of thought promoted Stalker to ask.

"And there is only one Queen egg?"

"That is so." An unpleasant inkling of what was stirring Stalker disturbed Kiri Ung.

"If I agree to find Arthur, what will you do to him?"

Kiri Ung sat down on his console panel, his legs failing him. He heard the alarms from distressed systems his weight activated. He felt vibrations through his hide, but he couldn't move. "A tiny skin sample would do." His numb mind tried to function. "The scrapings from inside his mouth. Any living tissue."

"Queen's Mate, can you move?" The hint of desperation in Sha Gru's voice showed in his hunched position over his wildly flashing console as he fought for control.

Kiri Ung levered upright on wobbly feet.

"Swear to me that is all you want from him." Stalker took a step forward.

"I swear we only need one living cell." Kiri Ung held his breath. *I need Stalker's guesses and his gift. I won't get them if I take over his mind.*

"A trade." Stalker marched over to face Kiri Ung. "If I find him and he agrees, I want you to transfer all Nestines from Moon Base to those arks, and then I want Moon Base destroyed." Angry brown eyes looked up into his. "Go find yourselves another home, and leave us in peace."

Kiri Ung's crest swelled. Every Nestines' crest erected with outrage. *Fly into the unknown? Leave all our heritage? Unacceptable.* "You're asking too much. Think about the alternative with Te Krull ruling."

Na Pan rushed forward to grab Stalker by the neck. "Let me free his mind now." Fangs hovered near Stalker's ear.

"No!" Kiri Ung got a certain satisfaction from Stalker's choking struggles and his thrashing, dangling feet. "Drop him. We might need him intact."

"How will we know where to start searching without this Terran's information?" Na Pan dropped his captive, who fell in a gasping heap at their feet.

"Arthur and all the mutants have an interest in that large water mass south of Tadgehill. Let's see if he has regrouped there." Kiri Ung marked Stalker's sudden stillness with interest.

*

Breathing, the simple act of breathing once taken from granted, and now a pain-filled experience became Kai's next target. Using his new found talents he focused inward. This time the glow came sooner. Broken ribs realigned to begin knitting together. Gasping from the effort, he heard the tramp of many feet.

A drip of water landed on his face. *Why is the rock leaking water? What has Rowan done that the ceiling leaks in Haven?* Water damage marred the wall pictures done by some long dead Brethren to enhance his quarters. The smell of mold permeated everywhere. Footsteps halted outside his curtain. *Enough of them to hold me down while they cut off body parts.* Kai began a calming mantra.

Goat stepped into his alcove followed by six other Brethren. Kai almost wet himself in relief.

"Rowan's gone to meet with the Submariners." Goat grinned. "We figured this was our best chance. Can you take him down in a duel if you get fit?"

"Could anyone best my sire?" Kai allowed hope to flower. "I learned fighting from him. Give me energy to heal, and I'll take him on."

Goat turned to his companions. "See? I told you. He's game."

"He's a wreck," a dark-haired Brethren objected. "Look at him. He's got a smashed leg."

"Let him prove his claims, Storm." Goat looked to Kai, his eyebrows raised. "We let him suck our energy and then we'll see what happens. No harm to us with Rowan gone."

"I sparred with Copper," a gray-haired veteran offered. "I remember this lad. We should give him a chance."

The others nodded and looked to Goat. They moved closer.

"What would you have us do?" Goat asked.

"Link hands and include me in your circle." Kai held his breath, unwilling to believe his luck could get so good.

Brethren shuffled into a ragged circle. Each reached out to his neighbor. Goat and Storm joined hands with Kai. He drove inward to that new part of his gift. A rush of instant heat flared within him while he tried to focus on his leg. Bones shifted, making him groan in agony. Sweat ran down into his eyes. The heat increased until his body was soaked with sweat. Thirst clawed at his throat. Pain diminished from his leg, but the heat continued. Kai focused on his ribs. More excruciating heat rushed through him. His breathing eased. Strength flowed in on cool refreshing waves. He broke contact.

A circle of white-faced Brethren met his gaze with hard looks. They'd given their energy, and now they expected a result. Pulsing with their strength, Kai reached down to his leg to remove the splint. He thrilled at the freedom from grating pain. Hands helped him, eager hands that hoped against hope. He eased his legs over the side of his cot and stood.

Shocked eyes met his. Hands trembling with exhaustion helped his first step, but he didn't need help.

"Copper's son is come to free us," Goat husked. "My loyalty to you." He knelt to Kai, offering his open hands in pledge. One by one, all the Brethren dropped to their knees in a gesture of fealty.

Shaken, Kai accepted their pledge with respect. "I'll duel Rowan for the leadership when he returns. In the meantime go get some rest. Come to me in the morning with as many trustworthy Brethren as you can muster. We need to make some changes around here."

Slow Brethren smiles lighted every face. As a group they rose, looking at each other with renewed hope.

Chapter 34

AVRIEL AWOKE TO voices raised in argument. She picked out Kai's name and submerged herself in her own world of wishful thinking. She didn't want to hear more hard facts from behind the safety of her shuttered eyelids. Someone must have stripped off her wet clothes, leaving her slightly damp in her undergarments. Her pleasant daydream of lying in Kai's embrace to the sweet rhythm of love dissolved in a heartbeat. Her eyes snapped open to see Haystack looking at the swell of her abdomen. Avriel grabbed at the fabric of a cloak to hide her body.

"When were you going to tell us?" His hard blue eyes riveted her like skewers of ice and a frown marred his pleasant features.

The sharp rumble of disagreement continued in the background from the forward section. Plush gray setting muffled the sounds in the aft. Slick gray walls reflected the flash of running lights. Those walls closed a fraction closer with their promise of no escape from Haystack's question. Behind the aft door lay both submersion chambers. A way out for any Submariner, but not a Terran. She met those twin icicles.

"So now you know." Avriel tried hard to swallow, but her mouth felt as dry as yesterday's ashes. *I won't be shipped to Avalon. I will stand in Kai's place.*

Haystack's face lit with a smile that made the cabin seem brighter. "That's a special babe you carry."

"Spare me the speech full of platitudes." She curled into a sitting position, her hand on her abdomen. "My child and my life. I make my own choices."

303

Haystack's smile blossomed. "Kai might want a say in the safety of his only child."

"He's gone." She thrust down the instant shaft of pain that the admission cost her. "I'll not cower in Avalon while I can fight for his son's right to a free life on the surface."

"Noble sentiments." Haystack squared his shoulders, and the frown returned. "The game's changed." He laid one calloused hand over hers. "Avriel, Kai's alive."

Part of her wanted to believe so badly, but her mind's eye showed Kai flying through the air like a wet rag. "You lie."

"Brethren don't lie." His hand squeezed hers. "He's hurt, and he's a prisoner in Haven. Huber found out when he delivered Linden to Avalon. Haven is . . . was our home base. Their leader is using Kai as a bargaining chip to get the supplies Haven needs."

"It's a trick." A faint fluttering like a butterfly's wings stirred in her mid-section. "I saw him hit water like a corpse. The saurian had him at its mercy."

"Shadow doesn't think so." Haystack reached out with his other hand to cup her chin, making her look at him. "She spoke to him. Do you think she wouldn't recognize her own son?"

Kai lives? Shadow thinks he's alive? Hope trembled into life. The butterfly wings stirred inside her again. *He's at Haven? Where's Haven?*

"Easy now." Haystack's eyes narrowed, marking his concern. "Don't go losing the babe."

Avriel's mind flipped. She viewed Haystack from a great distance. Hope began to wither. *This is not real. I'm fed pap to get me out of their way.* She thrust Haystack's hands away to roll on her side, facing the bland gray of upholstered seat backs.

Footsteps echoed on the metal floor. "Have you told her?" Arthur's deep voice said, so like Kai's that it cut a hole in her heart.

"She doesn't believe me."

304

Firm hands forced her to turn, facing her brother. "He's alive. I believe he's alive, so stop acting out."

"She's bearing his child." Haystack's words dropped like pebbles into a deep pool to send ripples outward.

"She's what?" A pulse began to beat in Arthur's temple.

"Going deaf, brother?" Avriel tired of this game to catch her out. She ripped aside her concealing cover. "Satisfied?"

Arthur's mind struck before she had time to draw another breath. She couldn't stop his invasion picking through the core of her being. He reached out to place a hand on her belly, his face lighting with a huge grin. The baby stirred within her.

"Got any boy's names lined up?" He settled back on his heels and removed his hand. "Kai will be astonished given his usual care to avoid paternity."

Anger flared through Avriel. She covered her body, glaring at both of them. "Why keep up the pretense that he lives now you know about the baby?"

"Losing your hearing, sister?" Arthur raised an eyebrow while his mouth quirked up in a grin. Haystack leered from behind him.

This was a cruel jest aimed at dumping her in Avalon.

Arthur's face settled into lines of concern. "I wouldn't mislead you over this. Kai *is* a prisoner in Haven. We are going to rescue him."

Avriel started trembling. She couldn't control her body. The light began to dim.

"He's alive." Arthur's voice cut through the cobwebs forming in her mind.

She fought to stay alert. "I'm not going to Avalon."

"That's a certainty." Her brother's mouth formed a hard line. "You're carrying a gifted son. I won't risk him falling into Seer hands."

"But I thought . . . Vortigon is there." Avriel tried to catch some sense of reality in chaos.

"Vortigon is safe because he isn't gifted." Arthur's eyes hardened into amethyst shards. "I won't risk a gifted child enduring the life I led."

My son will be free born. The thought fluttered away as feathers in the wind. *Kai is alive.* The fragile bud of hope burst into flower. Her eyes filled with tears.

"Easy." Arthur caught her hand. "I'll deal with our father, but you must promise me that you will obey my restrictions."

Avriel floated on a cloud of bliss. She didn't care what her brother demanded. "I agree."

"That's nice because I am restricting you to this submersible." He gave her a lopsided grin. "Kai will never forgive me if anything happens to the mother of his child."

Caught, Avriel looked into his incredible eyes, defeated. As much as she wanted to help free Kai, she had to protect their son.

*

The stench of carnage from gobbets of flesh fouled the air. Kiri Ung stumped around the deserted lakeside camp looking for some clue as to what had happened. He felt sick.

"Stalker!"

"Yes, master." The Terran's response came loaded with glee.

Kiri Ung let out a breath of relief. Stalker wouldn't be so sure of himself if Arthur were a casualty, would he? "Your take on this mess?"

Stalker looked around at the wrecked harness and blood spattered trees.

"I don't see any weapons lying around."

Stars, my pet is right. A sweep beam will take only living matter. Te Krull attacked an abandoned camp. He missed the prize. Relief coursed through him. Without Stalker's help, he couldn't begin to guess Arthur's next move. Kiri Ung glared over the rippling waters. *What did Arthur want here? If I find it, then I have a bartering chip.*

He turned to Na Pan. "I want echo sounding done in this lake." Kiri Ung ignored the look of studied patience. "Whatever might be buried in the mud of this sink hole is to be transported to our skyship. I don't care if it's the size of a grain of sand." He noted Stalker's look of horror. "Begin."

*

Kai strolled into the common room he remembered from his childhood with his entourage at his back. Shocked stares greeted him.

Games of dice ceased, and in one corner a multiple rape intention, died in the birthing. The girl involved edged toward him on her knees. He gestured to direct two of his guard to bring the young female into his orbit.

"There are going to be some changes around here." He stared down angry looks directed at him. "You all saw my condition when I was brought here. Anybody wanting to challenge me will raise his hand and then precede me to the fighting arena. I'll give no quarter."

Eyes turned down. They knew he shouldn't be able to walk, let alone issue a death challenge. A slow muttering began. The name of his sire reverberated in that cavern. One Brethren stood up against him. A burly brute, who towered him by four inches.

"Challenge accepted, but not in the fighting grounds." The burly Brethren grinned at his comrades. "Here, where all can see."

"So be it." Kai stripped down to his loincloth. His men touched him, trying to give him life energy, but he didn't draw from them. He didn't want that advantage.

Brethren cleared away benches and chairs. Others brought torches for more light. Kai advanced into the area of combat. He hefted a sword that Goat had supplied, testing its balance.

His antagonist stripped to the skin, leering at the young girl cowering behind Kai's supporters. He strode forth, confident of his strength and fighting powers.

307

Kai pushed down feelings of regret, not wanting to kill, but knowing he must to prove himself. He met an instant attack, parrying the blow that sent shock waves through his arm.

Circling, gauging each other, the two ignored their audience. Kai blocked an overhead blow that nearly sent him to his knees.

"Rowan will reward me for taking your head." the Brethren's threat came out in a hiss.

Kai broke off, studying his opponent. They circled. He struck an upward blow to the chest that was met by the Brethren's blade.

The Challenger screamed, leaping to deliver a devastating swipe at Kai's neck, but Kai wasn't there. He'd guessed the move to sidestep. The force of his opponent's own descent impaled him on Kai's up-thrust sword. Shocked eyes met his. Shuddering started. He withdrew the blade from a now quivering carcass. "Next?"

Silence wove around the cavern. "As I was saying before this minor interruption, there will be significant changes." Sweating, Kai faced them all down. "No forcing of women for a start. If you're not prepared to construct an enticing seduction, then expect to remain celibate."

Shuffling and angry mumbles followed his directive, but not one of the dissenters met his gaze. Satisfied smirks and sidelong glances from women spurred his next order. "We're Brethren, brothers and sisters who belong to the same family. That means all women will put their efforts into making Haven into a home for us once more."

Filthy rush mats littered the floor. The trestle tables shone with grease mixed with food remnants and dirty dishes. Kai sought out each of the women present, letting them see his disgust. Men now wore grins discarded from the women.

"I can see brothers with ripped clothing and who bear wounds. I see sisters terrorized by the presence of men." He paused, letting his words sink in. He almost had them. "Haven was our place to have the life denied us by forts. Let's work together to make it so again." Mumbling and whispers echoed.

Nearly. "What of our children? Where are the instructors of our young? Who brings our future family to their full potential?" Heads hung down. A small, wizened boy snatched a slimy mess from under the nose of a brother, bolting to consume his prize under a table. "Are we savages? Every male will stand father and every female will stand mother to any child."

Shoulders straightened. A brother hooked the now kicking child from under his refuge to put him in front of a full plate of food. The child's eyes bulged. He grabbed at this feast.

Voices started at a mutter to grow into a chanting roar. "Kai, Kai, Kai." Feet stamped, and hands pounded on tables.

Kai raised his fist for silence. The noise died as if sucked into a whirlpool. *Now they're mine.* "I know the rules. I call out Rowan for the right of leadership. There will be no ambushes. This fight is between him and me."

"But he's got implants." Ix's voice cut through the shocked silence.

"That's nice for him." Kai let the slow Brethren smile they could all recognize lift his features. "My strengths are part of who I am and growing. I healed in hours instead of months. Who thinks he can challenge me?" Not even a rustle of clothing violated the air. "Now let's get our home in order."

People started bumping into each other as they scurried to clear tables, sweep floors and dispose of rotting detritus. All of them, he noted with satisfaction. Men helped women and women sat men down to tend injuries with a confident, bossy air.

"Rowan's reflexes are beyond any here." Goat said as Kai dressed.

"I'll make a point to shit my pants when he walks in, then." Kai turned the same chilling slow smile on Goat. "My brother is on his way. If I don't take Rowan down, he will."

Every Brethren in his entourage drew close, listening. "Arthur is a Seer and a warrior. You wouldn't want to meet him in your worst nightmares."

"What does that make you?" A bone-thin Brethren asked, shoving the others aside.

"The next King of the Outcasts." Kai met that hard stare with one of his own. "Under my rule we will renew our alliance with Avalon. Arthur is going to be the next overlord of all the forts. Together, we will destroy our real enemy, the Nestines. We will reclaim our world to make it over into a place where no individual will ever wear a band."

Chapter 35

BLACK BLADE RESTED on an examination table attached to a bulkhead of Kiri Ung's ship. Not one of them could bear to touch it, not even Stalker. All of them gathered around, staring at it.

"Analysis?" Kiri Ung caught Na Pan's eye.

"Composition unknown, Properties unknown." Na Pan's shoulders drooped. "All I can tell you is that I get a death wish every time I reach for this cursed weapon."

"Stalker?" Kiri Ung rounded on his pet.

The Terran smirked, enjoying his moment of glory. "This is Arthur's sword."

"So?"

"You can't use it." Stalker's smirk widened. "Now we trade."

"Don't lose sight of the fact that you're food for us." He brought his gaze to bear on his pet, furious for the manipulation Stalker tried.

Every eye turned on them. Running lights illuminated the cockpit, winking off gray surfaces. Every chair swiveled to watch this confrontation.

"You want Arthur's cells, and he wants the sword." Stalker shrugged, relaxed in his position of power. "Te Krull wants to mate the next Queen, and that won't happen without Arthur. She won't draw breath unless I help you make contact."

"Your terms?" Kiri Ung made an attempt to prevent his crest raising, knowing Stalker would see it as a threat. He succeeded with an enormous effort.

"Almost the same as before," Stalker said. "Arthur's cells, only if he agrees, in return for the sword and the destruction of Moon

Base, which will follow your departure in the ark ships. A slow smile lit his face. "Your call."

"I generally like my meat raw." Kiri Ung let his claws extend, one by one. "However, singed Terran has a certain piquant flavor."

Stalker's cold smile didn't falter, but sets of muscles shifted in realignment. The Terran prepared to fight.

He's willing to die rather than bend to my will. Reluctant admiration held Kiri Ung's rage in check. "Stalker, your logic is flawed. If Te Krull takes Arthur, he won't worry if his prize is living or dead. There is enough genetic material in an intact hair root to serve the purpose."

"You control Moon Base." Stalker's jaw jutted, and his fists balled.

"The stakes have changed." Looking around at the other Nestines, their deflated crests and lost looking expressions, Kiri Ung accepted a trust placed on him by Shi Nom in its entirety. "Without our Queen . . ." He struggled to prevent his voice from breaking. "Te Krull will be granted access on my orders. I'll not allow my race to die for the sake of preserving my position, or my life."

Stalker suddenly froze. Kiri Ung prepared for a fight that could only end in his pet's death and the end of all hope.

"No!" Na Pan's roar of warning stopped the killing blow. "Don't hurt him! He's doing it again."

"Doing what?" Stalker didn't blink or move. Kiri Ung turned to his navigator for answers.

"He did that and then he started yelling for us to go help you." Na Pan edged to stand between Stalker and Kiri Ung. "Let him finish."

Stalker's eyes blinked into focus. "Arthur is in danger. Want to fight for your position as Regent, or would you prefer to curl up and let Te Krull win?"

Kiri Ung's crest pumped into full erection at the insult. Na Pan held out his arms to block any attempt at attack.

"I think I'm speaking for all of us." Na Pan glanced at Shu Gra and the sky pilot. "We served under Te Krull. We'd prefer any alternative that includes getting new Queens."

"Even if that means a generation ship? Terraforming a new planet?"

"Te Krull won't want multiple Queens." Na Pan's crest rose. "Look at the Terrans. We cull free thinkers and still they evolve. Look at us. Have we kept pace?"

"How many generations before all Terrans escape our control?" A chilling possibility thrilled through Kiri Ung. "Are you fertile, Stalker?"

The Terran raised his black slave bracelet for all to see. "Ask yourself that question."

The easy answer alerted Kiri Ung. *He's male, and he should be bitter. He's hiding something.*

"Stalker lies by misdirection." Na Pan grabbed the Terran's raised arm. "He's not as warm as he should be wearing that color band."

Stalker wrestled his arm free, admitting the truth by his action. The implications shook Kiri Ung. *This one and how many others?* Shi Nom's confession came back to haunt him. Without these special Terrans there could be no future Queens. *By the egg, we can't contain them, or eradicate them. Te Krull will though.*

"Readjusted terms," he offered Stalker. "We destroy Moon Base, leave in the ark ships, and give you the weapon in return for cells from Arthur and every gifted Terran male."

"That would be the Brethren with my gift of foreseeing." Stalker edged away from Na Pan. "What about Te Krull?"

"Your planet, your problem. There's no room in the arks for Te Krull and his followers." *That solves one problem, and it cuts down on the low-grade boneheads vying for position by pure brute strength. I'd be leading the intellectuals to a new future with many Queens."*

313

"There are a few class 'm' planets charted beyond this solar system," Sha Gru supplied. "Exploring would give us a challenge we've always lacked."

"We challenged the Terrans, and they've evolved. What could we achieve?" Kiri Ung looked around. Every crest stood proud. "Terms agreed."

*

Arthur piloted an erratic course in the deeps. A dull thump to the port bow sent the vessel sideways.

"We've got to find depth," Merrick called, fighting to regain control of the stabilizers.

"How the hells do they know where to find us?" Dragon hung onto the back of his chair, bleeding from a deep gash in his temple.

"Another incoming." Huber looked up from his console with a bleak expression.

"We've sprung a leak in the aft section." Circe staggered, white-faced around the shaking vessel, handing each Terran a stasis disk. "None of us can survive at this depth."

"We die if we surface." Arthur killed the forward thrust. A detonation from directly ahead rocked the craft. *And we're dead if we don't.* One Nestine ship might get lucky, but two would triangulate them. He couldn't risk going deeper with a breach.

"Shells," Huber stared at his screen, his mouth slack. "They're weaving around each other. They're fighting!"

"You sure?" *Eel's tits, what is going on?* Arthur set his course for shallow water to hug the coastline. The submersible shuddered at this change in direction.

"There's more water coming in," Haystack shouted from the rear.

Arthur turned. Haystack and Avriel held destroyed chairbacks against a fracture in the hull. Dragon gutted more seating to plug another split.

"Shit, I've got to surface. It's our only chance. We're going up. Merrick, send a call to Avalon. Tell them our craft is dying and that we'll be stranded. We're close enough to shore to swim for land if we have to abandon ship."

Huber's hand hovered over the emergency hatch control that would blow off the roof.

"Wait for my mark." The sound of water hissing out of fissures eased. The craft broke surface. Arthur killed another warning light. "Someone go get any container that'll hold vomit. This is going to be a bumpy ride without stabilizers."

"Land us then," Dragon yelled, pressing against a leak with a seat back. Water swirled around his ankles.

"Not yet." Arthur fought for control. "We're committed to Haven. I want to get us as close as I can and then I want a water exit." He met Dragon's angry glare. "The auto-pilot is about the only undamaged system left. When this craft dies, it must be in water too deep for any survivors. Huber, watch the position of those Nestines. If they head our way, then we evacuate."

*

Stalker spewed up his last memory of food into a reclamation chamber and then dry heaved. The ship dived, leaving his stomach near the roof. *Emrys, grant me mercy. Let me die right now.* Another violent lurch broke his grip on the unit. He skidded across the deck plates.

"They're losing speed," Na Pan called. "We hit their fuel cell."

"Head north," Kiri Ung ordered. "If we lose them, find a forest, land and turn off all power."

"They are going back." The sky pilot glanced around. "Do you want to draw them away from Arthur again?"

Stalker flew off the deck, held aloft by Kiri Ung's strong claws embedded in his tunic. The Nestine's muzzle curled in what might have passed for an expression of disgust on a Terran face.

Kiri Ung growled, shaking him, when another dry heave convulsed through him. "Stop it, right now." A second bone-jarring shake followed. "Have we bought Arthur enough time?"

Blood filled Stalker's mouth from where he'd bitten his tongue. He spat. "Might have."

"Te Krull's got reinforcements," Sha Gru called. He activated a hold screen to show three more Nestine ships quartering the area where Te Krull had dropped his last depth charge. Running lights glowed through the projected image.

"Let's hope our quarry made good his escape because we've just been outgunned." Kiri Ung shook Stalker loose from another heaving session. "Tell me if Arthur is clear."

"My gift doesn't work to order." Stalker braced for another jolting. His ears buzzed, and he had black spots swimming in his vision.

"Then make it." Kiri Ung retracted his claws, sending him to crash onto the deck plating in a heap.

Stalker tried. He concentrated on Arthur even as he distanced himself from personal cuts and bruises. Nothing happened.

"The mutant vessel is headed into deep water," Na pan called from his console. "I am getting signs of escaping air. They're in trouble and . . ." He swiveled round with a flattened crest to face Kiri Ung. "The vessel has just disintegrated."

"At what depth?" Kiri Ung's toneless question echoed around the gloomy flight deck.

"Not survivable, even for mutants." Na Pan studied the grid work floor as if it were the most fascinating sight he'd ever seen.

Shock sent fire blades into Stalker's mind. *No. Not like this. They can't be dead.* He tried to remember the inside of a submersible. *Was there a quick way out? Could any of them survive?* Silence thickened into a miasma of evil intent. Kiri Ung reached for his throat. Lights dimmed. Sound faded. A sensation of life and freedom overwhelmed him as his fey gift claimed his attention.

"Stalker?" Kiri Ung's yellow cat's eyes peered at him. "Someone go fetch the motion sickness hypo. I want my pet alert."

A cylindrical tube flew overhead to be caught in the Nestine's great paw. Pressure pushed against Stalker's neck to the sound of a quiet hiss. His stomach stopped contracting.

"What did you see?" The musky smell of Nestine from Kiri Ung intensified. "I won't hurt you. Just tell us the truth."

Stalker tensed in Kiri Ung's arms. He'd no idea how he'd come to be cradled by a Nestine, and he didn't like the proximity on many scores. Those immensely powerful arms clamped his own to his sides in an unbreakable grip.

"If Arthur's dead, I need to know." The cat's eyes of the Nestine narrowed to slits. "You're too valuable to damage. We know your worth to us now."

"The odds are in our favor." Stalker tried to swallow. He couldn't generate any spit in a dry mouth. His heart raced with his throat inches from Kiri Ung's predator fangs.

"And what does that mean?" Kiri Ung rocked him gently as if soothing a babe in arms.

"Arthur survived. I think all of them did."

"Queen's Mate . . . Regent, they couldn't withstand the pressure." Na Pan left his position to stand over them.

"Why do you think this is Stalker?" The gentle rocking continued as if to loosen his memories.

"I'd have gotten a sense of loss."

"Then why did the water boat blow apart at the depth it did?" A voice unused to patience tried to suppress frustration. Kiri Ung's muscles hardened.

"It must have been set to autopilot. Arthur wants to disappear." Mesmerized by those eyes, inches from his own, Stalker fought off Kiri Ung's mental compulsion with an effort that left him sweating. He became aware of the hard deck grid against his legs.

"Don't fight me," the Nestine's voice soothed. "We're on the same side now."

He's right. We are. Stalker merged his consciousness in sensations. He got a feeling of land under his feet. "Without the submersible they've got to find a base." The result of vomiting and injuries began to drain him. He yawned, exhausted.

"Shall I get a stimulant?" Na Pan peered down at him.

"No." Kiri Ung cradled Stalker against his chest as he stood. "Arthur will go to ground until all those searchers give up. I need our 'advantage' to rest before we start searching."

A padded sleeping mat met Stalker's back.

*

Fresh rushes crackled under Kai's feet when he led his entourage to a morning meal in the central cavern. Two Brethren playing dice looked up, guilty and scurrying to hide their game. He walked over to their table.

"Why did you stop playing?" Neither of them met his eyes. "Haven is our place to relax and enjoy ourselves."

The larger of the pair looked up, frowning through a mat of black hair. "We thought we had to work on cleaning."

"I want this place made over into our home, not a barracks." Kai looked around at all those trying to pretend they weren't listening. "Play is a part of that."

"Those two went out early to hunt." A woman looked up from scrubbing a tabletop nearby. "We'll be eating venison tonight."

"That will make a welcome change from rabbit stew." Kai grinned at the pair and continued to a very clean trestle table where a filthy child stuffed fresh-baked bread into her mouth. She started when he sat across from her, snatching her meal to her chest. Big blue eyes widened, and she tensed.

"Hello. I'm Kai, and your name is?"

"I didn't steal it." The wedge of bread crushed against her chest under the pressure of her frantic grip.

"No, that's your breakfast. Don't wreck it." His heart twisted at the sight of her sticklike arms. The smell of cooking bacon wafting on the air spiked his hunger. "Would you like something else to eat?"

"Bread's good." She broke off a hunk to stuff into her mouth; the rest cradled protectively.

"Do you like bacon?"

"Dunno. Never had any." A spark of interest flared in frightened blue eyes.

"Goat, would you tell the women that we'd really like some bacon? Maybe our friend will join us."

"What's the catch?" The child edged toward the end of the bench as Goat ambled over to the cooking fires.

"That you try something new to eat." Kai suppressed a gut wrench to keep his tone level. *What happened to these people?* "You might like it."

"What else?" She peered at him, brushing aside tangled brown hair. The scent of an unwashed body wafted from her.

"Perhaps you might consider a trip to the bathing pool?"

"That's off limits to us," a burly Brethren in his party cut in. "Rowan and his favorites have exclusive rights."

"Then they are the only ones now excluded." Anger made Kai hide his tight fists from the child. Turning to the man, he asked, "Your name?"

"Wormwood." The large man glanced at the child.

"Would you like to set up a bathing rotation for all?" Kai knew he needed a bath too. They all did. "Separate sessions for males, females and children. Make sure there are women to watch the children. I remember the pool being deep at one end."

"Your will, King." Wormwood grinned, moving off to implement orders.

"Is what they're saying true?" The child glared at him.

"What would that be?" Kai motioned his men to sit as Goat returned with two laden trenchers and a couple of women bearing wooden plates.

319

"Are you going to be our King?" The girl's eyes almost popped at the sight of bacon and scrambled eggs.

"Yes, I am your King."

"Can I have some of that stuff then?" Her eyes fixed on the steaming food.

Kai took a dish from one of the women and put what he thought the child could manage on it. He slid the serving over to her. She started to tremble.

"Are you my father?"

Kai battled to keep his voice steady. "No, but I can stand as your chosen father if you'd like."

"A real father?" Tension drained from the starved child. She managed a shy smile.

"Come to me with any problem," he offered, meaning it.

"Kai, you're going to get every waif in Haven claiming your attention," Goat warned.

"A ruler is supposed to be father to his people, whatever their size." Kai shrugged; aware the child had lost her fear of him. *How many more maggots infest this apple?*

Chapter 36

ERRICK SWORE AS he clambered down from a treetop. He jumped the last six feet, landing heavy and started to brush off twigs and leaves from his dark gray Submariner coverall.

"If I'd been intended to sit on treetops, I'm sure Emrys would have arranged a mutation to give me wings." He scowled at a hole torn in one sleeve.

Arthur emerged from under the shade of some low lying bushes where he'd left Huber guarding the stasis bound Terrans. Circe giggled from behind him. "Did you see any of those ships heading our way?"

"One veered off to the north, and another two joined the remaining one." Merrick grinned. "They are quartering the wreck site."

A fresh sea breeze ruffled Circe's hair as she ran past then to sniff some tall yellow flowers. Her nose turned up in disgust. "These don't smell nice."

Pleased to see her setting aside their near tragedy, Arthur ignored her comment. "Those Nestines might think we died if we're lucky. I like to make my own luck."

"They knew we had Terran's with us." Merrick hunkered down in a patch of shade. "They'll assume we'll take a river passage to stay out of sight."

"Then they'll decide we don't follow the expected path." Circe paused to sneeze, her nose covered with yellow pollen.

"Which is why we will take the river." Arthur grinned, beginning to enjoy the chase. "Just long enough to convince them, and then we revive our air breathers for a trek overland."

Merrick slapped a fly on his cheek, missing. "I'd like to see if Haystack has one of his insights before we leave."

"Best not." Arthur gently wiped the flower dust off Circe. "They'll be looking for heat signatures. If we keep those to the minimum then we'll make finding us inconvenient for them."

"Right. I'll go give Huber the bad news." Merrick stretched and headed into cover.

*

"Has your pet awakened?" Na Pan didn't turn as Kiri Ung closed the distance between them in the shaded grove of trees. The male seemed intent on a patch of sky just visible.

"No. He's drained." Kiri Ung unrolled a plas-sheet map of the suspected landing site and anchored it flat to the ground with two large rocks. Now he could see the details in topography. Turning off all power to their craft had disagreeable drawbacks. Lighting was one and food the other. "Have the pilots had any luck in their hunt?"

"They're stalking a herd of ungulates." Na Pan turned to face him. "They want tender meat and the adults are disobliging by clumping around the young."

One more hardship. "Total shutdown means no laz guns and no thought compulsion. I'd forgotten about that. How are they managing?"

"Once they figured their scent alerted the heard they split up to circle." Na Pan snorted. "I get the impression that they are enjoying themselves." He squatted down to study the map.

"This is where the water-craft wrecked." Kiri Ung extended a claw to isolate a deep sea grid. "It was headed south." Moving his claw due north, he hit on a river estuary.

"Too obvious." Na Pan studied the topography for inlets without high cliffs. "What about here?" He pointed to an area of sand dunes rolling back into scrub-land.

"No cover." He wanted Stalker, but his pet might need more rest for the strange ability to activate. "Arthur doesn't do the

322

expected." An incessant twittering of overhead birds distracted him. He repressed an instant urge to send them crashing into tree-trunks. "If I were him, I'd take the river route because it is the worst choice."

Na Pan glared up at the birds. "It would be nice to design our own world. Those pilots are having fun hunting."

"A world with no hoppers." Kiri Ung scratched at an angry welt in his fur. He wasn't prepared to let Stalker gain an upper hand, but a fresh beginning attracted him. The chance to break out of a rigid pattern and grow as a race. *How much fun have we ever had? We could take turns hibernating on the trip. No one need spend his life in travel, and we'd have a clutch of Queens in time.*

*

Clutching Dragon tight, Arthur rode an unexpected bore flood inland. Violent turbulence battered him, but it sped them all nearer their goal. *Submariners, we have to break free and head for shore.*

Why, when we're gaining ground? Circe objected, unencumbered by a Terran.

Nestines will track the surge to its fading point. Huber broadcast, his thoughts colored with warning overtones.

As one, they fought for the north shore to emerge, gasping with effort minutes later. Circe crawled to a bank of ferns, flattening a bed for herself.

Arthur leaned over Dragon to remove the stasis disk. He rolled on his back, blindly staring at a bank of fluffy clouds as his sire stirred to life.

"Where am I?" Dragon sat up, scanning the wide deep-banked river.

"A good way up the biggest river on this side of landfall."

"Then we're too close to Menhill for my liking." Dragon spat and stretched. "Hald held a grudge against me that his son has nourished with loving care. I'd be astonished if Keiran didn't try to take my head and mount it as a wall decoration."

Haystack's laugh rang out. "Menhill has a permanent contract for any Brethren willing to take you down. The price wasn't right."

Dragon's hand clamped to his sword hilt. He scrambled to his feet, eyes narrowed. "And what would've been the 'right price'?"

His arms locked around his knees; Haystack sat, grinning. "Oh, let's see, permanent reinstatement with all our faculties intact, the public execution of those that caused our sentence, a Gold Band for spouse and the treasure at the end of a rainbow. That sound about right?"

"Why?" Amusement warred with suspicion on Dragon's face. "I haven't welcomed Brethren in my fort for years."

Haystack shrugged. "You did once. We can't forget anything, ever. That's a part of our sentence."

"Any horses around here?" Merrick groaned into a tired sitting position. "I don't care how uncomfortable riding is. I want another set of legs under me."

"You're out of luck." Dragon extended a hand to haul Arthur up. "This is forest for leagues. No forage for wild horses. We're more likely to be hiding from flying lizards."

Shit! That's all I need. Arthur glared into the thick forest with distaste.

"Wings sound better than the jolting of horses." Huber raised an eyebrow, grinning at Arthur. "Can you go tame us a few birdies?"

Laughter erupted from all the Terrans. Submariners joined the fun, aware of the danger the creatures represented.

At least they can joke. Arthur dragged together the remnants of his energy to scan, but a thought worried into him mind. Saurians didn't have much of a brain. If he could tame a group of wild horses . . . he started to think through the concept. They'd need a way to harness the creatures and strapping to keep from falling off. Forests abounded with filament moss. He knew great tendrils of mutated moss hung from trees to lash into the faces of unwary travelers. It made a stout rope with a minimum of effort, but it stunk like a rotting carcass.

"Hey, Arthur?" Huber called, still laughing. "I wasn't serious."

"Maybe not, but I am." He returned the grin with a wicked one of his own. "Let's go find some filament moss."

Dragon grabbed his arm. "Arthur, these are flesh-eating predators."

"They're stupid, and they are an invisible form of transport." The more he thought about using the creatures, the better he liked the idea. "It would take us weeks to get to Haven on foot hiding from Nestines and other predators."

"I'm not happy with heights." Haystack frowned, shuffling his feet. "I also don't get a sense of threat from this plan."

"I'm not going anywhere near a flying lizard." Avriel marched over to him. "Count me out."

"Not a problem." Arthur patted her head. "We'll just put you in stasis for the trip. We'll also be able to land directly in Haven's compound without having to cross the Blanket Bogs."

"I'd prefer to get my feet wet." Avriel squeezed water out of her tunic.

"The Blanket Bogs are infested with thirty-foot long motion-sensitive snakes. They eat people whole," Arthur said, enjoying her look of horror. "Which would you prefer?"

*

Bugs flew in annoying circles around his head. Kiri Ung made a firm decision to view an ark ship database to see which ones were truly necessary for pollination. He didn't appreciate supplementing their diet.

The fire that Stalker made for them offered miserable warmth. Smells of charred flesh assaulted his sense of smell, but Stalker insisted on incinerating his portion of a very tender kill. Night closed in around the clearing bringing sounds of creeping creatures not worthy of eating. One drop of moisture landed on his fur followed by a succession of others. The Nestine pilots headed for their bunks in the ship, but he had to stay with Stalker until that lump of meat was burnt to his pet's taste. A creepy howl sounded, sending him into battle alert, but it didn't repeat.

"Those charred remains must be dust by now," he complained.

"I like my meat well done." Stalker turned the spit over a fire that didn't generate enough heat to warm Kiri Ung. "Go join your friends if a little water bothers you."

And have you sneak off? I don't think so. He resigned himself to getting wet. "What route do you think Arthur will take?"

Stalker paused, in the act of prodding the burnt remains. "Your guess seems a good place to start. I think he will leave the river before he needs to, though."

"In what direction?" Kiri Ung slapped at his leg to crush a bug.

"North. He has to contact Avalon, and the Outcast compound has the only transmitter that I know of."

"Will he take a direct route?" Kiri Ung knew of the place in the mountains. There wasn't a landing site big enough for a skyship.

Stalker removed the burnt mess from flames. "No idea."

"I thought I told you to keep a track on him."

Stalker looked up from his revolting feast. "I'm sure I told you that my gift doesn't activate on command."

Biting down on his frustration, Kiri Ung waited for Stalker to finish his meal before ushering him into the skyship.

*

Goat roused Kai from a deep sleep. He yawned, coming reluctantly awake.

"Riders are crossing the Blanket Bogs." Goat reported. "From the number, I think it's Rowan."

Is this my last day as King, or my first day of real power? Kai threw back his covers to begin dressing. *Avriel, this is all for you. Emrys, let me haunt him if I fail.*

"Do you need life force?" Goat's expression clouded with worry. "I can get a large group to fill your need."

"I'm healed. I don't need an unfair advantage." He wanted to win without the cloud of cheating over him.

Goat held Kai's weapons belt ready for strapping on. "Rowan has implants that make him invincible."

"Which is the reason I must meet him without your help." Kai shrugged. "I can't be your King unless I'm the best fighter. I won't use unfair advantage and leave that door open to all comers. I'll fight this duel in the way my father trained me. If I don't succeed, then Rowan will face my brother. Arthur won't cheat, either. He'll win by fair means."

"We don't want Arthur. We want you." Goat buckled up the belt.

"Fate falls where it will." Kai grinned. "I want to live."

"As challenger, it's your right to name the site of combat." Goat looked around the cavern as if already clearing a large area.

"Outside." Kai knew how much strength his mother gained from her replacement arm. Ix had hinted at so much more. *If I'm to die, then I want it to happen in the light of day.* All those hopeful faces looking at him dampened down the worm of fear that ate at his heart. *I can't let them rot in this hellhole. I need a home for Avriel, but I'm going to do this on my own terms. If I win, then it will be as rightful King.*

Events started happening at lightning speed. Brethren pressed him at their head to the cave mouth. Brothers scurried to clear an area in the forecourt of any debris. Others brought out trestle tables to lay them sideways for an area to protect onlookers. Most chillingly, a hurdle for a corpse was placed just outside the barricade. Sisters hustled children into the caverns, away from the death grounds.

Storm appeared from within, limping and bleeding from a cut leg. He handed over Kai's own confiscated weapon, shrugging. "I thought you might want your blade back. Someone else disagreed." A cold smile lifted his lips. "That brother just lost interest in the outcome of this duel."

Kai laid his sword on the ground while he stripped to his loin cloth. Rules of a death duel permitted no body armor. He shivered in the cool morning air.

"Watch his eyes," Goat advised as they waited. "Rowan has a habit of aiming at a man's privates. There are several worse than eunuchs in Haven who fought him."

Dirty bastard. Kai noted the warning with dread. He'd an idea Rowan might just try that with him. Hooves sounded in the entrance. Rowan pounded into the compound with his party. Shock widened those fat encrusted eyes. Chanting started. The word 'challenge' hissed in the air.

"So the mutant maggot wants to try his skill?" Rowan dismounted to leave his horse in the care of his men. "You'll not die, although you'll wish you had." He shed his clothing to reveal a bulky muscled frame. His ebony skin gleamed in the growing radiance of sunrise.

Birds twittered from nests in the heights. The rich smell of sweating horseflesh permeated the area. Kai braced for combat as Rowan lumbered toward him with a low held sword.

"I'm going to enjoy this." Rowan's teeth gleamed white. "You're going to crawl to me after this day is over."

Kai came on guard. The threats flowed over his head for what they were. "You killed my father, you bastard. This is for him."

Rowan charged. An overhead blow turned into a swipe at Kai's genitals at the last moment possible. Forewarned, Kai leapt out of range. Rowan circled, looking puzzled.

"So Ix has fixed your leg, has he? I'll take that courtesy out of his flesh, right around the heart."

Rowan danced into range. Blow followed blow. The extent of Rowan's implants surfaced. Kai barely held him off. They battled as the light died. Thrust, clash, parry. Kai's arm ached. Rowan began to breathe heavily. They broke off to circle.

"Give it up, mutant scum." Rowan gave Kai a death's head grin. "You can't beat me."

Kai concentrated. He'd established a pattern in Rowan's attacks; first the insult, and then the charge. It came, and he met it. Steel met steel. They circled once more.

Rowan began to favor his right leg, although Kai hadn't done any damage there. *A weakness. I have a chance.* Kai pressed his attack to focus on that leg. When they parted, Rowan bled from a cut to his sword arm.

"You're going to pay for that, bitch's whelp." Rowan plunged into a flurry of blows ending in a stab.

Kai looked at the sword sticking in his chest. He used his last strength to finish a swipe at Rowan's neck. The expression of astonishment from the severed head stayed with him as he dropped. His heart pounded, erratic, and light began to fade.

"Oh no, you don't." Goat touched him. "Do your thing. You can't leave us now."

He tried, reaching out for their energy. Many hands touched him to give him a supply of strength.

"Come on, lad. You've won," Storm cried, shaking Kai's tired bones. "Take from us."

He wanted Avriel to be there, but she wasn't. The heat from their input shook him.

"You can do this," Goat pleaded. "We've seen you. We need you to stay with us."

The erratic thump of his heart drowned out their voices into a senseless chatter. Light faded to a single point and then died.

Chapter 37

ARTHUR SAT ON a tree stump while he concentrated on submerging the minds of predators to obey his will. The others attached new-made harness to the now tractable flying reptiles. Controlling the beasts on ground was far easier than he'd imagined.

"We're set to go," Haystack called.

"Then divide up into groups." Arthur brushed leaf litter and moss off his pants to join the group. "Each of these beasts gets one Submariner and a Terran passenger except me. I'll fly alone so that I can maintain control."

He smothered the reptiles with his will while his group clambered into position, lashing themselves to the harness. His chosen mount, the male, looked perplexed when he mounted to a secure place over its neck. In position, Arthur transmitted his thoughts to the Submariners to haul up on the neck strap. At the same time, he released the lizards from absolute restraint. As a flock, they flapped from elevation. The jolt threw him back against the beast's spine ridge as it became airborne. For a moment the lizards parted, but Arthur grouped them with a thought of juicy prey to the north. His stomach protested at the sudden climb. Arthur caught sight of other pasty faces from unwilling riders.

The ground receded into tiny trees dissected by faint lines of trails. It looked so small from above. The formation set course to his direction.

Arthur, Nestine ship lights to the north. Huber transmitted.

Ignore them. Nestines won't be looking for us on flying lizards.

Huber's glee intensified as that ship passed overhead without altering course.

As the beasts climbed, their wings flapping, Arthur spotted a range of mountains. *There is my goal. I'm coming, Kai.*

*

"Regent, you told us to report anything unusual." Na Pan swiveled in his chair to face Kiri Ung.

He viewed his console screen, seeing a flock of mutant lizards under-passing them."And?"

"Lizards don't fly in formation, ever."

Kiri Ung caught an expression of shock from Stalker, lounging next to him.

"Make a wide circle, but keep these creatures in our sensor range." Kiri Ung noted Stalker tensing. "So my guess bears fruit! My prey can control animals at will. What else can he accomplish?"

"Are any Nestine ships following the flock?" His heart pounded.

"Te Krull is still concentrating on that river," Na Pan reported.

"Good. May he find the remains of a deserted site to his satisfaction." Kiri Ung almost smiled. "Follow that flock at a discreet distance."

*

Wind teared her eyes and the great flapping wings behind her created a lurching sensation. Avriel tried not to think of ground, so far below. Huber's strong arm around her waist stood between her and panic. *We're going to rescue Kai. I have to bear this. It is going to end.*

The beast began to circle, spiraling down on a current of air that sent Avriel's hair flying up. She smothered a scream.

"Steady, we're going to land." Huber hugged her tighter to his chest, his words coming over the rush of air. "There's Haven's

331

compound below." His arm went rigid, a band of steel around her. "Eel's tits, they're all out . . . there's been a fight."

The tension in him made her look. Far below, men ran for cover from the flock of descending saurians. Left in the panic, two bodies lay still in the forecourt. A glint of sunlight through the clouds lighted the long copper-colored hair of one of those fallen. The eyes of love picked out a bright red face veil on a heap of discarded clothes. One he'd stolen from her.

He's not moving. A scream without sound built to thrum its fear through her soul. The babe within her stirred, fluttering like a trapped bird.

Huber pulled on the makeshift reins to gain height.

"Land us now, or I'll take a shorter route." Avriel drew her blade, positioning it over the saurian's jugular vein.

"Let Arthur deal with this!" Huber stopped their ascent. He tried to grab her knife, but he relaxed his grip around her.

Avriel threw herself forward, lying along the bony neck ridge with her weapon now out of his reach while handy for a strike.

"Arthur's got them to stand down." Fear rasped through Huber's voice. "For pity's sake don't do anything stupid."

"Get this 'thing' on the ground right now or I'll do it my way." Kai hadn't stirred. Avriel strained to see a flicker of movement through the cloud of descending wings beneath them. She angled her blade to sever her lifeline even as the beast banked its wings for landing. The soft jolt of ground impact sent her into a flying roll. Winded, but not down, she started running.

Arthur was there before her kneeling by his brother. His expression told her all she needed to know before she glimpsed the deep wound in Kai's chest. Kai's gray face looked deathly. A brother with protruding brown eyes held Kai's head in his lap.

"Dragon!" Arthur looked over her shoulder. "Contain her. Get her away from Kai."

Arms closed around her, lifting her from Kai, struggling and kicking.

"Be still, daughter." Her father's deep voice husked in her ear. "There's nothing you can do to help him."

Helpless in that strong grasp, Avriel started to cry.

"You too." Arthur riveted the caring Brethren with a look of blank horror. "Stand clear from me if you value your sanity."

The man eased Kai to the ground, backing off with a strange expression. One that looked a mixture of hope and fear.

Arthur put his hand over Kai's spurting wound. His eyes closed to give him a stillness of person that went beyond the veils of death. A strange blue light flickered around him and then extended to Kai.

"Ocean's deep, a gestalt," Huber's shocked words came from behind. "Everyone, back off or we're all worse than dead."

Dragged away by her father, Avriel trembled, watching the light engulf both men until their shapes seemed to merge into one blue form. A cerulean light that pulsated with flowing tentacles of power. She blinked, unable to bear the brightness. Kai, with Arthur holding him, came into sharp focus. Kai's eyes were open. His face looked pale, but not tinged gray with death.

"Shit, what was that?" Haystack shouldered forward.

"They've done it again." Merrick wore an expression of awe. "They've formed a gestalt and gotten away with it."

"Kai?" Avriel sobbed wanting to go to him, needing to be with him and hoping against hope that she didn't dream.

White-faced Brethren drew closer to the brothers. Disbelief at what they had just witnessed wove through the air in a palpable miasma.

"Not yet, Avriel." Her father held her firm even though his arms trembled. "I don't have a name for what I just witnessed, but I'll not risk my grandchild near them until Arthur gives his leave."

"Arthur?" Kai whispered.

"I'm here now."

"Your timing could use improvement." Kai sucked in a deep lungful of air. "For a moment I thought I'd be joining the Wild Hunt."

"I had an interesting form of transport." Arthur dismissed the saurians with a flick of his hand. They took off for a roost on the heights of Haven. "I gather, from the decapitated corpse that you have been rather preoccupied?"

Kai sat up, looking around. His eyes fixed on Avriel. "I sort of needed a place to offer my Queen. That one got in my way." He grinned, looking tired but happy.

"Kai, Kai, Kai!" The Brethren chant started. They inched closer to the brothers, reaching out to touch Kai. Faces lit with a fanatical devotion that awed Avriel. Hands touched the wound that had healed. Hands separated him from Arthur to lift him high as they bore him into Haven in triumph.

Avriel struggled to free herself from her father's strong grip.

"No, you don't." Both his arms tightened around her. "They've just accepted him as their King. He belongs to the Brethren now. Let them give him his moment of glory. He's earned it."

"He needs to know of our child." Avriel tried to pick apart his interlocked fingers.

"And so he will." Her father rocked her against him. "He'll be dueling with me if he doesn't accept responsibility."

Brethren flowed around Arthur giving him a wide berth. They flooded into Haven on a surge of excitement leaving the renegades and the corpse of their former leader ignored in the compound. Arthur glanced up at the high crannies where saurians perched. Two of them swooped down to snatch Rowan's body and severed head. They settled on a lofty shelf to start a feeding frenzy.

"Sorry about that." Arthur's lips lifted in a feral grin. "I didn't want any of the Brethren to start thinking about trophies. Kai won't appreciate sharing his new home with a permanent reminder of the man who murdered his father."

334

"Rowan killed Copper? He didn't tell me that." Avriel wondered why not.

Something in her expression must have touched him because he walked over to her, his every step betraying his exhaustion. His hand felt cold as he cupped her chin, making her look into his sad violet eyes.

"Kai and I are a sword of the same forging." Arthur wrapped his free arm around Circe, who'd snuggled up to him with eyes brimming. "One side of the blade is him, and the other is me. What happened here was as much his doing as it was mine. When we form a gestalt, every memory is shared. Think hard about how different we are and if you want to share your life with one like us."

"What are you?" Her father's unsteady tone husked from behind her. His arm tightened in protection.

Arthur's bitter laugh rang empty on the deserted killing grounds. Huber and Merrick looked sad. Haystack reached out to touch Arthur's shoulder, and his face betrayed compassion.

"I'm Project Arthur and my brother is Project Kai. Both of us are the end result of a complex breeding schedule designed to create a creature with power enough to free Emrys from his captivity in Avalon." Hard amethyst eyes bored into her. His mouth formed a thin line laced with pain. "Both of us are something other than human. Our powers are growing. Can you bear us? Let Kai go if you have any doubts."

"Will Kai become like you?" Avriel feared this Submariner brother. A glance up at the heights showed her saurians now settled to roost. No doubt at his command.

"Kai is me as I am him." Arthur hugged Circe closer. "We are a weapon that was forged to fight for freedom. Only death will stop our tracks and even then we wait in a trap of Emrys' creating until we are born again to continue the battle."

"Keys of the Kingdom." The words flowed from Avriel. The childhood game of strategy now seared her soul. "Warriors will fight to the death for a cause if the women they love commit to rear their children alone."

Arthur took his hand away. "Release her, Father. She is a fitting Queen for the Outcasts."

Avriel stumbled forward in sudden freedom. *They aren't following me. Why won't they back me up?* Then it came to her. She needed to fight her own battle to establish a place with the Brethren. Fear warred with love and lost. She wanted Kai, whatever he was. She walked through ranks of Brethren in a huge cavern and was unnoticed, save for one pair of violet eyes. Those eyes gave her courage to approach a high table where her soul mate waited.

He held up a hand for silence. "We have a War Maid amongst us."

All eyes turned on her at Kai's declaration.

"What does a Gold Band lady desire from the King of the Outcasts?" Kai deliberately leered, eying her in a way that sent ripples of laughter through the gathering.

He's giving me a chance to reject him. He knows what Arthur told me. She accepted that if she continued she'd lose her status and become one of them for real.

"I want a father for our child." Avriel voiced her challenge, sorry that she had to broadcast her news in front of all but needing to see his reaction.

Kai's eyes widened. His jaw clenched, and his hands formed fists. "Is that all?" He stood, walking around the table to front her.

Silence cracked rocks. Eyes watched her breathe. Heart pounding; Avriel took another step closer.

"I'll trade being a Gold Band for the right to love the man I choose above all others."

A hiss of shock broke from many lips. Kai's smile lit the cavern as the first burst of sunshine after winter.

"There will be no going back if you join me." He took her hands in his.

Looking up at him, Avriel didn't care what he was, or what he might become. He was Kai, and that was who she loved. "I accept permanent loss of status."

A hum of approval rumbled through the Brethren. Slow smiles lit many faces.

"Does your father agree the match, and has he expectations from it?" Kai scanned the back of the cavern over the sea of heads.

"I have one demand for this union to take place." The Duke of Tadgehill's voice boomed with authority. "Continue to fight against Nestines. My sword will join with yours in this war."

"Conditions accepted." Kai embraced her. She could feel his heart thumping. "Haven has a Queen."

The chant started immediately. "Kai, Kai, Kai."

Amid the noise, Kai set her away from him, staring into her eyes, a frown drawing his eyebrows together. "A child?"

A wave of panic swept over her. Arthur's words about Kai avoiding paternity returned for a chilling visit.

"A gifted child, my brother's memories confirm." His eyes narrowed. "I can stop this pregnancy if that is your wish. The child won't be human."

Fluttering protest agitated inside her. "He has as much right to life as any other. I won't deny the product of our love."

"Keys to the Kingdom, indeed." Kai's lips closed over Avriel's to the cheers of Brethren. A tiny part of her wondered how he knew of Arthur's comment made after the gestalt.

Chapter 38

SCREENS FLICKERED INTO life, displaying a long-range view of the place Outcasts called Haven. A bleak black mountain blistered with spindly vegetation backed a flat area spotted with wooden and stone huts. Scabrous swamp circled a smaller rock formation hugging to the forefront of the complex with one narrow gorge permitting entry. On the peaks, a flock of saurians preened amid a small heap of glistening bones. Too small for a running beast.

"That was a man." Stalker leaned over Kiri Ung's shoulder, intent on the screen.

"Including an enemy in the food chain is the neatest form of disposal." Kiri Ung's respect for Arthur rose by several notches.

"That could be Arthur." Na Pan whirled around from his console. A violent move that clawed the pair of them into turning.

"That flock is still under control," he said, noting Stalker smiled in a way that chilled Kiri Ung. He continued, trying to ignore that look of triumph, "Na Pan, put up a force field around that compound. No one leaves, including those saurians. When they get hungry, things should start to get interesting."

Stalker grabbed his throat, squeezing. They fell in a heap, rolling on the hard metal grid work. Kiri Ung fought to get those hands from his neck without hurting his pet. He rolled on top of Stalker and by force of sheer weight crushed the air out of the Terran. Stalker battled to catch his breath, his hands now pushing to gain air. Kiri Ung rolled off and onto his feet in one fluid movement, his heart pounding. Every Nestine had a laz gun leveled at Stalker.

"Stand down. He's learned not to challenge me."

Stalker spasmed, whooping in air, helpless. Kiri Ung extended his claws to snag the front of his pet's tunic, hoisting him to dangle.

"I'll remember your behavior the next time I crave flesh." He got some satisfaction from the way Stalker's eyes bulged. "Na Pan, alter an implant for location and transmission only. I don't want a drone, but I do want a re-acquirable snack."

Stalker's screams sheered through his senses when Na Pan performed the procedure on his flailing and suspended victim. Once the implant was in, terrified brown eyes met Kiri Ung's.

"Listen and learn." Kiri Ung dropped his captive, amused when Stalker landed in an untidy heap. "I can get you anytime I wish, and I can see through your eyes, hear through your ears and know your thoughts." He almost felt sorry for the horror he could see thrumming through the Terran. "If you disobey, you will become aware of my displeasure in a way that will exceed your darkest nightmares. Do you understand?"

Stalker swallowed, wide eyed.

"Give him a taste of punishment." Kiri Ung glanced at Na Pan, holding a control unit ready. Stalker thrashed, screaming in agony. A wet patch spread from the Terran's crotch to drip down the grid work flooring.

"You will cleanse and then you will begin negotiations to acquire Arthur." Kiri Ung backed away from the odor of liquid excrement. "The terms are simple. He gets the sword in exchange for living tissue."

"And . . . the Moon Base?" Stalker looked down, his fists clenched.

"That is a decision for our next Queen."

"You promised!"

"We have the sword." His crest erected, full and pulsating. "Arthur wants it." Kiri Ung skewered Stalker with a thought cleanse command. The Terran scrambled to his feet, eyes bright with hatred, but helpless to resist.

339

*

Cheers reverberated in the cavern. Kai ignored them, lost in Avriel's blue eyes. *She bears my child. Our child. She gives up her status for me.* He drew her close, wanting her urgently.

"I take Avriel, daughter of Duke Uther of Tadghill to be our Queen with her father's consent. Let the celebrations commence." He swept her up in his arms, marching through ranks of cheering Brethren, who reached out to touch him on the way to his alcove. Once the curtain swished into place behind him, he kissed her, savoring her in a way that fired his senses.

She pushed him away, her eyes wide. "Kai, you've been wounded."

His hands already peeling away her clothing, Kai grinned. "Not anymore." The gestalt healed all wounds, and his Brethren gave him energy, but a trail of doubts disturbed him. He paused, trembling before her. "I can't alter what I am."

"You're the man I want." Avriel pressed against him. "I don't care how you survived."

Kai offered up a silent prayer to Emrys for the gestalt while he stripped her. Avriel unfastened his clothing, helping him free of them. Sweet soft flesh thrilled his exploring hands. He eased her down on his bed, throbbing harder when she opened to him.

One last doubt halted his entry. "Will this hurt our baby?" He paused on the brink, wanting her, yet not prepared to risk their child.

"There would be a lot of angry-looking men with pregnant partners if it did." She wrapped her legs around him, thrilling him with her silken embrace.

Kai thrust, and they moved as one enjoying each other in a gentle game of love. She closed around him, pulsating to create a release that made him cry out.

Sunk in the depths of her, Kai cursed when the curtain swished back. He withdrew to face Storm, who looked at the floor as if he'd never seen one before.

Yanking some cover over Avriel, he reached for his leggings. *Shit, this must be bad, or he wouldn't have burst in. What now? Storm's holding back because of Avriel. She's earned the right to share bad tidings.*

"Speak." His voice sounded rough even to his own ears. Kai didn't care.

"Perhaps you want to see for yourself?" Storm shuffled, darting a glance in Avriel's direction.

"I need to know what I'm going to face." Kai pulled his tunic over his head.

"Best not, in front of our Queen."

"Storm, she's a War Maid, who has seen more than her share of grief and death." His heart lurched at Avriel's white face and set expression. Meeting his eyes without any trembling, she pulled the covers tight around her.

"There's a Nestine skyship hovering over Haven." Storm's jaw muscles worked hard before he continued. "They've returned a captive. One of your group. Your brother wants to talk to him, but we're not happy letting a drone into Haven."

Kai glanced back at Avriel. "Join me as soon as you're decent. There will be no secrets between us."

"Be careful." Her beautiful blue eyes went wide with concern.

He tried to smile, hoping his expression didn't feel as false as he thought it might look. *Emrys help us, Stalker knew so much. What am I walking into?*

Kai followed Storm into the main cavern. All the women and children were gone. Eyes of every warrior followed him as he joined Arthur and Dragon.

"Where is he?" Kai wondered where they had Stalker confined.

"In the compound with thirty crossbows trained on him. Haystack and Circe are watching him." Arthur glared around at the gathered Brethren. "His mind is his own, but he's frightened. I didn't want to probe him until you were here."

341

"Do we need a gestalt?" Kai's stomach contracted. The thought of that joining terrified him. At the back of his mind sat the horror of permanent unification.

"If he is a drone that might be our only option." Arthur's lips formed a hard line. He looked as uncomfortable as Kai felt.

Avriel joined them to stand by her father. She'd chosen to wear a gray Brethren robe that covered her from shoulders to feet.

"Let's go see what the Nestines want from us." Kai squared his shoulders. That Nestines had located Haven sent ice shards down his spine. "They haven't attacked us, so they must have another reason."

He marched out to meet his fate. Stalker stood white-faced as a target for Brethren arrows in the center of the silent compound.

"Are you visiting?" Arthur called, stopping a few paces out of the cave mouth. "Or perhaps planning to stay?"

Stalker glanced up at the silver gleaming skyship. "The Nestines are offering a trade. They've got the sword. It's the real thing. I can't touch it and nor can they."

Arthur's face set in hard lines. "The terms?"

"Not good." Stalker shuffled. "They want a sample of Arthur's skin and that of every gifted Brethren. They are offering the sword and the destruction of Moon Base in return. Also, they will set out for a new home in the stars."

"Where's the maggot in this meat?" Kai didn't believe the Nestines would concede so much for so little.

"They're split into different warring factions." Stalker looked down. "My master is one step ahead of his enemy. He is going to lose unless he trades."

"And our alternative is?" Arthur's face lost all trace of color. He closed the distance between them.

"Fight a war against both sides and the sword will be dumped in the void of space."

Arthur grabbed Stalker's shoulder, pulling him around and lifting long brown hair from the man's neck. "What have they done to you?" He urgently gestured for Kai to join him. The raw edge of a recent wound betrayed the mark of an implant antenna.

Stalker's fist clenched. "Made me their eyes and ears, and they can drop me in screaming agony anytime I don't do what they want."

"How many Queens do they have?" Arthur released his hold.

Stalker groaned clutching at his head, his breath coming in ragged gasps.

Kai reached out for Arthur's arm. "He can't answer. Look at him."

"Enough! I withdraw the question." Arthur looked at Kai through narrowed eyes. "There is more going on here that we don't know. Kai, stay linked with me, we might need an edge."

He joined hands with Arthur, dreading the connection if it came.

"Nestines?" Arthur faced Stalker. "We want a meeting with one of you. I'll grant a truce for the duration." His hand squeezed Kai's. "If there is any attempt to snatch us into your ship you will find an enemy you can't contain. This is a promise."

A blue beam expanded from the belly of the ship to envelop Stalker, lifting him. At the same time, another figure descended. This one wasn't human.

"Hold fire!" Kai ordered, whirling to catch each archer in his gaze. "They are doing what we want. I don't want any accidents." He turned to confront the Nestine. It towered over him, a shaggy biped that couldn't conceal predator tusks in a face out of the seventh hell. Its arms spread wide in a gesture of good faith.

"State your real issue," Arthur ordered.

"What do you know of us?" The Nestine's crest pumped into full erection.

"Everything that counts." Arthur smiled in the Brethren way. A chilling challenge. "Why do you think I asked about your Queens?"

The Nestine unsheathed its claws. A cloud scudded over the sun to send shadows into the compound.

"I know about Greenly." Arthur tensed, battle ready.

"That's impossible!" The Nestine's crest wilted like a broken leg.

Through their link, Kai could see images of a man engaged in making a species for the sole purpose of his own survival. The human cells going into the final product created a Queen who could produce offspring.

"The Nestine needs us." Kai tried to shift aside the reason why. He didn't want to deal with the implications.

"Full disclosure, or there is no reason for you to remain." Arthur met his glance with a firm expression laced with horror.

"We have one potential Queen egg left to us." The Nestine's face muscles shifted into grief. "If we trade, then I'll have a viable daughter. Without her, our species will die."

Kai swallowed a gasp. *We have one of their leaders.*

"What of the other faction?" He wanted answers.

"I'm Regent. I hold Moon Base while my rival has every fort. If I take our people to find a new home, then he will eventually die without perpetuating more of us." The crest inflated. "Your people will gain freedom in time."

Shadows lengthened, and a chill wind whipped through the compound. On the heights, saurians flapped their wings to maintain heat.

"What guarantee do we have that you will honor any agreement?" Arthur's tone dripped acid.

"My word." The Nestine looked down at Arthur. "I am Kiri Ung, former Queen's Mate and now Regent."

"You've been honest with us. Now we must decide where we're going with your terms." Arthur glanced at the Brethren aiming weapons from various positions of cover. "Return Stalker to us without an implant."

"Not an option." Kiri Ung narrowed his cat-like eyes. "I'll return him as is. I can collect him anytime I want in that state."

"Keep him, then." Kai bristled at the idea of a spy in Haven.

"You're closing communication?" Kiri Ung's eyes went dark as the irises expanded.

"We'll accept Stalker if you let him speak freely." Again, Arthur squeezed Kai's hand in warning.

"Terms agreed." Kiri Ung opened his maw in the caricature of a smile.

The blue beam once more performed the exchange in the space of minutes.

"Guards." Kai motioned two muscular Brethren forward. "Escort our guest to an alcove and make sure he doesn't leave." As they took the captive away, Kai sensed Avriel staring a hole in his back. "I call a general council in the main cavern, and I want full attendance."

Now Kai experienced the full weight of leadership. Brethren ran to do his bidding, but he wondered at their reaction when they shared the truth that must be told. Arthur shrugged, releasing his hand. Kai turned to a white-faced Avriel. She joined him, holding her head high.

"You're not going to trade with our enemy?" Winter looked out through the ice in her eyes.

"That depends on whether we decide to meet their demands." He took her cold hand in his. "We need that sword and having half the Nestines gone will give us more than a fighting chance of ultimate victory."

"How can we trust them?"

"We don't. That's where Arthur and I show our strength."

Avriel reached up to trace the line of his lips. "That's the part I don't like."

"No more than I." His guts churned. "This is for survival, love."

Chapter 39

CIRCE JOINED HANDS with Arthur while they watched Brethren file into the central cavern. A tremor ran through her slight frame although her expression remained calm. "Copper would've been so proud of him." Arthur didn't envy Kai his chosen role. Kai had the upbringing to make a difference at Haven and Brethren listened to him, giving him almost god-like reverence.

Kai sat on a tabletop, gripping the sides with white knuckles, but swinging his legs as if he hadn't a care in the world. Arthur pictured his brother's dead sire from Shadow's memories. Copper's carefully concealed kindness and sense of humor lived on in Kai. Arthur hoped Kai's unborn son inherited those qualities because the infant might end up as the sole survivor from this development. Avriel's set face confirmed she sensed the danger also. The gentle tendrils of Circe's thought presence tickled at his mind.

Arthur, I've quickened with our child.

His heart lurched, pounding. *Why tell me now?*

Keys to the Kingdom. She nestled closer to him. *If this sacrifice must be made, then you need to know another will carry your burden.*

How long have you known? He counted back the days, resenting her reticence when he'd tallied the number.

I wasn't sure you really wanted a child or if you got carried away in the heat of passion. Her tremulous uncertainty conveyed in the flavor of her thoughts. *I knew the next day.*

I wanted our child. His heart swelled. *Raise him well.* A thought occurred to Arthur. *Or have I fathered a daughter as beautiful as her mother?*

We have a strong son, and I hope he looks just like you.

Kai held up his hand for silence from the noisy gathering. Voices hushed. With every eye turned to him, Kai took a deep breath.

"All of you know of Emrys," Kai began, "He was around when the Nestine species first came into being. He showed us why and how the Nestines were created."

Kai went on to tell the hushed gathering of a planet groaning with people and the solution of ark ships, to be manned by a species that humans regarded as disposable. He conveyed the horror of leaders on discovering those ships might not be safe and the subsequent development of Avalon as a shelter for the elite.

A shocked hiss resounded throughout the cavern. Brethren inched forward, their faces intent. Kai told them of the betrayal of Greenly, the Nestine creator and how this man destroyed life on the entire planet with the exception of Avalon. The air thickened with anger.

"Greenly was the first victim of his creations. The Nestines restored life to our planet because they need human cells to breed males, and now they must have the cells of the gifted to get themselves a viable Queen." Kai looked around the swaying gathering that almost crooned venom. "Kiri Ung offers the sword, total destruction of their Moon Base and his faction relocating to another world with their only Queen in exchange for these cells." He paused, letting the information sink into them. "Every fey Brethren must agree before we continue. We get an abandoned and sterile enemy left with no home base. Their numbers will be halved. What do you say?"

Goat raised his hand. "Why fey brothers? Why not just you and Arthur?"

"They need a viable gene pool to draw from." Kai stood up, facing them. "We breed horses and know the danger of limiting our stock."

"How do we know they'll deliver?" Storm's voice rose about the muttering.

"It is possible Arthur and I won't survive another gestalt, but neither would the Nestines."

Arthur's innards contracted. He dreaded the bonding, aware of other fatalities. They'd been lucky so far.

"Can I get a show of hands from all fey brothers?"

Sixteen hands shot skyward, including Kai, Haystack and a tentative Dragon.

"Keep those hands up if you agree the terms." Kai's own hand remained high. Not one of the others lowered.

"So be it." Kai looked over at Arthur with a dead expression. "I'm going to change leadership rules because we can't afford to lose our best fighters. If I don't return, then I want you to vote for the strongest leader in your ranks. You won't have time for duels. Is that clear?"

Muttering started and then they began to sway and chant. "Kai, Kai, Kai . . ."

By the deeps, he has them. He's made sure they don't fall apart if we fail. Arthur drew Circe's hand up to his heart. "I love you, and I always have. I'm so sorry."

"Do what you must. I love you too, and I always will." She hugged him, fitting herself to him in a way that made Arthur want to weep for a future that hung in the balance.

"Keys to the Kingdom, my love. I'll come back to you if I can."

"I know you will."

*

Kiri Ung faced his Nestines. "The Brethren have strong leaders. Stalker was not exaggerating, and I don't trust them. Suggestions?"

"We have to have those cells." Na Pan's claws extended. "Without them we are a dead race."

"I can triangulate Arthur to bring him to us the next time he walks out into the compound," Sha Gru offered.

"What if we can't control him?" Kiri Ung voiced his biggest concern. "Something unusual happened on the surface. Stalker's mind is filled with whispers, and he is concentrating hard to ignore them."

"Zap him." Na Pan reached for the control.

"No!" Kiri Ung held a claw over the abort button. "He's telling us more with his attempt at evasion. He's giving us a focus."

Sha Gru stretched, rubbing his lower back. "I'm hungry. Daylight fades and we will stand out like a flare in the night sky for Te Krull if we don't land soon."

"Hunting was that much fun?" Kiri Ung's heart beat harder. "We need fresh meat. Why not?"

The crests of both pilots rose, giving him an answer.

"Set us down where we have ground cover." Te Krull wasn't the only enemy with air power now, and the force field over Haven was only good for as long as their ship hovered there. Kiri Ung didn't trust Arthur, for he'd seen the glint of laz guns in the compound. "Let's catch some tender meat."

*

Dragon sat down with the beer he'd just collected, joining his group at a trestle table that squeaked of scrubbing. In the background, he heard Kai barking orders with Avriel's soft comments taking the sting out of commands. She'd not let her man out of reach since his recovery. Dragon's heart swelled with pride for the way she'd handled herself, yet a feeling of wrongness jarred at him. Brethren touched Kai as if they couldn't believe he lived, and he seemed to have the energy of ten men, yet Arthur's face was gray with fatigue.

349

"Are you feeding him energy?" Dragon jerked his head at the flame-haired King sending his people scurrying.

"Not me." Arthur's face lifted in a feral smile. "Them. All of them. They know now what he is, and they're making him over into one of them."

"We're not included." Haystack raised his glass to his comrades with unspoken mourning.

"But you're an Outcast." Dragon failed to understand the difference.

"Seems I am indeed." Haystack's lips lifted in a mirthless smile.

"He means he's clumped with us now." Merrick looked over the rim of his cup. "We don't belong here."

Arthur adjusted Circe, sleeping in his lap, to a more comfortable position that didn't impede his drinking arm. "Brethren are warriors, an army who'll follow Kai to each of the seven hells and back. We have another function."

"Which is?" A sinking sensation dropped Dragon's guts to his feet. Brittle laughter echoed in the cavern. A woman's squeal of pretend outrage brought more of the same. He knew what such behavior meant. Brethren prepared for war.

Arthur's mouth thinned into a hard line. "I'll know when I get my hands on that sword."

"You'd trust Nestines after all they've done?" He couldn't believe he'd heard aright.

"Having second thoughts now that we're on the outside?" Arthur frowned.

"Since when do I really count as fey?" Dragon shifted, uncomfortable with all the eyes from the men on him.

"Try thinking back to the first time you got fey sense." Huber stared at Dragon with a steady gray gaze. "Your mating with Shadow created Arthur. Try thinking about that."

With Arthur's violet eyes on him, so much like Shadow's, Dragon yielded. "I'll do what I must for the sword." *And for you, my son.*

350

*

Awakening regenerated, Kiri Ung enjoyed the sensation of fullness in his stomach. The hunt had exceeded his wildest dreams of pleasure. *I can't go back to how we were.* The others stirred, a picture of health. *Neither can they.*

"Policy meeting," he announced to the stirring Nestines curled around a dead campfire. "The thrill of the hunt raised the stakes for me. What about you?" He caught each set of eager eyes in turn. "Do we agree we want a better life?"

"The hunt throbs through my veins." Na Pan's crest rose and his claws snapped into view.

"Moon Base is not where I'd choose to spend my life," Sha Gru agreed and the other pilot nodded.

"On the one hand, we will be fighting for such a life on this planet against two factions. Even if we renege on our agreement with Arthur and try to steal what we need, we are fighting against Te Krull." His council, for that is what they represented, looked sour.

Sunlight glittered in the dawn dew. Birds began that irritating noise. Kiri Ung's crest rose with the desire to send them crashing against rocks.

"Our second choice is to play fair. We give Arthur all he wants in peaceful exchange for what we need to make a fresh start. One breeding Queen can generate more with those cells. It will mean a leap of faith to venture into uncharted space." He looked around at them, catching their rapt expressions. "We also have an opportunity to create a world best suited to our needs, without Te Krull."

Na Pan stood up. "All of us want to mate. Te Krull will not permit more than one Queen." He glanced down at the pilots. "And this crew likes the hunt. I can't think of any Nestine that wouldn't kill for a chance to take part."

Crests rose in agreement. They wanted a life that allowed them to grow despite the risks involved. Kiri Ung scratched at a bug bite, determined to eliminate that particular insect from ark databases. *We can do this. We can create a perfect world.* His hearts beat faster.

"Then we trade fair?" Tusks bared, Kiri Ung tasted defeat and found it foul. *We risk our survival, and Arthur gets all he wants. The slave race wins against our might because we must have their genetic material.*

"A third course would suit our needs more." An idea at the back of his mind slotted into place with the snap of perfection. "We trade as agreed, but invite Arthur to witness the destruction of Moon Base. He doesn't stand a chance of overpowering four of us."

His Nestines swayed, bright-eyed and thrumming a deep note of triumph.

"We take him with us to the stars, ensuring we have the quality material we need into eternity."

"Yes!" The word hissed from each Nestine.

*

"Kai, the skyship is back." Storm looked down as he stood by Kai enjoying breakfast with Avriel.

"Get my brother and his group." Kai wrapped an arm around Avriel, thrilled by her growing girth, yet disturbed by this projected meeting that could wreck his life. "I also want the Nestine drone. We'll need him to communicate."

"Your will be done." Storm bowed and started shouting off a series of crisp commands that send Brethren running.

"Kai, I'm frightened." Avriel's big blue eyes glistened with unshed tears.

"So am I." He leaned down to kiss her cheek. "We must take this chance. The alternatives are unthinkable."

"Promise me that you'll stay near Arthur."

"That's a given." He smiled, catching sight of his sleep-ruffled brother striding to join him. Stalker also shambled forward under the escort of two burly Brethren.

"They want a meet in the compound." Stalker rubbed at his eyes. He shook himself awake. "They agree all terms."

"Where's the maggot?" Arthur looked doubtful.

"I'm getting a feeling of excitement," Stalker said. "Don't know what that means."

"That's a promising start." Arthur stood up. "Kai, don't stay more than a pace from me."

Arms linked, the brothers went to meet their future with a sea of Brethren in their wake.

Kiri Ung waited in the compound for them. At a distance from him, a black sword encrusted with runes lay on the dirt. Dawn light turned those runes to writhing worms of blood.

"As a gesture of faith, we surrender the sword." The Nestine glared at all, challenging.

Both Kai and Arthur walked forward, and Arthur's hand reached for it.

Bright blue sparks flew from Arthur to the weapon as if they recognized each other. He glowed a cerulean blue with the sword in his hand.

"Kiri Ung speaks the truth." The certainty of that statement shone in Arthur's face.

"We want a life that we've never had." Kiri Ung bared his fangs in an almost smile. "We give the sword as a mark of our intentions."

"Fey Brethren, line up for tissue samples," Kai ordered. When only he and Arthur remained he faced the Nestine. "Our hides are the ones you want the most. Forgive us if we doubt your intention. We want proof of the destruction of Moon Base before we continue."

"Our home has been evacuated." Kiri Ung looked around at them all. "The last act is to retrieve the Queen egg. Arthur, will you come with us? We need you."

"Not without my brother."

Kai nodded, saying goodbye to Avriel in his thoughts. The way Arthur claimed him sent a chill warning through his bones.

353

His hand curved around the hilt of that black sword Arthur carried as if he held it in truth. The air vibrated with tendrils of treachery. *Arthur is right. We must see this through, whatever the personal cost.*

Arthur turned to Dragon. "Father, keep this safe for the rightful bearer." He glanced at Avriel and then longer at Circe. "Our ladies are also in your care since both carry sons.

Dragon tensed, his hand sliding to his sword hilt. He locked gazes with Arthur, finally taking the sword with both hands stretched out to bear it on his forearms. For a split second Dragon appeared etched in cerulean blue. His eyes widened and then narrowed in an expression Kai recognized from Brethren faced with impossible odds.

Arthur wouldn't risk a thought transfer this close to a Nestine. It's not him! It's the sword! Dragon knows. That thought helped him join Arthur. Together they stood with the Nestine while a beam descended from the ship to lift them into a place where deceit held sway. Arthur's hand reached out for his, clasping him as they ascended. The bowels of the ship opened to envelope them into a metal tomb.

Chapter 40

THE PORTAL SEALED beneath their feet. Dark gray metal walls shone with flashing control panels. Three Nestines hunched over those winking stars of brightness in the night of Kai's despair. *My son and Arthur's will finish this. Our lives are well spent.*

"Come." Kiri Ung gestured for them to proceed over metal grid-work flooring. The Nestine indicated two hard shelves, not fit to describe as seats. "Wait there. The passage to Moon Base will take approximately one hour."

Still holding hands, they sat. A holo projection of their flight path overshadowed the drab nonentity of one wall. Smells of metal and blood permeated the atmosphere.

"You know?" Arthur asked, not looking at him.

"The sword came to my hand, too." His brother's hand tightened on Kai's in warning not to alert the big Nestine. "Dragon has enough control to continue in our absence." Kai tasted the lie on his tongue, hoping Arthur saw beyond it to his real meaning. *Yes, brother, I know Kiri Ung means to betray us, and I wish we could share thoughts.*

"We're both to be fathers." Arthur met his gaze. "I wonder how our sons will turn out."

A wealth of wishes flavored that remark. With Dragon as mentor to both boys, Kai envisaged strong warriors emerging. The thought helped him.

Time dragged, and the moon glowed larger in the holo projection. Arthur's hand was as sweaty as his own, but neither relaxed their grasp. Project Arthur and Project Kai sped toward their destiny.

As the orb of the moon filled the screen Kai identified three giant ships in orbit. Looking around at these craft Kai found himself lost in awe. One thousand years old and still functional space arks now prepared to make the journey for which they were intended. Once the conveyance of humans, these ships now carried the hope of the Nestine race for a new life.

"Impressive, aren't they?" Arthur commented.

"So much lost through greed and fear. That should have been our ancestor's chance of escape. What were they thinking?"

"Moon Base is now operating with minimum staff," Kiri Ung said, his furred digits flying over the console. "See the landing beacon on the surface?"

"Why aren't they leaving?" A crackle of unease raised the threat level generated by Kai's fey sense. A swarm of skyships loitered near the shining light.

"Our science station is required to analyze the tissue samples of the gifted." The big Nestine turned; his cat's eyes pits of fiery darkness in the gloom. "You will be privileged to attend the vivification of our new Queen."

"A great honor that I decline for both of us." Arthur's jaw thrust out in a belligerent denial. "Find other meat to feed your hatchling. I'll not stand in Greenly's place for her first banquet."

Nestines swiveled in their chairs to front Arthur. Each visage radiated disbelief and shock.

Arthur met each pair of eyes in turn. "I know that you Nestines fed your creator to the first Queen. Don't anger Us."

Even in gestalt he hid this from me. Horrified, Kai stared at his brother. *Arthur used the royal prerogative.* For a moment, another, older man occupied Arthur's place in eternity. Wheat-colored hair and a darker shade of beard replaced night-colored locks. Eyes of periwinkle blue radiated wisdom. A mantle of power and authority permeated from this ruler. The sensation of a cool, smooth hilt filled Kai's free and empty right hand. Kai blinked, and Arthur was himself once more.

It's the sword. Emrys told us it cleaved through deceit, but it also shows that which was. Ice ran through his veins. *I saw that man with the Wild Hunt just before Arthur called me from death. He's the first of Project Arthur.*

Nestines appeared not to notice. It was as if time, that moment had not happened for them.

Kiri Ung rose, towering over Arthur and Kai. "No one knows of Greenly."

His guttural voice cracked, riddled with tension. "All surface Terrans died that day. Avalon never knew the extent of Greenly's treachery. We controlled Moon Base. His fate is sealed to us. How can you know?"

"Emrys sees all." Arthur smiled a slow smile that carried the promise of carnage.

"Impossible." Kiri Ung's tone wavered between uncertainty and fear, evident in the deflation of his crest. "Our Queen will be many months in hatching. I intended to honor you as respected enemies."

Kai detected a ring of truth in that statement. *They don't want us dead. Kiri Ung said 'enemy' with a power of hate behind that word. He has a different betrayal planned.*

"My brother and I will accept your offer." Arthur caught Kai's eye with a brief glance of warning.

"Prepare to witness a sight no free Terran has ever seen. Moon Base, the location you demand destroyed as part of our pact was built by your ancestors." He signaled his underlings back to their tasks.

The ship descended to an orifice of metal on the surface that opened up like a ring of shark's teeth. Bright lights blinded Kai. A gentle thud informed him the craft had landed, but he resisted the urge to break link with Arthur to rub his eyes.

"Docking clamps in place," one of the Nestines reported. "Hatchway open and stairs extended."

"Come." The Nestines invitation was imperative.

Kai stood up with Arthur, only aware of gray shapes against a darker gray that swirled with brightest stars. *They have a protective membrane to their eyes that we lack.* He blinked, his eyes tearing while vision returned to normal. Hands locked with Arthur, Kai followed Kiri Ung out of the ship into a cavern that made Haven look like a rodent's burrow. Metal walkways ringed the outer walls and had joint and pulleys attached to relocate them at will. Already a service crew, bristling with equipment, advanced to the ship. Shoulder to shoulder with Arthur, Kai entered an elevator with Kiri Ung and his crew, who carried genetic material from gifted Terrans.

Down along corridors that smelled of cleanliness they walked, into an area that looked new made in its pristine perfection. More Nestines took the containers from the crew to begin an immediate assessment. Arms suddenly circled around Kai to hold him still. A Nestine advanced to run a swab around the inside of his lips. Arthur endured similar treatment. Equipment buzzed and flashed. Suddenly, all eyes centered on the brothers.

One older Nestine extended a claw in their direction, his jaw muscles working as he looked at Kiri Ung, who nodded.

"Both of them, Te Pa?"

Kai tensed. *Is this the moment that we meet our fate?*

"Together they possess the missing factor. This Queen will be viable." Moisture extruded from those aged eyed to run down sagging jowls. "She'll produce fertile young daughters."

Kai wanted to vomit. Arthur looked a sickly shade of green, too. *What have we done?*

Kiri Ung stepped forward. "Our race can now perpetuate. Our agreement is almost complete." The old Nestine handed him a syringe. "Come with me to witness the final result of your part in this."

Kai's hand itched for his belt knife, but that remained in Haven. Nestines flocked in their wake down endless corridors until they came to a strange sight. A gray membrane of threads covered a part of one wall, approximately door shaped.

358

Kiri Ung drew a knife to run it across his paw. Blood flowed. He smeared his dripping wound across that sticky looking surface. It began to flake into hard shards that peeled away from the surface. The reaction spread and more solid clumps sloughed until the doorway appeared clear from obstruction.

Still bleeding, Kiri Ung advanced into a gloomy cavern with muted light. The stench of death and decay gagged them all. A huge insect form lay near one glistening egg case. The legs curled up around a body leaking fluids, creating an acrid aroma that made Kai's eyes water. Different moisture filled every Nestine eye. *They're crying. This was their Queen? They love this?* A harsh sob tore from Kiri Ung, who knelt by the monstrosity's head. He laid his paws on the stinking carcass in reverence before advancing to the pearl that glittered on the floor. Syringe extended, he delivered the genetic material. Surrounded by swaying Nestines, Kai couldn't stop the process.

A moment extended into eternity and then a steady throb of life filled that vast darkness. The egg pulsated. Kiri Ung now cradled it in his arms.

"Shi Nom is at peace." Facing the Nestine congregation, he looked at the remains of his Queen. "None shall disturb her tranquility. Her essence shall grace the cosmos. Now we set forward on a new journey of hope to create a world for our kind. To the future." His free hand punched the air in a gesture of victory and defiance.

Arthur's hand gripped his tight as they were swept outward amid a flood of Nestines. Breathless minutes later ships soared for the orifice. The brothers clung tight in the jostle. Then they boarded with Kiri Ung and at least fifteen Nestines crowded around him in adoration of the pulsating egg.

A lurch betrayed take-off. Pushed against a bulkhead into the crush, the brothers gazed at the holo screen, once more activated. Moon Base receded to a point of light.

Kiri Ung stood, the egg held against his chest with both arms. "Destroy our home," he ordered, his face set.

Bursts of orange light streaked toward the lonely beacon of Moon Base. Bright white light and then dust flared high about the point of impact. A crater lay in the former position of the Nestine home. Nestines on the ship parted to expose the brothers to Kiri Ung's glare of pure hatred.

"Our bargain with these Terrans is complete." Kiri Ung's mouth flaps raised in the caricature of a smile. "They have no further use. Eat them."

Arthur's surge met his own in that last moment of individual existence before they merged.

Cerulean blue light brightened the inside of the ship to a sunburst. Nestines cowered before the glowing being that flowed with tentacles of power. "We warned you not to anger Us." Laz fire passed through the united being without damage. It exalted in its supremacy. Tentacles reached out, through helpless Nestines, taking over controls. The ship altered course for Terra.

Now the entity focused on that glistening egg. Power swelled to annihilate this monstrosity. Reality lurched sideways into a cave where an old young man sat before a fire. He looked up, his coal black eyes bearing the weight of forever.

The cave sitter smiled the slow smile of Brethren, full of malice. "Have you learned nothing? If you destroy their Queen, why should they spare your world?" His eyes pierced through to the heart of the entity. "Revenge is a bitter fruit best left unsavored. Let them go in peace, or reap the reward for removing a species from the weft of the universe. She doesn't forgive transgressors."

Water fell, drop by drop in that dark cavern. The sound of a heartbeat, of a child, of three children, only one wasn't Terran.

The beat increased, consuming the attention to the entity. Lights swirled, and the ship interior came back into focus. Terrified Nestines formed a ring around Kiri Ung and the egg. A decision solidified.

"You have now seen us in our true form. We traded fair while you reneged." The being still wanted some satisfaction. "In this form, we could destroy your ship without harm to us. Do you understand?"

Every Nestine dropped to his knees.

"We will release you when we are at our destination." The being noted thoughts of revenge from some of them. "If you turn on us, then your Queen will die. Don't doubt our power, for she is a part of us."

The smell of urine and feces filled the air. Fear throbbed with a life of its own. Time inched by in suffering for all until Haven came into sight. Activating controls, the being transferred to ground. The skyship accelerated away as if the worst hell of all chased its tail.

Terrified Brethren and two women circled the being. The chill pull of star metal demanded attention, but the gestalt couldn't divide. Pulsing power held it enthralled.

"Kai," one dark woman sobbed.

"Arthur," a blonde woman wept.

Dull thuds sounded. Separate heartbeats. The song of unborn sons thrilled through the being, calling for fathers. Each infant voice shouted a claim that couldn't be met. Each cry created a crack in the whole. The combined wails of both boys divided the being.

Kai fell to the ground, hitting hard. His cheek hurt from the impact. Avriel landed on him, crying and laughing, mad in her joy. Beneath it all he heard a quiet and still child's voice. *You're home now.* And he was.

Struggling to his feet with an excited and happy woman in his arms, he exchanged gazes with his similarly occupied brother. Beyond the relief was the horror. Neither of them would ever forget that.

Brethren pushed close, wanting answers. They'd suffered enough. Kai formed the words to explain. "Moon Base is no longer. The Nestines have taken their Queen to find a new planet." Cheers sounded. "Those who are left will die in time. Without a Queen, they can't breed. We will prevail." They started chanting his name again, but he let it slide over him as he drew his woman into his arms.

"Where are my saurians?" Arthur scanned the heights.

Circe shrugged. "They were birds at heart, Arthur. They could see all those large worm-like Vortai from the heights, and they went to pull a feast from the bog as soon as the ship left with you aboard." She pulled a moue of distaste. "None of them survived. We lost a few Vortai, too."

Goat came running out of the caves. He skidded to a halt when he saw Kai and Arthur, his face breaking into a wide grin that vanished in a second.

"Avalon is transmitting. Does one of you want to answer? They won't tell me what they want."

Arthur shrugged, holding Circe close. He glanced at Kai and the excited Brethren. "I guess this is my call."

*

Arthur kept his arm tight around Circe as they entered the caverns. He didn't want to think about how close he had come to losing her and tried to concentrate on where Goat was leading him.

Off the main cavern, an alcove contained a transmitter. Arthur settled Circe on a bench while he sat on a hard stool in front of the screen.

Ector's face stared out at him. The drawn gray look of the Submariner sent Arthur's guts into downward spirals.

"We eliminated Moon Base, have half the Nestines headed out to another planet home, and we have the sword." His heartbeat skipped when Ector's expression didn't change. "Why do I think your tidings are bad?"

"I don't know how to begin." Ector shut his eyes for a moment, the pain on his face etched clear. "Evegena began acting strangely. We thought it was age and the fact that her Seers had been compromised with a few drones." He swallowed. "I don't know when it happened, but Evegena became a drone."

Pinpricks of ice ran over Arthur's skin. He'd begun to like the matriarch of Seers. "So who is her successor, since I assume she is no longer with us."

Ector breathed hard, and his voice cracked, "Evegena isn't dead. She snatched Morgan and headed for the surface. Shadow hasn't eaten or spoken since."

"I'll find her, Ector." With Kai and the Brethren at his back, finding Morgan was going to happen. No one was going to keep his sister from him. The screen when blank.

Acknowledgements

A special thank you to Sammy H.K Smith, Zoë Harris, Ken Dawson, Evelinn Enoksen and Carol Powney for making this book possible, and for making the process such fun.

In no particular order, these are the awesome people who helped in the shaping of this book and to whom I am truly grateful. Giacomo Giammatteo, Jeanne Haskin, May-Lin Iversen Demetriou, Jennifer Dawson, Lisa Smeaton, Corie Conwell, Elissa Hunt, Dena Landon Stoll, Crash Froelich, Kendra Highley, Ursula Warnecke, Rhonda S. Garcia, Susan Elizabeth Curnow, Victoria Kerrigan, Charles Coleman Finlay, P.J. Thompson, Laura Waesche.

About the Author

C.N. Lesley is the pen name of author Elizabeth Hull, who lives in central Alberta, Canada with her husband and cats. Her family lives close by. As well as writing, Elizabeth also likes to read, paint watercolors, and is a keen gardener, despite the very short summers, and now has a mature shade garden. Once a worker in the communications sector, mostly concentrating on local news and events, she now writes full time.

Lesley's first book, *Darkspire Reaches*, was published in March 2013 by Kristell Ink, and her second, *Shadow Over Avalon*, the first in the *Shadow* series, published in October 2013, is an Amazon bestseller.

For more information, check out her website at cnlesley.com

A Selection of Other Titles from Kristell Ink

Healer's Touch by Deb E. Howell

A girl who has not only the power to heal through taking life fights for her freedom.

Llew has a gift. Her body heals itself, even from death, but at the cost of those nearby. In a country fearful of magic, freeing yourself from the hangman's noose by wielding forbidden power brings its own dangers. After dying and coming back to life, Llew drops from the gallows into the hands of Jonas: the man carrying a knife with the power to kill her.

February 2013

Darkspire Reaches by C.N. Lesley

The wyvern has hunted for the young outcast all her life; a day will come when she must at last face him.

Abandoned as a sacrifice to the wyvern, a young girl is raised to fear the beast her adoptive clan believes meant to kill her. When the Emperor outlaws all magic, Raven is forced to flee from her home with her foster mother, for both are judged as witches. Now an outcast, she lives at the mercy of others, forever pursued by the wyvern as she searches for her rightful place in the world. Soon her life will change forever as she discovers the truth about herself.

A unique and unsettling romantic adventure about rejection and belonging.

March 2013

Shadow Over Avalon by C.N. Lesley

Fortune twists in the strongest hands. This is no repeat; this is what happens next.

A man, once a legend who bound his soul to his sword as he lay dying, is now all but a boy nearing the end of his acolyte training. Stifled by life in the undersea city of Avalon, Arthur wants to fight side by side with the air-breathing Terrans, not spend his life as servant to the incorporeal sentient known as the Archive. Despite the restrictions put on him by Sanctuary, he is determined to help the surface-dwellers defeat the predators whose sole purpose is to ensure their own survival no matter the cost.

October 2013

In Search of Gods and Heroes by Sammy H.K Smith

Buried in the scriptures of Ibea lies a story of rivalry, betrayal, stolen love, and the bitter division of the gods into two factions. This rift forced the lesser deities to pledge their divine loyalty either to the shining Eternal Kingdom or the darkness of the Underworld.

When a demon sneaks into the mortal world and murders an innocent girl to get to her sister Chaeli, all pretence of peace between the gods is shattered.

In Search of Gods and Heroes, Book One of Children of Nalowyn, is a true epic of sweeping proportions which becomes progressively darker as the baser side of human nature is explored, the failings and ambitions of the gods is revealed, and lines between sensuality and sadism, love and lust are blurred.

June 2014

The Sea-Stone Sword by Joel Cornah

"Heroes are more than just stories, they're people. And people are complicated, people are strange. Nobody is a hero through and through, there's always something in them that'll turn sour. You'll learn it one day. There are no heroes, only villains who win."

Rob Sardan is going to be a legend, but the road to heroism is paved with temptation and deceit. Exiled to a distant and violent country, Rob is forced to fight his closest friends for survival, only to discover his mother's nemesis is still alive, and is determined to wipe out her family and all her allies. The only way the Pirate Lord, Mothar, can be stopped is with the Sea-Stone Sword – yet even the sword itself seems fickle, twisting Rob's quest in poisonous directions, blurring the line between hero and villain. Nobody is who they seem, and Rob can no longer trust even his own instincts.

Driven by dreams of glory, Rob sees only his future as a hero, not the dark path upon which he draws ever closer to infamy.

June 2014

Atlantis and the Game of Time by Katie Alford

A tale of two great powers and a battle across the breadth of time as Atlantis, a peaceful culture of academics intent on conserving the flow of time, struggles against a new rising power determined to reform it.

After decades of quiet time watching, the Atlanteans are caught off guard by a sudden wave of destruction, travelling up the timeline from the distant past, threatening to destroy all known civilisations and even, finally, that of Atlantis itself.

All that remains behind the time change is a single culture, one world and one history. Can the peaceful culture of Atlantis find the power to battle this new war ready culture and return history to its former glory or is the history they have protected for centuries doomed to be lost forever?

August 2014

Non-Compliance: Equilibrium by Paige Daniels

The alliance with the Magistrate is now in shreds, and the sector is descending into chaos as sickness and starvation spread. The crew must figure out how to solve the detrimental supply shortage, and the dangerous secrets hidden in the vaccine, before the whole Non-Compliance Sector revolts. Shea faces heart wrenching personal news that forces her to weigh her family's welfare against her belief for truth and justice. In this conclusion to the Non-Compliance series, the crew will face life-altering decisions while revealing the plots that have twisted all of their lives.

October 2014

www.kristell-ink.com

Lightning Source UK Ltd.
Milton Keynes UK
UKOW04f0609261114

242164UK00001B/6/P